THE PROVIDER

THE PROVIDER

a novel by
Carter Wilson

Bankilal Books

THE PROVIDER
Published by Bankilal Books

ISBN (paperback): 9781662952951
eISBN: 9781662956225

"…marriage, the old full stop, is not an end at all…"

—E. M. Forster

ONE

Jake Guarani had just come in from a Sunday afternoon run, nothing excessive, a lope more than a run really, down as far as the junior high, a scramble up over the chain-link fence, around the track a couple times, back along the quiet streets of the older part of Skokie. In the shower when he heard the faint ringing of the phone. He thought someone else could get it before remembering he was alone in the house—or as good as—so he made a dash for it. And just missed it. Gone to message, which for some reason only registered on the machine downstairs. Standing there towel at his waist and making a puddle, he had the somewhat fucked experience of knowing someone was maybe speaking to him but he couldn't hear them.

He went back and rinsed off, dried off, combed his hair and got into shorts, then laid his towel over the water by the bedside table before going down to check and see. He expected it would be his wife Angie, who'd taken their daughter up to her mom's cottage at Delavan for the long weekend.

But no, it was a voice from the past, as the caller began. Then she laughed at herself and said, "Oh how corny," and then, "Jake? It's Felicity Stiles. Your old Fleas! We're all so looking forward to seeing you. Angie too. I was just wondering what you're up to right now and if it's possible could you do me a really big favor? If you are available, would you just come over to the house for a minute? Needn't call me back or anything, just come. We're in the midst of everything here. It's a real circus." She laughed again, breathed. "I mean that literally. Looks like they're just about to raise the tent this very minute!"

In the Stiles family they said 'Fleas' was the name her little brother Ian gave her from the time he learned to talk. 'The house' would be their parents' place at the end of Pine Street in Winnetka, only fifteen or so minutes' drive for Jake. Ian, his friend from childhood, would be there and the rest of the clan too probably. Fleas' only son was getting married the following afternoon in the garden behind the house, and the tent mentioned would have to be in the field down below for the dinner and dancing afterwards.

Not knowing what he might be called on to do, Jake put on an older polo shirt and his sneakers and loaded the smaller of his tool boxes into the back of his truck. He was a contractor, or had been, and had no doubt he could probably fix whatever it was. Or at least patch it long enough to get the Stiles through their festivities.

The Pine Street house was a pretty grand business, a brick mock-Georgian from the 1920s with a slate roof and a lot of land behind. It had belonged to Fleas' and Ian's grandmother Bowen and then passed to Nancy, their mother, who had grown up there. Well, in a way Jake could say the same, he thought, since for a lot of his later childhood and on up into high school he had spent as much time at the house as he could manage.

He snugged his little pickup right against the hedge at the side of the property and went around. The front door stood half ajar. He called, heard voices but no one answered him, so he went in, through the big echoing entry hall, down the corridor into the butler's pantry and the kitchen, calling softly again as he went, then out back into the sun.

Rows and rows of wooden folding chairs had already been set up, probably a hundred and fifty of them. They filled the lawn in the middle of the garden right up to where the borders of Nancy Stiles' English-garden jumble of flowers began. No tacky add-on bower at the front, just a one-foot platform for the happy couple and the minister. Though the platform was placed where the trees behind would keep them in the afternoon shade, a simple wood frame had been erected and draped with silvery swag. A paper runner was already tacked down in the center aisle. Leonard Nelson, Fleas' husband, had dragged one chair over to the darkest spot against a wall and sat there, slacks and a striped business shirt with the cuffs turned back, attending to the screen of a thin laptop.

"You're Jake, right? I know you." Black eyebrows arching but eyes back to his screen.

"Hi, Leonard. How are you?"

"Oh, I'm well, thank you, very well. They've been hoping you'd be able to come. They're down below still, I think."

Leonard made a slight indication with his head toward flagstone steps which led to the two lower levels of the property. (And Jake made a conscious effort to keep Leonard's tone and his apparent indifference assigned to his being English, or preoccupied with his computer, or something.) From the top of the half-flight of steps Jake looked down directly on the blue rectangle of the Stiles' swimming pool and its squat changing rooms. Beyond down the hill the white canvas of the tent Fleas had mentioned, men in blue coveralls finishing putting stuff into a van wheeled out onto the grass. Nancy Stiles was coming up the steps toward him using the railing, her other hand already extended and a big smile on her face. Behind her, Fleas and Ian.

"Oh Jake!" Her hand went back flat against her chest. "Whew! Guess I'm a little winded there! Sorry!" She breathed, then both hands came up and Jake leaned in a bit and she pulled him to her and pressed her cheek against his.

"Sorry I didn't have time to shave, Nancy."

"Oh poo! What woman minds a little abrasion from a handsome man? You know, I was thinking about you just the other day. You and Ian—"

Fleas and Ian had come up now too and stood, waiting for their mother to go on.

"Just how long's it been since you boys have seen one another?"

"I was trying to figure that one on the plane," Ian said.

Nancy said to Jake, "Was it when you married Angie Moore?" She sniffed a little, recalling. "Ten years ago? Twelve?"

"That was ten. But I think Ian also happened to be back from Europe when my daughter was christened. So that would be only six years now, seven max."

"And are your parents still down there in Wilmette? In that same apartment?"

"Yes."

"What I was remembering," Nancy turned to Ian, "was when we were still there how those little hoodlums on our block would get together and just whomp on you. Until Jake here put a stop to that."

The Guaranis had rented the second floor of a gray three-story, six-flat building on Prairie Avenue next door to the Victorian where the Stiles lived. Opposite though the two boys were—Ian hang back, shy, Jake a little powerhouse, outgoing even then—from kindergarten on they became inseparable. Jake would sometimes play with the other neighbor kids, but having one true friend seemed to leave Ian with no need to look further.

For a moment, Nancy seemed lost. Then she said, "Before Jake came into our life I just could not see how you were going to make your way, Son."

Ian looked to Jake and to Fleas for help, but then himself said, "I was five, Mom, wasn't I?"

"Well, yes, you must have been—"

"And already a lost cause? at that age?"

"No, but still. Jake <u>was</u> your protector, you know."

"Oh, no one contests that. He was."

"And at a later date mine too," Fleas said.

"How is that, dear?" Nancy touched her daughter's wrist. "I didn't know."

Fleas regarded Jake with her chin up, as though contemplating a vase or a painting she might bid on. "When we were all at New Trier. Jake took it on himself to defend my honor. Big job, you know."

Again Nancy seemed somewhat puzzled. Then she looked down and there was a little smile on her mouth. Had she known at the time her daughter had a reputation for being fairly wild? Or was it a later revelation?

Fleas went on, "Jake'd threaten to punch 'em out if he thought they weren't treating me with the respect I deserved. Guys way bigger than him—"

"It was puppy love, Fleas. Wasn't it?"

"You think? It was more than that, Jake. You were so devoted to me. Remember?"

"I do," he admitted. "I was dazzled by you. Still am you know."

"Oh—" She laughed, threw her great hank of hair back.

Things that don't change. There were girls in school Jake and Ian called 'whinnies,' not just the ones who actually had horses but also their friends who wore their hair long and could be counted on to give it a good toss now and then. Though Fleas didn't ride in those days, she traveled in the whinnies' set.

Nancy said she was going in. Did anyone need anything, an iced tea or something?

No thanks, they said. They stood and watched her go.

Ian had now been living in Paris fifteen years. Hair cut high on the sides and left long on top, milk paleness of his skin down in the 'v' neck of the skimpy little blue sweater—none of it read as American anymore. But Jake caught himself about to say that and went instead with, "You're nice and skinny, man. They not feeding you over there?"

"It has to do with the different way we eat, Jake," Ian said earnestly. "I—"

Jake grabbed Ian's upper arm and pressed. "I'm kidding you, pal, get it?"

"Sure, I get it. And you—" Ian looked him up and down. "Remember that coach who used to call you a bullet?"

"The one at North Shore—."

"Because of the heedless way you'd crash right on through the line when you had the ball."

Jake took hold of two or three inches of the flesh at his right hip. "More cannonball than bullet nowadays, hm?"

Fleas said, "But then, which of us?"

Not her, certainly. A tall, athletic woman with a great lean build.

"So Fleas, what is it I can do for you?"

"Oh," she said, "nearly forgot." She checked the large-faced watch on her wrist. "Jake, tomorrow for the wedding proper we've got ushers. Ian's in charge, and it was supposed to be split even steven right down the middle, three from our team and three from the bride's. And now there's been a no-show, on their side actually, and I was wondering if you'd be willing to fill in?"

"Sure, Fleas, no problem."

"Great." She looked again at her watch, turned to see what Leonard was up to back in the shade. "So I need to get cracking here. You remember how bossy I am—"

"No, I don't remember that."

But Ian behind her was nodding agreement.

"Well, it's the way I am. So I got it in my head I didn't want the ushers to be dressed all differently, higgle-piggle, and I went and ordered them outfits."

"Tuxes and blue ruffle shirts?"

She laughed. "That would have been fun, wouldn't it? And we could all have driven to Bubba Gump's for the reception. No. Sorry to disappoint. They're just nice summer-weight gray suits, different color ties. If you've got a minute, Ian will take you up and you can try yours on. Or at least hold the pants up to see they're the right length—" She turned to Ian. "Or however it is you all do that sort of thing."

"We'll figure it out," her brother said.

"Good. Oh Jake—" Fleas gazed at him, head a little to the side. "We're so glad to see you! And I am <u>so</u> entirely grateful."

Her hair had come back forward and he thought he might be in for the pleasure of watching her toss it again, but she didn't. "You and Angie'll be there tonight for the rehearsal dinner, right?"

"Angie won't be able to make it, I'm afraid."

"Oh too bad. But at least we'll have you. At the Club, at eight, right?"

"Sure, Fleas. Coat and tie, right?"

"Still a requirement there, can you believe?"

*

The third floor at Pine Street was mostly attic, rough beams leaning in at the angle of the roof, no real flooring, just some loosely nailed board paths across the joists. But in the middle there was one large finished room with dormer windows which had been Ian's when they were young, and across the way a full bath. As they climbed the stairs Ian explained the bedrooms on the second floor were all taken or assigned to the major participants, so Fleas had put the ushers up here.

Hot and musty smelling. The two single beds where Jake and Ian used to sleep were still there, Ian's desk for doing his homework, his bookshelves and his prize David Bowie poster up on the wall, somewhat light-faded by now. A rack of suits in plastic bags had been wheeled in.

How long since Jake had been up here? He and Ian were facing forty, and if he stopped coming to stay over when he was fifteen, sixteen, then almost 25 years.

Ian went through the clothes, checking the white sheets of paper stapled to each bag at the shoulder, brought out the one for somebody named 'Pearson.' "Do you want to try any of it on?"

Jake surveyed the list. Fleas' guess had been very good. He himself was 5'8," 190 pounds, and the missing Pearson was same jacket size, waist, even pant length. "I don't think I need to really," he said. "What time you want us tomorrow?"

"Show's at four, so why don't you come two-fifteen or so?"

"When do you guys fly out?"

"This is a real short visit. Tuesday early."

"I was hoping we could find a little chance together, you and me."

"Well come earlier then, Jake, and maybe we can get a minute or so, amidst all the confusion."

"I'd like that."

"There're shoes that come with the suits too, but maybe you have black ones of your own?"

"I do. For sure."

They were back in the hallway. Ian went ahead, but Jake peered a moment into the bathroom. Nothing different here either, the little-block green and maroon patterned linoleum, the high outsize old bathtub on its claw feet, the circle shower curtain ring, a milky plastic curtain tucked back behind the tub.

"You know," he said, trailing after Ian, "something that happened with your mom one time I don't know whether I ever told you—"

But Ian was halfway down the stairs and hadn't heard him. When Jake caught up, Ian said, "Too bad Angie won't be here."

"I know."

"What happened?"

"She and Lisa received a summons." Ian's half-worried look made Jake laugh. "They're at her mom's place up in Wisconsin. Some sort of girls-only Labor Day weekend weenie roast the old lady cooked up. And as you know my wife is helpless in the face of that kind of demand."

"I remember."

Ian was a psychologist. He and Jake had long since covered the territory about Angie always being compelled for some reason to be the extra-dutiful daughter.

"And Angie's boy? I'm sorry, I forget his name."

"Earl. Good old Earl."

"He still at home?"

"You bet. Actually, out of rehab and back in college and going to be living in the dorms down at Chicago Circle. He was supposed to move down there this weekend, but when I left the house just now he was still up there in his room snoring away."

"And you guys are still supporting him?"

"Yes. <u>Me</u>, I'm supporting him. Along with everyone else. Pain in the ass. Not to mention the drain on the finances."

"So are you somewhat strapped then? Is that it?"

"Not really. I pull down a hundred and twenty thou, you know."

"Wow! In construction? Isn't that very good?"

"At my level? Given what I manage, the clients I bring Mike Tanner? It's only OK. Not great. Not what I'm worth to the company by a long shot."

Reaching the ground level, the two men went out on the front. The afternoon had cooled off a little and a white SUV neither of them recognized was pulled up in the driveway gravel right to the steps.

"So what's really going on?" Ian said. "You and Angie on the outs?"

"Not really. Well, sometimes. Knocking on the door to middle age, you know—"

"Since I'm also knocking...."

Jake shrugged, nodded. "Right. So anyway, I get worn out with being the provider. It can get to look like that's all I am to them. The checkbook, the bottomless pocket they can always dig into when they need to score some change. The fucking inhouse ATM machine." He shook his head. "Sometimes I just think I may not have been cut out for the married life."

Ian looked closely at him. "That really true?"

"I don't know. It's an honest feeling." He laughed a little. "And if I can't be honest with you, then there's not much anybody else around to be honest with, you know."

Behind them in the house there was talking. Fleas' voice coming through, another woman's, but not the words. Pleasant enough, but serious, arguing and then agreeing in turns.

"Oh. The lady in charge of the catering," Ian said.

"Ah—" The explanation of the SUV at the odd angle. "Let me ask this," Jake said. "Fleas and Leonard, they've got a lot of residences, right?"

"New York, Georgetown, Jamaica, Winchester—" Ian counted them on his fingers, grinned, "—if you think that constitutes a lot. Me, I have the use of one apartment that doesn't belong to me, so Fleas and Leonard's holdings do seem numerous to me sometimes."

"That place down in Virginia, Mayflowers?"

"Mayfields, yes. 'The Farm' as they call it."

"From the way you described it, I thought that would have been the place they'd want to put on Ezra's wedding."

"Well for sure Mayfields would be a great spot. The bride's from Texas, Houston, and usually the location would be her family's choice, but no one wanted Houston at this time of year. And they, the Johnsons, and their entourage turned out to be entirely movable." Ian paused, reconnoitered. "There's also another consideration involved, Jake."

"Which is what?"

"My mother really wanted to have it here. She said, 'I was married from this house and I want my Ezra to be too.' You know how she loves to show the place off, and her garden too, now especially with all her late-summer flowers doing their thing." Ian paused again. "Even harder than usual to go against Mom's wishes right now."

"How come?"

"Well you know she's been fighting cancer, right?"

"I did not know that, no."

"For the last several years really. But now according to my parents it's come back in what the doctors call a 'virulent manner' and there's not much anyone thinks they can do for her."

"So she couldn't travel to a wedding anyway."

"Oh she could still do that. Though maybe at some cost to her energy levels. She's not quite through yet, you know."

"Where is it, the cancer?"

"It's in her colon, Jake."

Jake made a face, shook his head. "I'm so sorry, man. I'm completely at your disposal, I hope you know that. I mean, me being nearby, if you should need something and can't get over from France fast enough or whatever, or if Fleas can't get here, you guys just call me, hear?"

"Yes, I hear, Jake. Thank you."

After a moment, Jake said, "A very special lady."

"My mom? She is, isn't she?"

*

Dumb luck and nothing else that Ian had not been in hearing range as they were coming downstairs.

What Jake had been about to relate was a memory of one still suburban midday, him 12 or 13 and staying at Pine Street, by then his second and happier home. It must have been summertime, only Nancy's car in the Stiles' driveway, Mary the black lady who came up from the South Side a couple days a week to clean and sometimes cook for the family not in the house. Sure he was alone, when Jake had to pee he didn't think anything about the door to the attic bathroom being closed. Had to go so bad he was already fishing it out as he pushed his way in. And there was Nancy, her long blond hair loosened and dangling almost down as far as the old tub's feet, her brown nipples, the round island of her tummy and her dark furry muff looking as though it was floating on the soapy water. Jake was stammering and apologizing and backing out before he was all the way in, a real cartoon of confusion, Oh sorry sorry Mrs. Stiles. No no, said she, it's OK, Jake, you couldn't have known I was up here. Then, door safely closed again, he thought he heard her laughing.

So what did he do? Ran down to Fleas' bathroom and pissed, so boned up only about half of it got into the bowl. Snuck back upstairs, remembering only then a blue thing, washrag or sponge in the clouded water next to Nancy's sleek legs, that and the fact she hadn't moved to cover herself. Carefully he locked Ian's door from the inside, lay on the bed away from the window, the one he slept in, yanked his pants and shorts down to his knees and started jerking it, eyes fixed on the ceiling. Even as he whacked away, he could hear the suck and smack of her getting out, imagined at least he was hearing the shoosh of the towel against her body as she dried off. The creaking of the door as she came out, her bare feet on the thin hall carpet.

After that he started bumping into her when they were the only ones in the house, her in a little bathroom wrapper, not the big terry cloth floor-length thing she wore Sunday morning when she was producing French toast for one and all. Repeated peeks—flashes—of Ian's mom emerging from her "soak" as she called it and passing the open door to Ian's room rapidly buffing her hair with a towel, the shorty Japanese robe hanging pretty much unbelted.

As his first real naked woman, Nancy was more important to him than all the top-heavy girls in all the <u>Playboys</u> he'd ever thumbed through.

*

What always struck Jake now when he saw Ian again was how time and a couple thousand miles seemed to have no effect on them. Which in turn always brought back how when they were ten or eleven a single move could have ended the whole friendship. Ian's grandmother Bowen died and Nancy came into her inheritance, which included the

Pine Street house. Later Jake learned Ian's father was the one anxious to get away from Wilmette, the one who did not like living around working people or next door to an apartment building. The Stiles occupied Pine Street as soon as the downstairs could be cleaned and repainted. But for him and Ian at first nothing seemed to have changed. Jake's uncle Gio had decided it was time for him to begin to help out in the family business, a Winnetka nursery and florist where Jake's father was the number-two man. On his trusty bike Ian could power from his grandmother's in a single straight shot up Pine to Guarani Flowers at the corner of Green Bay and, when Jake got free at noon, they'd take their sandwiches out behind the greenhouse by the big bins of shavings, sand, and gravel and talk. Weekends and even some week nights Jake was allowed to come to his buddy's new place for swimming and then to stay over. Neither of them seemed aware that come fall they wouldn't be in the same school anymore.

Then at the last minute, September already under way, people from North Shore Country Day went to Jake's family and offered to take their son on a sports scholarship. His parents were late immigrants, brought over by Uncle Gio only in the 1950s, so they were cowed by these men—a principal, a coach, a trustee—and failed to understand how odd the proposition was. Private school tuition waiver because a sixth grader was such a "promising backfielder" and excelled at basketball and baseball too? Somehow the Guaranis got the idea that the offer came about because Jake's sister Claire worked in the school cafeteria.

Later, in carpools or at games, other kids let it drop that their dads, tennis friends of Ian's father, had co-sponsored Jake. But apparently at no cost to them. Ian and Jake were both gone from North Shore and in high school at New Trier by the time they figured out that for three years Ian's parents had funded Jake's education.

Though there was a public golf course right across Hubbard Road from Pine Street, for the Stiles what Felicity called the 'Club' would mean only Indian Hill down at the south end of Winnetka. When Jake got home he checked the large creamy white envelope Angie had left propped up on the kitchen counter. Across the front she had written, 'You need to go to this. I accepted for us.' But inside, the only invitation was to the main event tomorrow, Labor Day. "Mr. And Mrs. Henry Johnson request the honor of your presence at the marriage of their daughter Olivia Bowman to Ezra Peter Nelson..." and so forth. No separate little card about a rehearsal dinner or anything.

So. Nothing fabulous in his plan for the evening he'd have to cancel. Water some out behind the house, then TV and a pizza he'd go for but which old Earl would probably hoover his way through most of. Even kind of sweet if Fleas felt calling on him at the last minute to usher meant she needed to slip in an extra place-setting for him tonight.

*

Just as the last of the plates were being cleared and a microphone set up at the head table, Ezra Nelson and some of his groomsmen pulled a fade. After a few minutes word filtered back into the Indian Hill private dining room that they had stepped out onto the golf course or gone over by the pool to lay on some chemical fortification to get them through their toasts. Pot? Coke? Other powders? Jake was fairly aware of the things the men on his work crews dosed themselves with, and knew more than he cared to about his own stepson's substance history, but he didn't have any sense of what these Ivy League guys might be into these days.

Fleas had put him with Ian and his family, Ian's wife Beatrice next to him, their boys Paul and Isaac, twelve and ten now, across the table. Super-polite kids in blue suits Jake hadn't seen since they were toddlers, already growing gangly. Beatrice confided in her low voice that Paul was doing so well in his present school there was speculation he might get into Condorcet.

"That's good, right? Some really good place?" Jake said.

She laughed. "They themselves have no modesty about claiming to be the best."

Her English was nearly perfect. She had attended Mt. Holyoke for a year and Ian had met her through her brother, also an exchange student and Ian's roommate for a while. It pleased Jake for his friend to have such a beautiful wife. Boyish short red-blond hair, a tiny pass of lipstick, tonight little touches of eyebrow pencil you'd only notice close up. For the occasion a fitted cocktail dress scooped in front to show off the smooth expanse of her upper chest. It was a rich plum in color, which made the whole effect less severe. He had asked once what she did and Beatrice said she had a career in magazines. Then added, 'You know, the ones without pictures that no one reads.'

But Ian told him that was false modesty, since Beatrice worked at one of France's very top intellectual journals.

"Funny isn't it—ironic—that I'd have a girl and Ian would get boys."

"I don't understand. What is the irony?"

"Well if I had boys at least I'd know what to do with them."

Ian said, "And I wouldn't? Don't, somehow?"

"Sorry, don't mind me."

"Oh, I don't mind you, Jake. Never have. You know that."

"What I should have said was the problem is—and don't get me wrong, I love my Lisa to pieces—but I sometimes just don't know what to do with a daughter."

Beatrice said, "I see. With boys at least you could throw an old football around or something."

"Or something."

"But your little girl, she does love you?"

"Oh, I'm sure of that. I get her everything. Proud proper papa, attending her little recitals and all." A beat, Jake glancing down. "Sometimes she acts a little scared around me."

Ian leaned forward. "Because?"

"You going to shrink me right here and now, at the table?"

"No, that wasn't in my therapist voice at all." Ian appealed to Beatrice. "Was it?"

"Not at all." She touched Jake's hand lightly. "The shrink voice is quite different, I can assure you."

"The big issue, I guess," Jake said, "is that I'm too critical. I notice everything and if there's anything wrong I can't help bringing it up."

"I remember your saying it was why you were good at your work."

"Yeah, on the job I do catch things. And if my men don't do it right, I get on 'em. But with the girl—fuck man, with Angela too—" Jake checked himself. But Paul and Isaac weren't paying attention. They were tracking the small clutch of kids around their age standing talking across the room. He went on, "Why couldn't I just lay off once in a while? I think I scare them sometimes. If I tell 'em and they don't do, I start yelling."

Ian waited. And now his silence did make Jake think of the way a therapist might hold off to see what the patient would say next.

So he changed the subject, asked Beatrice, "Does it feel funny coming all the way to Chicago for just a long weekend?"

"Quite disorienting," Beatrice said, "exhausting, actually. But Fleas called and asked me especially, and then she embarrassed us by offering to pay not only Ian's airfare and mine, but the boys' as well. It was sweet, perhaps, but I sometimes wish she wouldn't do things like that." She brightened. "But anyway, I went to my editor and he said of course, take whatever time you like, and so here we are."

"Fleas can't help herself," Ian confided. "I think it's genes. We had a great-uncle who was an admiral and she must have inherited the will to rule from him. And as time goes by she's only getting worse."

"Why do you think?"

"Don't know. She manages her and Leonard's social life, all their complicated comings and going amongst the various residences. Which leaves Leonard free to work his numbers and play his hunches, profitable as they are usually. Quite the team they are."

Beatrice said to Jake, "Do you think there's some sibling rivalry or some envy in evidence here?"

"None at all," Ian said. "Just a little disappointment maybe. Fleas won the Barker Prize at Harvard, you know—"

"For what?" Beatrice asked.

"Her undergraduate thesis. It was called, 'Reduplication in Infant-adult Communication Sequences.'"

"Whatever that means," Jake said.

Beatrice shrugged as though she didn't have any idea either. Then looked up and her eyes widened, a small warning.

Fleas herself was bearing down on them, bringing along a dark-haired woman from the bride's end of the head table. Ian and Jake got to their feet.

"I want you all to know Mrs. Mudd," said Fleas. "She's been asking to meet you."

Fleas introduced the grownups and the lady offered her hand to the men. Scarlet nails, wide lipstick smile.

"I usually tell 'em my name is Mudd, but I'll spare you all that one." She laughed one short breathy laugh. "I'm Elva, from Houston. And you all are from here?"

The lady had the edge of a Texas accent.

Felicity said, "My brother and his family came all the way from Paris for the occasion."

"Really! And what part of the city is it you live in, Mr. Stiles?"

"At the moment right off the Boulevard Saint-Michel across from the Ecole de Mines."

"Well good for you! That is a lovely neighborhood."

"It's my wife's really, her parents' intown apartment. And you, Mrs. Mudd?" Ian asked, "Are you a real one?"

"A Mudd of the Mudds?" The accent was deepening. "Only by marriage. My late husband was related somewhat distantly to Roger the TV commentator and much more directly to the doctor who went to prison for fixing up John Wilkes Booth the night he shot Lincoln."

"The Prisoner of Shark Island."

"The one." Elva Mudd smiled broadly. "John Ford made the film. And you, Mr. Stiles? What occupies your attention there in Paris?"

"I'm a psychologist."

"People? Rats?"

Ian laughed. "I'm on the people side, but some would say on the rats' team."

"How ambidextrous of you," Elva said.

"Ian heads counseling for PNG, which is a financial group based here but with a large presence in Europe," Fleas said.

"And they prefer to have their executives' little problems dealt with inhouse and so avoid...what do they call it? Leakage."

"You understand it all very well,"

Elva nodded. "My husband's outfit did something similar. So do you do the spouse weepin' on her bed over hubby's next dreary postin' and facin' up to one more unsettlin' move, Dr. Stiles?"

"I specialize in it."

"You should think about pitchin' that as a TV show, you know."

Ian laughed and shook his head. "'Distraught Corporate Wives?'"

"Or maybe just 'Tears on My Pillow' you could call it."

Fleas had become impatient. "I need to find my darned son so we can get this next part rolling or we'll never get out of here tonight. Boys?" she said to Paul and Isaac, "you want to come help me look?"

Both nephews seemed glad for the chance to get up and move around.

"I think I'll sit with these folks a bit then," Elva said. Various chairs were offered and she chose the one next to Jake. "You know Rebecca? the bride's mother?"

"I don't, no," he said. "At least not yet."

"Well no matter. She's my best friend in the world, but she <u>does</u> have a mouth on her, and it can become a bit...what? Tiresome."

"How's that?" Jake asked.

"Oh, just now for example. They were talkin' about country music, and there was general agreement that old Hank Williams was not only the greatest singer but also the greatest song writer ever in that field. But then someone asked Rebecca where she would place the son, Hank Williams Junior. And Rebecca announced, 'I always say the better part of <u>that</u> man must have dribbled down his daddy's leg!'"

Neither Beatrice or Ian said anything, but Jake, surprised, laughed.

Elva Mudd might well be somewhere into her fifties, but he felt sure it wasn't an accident she had chosen to plunk down next to him. Or, when he thought about it, that she had chosen that little story to tell.

And then, as though in confirmation, she looked directly at him and said, "And it's not that I'm a prude, you know, not by any means."

*

"How long you think this part'll go on?" he asked, voice low, leaning in close enough to Elva Mudd that he could feel her body warmth.

"Ha! Only slight longer than you'd think humanly possible," she whispered back. 'Just be patient now, young man, OK?"

He tried, but the day had been long, he was at least mildly toasted, a couple drinks before dinner and wine with and now the champagne toasts, and he had trouble staying with the youngsters at the mike as they rambled through their in-jokes.

Ian's parents were seated at the head table side by side shadowed by the bright overhead light, Peter Stiles shifting and sighing, dangling his arm off the back of his chair, no disguising his impatience. Nancy beside him, head down as she listened, turned out nicely in a gray jersey dress and still, though from time she touched the blue enamel watch on the silver chain at her breast. A family piece, her own mother's Jake knew, brought out these days only for big occasions.

When it came time for the grandfather of the groom to make some remarks, Peter Stiles got up unsteadily, blinked out onto the darkened room, fumbled out his half-frame reading glasses, but then pulled out no notes. He was big and beefy, florid large face, large hands, at 70 still plenty of curly white hair.

For the outer circle of guests, what he said would appear what you might expect. The proud grandpa representing the Stiles side of things. Even on short acquaintance what a fine young woman Olivia Johnson struck him as being. Thanks to Henry and Rebecca Johnson for creating her, praise for his son-in-law Leonard and his dear daughter Felicity for this evening and for the even more fabulous hospitality they would all encounter tomorrow. A somewhat choked-up accolade to Nancy for seeing a difficult fellow such as himself through almost 50 long years, mention of Beatrice as mother of Paul and Isaac, a nod to those two boys and their progress with their studies over there in *la belle France.*

And finally he told how several years ago now he'd been in New York and got an impulse and showed up in New Haven on Yale-Harvard weekend and could not for love or money find a hotel room. And how Ezra Nelson, now the man of the hour, came through and gave his old granddad his bed and himself slept on the ratty couch in his college dorm living room.

It was maybe a better performance than it looked. Afterwards when Felicity came up with her father by the arm, half supporting, half leading him, it was clear he was very drunk. Though he'd been competitive at tennis until he was into his fifties, his general way of moving was blundering, almost alarming. But now he swayed, head down, and when Felicity said, "Dad, you'll remember Jake Guarani," he had trouble focusing. Then said, "Sure, sure. Fact I was looking for you this afternoon. They said you were there at the house."

"Yes sir, I was."

"You still do plumbing?"

Jake smiled, looked to the others. "I did plumbing, sir, starting out. Some work under your own kitchen sink if I remember right. But I haven't actually plumbed anything in a long time now—"

"Well it doesn't go away, does it? The ability to plumb?"

"No sir, probably not."

"There's something going on in our pool filtration or the heating system, the boiler or something— We can still use it, but—"

"Well, I could at least have a look. And if I can't figure it out, I can certainly get you to the guy who will be able to."

"That'd be good. What I need is—"

Fleas said, "Dad, what we need right now is to get you home." Her grip on her father's arm tightened, pulling him up a little.

"I'll call you, sir, next week," Jake said gently enough.

"Huh," Peter grunted, turned to Fleas and shook his head as though he had been insulted. "I still don't get what this guy's doing here anyway."

"Dad!"

"Mr. Stiles?" Elva Mudd said. "Among other things Mr. Jake's presence here is yet another example of your girl Felicity's genius. His job is to deal with the problem of the lonely rich widows at this wedding and he is doing so in a superb manner, I can tell you."

Jake asked her, "I didn't know. Are you a problem?

She smiled. "I try my best not to be."

*

Jake found Ian in the men's room, stepped up to the urinal next to him.

"What's the story here, Jake?"

"What do you mean?"

"About the widow Mudd."

"She's a dish, isn't she?"

"I like her. How old do you think? I couldn't tell."

"Older than she looks, I'm pretty sure."

"Well, your range always included older women, as I recall."

"Did it?"

Once they were finished and zipped up, they went back out to the sinks. Fresh hand towels were stacked in neat piles on glass shelves above the faucets.

"So is there something in the offing?"

Jake regarded his own face in the mirror. "What do you take me for, man? I'm a gentleman, remember? Just met the lady."

"Sorry, guess I'm just lost in the old days. You worked fast as I recall."

Jake raised his eyebrows at his own image and at Ian, fainter, watching him from behind. "You know as well as I do, man, a lot of that was talk. Buzz."

"But not all."

"No, not all," Jake admitted. "Not all."

The private dining room was emptying out. Waiters were hastily clearing the tables, making a clatter, beginning to pull off the linens.

"You know, I've never cheated on Angie," Jake said, and then, because he was skating along the edge of honesty, added evenly, "not with any other woman. Does that surprise you?"

"Not really."

"I made it kind of a vow to myself when we got married and I've managed to keep to it. Ten years."

"That's good, Jake. Don't you think?"

Jake didn't answer.

To avoid the noise and the stir, they took glasses and a bottle of champagne and went outside. The fairway stretched out downhill in the moonlight, the tennis courts and the artificial lake nearly hidden off to the left, patches of near-black green where the club's huge old willow trees were clumped.

Ian said, "I hope you noticed how polluted my father was. Not that that forgives his behavior."

"Don't you apologize, Ian. Certainly not any fault of yours. Or Fleas'."

"Unwarranted, though."

"You think?" Jake laughed. "He's still pretty sharp, your old man. Knows how to put his thumb right on the old insecurities. You remember them, of course."

"Yours? I think I could still make the list."

"Go on."

Ian laid them out on his fingers. "Having to work Saturdays when the rest of us were free to play, being short—

"And hairy—"

"And hairy and dark in notably tall and fair Winnetka. But tell me, any new ones I should know about?"

"Ways of feeling inferior? Why'd you ask that?"

"In my practice I'm often surprised when clients come back to see me. Often they've forgotten their old problems and have replaced them with an entirely new set."

"Not me, man. I'm same-old same-old, I promise you." Jake laughed. "I often think of how fucking right you were to get out."

"Of Chicago? Winnetka?"

"Though, of course—" Jake spoke slowly, considering, "if you still lived here, it would be entirely different for you—"

"Because I'm a Stiles—"

"Or a Bowen—"

"Or whatever it is I am."

"A 'whatever' you are indeed," Jake nodded.

"I'm missing the direction here, my friend," Ian said. "You just trying to make me feel cut off from you 'cause I'm so pleased to see you?"

"Of course not." Jake bumped Ian with his shoulder, a feint at a football block. "Just marking it, that's all."

"You're probably right, though, about the North Shore not being the best place for you."

Jake laughed, scuffed the gravel with his toe. "Just got a nice offer, you know."

"Really? What was that?"

"Houston. From Mrs. Mudd should I happen to be free."

"But you're not."

"No. And it's not just Angie and the little girl. I'm not going anywhere. Know what I have in the bank? Ten thousand dollars. Otherwise, I'm paycheck to paycheck."

"So where's your salary go?"

"Beyond the mortgage and the supermarket and the insurance on house, car, and every damn thing but my nuts? Bogus therapists, bogoid 'life coaches,' orthodontists—"

"Already?"

"For Lisa, yes already. And God forbid at this point Angie should go out and earn some money. Too busy being the full-time little mother. Which apparently she plans on being for a number of years now." Jake paused, drank. "Little girls come with a lot of extras these days, I guess you've heard. Piano lessons, ballet lessons, reading tutors, girls' soccer clinic."

He stopped. Then asked, "Do you remember my old man?"

"Sure. From Prairie Avenue, out in the backyard Saturday or Sunday mornings still as a stick in his shirtsleeves, cigarette in the corner of his mouth."

"My mother didn't allow him to smoke in the apartment."

"Even as a kid what impressed me was how your dad didn't seem to feel called upon to say hello to little neighbor boys like other grownups did. They said when your uncle died and your father took over Guarani's he nearly ran the business into the ground."

"No one's ever liked him much," Jake said. "My mom either. You know, if there was an exorcism to get your fucking parents out of your blood and your bones and most of all out of your head, I would pay the price. To the damned priest if necessary. But I guess there isn't."

"Not that I've heard."

"All the old man's impatience and my mom's shit—those terrible explosions—I inherited all of it, lock, stock, and barrel."

"Jake, you're nowhere near as unhappy as either of those people were."

"Are. They haven't changed, you know. Worse now than ever. Angie doesn't like taking our daughter around them."

"I suppose that makes sense, doesn't it? Beatrice isn't exactly enthusiastic about our boys spending much time around my dad either."

Jake shook his head a little. "I don't think he'd go after his own grandsons, do you?"

For a moment, Ian looked dubious, baffled. Then he said, "That wasn't what I was getting at. Beatrice just doesn't like the unreasonable way my father gets when he's been drinking."

"Oh, sorry."

"But what was it you meant?"

"Well, you know, he used to touch me. We've talked about that."

"No, I don't think we ever did."

Jake laughed. "Really?"

"When, Jake?"

"Starting I guess when we were 11, 12 maybe? When you moved to Pine Street and I started coming to stay over. Sometime in there."

"Grab ass kind of stuff?"

"Yeah, that—" Jake smiled, shrugged, "—full-on pats on the butt when we were in our pajamas on our way up to bed, you know, his hand laying along my leg when it was me in the middle and you on the outside driving us home at night, getting a look at me in the bathroom when he could."

"And you didn't say anything?"

"To who?"

"Well, not to me certainly."

"No. Not at the time."

"And you didn't confront him?"

"No."

"Was there more to it?"

"What do you mean? There was one time he kind of showed himself off to me. Remember we went camping out beyond Elgin that time? There was a lake—"

"Yes."

"—and we all went skinny dipping. The rest of you had already gone to dress, the sun was down, and I was getting a canoe moved up and the paddles shipped and your dad came up out of the water and was just standing there watching me and chatting and he was brushing water off his chest and then he started tugging on himself some and it looked like it was getting thicker. That's all."

"I don't know what to say, Jake."

"You don't need to say anything."

"You weren't upset by it?"

"Not really."

"How long did it go on?"

"I don't really remember. Until tenth grade maybe?" Jake stopped, thought, then said, "You know what I thought at the time?"

"No."

"I wasn't up to going after girls yet, they were still a complete mystery to me. But I was certainly already primed. Some nights at your house I could hardly wait for you to start breathing regular so I could jerk off. And it seemed to me your dad saw that about me. Not that I was whacking it three, four times a day, which I was, I don't mean that, but that I was—you know—ready somehow."

"But still—"

"Your folks were extremely good to me—all of you, you and Fleas too, of course—but I wonder sometimes if Peter and Nancy's attention didn't matter to me so much at the time because my own parents are such cold fuckers."

"That could be, sure. Still, this is really distressing news."

Jake waited, then, turned away, his voice low, said, "You know, I sometimes think marriage isn't really my thing, built the way I am."

"So you've said. Do you often consider getting out?"

"Now and then. But I've told you, I've got my daughter to consider, and I won't be the one responsible for her coming from a broken home. Angie says the problem is that she and I are going in different directions."

"How's that?"

"That she's growing and I'm not."

"Is that true?"

Jake laughed. "If she only knew——" Then suddenly, "I think I can tell you this. I could be with men too, you know. Quite easily. What do you think of that, pal?"

"Is that theoretical, Jake? Or have you had some experience?"

"It's been a possibility since I first ever had sexual thoughts. When I figured out how to masturbate, sometimes it was to girls, but also sometimes guys. Grown men."

Silence on Ian's part. So Jake said, "Maybe your dad saw that in me too, you think?"

"Even if it's true, Jake, it doesn't let him off the hook."

"Then let me ask this. You ever happen to see Walter?"

"My brother-in-law? Yes, but not much. Mainly at holiday things at Beatrice's parents' place. They live out in Nanterre. Why?"

"Beatrice was noticing your father left you out of his speech. She said he often neglects to include you in things."

"And you think that might go back as far as Walter?"

"It's a possibility, isn't it?"

"And how did you find out about the business with Walter? Did I tell you?"

"You, yes. Or maybe it was Fleas."

*

It had been Fleas, Jake was sure. Told him as the kind of gossip so juicy she couldn't keep it to herself. The year Beatrice's older brother Walter came to Hampshire he was assigned to room with Ian. Impressive guy in the beginning, a smart redhead, cross-country runner. When he and Ian found themselves confounded by the dense reading for a politics course, they took to propping themselves up across from each other on a couch while one read a sentence aloud and the other tried to paraphrase it. But big-time theories sometimes cause young scholars to doze and one night Ian woke up surprised they had been out an hour or more. He poked Walter with his toe and asked was he going to move but Walter said he didn't think so. Then one thing led to another and there was some grappling and then some sexual stuff between them. Ian told his sister he wasn't alarmed by it, in the beginning he really just enjoyed the creature touch of Walter. No daytime expressions of affection in front of others which made Ian think in fact there was no real affection there. The sex might as well have been a new sport they were trying out. Extreme foo ball or something. Ian searched himself for worries about being gay, but at nineteen what little of his future he had sketched out included having a wife and a family.

Walter came to Winnetka for Christmas and took the other bed in Ian's room, the one that had been Jake's. Early Christmas morning when not even a mouse was supposed to be stirring, Peter Stiles came up to collect presents he had stashed in the back of Ian's closet and blundered in on his son face down with Walter on top of him. For the rest of the visit, Fleas said, her father remained entirely civil to both boys. But at the end of January Nancy announced on the phone that she and Dad would like Ian to 'go to someone to sort some things out.' Ian tried to tell her Christmas Eve had turned out to be the end of it with Walter and both of them were now seeing women, him Walter's sister for whatever you wanted to make of that. But his parents insisted.

The therapist they sent him to was a man named Lewis Keyes, who had been Fleas' psychology professor at Harvard and ran a small clinical practice out of his home in Cambridge. Ian took the bus down from Amherst for his sessions. Though Keyes had been Peter Stiles' own college roommate, he and Nancy somehow remained oblivious to the fact their old friend was in a long relationship with another man. Ironic, huh? Fleas said. She and Ian had a good laugh over what their dad would say if he found out he was shelling out for Ian to be set straight by someone gay.

*

Rain in the night starting at about three, hard, coming in gusts at first then settling into steady downpour. Thunder far off. Booze at the dinner and confession time with Ian kept Jake awake for quite a while, listening and waiting for the occasional flash of lightning.

Morning began dark, clouds low in, the air as warm and uninviting as bathwater left to sit. About ten, another big gush followed by on and off drizzle. At 1:15 as Jake was leaving Skokie (he thought to get there early to see what help he could be with whatever the new plan was), the sky lightened and the rain stopped all at once, as though someone had shut off a spigot.

When Jake pushed through the swinging door into the Pine Street pantry, he came upon Elva Mudd in a sleeveless turquoise satin dress, her luxuriant dark hair all carefully pinned up.

"You look terrific," he said.

"You think? Wish I felt so good. I used to be able to get into this dress without a girdle, but I guess those days are gone."

She came to him and put her arms around him and her head against his chest and hugged him. "Umm," she said, "just as I thought."

"How's that?"

"You are one <u>nice</u> feelin' fellow."

He was holding her too, catching little whiffs of a light, flowery perfume. "You too, ma'am," he said, imitating her cowgirl accent.

She pulled back and looked up at him. "But not really available, are you? You've got a handful of cards to play already."

"That's right. At least a handful."

She sighed, squeezed him again, let him go. "It's too bad, isn't it? I could use a man like you in my life right now."

"It is," he repeated, "too bad."

In the garden the sun was out full. Commander-in-chief Felicity paced the aisle in a sun dress assaying the damage, lifting up clumps of the sopping paper runner here and there. Rebecca Johnson was following her with her eye. "Wouldn't have had this problem, would we," she sang out, "had we gone with that Christ Church over there at the Lake as I originally suggested."

Felicity sighed and seemed about to snap at the bride's rail-skinny mother, but then she recovered herself and said, sweetly enough, "I'm sorry, but you know my mom loves this old place so much and what's the use of hanging on to it if they can't show it off from time to time?"

Leonard Nelson said, "I don't really see the problem. As long as Charlie shows up, who cares what happens?" His little joke was that the large number of acceptances for the wedding was due to the fact word had gotten around that his school friend Charles Gibson, the retired ABC News anchor, would be there.

Rebecca Johnson called out to Elva, "Hon? What is that thing you've got on?"

"This?" Elva spread her dress's flared skirt and made a little curtsy. "This is that old Bill Blass you have seen on me a hundred times before, lady."

"Oh Bill! Is there one girl left down in Texas who isn't a Friend of Bill's? I ask you!"

Olivia Johnson had not yet gotten into her gown. She said she wanted Ezra's opinion about what to do, but the groom was nowhere to be found. Her father cocked his head up and squinted at the sky and said, "We've got an hour. If the men'll pitch in to wipe down the chairs and we get rid of all this paper crap, I don't see why we can't just go ahead here."

Olivia stooped and pulled aside a piece of the runner and felt in the grass under it. Standing, she said, "I could go barefoot..."

"Oh darling! You can't get married without your shoes on!" Her mother's thin mouth turned down as though she was going to cry.

But Fleas and Olivia decided to go ahead with Henry Johnson's suggestion. Armfuls of bath towels were brought from the linen closet upstairs and Paul and Isaac were recruited to help. Mr. Johnson peeled off his jacket and squared his big shoulders and went to work.

With all but the last rows finished, Ian took a moment to clear his glasses and dry off his face. "Here, let me," Elva said, taking his handkerchief from him and reaching up to pat at his forehead. "You should really have a hat of some sort, you know. You're way blond—"

"I know."

Jake came up on them, his face and neck and arms glistening. "You may make do with a wipe down, but this man's going to need to wash," Elva said.

Ian checked his watch. Already 2:30. "OK, but we're up against it now."

In the downstairs hall Felicity was talking with a tall gentleman in a linen jacket and tie, long silvery hair draped behind his ears. He had a confident bearing, head high like some animal that only browses from the treetops. This was Lewis Keyes, Fleas' old mentor and, in a different way, Ian's.

Ian offered his hand, but instead Lewis put his arm around Ian's shoulder and hugged him. Fleas introduced Elva and Jake, then told Lewis, "You better go up with these gentlemen quick and change."

Lewis spread his arms and glanced down as though taking a small bow. "Do I not pass muster as is?"

"We get rental clothes," Ian said.

"Oh, alright, how fancy. I wasn't aware."

*

When Jake came out of the shower, the hum and chatter of guests arriving was already drifting up from below. The other three ushers had gone down, and the boxes the shoes came in and shirt wrappers and plastic bags and coat hangers lay strewn on both beds and on chairs. Lewis Keyes had his rental pants and shirt on, but the tails not yet tucked in, a blue tie in under the collar still untied.

"Do me, would you?" he asked Ian.

"Don't tell me you don't know how to tie a necktie."

"Of course I do," said Lewis. "It's just yours looks so nice and I want mine to look just like it."

Ian pulled the big end of the tie down, measured with his eye, then turned to Jake and said, "Lewis here is one of the great narcissists."

Lewis's big chest rose and fell with the tiniest singing wheeze. "I assume you say that in complete fondness."

"I do."

To Jake Lewis said, "I permit myself vanity."

Ian laughed. "Lewis is the one who came up with the idea for my masters that I should try to figure out the difference between positive self-regard and narcissism."

Jake was toweling himself off. "Well you got me. What is it?"

"The difference?" The other two men only laughed.

Ian had Lewis's tie done. He reached for the shorter tail, inserted it through the label on the back of the front piece, then pressed the whole thing against Lewis's chest with the flat of his hand. "There."

Over Ian's shoulder Lewis said, "It's a pleasure to finally meet you, Jake."

"Yes sir, me too."

"Is it actually Jacob?"

"Actually it's Giacomo, but I didn't ever like the idea of being called Jim or even Jimmy."

"You and Ian were great pals in childhood I recall."

"We were," Jake said, turning to Ian as though to be reminded who this guy was. "We are pals. Still," he added.

"Lewis was Fleas' teacher at Harvard and helped me too, remember?"

"Oh. Then this is the guy who did your shrinking."

"That's right." Ian looked yet again at his watch. "Gentlemen, we need to get on with it, please."

Jake put one leg up on the blanket chest at the foot of his old bed, dried it, changed legs, then wiped at his belly and chest.

Lewis loosened his pants, tucked in the shirt and buttoned back up. "I recall Ian saying you were the one who taught him when it's not necessary to be afraid."

"Well, physical stuff—that kind of danger—doesn't affect me much, it's true," Jake said. "I was just built that way I think. I got us into some nice trouble over time." He looked to Ian for confirmation, got it.

"Like what?"

"You live around here?"

"Down on the South Side by the University. I just recently moved out here from back east."

"You know the Baha'i House of Worship there in Wilmette by the Lake?"

"Extraordinary, exotic thing, that great white lacy dome, all the ponds and gardens—I was taken to see it first off."

"When we were kids we called it God's Little Orange Squeezer. I'd con Ian into going over there on our bikes. Way out beyond the distance either of us was allowed away from home."

"I'd have been such a stinking good boy if I hadn't ever met Jake," Ian said.

"What was the worst?" Lewis asked.

"Trouble?" Jake draped his towel over a chair, stepped into his shorts while he thought the question over, then sat and pulled on the thin black socks that came with the outfit. He stood and got into the pants. Ian unwrapped Jake's shirt, shook it and held it for him, waited for Jake to button up and put up the collar, then handed him his tie.

"You know about skitching?"

"I do not," Lewis said.

"When was it? Starting in sixth grade maybe?" Jake asked.

"Sixth or seventh, yes," said Ian.

"In the coldest part of winter—January, early February—when around here the streets are all a sheet of ice at night, you wait out of sight and when a car goes by you grab the bumper and 'ski hitch' yourself a ride."

"Fun."

"Sure—until the car brakes suddenly and you go under the back tires," Ian said.

"Which can happen," Jake added, laughing. "Or when the people in the car notice you in their rearview mirror and slam on the brakes and jump out and grab you and drive you down to the Winnetka Police Station and your parents are called…"

"Which did happen," said Ian. He held Jake's jacket up for him. "Gentlemen? I don't want to rush you, but shall we?"

Coming down the main hall stairs, Lewis paused at the landing. He said to Jake, "One other thing I remember about you."

"What's that?

"The January of getting laid."

"I don't know what you mean."

"Ian told me once you made a wager with two friends—you were in college I think—to see how many days in the new year each of you could go having sex with a woman."

"Oh, that—"

"And as I recall the other guys only made it through a week or so, but you—"

"It was never really a fair bet," Jake said. "I was the one who had the apartment, those guys didn't even have a place, you know? And I had four or five different girls, regulars I could call on at that point, and those bums, they had to hustle theirs up pretty much from scratch. So after six or seven days they pooped right out and I managed to get through until—I don't know—sometime in February maybe before I finally just had to knock off and get a decent night's sleep."

*

After the dinner and the bride and groom stuffing cake in each other's mouths, a six-man band set up at the far end of the tent. The players were college pals of Ezra Nelson's, the singers a very light-skinned black man and a Pakistani fellow. The young had no problem with how to gyrate to the music, a mix of reggae and ska, and some of the older guests seemed to decide there was no mystery here, just wave your arms and get funky. Others thought you might get by with a kind of exaggerated, tipsy foxtrot.

Late, midnight or after, when Ian noticed that Jake was no longer close-dancing Elva Mudd around the floor. The bride's parents had departed and Elva was nowhere to be seen.

Jake stood in his shirtsleeves, tie loosened and suit jacket over his shoulder. "Well," he said, "time for Luigi to pull a fade."

"You have to go?"

"I'm an early riser you know, and I work in the morning."

"How'd you leave it with Elva?"

"Kiss on the cheek." Jake laughed a little, shook his head. "No. When they left for their hotel, she said, 'Don't forget to call should you ever happen to get free...' Such a sexy lady!"

"You drunk?"

"Some. But I can drive. You?"

"Also. But I could have one more with you."

Though the bartenders remained pleasant and helpful, they were discreetly beginning to put bottles and equipment away in crates. Jake and Ian got short brandies and climbed up two levels to Nancy's garden, pulled chairs around so they could sit side by side and look out toward glow of the west suburbs.

"Remember at New Trier...?

"What about it?"

"When I informed one of the guidance counselors what my career goal was?"

"Mrs. Carrier. You told her you were thinking of going into garbage." Ian laughed. "You're not still of that frame of mind, are you?"

"I guess not. But you know, I do veer in the <u>direction</u> of screwing myself over. Like working for Mike Tanner. Not finishing college because <u>he</u> wanted me to go full-time and the money was sweet to have and I was 21 and stupid. Or later when Mike wanted to take me in the office. My logical next step, Mike said as much. But I didn't want to put on a tie and do nothing but estimate and massage clients, couldn't see myself nailed to a desk all day. I was cool. I had my own crews by then, guys I liked, felt responsible for. So I stayed the on-site man, and I may have fucked myself for good that way. Now Mike's got himself a handful of suits who may know 'business' but they don't know construction at all, I can promise you."

"I do recall there was some considerable shit you were taking when you first left DeKalb."

"Yeah? What was that? Enlighten me."

"Mike Tanner put you to overseeing a bunch of major residence renovations he'd gotten too busy to handle himself and some of them were for the families of people you and I had gone to school with. I said it couldn't hurt, them knowing you. And you laughed and said it couldn't hurt <u>them</u>."

Jake shook his head. "Why don't I remember any of this?"

"You said you'd be in there with the owner running through decisions and it'd be all buddy-buddy 'want a brew, Jake?' or whatever—and then the wife would call him to come get his lunch and you could hear her saying, 'I don't have to feed <u>him</u>, do I?'"

"It's changed," Jake said, "some at least. We're a lot more into commercial these days, big jobs west of the city and lately some pretty lucrative stuff at Northwestern— You know Mike's closing in on Mc-Closky in volume, don't you?"

"And you're still the boss's bright-eyed boy, aren't you?"

Jake screwed up his nose in doubt or maybe distaste. "I guess. But now Mike's got to find some way to snug his idiot Wharton MBA son onto the payroll."

He shifted gears a little. "Can I ask something?"

"Shoot," Ian said.

"In school, in your training, did they ever mention why when it comes to sex people seem to have such different needs?"

"No." A pause, then Ian said, "Sorry if I'm slow. Not functioning on all cylinders right now." After another moment he said, "Natural differences aren't really paid much attention in psychology. For a clinician like me, the major concern would be about what kinds of trouble their sex lives might be giving the client."

"Are there people who are actually <u>addicted</u> to sex?"

"It's a popular idea these days certainly. But not a way I prefer to think of it. Some people seek out a good deal of sex because of how it affirms them."

"Makes them feel better about themselves."

"That's right. Another thing which doesn't get mentioned very much is the motivation to please. For their own reasons, some people get a great deal of re-enforcement from providing others pleasure."

"Me, right?"

"I would imagine so, yes." A minute passed, and Ian said, "Funny, you asking me about sex."

"Well, I thought maybe you could help me."

"Is there a problem?"

"That I need to have it the way I do? Yeah," he laughed, "it can be a problem."

"And Angie's not up for that?"

"No, she is, but— It's about what I told you last night, my thing about guys. You asked had I had any experiences."

"Yes."

"A couple. The internet, you know, makes it so convenient. Though most of the men out there..." Jake trailed off. "They turn out to be real tire kickers, you know?"

"Tire kickers?"

"You know the guy who comes on the car lot and kicks a lot of tires but really isn't planning on buying anything. There was this one fellow, in real estate he was. He met my specs—fifties, hefty, not bad looking."

"And what happened?"

"Nothing. We had coffee. He's divorced, grown kids, lives alone now. Gave me his cell number, but I haven't called."

"Why not?"

"Guy struck me as being needy. And I don't need needy, do I?"

"I guess not."

"I tend to like the ones who want to be taken. I guess that makes me what they'd call a top."

"That's what we'd expect, isn't it?"

Jake shrugged. "They're in demand, the tops. Or so it seems." He paused. "Your friend Lewis seemed to like me."

Ian said, "Is that why you two were so slow getting dressed?"

"You didn't notice he had his eye on me? I didn't mind at all. He's got someone though, right?"

"Yes, Jay Carlson is his name. He teaches linguistics at the University of Chicago. He was here tonight, redheaded, skinny fellow. They've been together a long time."

Silence. Then Ian said, "Let me ask this. Regarding men, why'd you wait till now, Jake? Do you know?"

"Well, we're 40 or as good as——."

"As you keep reminding me."

"So I figured it's now or never. You're not shocked?"

"Why should I be?"

"Oh come on. This must change what you think about me somehow, old buddy."

"Let me ask you then. When you came to know about me and Beatrice's brother... It was Fleas who told you, right?"

"Must have been. She found the whole thing pretty amusing as I remember."

"And did that change your opinion of me?"

"In terms of being your friend? What kind of an asshole do you think I am?"

Ian laughed.

After a minute, Jake said, "What about it? Should I stop right now, while I'm still ahead?"

"I can't decide that for you," Ian said. "But if you go ahead 'exploring' with men, you will want to be careful. People who step outside their marriages for whatever reason can't imagine they're ever going to be found out. It's like bank robbers. They never figure on getting caught."

"Why's that? Is it guilt that trips 'em up?" Jake asked. "You know I don't have a lot of ordinary sense of guilt, especially when it comes to sex."

"I remember," Ian said.

"So is this your pal Freud then? You slip up because you <u>want</u> to get nabbed?"

"Not necessarily, sorry to say. It's nothing theoretical, just an observation. The thing about bank robbers came from a police detective I consulted with on a case one time."

"Ian? Don't start thinking my wanting to be with guys comes from the attention your dad gave me, OK?"

"No," Ian said, sounding a little reluctant, "I don't."

"Because he's not to blame. In fact," Jake laughed curtly, "there's no one to <u>blame</u> here."

"OK, if you say so. But tell me this. Do you think of yourself as being in trouble, Jake?"

"Me?" Jake barked out a little laugh. "You kidding? I'm <u>fucked</u>, man."

"Oh—"

But Jake cut him off. He squeezed Ian's shoulder right up by the neck. Then he came close and kissed him on the cheek. Ian did not pull away, but Jake could tell he was a little surprised maybe or nervous. "What the hell?" he said, "if anybody sees, we'll tell 'em we're just doing like the frenchies, right?"

TWO

Thinking over his talk with Ian on the way to Evanston in the morning, Jake only wished he'd said more. At least he could have laid out some of the amusing stuff. Like how the real estate guy he mentioned turned out not to be just a cup of coffee but a full-on effing farce. They agree on e-mail to meet 11 a.m. one summer morning at a house in Lake Forest. The guy is showing the property to prospects at noon. Hard for Jake to make up a reason to go off the job at that hour, but he manages. Gets there, guy's entirely OK, ex-football player is what he advertised and it's probably true, but turns out the owners have come back to the house unannounced and are futzing around the upstairs. So real estate guy draws Jake into the garage, lets down the double doors, gets him in a corner and starts feeling him up, which makes Jake super hard and hot for it. Funny the one to be done to for once when you're used to being the one who does. Jake relaxes, sighs. Real estate's on his knees rubbing his face against Jake's pants and trying to unzip his fly when they hear the tap tap tap of high heels and women's voices out on the flagstones. In a flash real estate's up and out to meet and greet the client and her lady friend, Jake waits a long anxious beat, then skirts out going toward the street face turned away, hears real estate explaining him as the pool man. But there is no pool, you jackass! Distantly Jake hears real estate correcting himself, saying…um…must be the gardener.

Luckily Jake's had the sense to park his little truck well down the street.

*

He was off the elevator and by his watch inside the office door with at least two minutes to spare before Mike Tanner's 8:30 a.m. Monday meeting, scheduled for Tuesday this week because of Labor Day. But there was no applause, nothing except half a smile from Cheryl the receptionist with the silver-blond hair and the big hazel eyes. And she opened with, "You needn't even have bothered coming all this way in, Jake."

The "guys" as he called them, five of them in fresh blue or white shirts and ties and one in a seersucker suit and no tie, flowed noiseless as goldfish behind glass in the big conference room at Cheryl's back, Dave Preston holding up a wire wastebasket and swooping about to catch crumpled paper balls the others lobbed toward him from their tilted-back chairs. The carpet around the table had blossomed into a white and yellow field of missed shots.

"Meeting's tomorrow instead, same time. Mike is at the doctor's."

"What's that about?"

"Chest pains. Mike says indigestion, nothing more than excess barbecue, but Meg insisted she take him anyway. "Here," Cheryl ripped a pink slip off a little pad and handed it over, "he just called from the waiting room. You can inform the basketball team yourself," she raised her lovely gray-shadowed eyes to Jake and smiled again.

He didn't look at the note. "What else did Mike say?"

"Well, you know how well he handles being made to wait. He said if it wasn't a heart attack before it's gonna be one by the time he gets in to see the doctor."

Jake was surprised, but not exactly worried. Mike was a bandy, thrust-chested little Irishman just short of 60, ruddy, a reformed smoker, overweight but light on his feet. He bounded up from chairs to glad hand as though electro-shocked, ran all day from problem to problem. His lunch was usually a sandwich crammed in and hardly chewed while he talked, which did not make him easier to understand when he happened to be on the phone.

Jake laid his shoulder against the panel of the glass which was the conference-room door and pushed in. Noticeably chillier in here than in the reception area. Out the four ceiling-to-floor windows black-tar downtown Evanston rooftops and green treetops poking up in pale yellowy hazy sun. "Hey Jake! Hey man! Hey!" the guys grinned, "Didya hear about Mike?"

"I heard." He glanced at the slip Cheryl had given him. "Meeting's off till tomorrow, same time."

The guys nodded a little, then went on grabbing sheets off the tablets printed with the MIKE TANNER BUILDER logo, scrunching them, winging them in the direction of Dave's seductively dancing wastebasket. They treated Jake like some kind of ongoing joke they had among themselves. Only Kevin Tanner, Mike's son, the one in the seersucker with a pink polo shirt and white tennies, moved to swivel around the leather chair next to him. "Good weekend?" he asked, patting the seat cushion with the flat of his big hand.

Jake sat, not answering.

"What'd you do?"

Jake thought maybe he would just drop in casually, 'Oh, you know, I had to usher at this big society wedding.' But even if he explained, none of the yo-yos except maybe Kevin would necessarily believe him. And though Jake had known Kevin since he was nine, he could never be sure how much about him the kid actually tracked. Sometimes he acted as though Jake was just some joe who'd been on Dad's payroll since the beginning of recorded time. The current book on Mike's boy was that now finally at 30, married, busy school degree in hand, wife expecting Mike and Meg's first grandchild, he was back on track. The bopping in and out of school, throwing up nice jobs, the time outs lolling about in Thailand and Malaysia and the excessive amount of powder he'd snugged up his snoot? According to his hopeful parents, these were things of an over-long adolescence all now put aside.

Having been let hang, Kevin's little question had caught the interest of the others. Even Dave Preston had grabbed a seat and was leaning forward, still stupidly cradling the wastebasket in his arms like a man expecting he was going to barf. Almost under his breath, Jake said, "Went to a wedding."

"In Winnetka," Kevin said.

Before Jake could say anything Pat Nellums down the table chimed in, "If it was Winnetka it could hardly have been any big old Eye-talian wedding, could it?" and the rest of them laughed. Jake got to his feet, gave them a pale smile, showing them his teeth. Policy was to never let them know when they had gotten to him. Nellums was supposed to be Mike's lead contract scout and Jake was sure the man had it in for him.

It would have been nice to have something—a set of papers or files to straighten with a whack against the tabletop—to emphasize the fact that it was he who was now done with them, at least for the time being. But having nothing in hand he simply said, "Gentlemen," giving it a bit of a military snap, and headed for the lobby.

He was at the door when Kevin sang out, "So Jake, you never let on what wedding this was."

Jake only half turned, not allowing them to see his anger and mumbled, "Friends." Then he washed it out of his face at least and did turn all the way back to them. "Charlie Gibson was there."

"Who's that?" David Preston leaned toward Nellums, who was seated beside him.

"The retired CBS news guy, I think—"

"ABC, you jerkoff." Jake couldn't help saying it, but he did manage to smile as he did.

But still, except maybe for Kevin, their eyes all got big. "Ooooh!" some said it, some just looked it. Charlie Gibson. A funny claim to make. True? They didn't seem to care. The good part was they had succeeded in getting under his skin.

"I'm interested. How'd you happen to know my whereabouts?"

Kevin said, "My mother-in-law's here on a visit and we were showing her around and on Pine Street there were all these cars, obviously some big do, and my wife noticed that little Toyota you so love."

"In amongst the Mercedes and the Jags. OK. So?"

"If you really insist on using that vehicle, Jake, I think what we agreed on was that you'd return it to the office lot at the end of the day."

Jake nodded. That had been the deal. "It's just—" he sighed, having made this pitch before with no luck, "—it's just a long drive in here from the sites we're working right now and a waste of my time to have to return it every night and then drive halfway back out to get home."

"Yeah," Preston said, "but remember, Jake, when you're in that thing you are an advertisement for the company."

"So?"

"So we're back to the question," Kevin explained. "What's that little old Mike Tanner junker in the wrong color doing there where it was?"

Jake shrugged and shook his head. "You'd have to list for me who other than your wife it might be who's clocking that kind of thing," he said. "Otherwise, I got plenty of other stuff to worry about." And he went out.

The vehicle in question was a '94 regular-length pickup, fire-engine red with the company name in black on the driver's door and an out-of-date phone number Jake had painted out himself, though in certain lights he would admit it still ghosted back into view. To celebrate the new millennium Mike had gone for all new vehicles in blue with gold lettering. Cheryl's mother Olivia still ran the office in those days. She told Jake it must have been an oversight the red truck wasn't sold off then. Jake happened on it more or less abandoned in the back of the yard out off the Edens where they kept the big equipment. It turned out to be what he expected, a very peppy little gun, a rough ride but fun for zig-zagging in and out of traffic. Jake put some time and his own cash into it—seat covers, battery, plugs, later a radio—and hoped Mike would eventually just give it to him. But instead, the Toyota blew up into being an issue. Jake couldn't figure out exactly who in the office wanted it gone, though he didn't think it was Mike himself.

He stood bent over Cheryl checking a couple phone numbers he needed against her Rolledex. Nellums was holding the conference room door ajar, but none of them came out. Their voices ran together, humming, indecipherable, and occasionally they let go a little confidential laughter. The guys' main job as far as Jake could tell was looking busy, so without Mike on the premises there was no special reason for them to saunter on down to their nice clear desks. Not likely any of them had a fistful of urgent calls to return.

Out of downtown Evanston heading west he breathed easier. Except for helping out at his uncle Gio's flower business up through high school, Jake had never really worked for anybody other than Mike. Loyalty usually made it possible to get through the weekly meeting simply by concentrating on figuring out what Mike himself currently wanted from him. Or if it was presentation time, he waited through the flapdoodle the guys generated and then came in under them, direct to the prospect as practical as he could be. Which almost always had the desired effect. In his check shirt and jeans, in cooler weather his leather jacket, Jake stood out as <u>not</u> a suit. Reliable know-how his stock in trade, his part in setting the hook.

Otherwise he pretty much dreaded having to drag ass in to the main office. He never understood why Mike wanted to buy the building and renovate the labyrinthine fourth-floor in the first place. True, the decision came during a period when their business was expanding rapidly, but as Jake pointed out, they had grown nicely while they were still operating mostly out of the on-site trailers, with Olivia and just one girl to pick up for the boss and take his messages in a three-room main office on the ground floor. 'Shit, man,' he told Mike at the time, 'if you just want to dazzle 'em, forget Evanston entirely and go into one of those high-rises downtown.'

But Mike hadn't listened. On many subjects. The college boys with their packaged software estimates, their business economics degrees and their pie-in-the-sky promises to clients. Mike held out hope for them, upped their salaries when they threatened to walk, apparently never noticed that year after year Jake continued to bring in the second most business, very close behind what he himself brought in. When Kevin came along, his father created "Operations Manager" for him. And what was that? Apparently it meant doing all the stuff Olivia Livieros had done for years with no apparent sweat, but badly and for more than double Olivia's salary. The poor old girl got so frustrated with being shadowed she quit, or "retired" as Mike spun it, getting nothing much out of her years with the company except the receptionist's job for Cheryl. Which in itself was good, since the daughter turned out to be nearly as efficient as Olivia herself.

His way passed within a mile of his own house, so he decided to head over and see if Angie happened to have gotten back yet. The streets were silent again, no bikes, no kids in the yards or on the pavement. But from the elementary schools came the excited roar of all the little bees returned to the hive. His own Lisa all last week on edge but happy too, coming out to the garage to use his electric sharpener on her new pencils, coming again to show him her set of highlighters from the dollar store.

Angie's car was gone, the door into the kitchen locked, but her bag and Lisa's smaller one stood at the foot of the stairs. So maybe she'd managed to get Lisa to school on time. He was about to go, but then instead took their stuff up, dropped Angie's in their bedroom and put Lisa's in hers. Angie's son Earl had been released from 'the farm' as they called it the first of May and had been staying with them all summer. Angie would tell Jake he shouldn't snoop, a young man deserves his privacy, but Jake didn't count knowing what's going on in your own house snooping. He tried Earl's doorknob but it wouldn't turn. He stood still and listened, heard the heavy slow breathing of a fairly plump young man sleeping with his mouth open.

Ten-thirty a.m. Jake sighed. Even Angie, so goddamn loyal to Earl, was anxious to have it be just them and Lisa in the house again. Back down the hall, he glanced in on the master bedroom and all at once it came in on him in a black wave how tired he was. He thought about stumbling in, kicking off his shoes and lying down for an hour, but he forced himself not to, went in the bathroom and threw water on his face and ran a comb through his hair, jogged down, locked up and got back in his little truck.

His current assignment was no big deal, the tear-down of an old house on a large lot in the center of Barrington and the construction of four floors of new offices for a community foundation and a medical consortium. Two boxes basically, elevators, reinforced flooring and additional electric for diagnostic equipment the client was planning on putting down the basement. They had the shell completed and most of the glass in, so it was the hour of the subs, the heating duct guys, the plumbers and the electricians. His own men had not progressed much this morning, but he had not expected them to. And unlike the guys at the Evanston office, they were happy to see him. Questions for him to decide, reasons to go into his trailer and pull certain plans out of their pigeonholes and unfurl them one more time just to be sure.

*

"Girls?" Angie called from the foot of the stairs.

A sudden cease to the giggling, chatter, and occasional wild shriek from Lisa's room.

"Heads up now, this is important. It's your father, Lisa. Come down and give him a kiss."

Silence. Now that she was a second-grader, Lisa was in the process of training herself not to come automatically when they wanted her. Her pal Trudy Meyers seemed to have that one down pat already.

"I've got stuff for you," he called up.

Angie frowned just a little even as she smiled at him. The thought seemed to be, 'You have? Really?'

Just that much started him hoping there might be something up. Some of her sweetness to be had. Coming soon, maybe tonight? He felt he <u>deserved</u> it. And not just normal kid's-asleep lovemaking, but some real extended getting loose. In a word, some banging. After all, he'd held out against Elva Mudd, her big Texas-size compliments, her face against his shoulder when they danced, her breasts pressed against him.

The problem of course was how to get Angie to want to without ever knowing what it was he'd taken a pass on in her honor.

He went ahead of her into the kitchen, where her grocery bags stood on the counter. He was bent over getting a bottle of wine from the cupboard when the girls came tumbling noisily down the stairs. Lisa ran in and threw herself on him as though he was some big field rock meant to be climbed. Lucky his legs were strong. He straightened and she still clung to him, a scrawny monkey. "What is it, what is it, Daddy?"

He had been smart enough to ask could he take two. Delicate little lacy ceramic candy dishes with clusters of tiny red and yellow roses along the rim. Both girls suddenly subdued, pleased, admiring. He'd struck out.

Angie put the milk away and closed the refrigerator door. "And for me?" she asked.

"Big kiss."

He came down on her quickly and before she could duck out of his way pressed her back up against the refrigerator magnets and postcards and planted one on her. And got no nervous resistance, the push-off which often came when Lisa and her little friends were around. She gave back as good as he gave her, her mouth soft against his, his tongue easily parting her lips for a second.

The girls watched, for a moment still.

He let Angie go and she came back to the counter and picked up one candy dish and turned it over, looking for a name, a mark. So like her that he laughed. It was a trait picked up from her mother. "Saint Alice Collector of Name Brands" he called the old girl behind her back.

"Classy," Angie said. "From the wedding?"

"The dinner last night. For the mints."

"So you just snagged them?"

"No, Fleas asked if I would like one to bring Lisa and so I mentioned Trudy too and she said sure."

"Always so thoughtful, Felicity." Angie set the dish down.

She had been girls' JV volleyball at New Trier when Fleas was a senior star. In fact, Jake first met Angie when Felicity took him along to her crowd's parties. Dark-haired, compact, foxy Angie Moore was two years older than Jake so he figured well out of his league. She remembered thinking him cute and one time to let him know she ruffled the hair on the back of his neck when they were dancing. He wasn't even sure that had happened, and it didn't matter anyway. In those days a dozen girls could have been hitting on him and he wouldn't have noticed.

"What?" he said. "Did you think I swiped a candy dish?"

"No."

"I'm not a thief, you know."

"I know. And Richard Nixon was not a crook."

"That's kind of a shitty thing to say—"

She shrugged. "I didn't mean anything, Jake. Forget it, OK?"

He took a deep breath. "OK."

She unpacked groceries, leaving out a package of chicken pieces, onions, celery, a box of rice pilaf, the butter. When she reached to stow cans in the cabinets her shirt rode up, exposing a strip of suntanned back above her jeans. They'd been together almost 12 years and married 11, but a sighting of her flesh still drew his attention. At 42 she was of course a little fuller than she had been, but in Jake's opinion the extra flesh on her belly and hips only made her sexier.

She reported the news from the weekend at Delavan. Lisa swam out to the raft by herself. With a life jacket, of course. They helped Grandma Moore make cookies all Sunday morning and wrapped them in Cellophane and tied bows on them and sold a bunch at some Labor Day picnic Monday. Coming home Angie's car sounded funky, it worried her the whole way, maybe Jake should have it looked at.

"What happened with Earl?"

"What do you mean?"

"I thought he was supposed to move down to campus this weekend, but he's still upstairs—" and then in a lower voice because of the girls "—whacking off."

"Actually, he's gone out," she said curtly.

Jake looked out the window over the sink. True, no Earl's car in the driveway or, craning a little, out at the curb either.

"He says there's no real reason to stay down there this week, it's only registration, which he can do online, and one day of classes, and the rest is freshmen moving in and noise and hassle and—"

"A deal's a deal, Angie."

She stopped dead, eyed him. "You really want him gone, don't you?"

"You were the one who said you could use the break. I—" Having risen once, his bile seemed to know the way up again. He fought it. If he spoke his mind now there would be hostilities. And no nooky.

"There's no reason to pretend, Jake. Earl is my problem, not yours. You've made that clear enough."

"How do you figure? Who wrote that fucking 'farm' in fucking California a check for two thousand dollars every month for a year-and-a-half to keep Earl in tennis togs?"

"You 'write the checks,'" she mocked him again. "And me? 'I write the songs that make whole world sing!' Fuck you, Jake, just fuck yourself!"

He looked around. They had agreed to try not to swear in front of Lisa. But she and Trudy had snuck off, leaving the candy dishes on the counter.

Once again he mastered himself, pulled up the reasonable voice. "You're not being fair to me, you know."

She turned away. Her shoulders rose, fell. Her breath caught. He got her from behind this time, arms fully around her, locked across her chest. He pushed against the curve of her neck with his chin, gently, raspy, and she stayed still. Her chest heaved again, there were tears he was sure.

He nuzzled again and she moved her head off a little, but didn't try to break free of him. "You're like sandpaper," she said.

"You should watch it with the 'fuck yous,' honey. You've been doling out a lot of them lately. Save 'em for special occasions, OK?"

She smiled. Nodded. Whispered, "I know. I'm sorry, Jake."

He rocked her a little. "Wish you could have been with me instead."

"I do too. Was it grand?"

"You know Felicity. No jar of caviar left untapped."

"Our weekend was a nightmare. Lisa was all needy, whiny. My mom brings it out in her. She caters to her, then traps her in her own stupid agendas, crap that Lisa couldn't care less about that just drags on and on."

"Like?"

"Those damned cookies. Not as much fun as I made it out to be. Sweltering weather, oven blasting away, hotter than the hinges of Hell in that dinky kitchen. Lisa got so worn out, by the end of the day she was frantic. It was really sad."

Angie always saw clearly the effect her mother had on the little girl, never when old Alice conned her in exactly the same way.

"We should try to get away, just you and me, even if only for a couple of nights."

She nodded, but also said, "And do what?"

He shrugged. "Check into a hotel, have a nice dinner. Downtown if we don't want to get on a plane. Chase each other around the room all night."

She raised her eyebrows, smiled, looking down. Modesty? Maybe some amusement over memories? They had spent some pretty wild, happy nights in hotel and motel rooms over the years.

"You and Merle—"

She always made mild fun of his love for Merle Haggard. What's that all about? she would say, it's not as though you're a cowboy or some lonely long-distance trucker out there on the road.

No way to tell her he did often feel lonely, not out there on the road but out in the dark and cold for sure. Saying that would be taken as direct criticism of her. He had tried to explain it in a joking way, though, pointing out he shared Ol' Merle's faith in some good sexual times to reset the buttons between a man and a woman.

Going up to take his shower, he found the girls in Lisa's room arranging the seating order of dolls and stuffed animals around a play table. More subdued now. They didn't look up when he came in.

Had they even been aware of the squabbling between the grownups? He was sure. Always tuned in, little listening posts. Jake had been one too, in the poison, often nutty atmosphere of his own childhood he had to be.

*

He lay splayed across the bed in clean undershorts waiting for sleep, windows open to the late afternoon stillness, the lightest of breezes playing the hair of his torso and upper legs. The shorts were a concession to having a daughter. Though she'd been asked to knock, Lisa hadn't yet developed any real sense of him and Angie deserving any privacy.

Not a summer breeze. Anyone who marked and loved the signs of the seasons changing as he did would sense that. Fall. The storm windows to put up some weekend next month leaning only a few degrees off upright against the wall in the garage. His critical eye for work done wrong also made Jake take notice when things had been done right. The windows stacked like that by the previous owner had helped sell him on the house, a brick ground-floor and white frame story-and-a-half with four bedrooms, two-car garage, half finished basement. When Jake was starting out the men used to call these ample places from the 50s 'Ozzie and Harriets,' but he had come to admire them. Not only were the rooms larger and the craftsmanship better, in these older models even the hardware and doors and fixtures were more solid and durable.

Though Angie's mom had not been asked her opinion, when she first saw the house she pronounced it much too big for their needs. But then to her surprise they didn't ask for any help with the down. The day Jake and Angie married he had forty thousand in the bank, the next week his savings amounted to a hundred dollars and change.

He had never minded. What was the fun in life if you couldn't put all your hopes on one throw now and then? He knew Angie was a princess when he asked her to marry him. Not on the level of a Fleas Stiles, not a Winnetka princess, but a coddled half Jewish Wilmette one. At the time buying the Skokie house was part of his plan to spoil her further. The way her asshole first husband had rubbed her face in the dirt offended Jake. The hope was he could make Angie once again as carefree as he remembered her from New Trier.

After she was divorced, Angie continued living in Santa Barbara. When Jake went out there to get her to marry him, he found her in a cramped little place where Earl had to sleep on the couch and had nowhere to put his stuff. When they came back, Earl got his own bedroom with plenty of carpet space to spread out his things. Jake was 29 then and took pride in the instant family effect. He offered Earl fishing, the chance to go target shooting and learn to use his guns, hunting in the future. And for a little while it looked as though the boy was going to go for it. Then something changed. 'I have a father in California, Jake,' Earl said one day. And it wasn't as though he didn't understand his real one was a jerk and a welcher. He still had nightmares about the landlord pounding the door nearly down yelling for the rent when real dad slacked off on the child support.

The boy started getting into trouble almost as soon as he and his mom moved back to Chicago. Detention, bad report cards, vandalism, other mothers complaining he was foulmouthed. At first Jake thought there might be an opening for him here since he knew the drill, had been considered a trouble kid himself. Counselors claimed the acting-out was Earl's way of testing to see how much he was really wanted in this new family. For three or four years his main problem seemed to be an inability to stick with anything for very long. Then he became entirely dedicated—to getting high. Booze and pot first, then coke and probably even before the end of high school some heroin. And of course lying, cheating and then bigtime stealing from them as he began to drown in his needs. Jake got so angry at one point he told Angie the boy was a write-off. She came back at him with stuff about you can never write off what was born out of your own womb and so forth. As his punishment she took Jake off the case, so often he had little idea of what was going on except when she came to him for money. Money for Earl to go learn how to cook up bark and weeds and grill a snake at a survival camp in Maine, then for a court-mandated ten-week tough love program neither the feds or the State of Illinois would spring for. Angie's own parents were both sitting pretty in their separate ways, but neither of them opted to contribute to the salvation of their only grandson. Earl moved back to California to live near his father, completed junior college, seemed to be shaping up. Then he was arrested for going 90 miles an hour the wrong direction down the freeway at 3 a.m. with a blood alcohol level nearly equal to a martini's. Angie had to go, ex-hubby's parents had to pull strings to get Earl a year at a rehab "farm" instead of jail. ("Strange farm," Jake said when he had looked through the brochure, "swimming pool and barbed wire, no cows or chickens.")

The farm seemed to do the trick. The kid came back to Skokie, went to school, managed to stay in. Jake kept his fingers crossed, being of the opinion Earl was one of those people whose biggest kicks come from disappointing the ones who care about him.

*

It was funny, Angie astride his thighs in only her panties tugging down his undershorts and him still zonked and trying to come to reaching reflexively to pull his shorts back up. She paused and then as she tugged again Jake's eyes half opened and he swam up enough to figure out what was going on and also get a laugh out of it and let her pull the shorts off him.

He rolled, looked toward the door. Shut. Whispered, "Where're the girls?"

"They went back down to the Meyers'. They have homework."

"Already?"

"I think it's writing their names and addresses in their school things."

"What kind of time we got?"

"Maybe a half hour."

She had him hard already. He sighed, watched as she slowly licked his cock, then swallowed it. He reached and lightly touched her breasts, thumbs pushing in on her nipples.

She came up, lay full out on top of him, her whole body flushed, warm.

"Lift up."

When she did, he lowered her panties, reached down and in one long stroke pulled them off her legs, tossed them toward a chair, settled back. Held her butt and kissed her and she squirmed and rubbed her sex down against his cock.

"Can you sit on it a while?"

"Sure."

She got back up on her knees, eyes on him, fixed smile, got hold of his penis, lifted, rubbed the head against herself and slowly sat to introduce it.

"Just hold a minute now," she whispered.

"I'm not going anywhere."

She was already quite wet. He let it all settle, waited for her to make the first move. Meanwhile, he held her lightly at the hips, swept his hands up along her sides, cupped her breasts, put spit on his fingertips and applied it to both nipples, lightly tugged them, friendly tug.

"Hello."

"Hello, husband."

She began to rock, hands on his chest, head back, neck extended, eyes closed. Soon it began to feel too good. Not wanting the trip to end right away he pulled her down against him and rolled them together onto their sides to put himself more in charge, paused, then began giving it to her gentle and regular, sweeping her long hair out of the way and kissing all over her face as he went. She squirmed but he held her tighter to him and she seemed to like that, snuggled down into it. Her cheek hot against his. Mouths and tongues, dick and cunt, her free hand full cupping on his ass, pulling him in on her, letting him know when it felt best.

Like this, he thought, it could just go on and on. But then all at once Angie was biting her lower lip and her eyes were closed again and she was tense. Maybe beginning to come? Not sure of that, only sure of his own need to shoot it coming right up through him. If he didn't stop or back off—

"I'm going to have to do it honey, soon now."

"It's ok, it's ok," she said, her mouth tight, "go on. I'm fine."

He came hard, breathing, noise in his throat, all that pent-up desire, and held her close even after it was over. Pretty sure she had gotten one too, although he didn't ask. Little kisses, gently. Her breathing, his.

The house quiet around them like a giant cocoon. It was a long time before he loosened his hold on her, and even then she was slow about rolling even a little away from him.

*

Jake had no trouble getting started in the morning, loved being up and out in the dark while the rest of the world slept on, having the jump on the day. He usually woke with a kind of shock. If he made Angie stir he'd just kiss her cheek or her exposed shoulder and then would be across the bare floor into the bathroom, light on, blinking, shucking his pajama bottoms, a mirror glimpse of his body momentarily startling as though there were a stranger in the room, starting the water, taking his first leak, only in the shower stall face up to the hot water coming finally fully conscious.

Clean, dried-off, as he moved through the bedroom gloom gathering his clothes Angie shimmied over, found the warm indentation where he'd been. "Ummm," she sighed, "why don't you come back for a little, honey?" Her voice hoarse, deep, unconsciously at its sexiest.

"Wish I could." He was tempted. There was an electric plug-in razor in the truck he could use if he needed to. Get to the job <u>at</u> seven <u>with</u> the men, instead of before…

But no. Keys, handkerchief, wallet, no coffee, he was out the door and in the little Toyota all on automatic. Earl's Nissan at the curb. Jake had heard him come in late, but hadn't bothered to check time when.

Out there zipping along in the blue, the lifting dawn at his back, no traffic to speak of, he thought of himself as one of those responsible for all those still sleeping. Should have been a cop, he sometimes told himself, or a fireman. Protector, caretaker, the guardian in his nature. (Or garbage man. Why'd he ever let the New Trier guidance lady in the big black-framed glasses and the check suit talk him out of that one?) Same feelings when he was twelve and had his paper route, crisscrossing happily through the dreaming streets of Wilmette.

He matured before a lot of the other boys, though he didn't shoot up the way some of them did. No memory of what his genitals had looked like before, but what he got was OK with him, a dick about six inches when it was hard and fairly thick, balls that swung a little, bush when it came in dense, fairly coarse. The first fall he was at North Shore the coach took him aside and told him he needed to get himself a jock strap. Now how in hell was he going to do that? Not something he felt he could ask his father about or his sisters either. Two of them were already gone, married, anyway. So he got the paper route and with his first pay snuck into the sports shop down in the village and, head lowered, mumbled something to the manager about where to find them. "Athletic supporters?" the man said, and pointed him toward the back. Hard figuring out about what the size labels meant, red-faced as he took the slim Bike box up to the counter. Before on the way into the shower at school he'd felt the other kids' eyes on him. But after he started wearing the jock their sniggering stopped and he sensed he made some of them a little envious.

He kept the paper route. One morning in the dark as he was flinging one customer's Trib he noticed a lamp on low in the picture window
and a man standing there naked. The account was an older lady, so this
had to be her son. Jake had trouble believing what he'd seen. (In the
movie "Airplane" the nasty pilot asks the kid, 'Have you seen a grown
man naked?' Except for Peter Stiles that time at the lake, Jake didn't
think he had. In his family there was always strict modesty, him and his
father always in pants coming out of the bathroom, his mother with her
wrapper clutched about her.)

The guy in the picture window…how many times did that happen? Maybe five or six. Once Jake figured out he was the entire audi-
ence for the show he began looking forward to it, was disappointed if
he didn't see the light on as he came down the street. College kid home
for the summer. The guy would be holding his dick, but whether that
was some kind of offer Jake didn't know. To avoid actually meeting up
with him, he went by to collect when he figured it would be only the
mom in the house (the guy worked, Jake saw him downtown one day
scooping ice cream). One time she told him to come back and when he
did, near dark, it was the son who appeared at the door. He invited Jake
in, but Jake just stood there. The screen was between them. The guy
went to look for money, came back, said he couldn't find it yet, just
hang on. Asked again, 'Why don't you come in?' Jake couldn't even
find his voice. Then the mother called from upstairs that there were
dollar bills loose in her purse and Jake felt relieved. The guy brought
the purse, opened the screen, counted out paper and silver—the exact

amount—and carefully passed it to Jake. He had a funny little smile on his face that seemed to say, 'We know each other, don't we?' and his hand trembled just a little. Before Jake could turn away, the guy touched himself, placed his hand on his basket and "adjusted" himself as they say. Jake caught it more out of the corner of his eye and didn't turn back to really look, didn't want the guy to see him looking. In fact he ran down the front walk, got to his bike and power-pedaled away.

*

"And finally," Mike Tanner was saying, "there's the one piece of really good news."

So much had gone on in since Friday that Jake first began glancing around the table to see which one of the bozos was getting that puffed-out canary look they took on when it was announced they had landed the company some action. But then Mike mentioned Jake's cultivating the Miller brothers over the years and Jake abruptly looked down instead, drummed the edge of the table with his thumb and index finger as though impatient while Mike began heaping on the praise. When the boss finally rolled out the figure—a twenty-point-five million dollar office building beyond O'Hare—there were several low whistles and then a little round of applause. Jake looked up and glared. Given their performance yesterday, he wasn't even going to expend the energy to figure out which of them might actually be pleased for him.

The meeting began to break up, Mike hurrying down the hall toward the men's room. Jake caught up with him coming out still rehitching his belt. The boss could look fairly spiffed—blazer, tie—for a presentation, but around the office he was shirtsleeves rolled and shirt half out and bagging around his big middle. He had a way of steering you along in his direction by bearing down on you with his bulk. So without his boss even touching him, Jake now found himself pushed into Mike's office and waiting in front of the big messy desk while Mike went through drawers.

"What're you looking for?"

Mike stopped. Straightened. Big smile. "I thought I had a half-pack of cigarettes here somewhere." He indicated a skinny foam-rubber padded couch against the wall if Jake wanted to sit. But Jake stayed on his feet.

"Forgot they want me off 'em completely now."

"So did you have an episode or something?"

Mike shoved a drawer shut, sank into his big desk chair, swiveled back and forth. "Seriously, Jake?"

"Dead serious."

"Between you and me, I still think the whole thing was a burp that got down the wrong tube. They did some tests and all and there'll be results, but man, I feel good today. And if I'd had an incident, that wouldn't be true, would it?"

"I don't think so."

"So let's see." Mike moved some papers around, appeared momentarily interested in one, put it back. Given the size the business had grown to, he still carried too much of it in his head. He was always bellowing 'Cheryl!' and she'd come running in, headset cord dangling, and he would demand to know where some document had gotten to. But Cheryl couldn't be of much help, really, because even if she had the time Mike usually wouldn't let her touch his desk.

"Oh—" He smiled broadly at Jake, "About that little truck you've appropriated—"

"Yeah?" Jake thought, Let it go, if need be just let it go.

"I don't see any reason you have to bring it back into town here at night. That's bullshit. Your time's valuable, you know."

"The argument was my leaving it wherever might be bad for the company's image."

"You weren't going to park it in front of the whore house, were you?"

"No, I'd take it around back."

Mike hefted himself to his feet, came and put his arm around Jake's shoulder, started him toward the door. "Jake, you are the best advertising we got."

Kevin Tanner stood in the hall waiting to talk with his father. Mike said, low, "Some people around here may be getting a little fuddy-duddy in my opinion." But Kevin appeared not to register what the remark was about.

"When do you see the Miller brothers?"

"Tomorrow, meet with them and the architect again, then we'll all go to lunch. There's a whole slew of engineering questions still that have to be dealt with, so I'm taking John Heinemann along."

Mike called out to Kevin, "What you got on for tomorrow, Son?"

"Nothing much."

"Jake, why don't we put Kevin in that meeting with you?"

"What would that do?"

"Well—" Mike hesitated. "My thought here is that you've got a very full plate right now and you could get spread way too thin the next couple of months. If we give the Millers the boy here as an additional contact person—"

Why don't we just give them a nice dose of the clap instead? Jake thought. But of course he didn't say it. Instead he said evenly, "OK, sure, why don't you come along, Kev?"

*

"And what major event draws <u>your</u> attention tonight, young man?"

Alice Moore stood looking down on him from the last landing of her main stairs, a five-foot-two ball of judgment in a floor-length dark blue gown with sequins on the bodice. She carried her mink jacket over her free arm, flat purse and little opera glasses in hand. In the harsh overhead light Jake could not make out her eyes.

"Gym," he said, glancing down at his beat-up rubber-sole shoes, "thought I'd do a couple of hours on the machines."

"I see." His mother-in-law came on down, stood before him, tugged lightly at his jacket as though fixing him, as though fond. "I'd have thought you'd get enough exercise building your buildings or whatever."

"Well, I'm more in the trailers nowadays than I'd like to be, Alice. Not much physical work I get to do."

She pursed her lips, shrugged. "Where're Angie and Lisa?"

"Down the hall. One last pit stop."

Alice was taking them to the ballet downtown at the Auditorium. It was one of the big-ass troupes from New York whose name he forgot in the third act of something and scenes from something else. Lisa was supposed to be enthralled because she was taking lessons. Jake had gone along last spring to a ballet version of "The Wizard of Oz" at Northwestern and both Lisa and her pal Trudy squirmed and looked around through both acts. So did they really give a rat's ass? What he was sure the little girls did like was putting on their party dresses, getting to stay up until unimaginable hours, the crowd milling around during the intermission and wheedling ice cream bonbons and sodas out of the grownups.

Alice laid her fur jacket carefully across the banister and patted it like a baby. "Come, Jake, I have something I want your opinion on."

Unlikely she cared bugger all about his opinion, he thought, but when she led the way into her breakfast room he did follow along. Her computer screen glowed in the darkness. Alice bent over the keyboard and started typing and moving the mouse, brightening the screen and pulling up images. Dithering. "No, not that...let's see...maybe here..."

A white square with a jolly cartoon grandmother in a red-checked apron and the words "GO ASK ALICE" swam up. Beneath, smaller, in italics, it said, "*Heavenly Cookies.*"

Alice stood back. "What do you think?"

Jake's turn to shrug, although he remained polite. "Nice. I don't suppose Jefferson Airplane can sue you, right?"

"Who's that?"

"A band. 'Go ask Alice' was a line from a song of theirs."

"Really? I knew there was a novel, but the author is 'Anonymous,' and I didn't figure 'Anonymous' could sue anybody."

Jake laughed. "Anybody can sue anybody these days, Alice. And the song was a thousand years ago, so don't let that stop you. What's the deal here? You serious about cookies?"

"I am," she said. "The model is the Pepperidge Farm lady... Whatzername... Start local with a superior product out of my own kitchen and let word of mouth make it just expand and expand. What do you think?"

What Jake remembered was the way a business prof at DeKalb charcterized Alice's very dream. 'The foredoomed escape strategy of every American housewife who ever baked a chocolate chip or a pan of sweet rolls,' were the man's words.

But what Jake said was, "Sure, why not? Go for it."

Who knows? he thought. Might keep you out of our fucking hair for a while.

Even in the dim light of the screen he could see her eyes as she appraised him. "You're such a downer, Jake! Jesus!"

"Me? No. Not so, Alice. Listen—"

She had turned and he found himself trucking after her bustling plump little rump back into the hall, her trilling after Angie and Lisa, "Hurry it along, we're going to be late if we don't go now, kids." They were coming, Lisa in her white organdy princess dress skipping in the lead. Alice picked up her mink and put one arm in the sleeve. Jumping to, Jake held the coat for her while she fished for the other sleeve several times, then slid in.

No thanks for that.

Alice handed her keys to Angie and made for the front door. With it open she turned and said, "I wish you'd at least pretend to care about cultural things, Jake, at least for the little girl's sake."

"I—"

"I know. You just love to watch the fairies flitting, right? Isn't that your quote?"

"What I said was—"

"Then at least we'd have someone to drive."

"Yes'm." He tried to catch Angie's eye to make sure she'd heard that one, but she was already on the move, out into the chilly night and down the front walk.

"Would you lock up, Jake?"

"Yes'm," he repeated.

The truth was he'd been planning on going until he remembered the amount of time he'd have to spend cooped up in the car with the old bitch. He didn't like the way she whacked on him, of course, but he had reached a point where he could see there was no reason to take it personally.

Any list of Alice's reasons to distrust men would be headed by her own choice of husbands. And the Miserable Shit Lifetime Achievement Award goes to…Norm Moore! According to Alice from the day they were married the man turned out to be entirely preoccupied, a workaholic, secretive, always away on unexplained trips. A wholesale liquor business. Though Alice was sure there were other women from the get go, Angie was less convinced. Her own claim was in her childhood she never had a single talk with Norm where he didn't have a phone in his hand. Despite this, Angie loved her old man, would move heaven and earth to spend an hour with him when he passed through Chicago. Her parents' divorce, which came along in her first year of college, tore at her. Norm ceded Alice the Wilmette house, but managed somehow to squirrel huge chunks money away offshore or in trusts of some kind and to convince the judge his net worth was only about 30% of what Alice's lawyers calculated it to be. Though she would have been better off dumping it, Alice clung to the house, rattled around in it. It was a 1920s faux-Italian palazzino with a pool she hardly used and a gravel-pathed garden with rosebushes kept severely trimmed up. She employed a Mexican fellow nearly full-time as her gardener and house man.

When Jake first knew Alice, she was quite different with him. Somehow she'd found out about Jake and Angie hooking up in Paris

(Angie thought because of a letter of hers that had bounced back to Wilmette which her mother had no business reading). Alice called him, invited him to breakfast, painted a picture of Angie down and out in California slaving away to support her little boy, driven crazy by uncertainty over whether her alimony checks would arrive. Alice encouraged Jake to get out there, told him she just knew Angie was deeply in love with him. He said he planned to go, was only waiting for the right moment to ask Mike Tanner for the time off work. Alice gazed at him openly, admiringly, as though he was the greatest thing.

Even at the time he knew Alice was using him. But he was not aware that once he got her precious daughter and the boy back to the North Shore she would be done with him. In the lady's book Jake became at once The Husband and therefore someone for her to snip at, undermine, mock when she got the chance.

*

Jake was aware there were guys on his crews who covered for each other when they went off the marital grid a couple hours. So why didn't he have a friend like that? Ian Stiles, sure, but Ian lived far away. Do you lack trust? he asked himself. No, he trusted Angie, or at least did once. Now he felt more like a squirrel with a mouthful of rescued nuts crazy anxious to find a safe new place for them.

Before coming to bring Angie and Lisa in to Wilmette tonight he had even bothered to stop by the TV room to mention where he was going to Earl, who had unfortunately bounced back home for the week-end. It was hardly a necessary precaution, since Earl did not deign to keep tabs on his putative stepfather anyway. Slouched lizard-eyed in an armchair in front of an old movie, he probably didn't even register what Jake was telling him.

Leaving the dead quiet of Alice's street in Angie's Volvo, Jake hummed along a couple of blocks east, waited at the light in the un-natural glow of the bright white stack and store windows of the Plaza del Lago. Then as he made his turn north onto Sheridan Road, excite-ment ran all through him like current. He imagined he could hear his heartbeat, felt sure that his chest was constricting, making it harder to breathe, although not in any scary way. Just on the possibility you might get laid in a little while, he mocked himself. It was a sensation he remembered in a weaker version from times fifteen or twenty years ago in the moment he realized a woman was telling him 'yes' and 'now' or 'soon.' The difference in intensity? He didn't know. Because this was cheating? Because it was a guy? A threat to everything he had built up in his life? Hard to say.

With one notable exception, the only contacts he'd made so far had come about through the net. The guy he was meeting tonight was off Craigslist, not one of the usual sites Jake worked. At the guy's house, but agreed upon only as a take-a-look kind of thing.

The way he'd met the exception still amused him. Back in the spring when he and Angie were at each other a lot, he'd agreed to go one time only with her to her therapist. Toward the end of the hour the therapist turned to him and said, "I'm going to say something in front of your wife, OK?"

"Why not?" said Jake. "Shoot!"

"You've got anger management problems, my friend."

And though he didn't like the therapist, didn't trust her, in the moment Jake agreed with her, amiable enough. And suddenly, bang, he was in a loop where he was signed up for some classes. A men's group that met in an upstairs room in the hall adjoining a Lutheran church ten minutes from the house. The other men were such low-lifes and fuck-ups he was ashamed to be in the same room with them. Though actually a lot of what they admitted to sounded familiar to him. (Not the hitting, he'd never in his life hit a woman.) The leader's big message was about how verbal stuff—especially denigrating your wife or partner, making her feel small—was just as bad if not worse than the physical abuse.

After five or six Thursday nights, Jake had had it. He didn't tell Angie he was quitting yet, but went one more time, early on purpose just to let the leader know he was dropping out. He didn't see the counselor's car in the lot yet, but on the stairs up to the meeting room there was a man, late 50s, sitting waiting, smoking. He was from a time slot on another day of the week, he said, but had come to see if he could change to Jake's group.

Jake sat a few stairs above the other man and there was silence for a minute. He had already caught something about the other guy, a diffidence maybe, willingness of some kind. He asked, "What do you do?"

"Foreclosures. Mercy sales. I'm what they sometimes call a bottom feeder."

Jake stood up, stretched. "I guess I'm more of an active guy myself, go out to the clients, reassure everybody…take charge."

"Are you? As they say, a good top is hard to find…or is it good to find hard?"

What Jake recognized as a gay remark put him off a little even as it excited him. But the guy looked OK, thickset, red complexion, white hair, mustache. Jake pulled the back of his hand up along the join of thigh and belly, actually needing to realign since he'd already halfway sprung a chub.

The other man watched him.

Now Jake's heart was beating. He checked his watch. "I can't wait for this motherfucker. You want to go get a drink?"

"Sure." The other man stood up. He was an inch or two taller than Jake. They would fit OK, if it came to that. "I'm not much for bars, anymore at least…. Want to come by my house?"

"You live alone?"

"Virtually," the guy grunted a laugh. "Wife and I have a grandchild, it's our first one, and she spends about half her time down in Lexington fussing over the little thing. I admit she's cute."

"Your granddaughter…"

The man looked at him, shook his head. "Well I didn't mean the wife, did I? She's ready for the side show by now." They had reached the street-level door. The man pushed it open, ushered Jake out before him. "Let herself go, you know, long time since."

He had lowered his voice, as though this were a secret, something shameful.

"So you lost interest?"

The man stopped, thought about that, as though the idea were new to him. Shook his head. Smiled. "Something very like—I suppose. To the extent I ever was much interested. Drinking was my problem, but now I'm pretty much in AA," he said. "And drinking for me turned out was just a cover for another problem."

"What would that be?"

The other man looked around, although they were alone in the expanse of the church parking lot. "Guys." He said it straight ahead, almost defiant. Then, softer, "I sometimes like to do a buddy a favor."

"Without him doing any favors back?"

"I don't really care. If he wants to beat me off at the same time, or whatever, play with it and keep it hot, I'm not going to tell him 'No, No, Nanette' you know…"

His name turned out to be Wally. That first time they went to his house, every room claustrophobic with bric-a-brac, tiny framed pictures tacked up in rows, and they were careful, spreading towels on the bed before getting down to it. Wally was as advertised, entirely into being of service. When Jake asked him to, he got on his knees and turned his big white butt up and moaned and begged while Jake fucked him.

Jake acted as though he was still in his group so he could see Wally during the meeting times. The wife had come home from Kentucky, so they moved the action to an out-of-the-way motel. Wally was so compliant in the sack it took Jake three or four weeks to figure out why he might have been sent to Anger Management. The wife knew all about Wally—he'd been arrested in a park down in the city—and was suspicious of his every move. It sounded as though they were completely contemptuous of one another, she said terrible things, he said terrible things, but neither of them was willing to call off the marriage. Wally's ongoing complaint was tiresome, filling entirely the brief time he and Jake had for talk. But what tore it finally was the thing about the motel. Jake seemed always to get there first, so he booked the room and laid out the cash. Each week Wally made a point of promising to pay his half and then didn't. But if he was a broker he couldn't be destitute, could he? The sex was good enough, but increasingly Jake felt taken, so he told Wally he'd run out of excuses for being out Thursday night and this was it.

*

As soon as he turned off Sheridan, it got very dark. It took him a moment to realize what had happened—he'd entered a dense tunnel of trees. Thick black trunks in his headlights. A strong hit of déjà vu, puzzling since it was unlikely he'd ever been here before, the Winnetka lakefront mansions never exactly his stomping ground. The address given by the Craigslist man (he said his name was "Chuck") certainly wasn't familiar.

Jesus you are one hard up sonovabitch! he told himself. He hated Craigslist, actually feared it some. Not this guy, but usually when you looked it was almost all men in their 20s or 30s hanging in hotel or motel rooms someplace, saying only for a few more hours, wanting a blow job, no reciprocation, sometimes an iPhone pic of the hardon in question. Or, if they admitted to wanting it fucked, a rounded butt. The whole thing smelled to Jake of risk and the desperation of flying under the radar.

Here the abrupt turn to the left "Chuck" had warned him about. The broader road went on to the right toward what appeared in the gloom a castle of some sort, towers and things, mass. The way Jake was supposed to take wound through smaller trees already losing leaves, then suddenly came out into a graveled courtyard before a very modern house given its form by a single down-raked plane of roof cut funny, some kind of trapezoid. He parked, turned off his headlights, got out. The Lake would be on the far side, a big drawing emptiness he could sense but not really see.

The front door was black even in the blackness, hard to locate in an expanse of six-foot-high concrete wall under a wide overhanging edge of that dominating roof. A recessed light up above popped on— from a sensor?—making a precise circle on the doorstep like a place for an actor to recite his to-bes-or-not-to-bes. Jake punched the bell and stood, suddenly self-conscious, glancing around, suspecting there must be a way to watch him. Yes, a tiny speck of red light had winked on up in the crevice between roof and wall. He turned up toward it, wanting to be seen, let the guy know he knew he was being examined. He grinned broadly. Go on, something in him said, show 'em the wolf teeth up front.

The front door pulled open and a man said, "Well all right," in a soft deep voice. "Come in, come in."

He was six foot and burly as advertised (his own word for himself in his ad), wide-faced, prominent but not hard jaw, soft hands, wedding ring. A dirty blond, the hair thinned and soft but cut longish. An attorney or some kind of arts guy? Immediately Jake was uncomfortable about his own hoody and sweats and the gym shoes, necessary as they were to his alibi. The oxblood loafers, the wide-whale gray corduroys, the maroon and green-striped tattersall shirt and the unbuttoned suede vest—Jake estimated "Chuck" must have on several hundred bucks worth of goods.

And besides, he was too good-looking, the whole of him fleshy and yet fine at the same time. Jake had an impulse to turn and run. But instead he said, "I should tell you I don't have a lot of experience with this kind of thing."

"That's OK," the man said, "I have some."

"A lot? With married guys?"

"Over time," an easy smile, "some married, some not. I'm not a slut, if that's what you're asking."

"No, I wasn't—"

"What do you do, if I may ask?"

"You mean in bed?"

"No, well, I meant for your work…" A smile spread across the guy's face. "Though if you want to tell me about the other…"

"I'm in construction."

Silence. Chuck's eye on him. A reappraisal? Reconsideration? Apparently not, because Chuck nodded and said, "Why don't we go in there?" and, without letting on anything further about what he did for a living, he closed the front door and led the way through into a large living room where there was a fire going. Everything sleek and low and heavy. The glass top of the long metal-framed coffee table green-edged, three-quarters-of-an-inch thick. Long windows, black reflectors now, in daylight the Lake would be out there down below in all its colors and moods. Three very bright-lit paintings in gilt frames the only things on the walls. A Barcelona chair by the fire was indicated for Jake.

(Or "Eugene," which was the name he had to remember he'd given himself in the emails. "Eugene Gorham." Why that? What had he been thinking?)

'Drink?"

"Sure."

"Prefer scotch?"

Though he didn't actually prefer scotch, in the moment Jake said, "Sure."

"Ice? Soda?"

"No, just neat, thanks."

A silver bucket with ice had already been set out. And classical music, churchy sounding, a choir, men's voices, monks maybe, playing low. So. A seduction had been thought of, thank God.

Chuck came across and held out a glass, unexpectedly heavy when let go in the flat of Jake's hand. Crystal. The finer things. Felicity and her girlfriends summer afternoons out by the Stiles' pool dipping their fingers and then rimming their glasses to make them sing a clear high note.

The gold-frame pictures were bright and full of color, a little hazy but realistic enough so you could make out a woman in a straw hat by a boat with a little girl, several women in long skirts with sunlight raking across them, a big spray of blue-gray lilacs in a vase.

Chuck followed Jake's gaze, eyebrows raised as though he too were viewing the paintings for the first time.

"Impressionists, right?" Jake said.

"Well—yes. They're Cassatts, you know. She happens to have been my mother's great aunt."

The way he shrugged the connection off so casually make it clear "Cassatt" was not just some poor relation Sunday painter. Jake looked again, wondering if he hadn't seen these very pictures himself reproduced somewhere. On calendars? Or on the notecards his sister Nica got from the Art Institute?

"Cheers!"

They raised their glasses to each other, drank.

A moment's silence. Then Jake said, "Nice house."

"Thanks. My parents had it built—the architect was a friend of the family—and they were going to move down here from the big house but somehow never got around to it. Then Dad died and my mother continued to rattle around over there—it's 18 rooms—and the older she got the more stuck she became. My first wife and I had to move in here more or less as a way of looking out for her and for the property too. We modified it some, to our own needs. Not that there's much you can change in a building like this."

Jake stretched in his chair, lengthening out every muscle he could, wiggling his toes. "Your mom still with us?"

"No, she passed on too."

Silence. Both men drank, peered into their glasses.

So many ways to go—ask about the second wife, comment on the workmanship of the place, obviously so first-class—but Jake felt bound, tongue-tied. He drained his glass, jumped up.

Chuck was on his feet too, reaching for Jake's glass.

"Neat again?"

"No, I'll have some ice this time, please." He could use the cold. Throat all dry despite the big slug of scotch.

He trucked along after Chuck over to the bar, a recessed area with a sliding door to hide it as desired. Chuck made the new drinks, handed Jake his. Jake took it and suddenly downed the whole thing as though he was chugging bitter medicine, gave the glass back.

"Well, I better get going."

Chuck was standing so close to him Jake thought for a moment he could hear the other man's heart, boom, boom. "Really?"

"Nice talking with you." Jake stuck out his hand.

"You don't want just another—"

Jake checked his wristwatch. "Running a little late. My wife and my little girl—" Blurted. For some reason he just needed this asshole to know <u>he</u> had a life too.

Chuck touched his arm, searched his face. "What <u>do</u> you want, Eugene?"

Jake looked up at the older man, impressed by how kind he sounded. He laughed. "I want you to know my real name is Jake—"

"OK. Jake."

"And I want to make love to you."

Chuck let out a breath. "Do you? That's what I've been wanting too." He set both glasses down gently on the bar counter. "And you should also know my real name is Guy."

*

The room Jake was led into was big enough if not for football then at least for a soccer scrimmage of some sort. And you wouldn't even have to take out the low-lying king-size bed.

"So who is it usually sleeps here, you and your wife?"

"That's right."

"Your second, right?"

"Yes."

"And she is? At the supermarket? Due back in twenty minutes?"

Guy laughed patiently. "Christmas shopping in New York and going to some shows with her lady friends for four days. Back Sunday. Tomorrow."

"You have kids?"

"Yes. At college."

"Mine too," Jake said. "One of them. You got a bathroom?"

"Go either way, take your pick." Guy pointed index fingers across one another like the clown cop at the circus directing traffic. Through the doorway Jake chose he found himself in a full-sized dressing room, dark wood drawers, dresses neatly hangered, some under plastic covers, high heels lined up in rows on wood tiers at knee level.

He turned back. Guy seemed amused. "That's the distaff side."

"The what?"

"The girls'. 'Gents' is the other way."

What was wrong with him? Couldn't piss in the ladies' pot? Jake felt stupid, clumsy. But why? He never felt like that.

Through the other doorway he found a second dressing room, mirror of the first except in this one hung broadcloth shirts and many colors of polos, some soft-shouldered English or Hong Kong wool suits in gray and blue, tweed jackets, one tuxedo. On the wall opposite was a three-quarter-length oval mirror and dowel racks for ties, conservative diagonal stripes and soft purple and green silks.

Jake peed and flushed and returned to the bedroom. Guy had taken off his loafers and was lolling on a little settee under a window on the Sheridan Road side of the room.

"Nice duds, man."

"Thanks."

"Where do you go for them?"

"Do you know J. Press?"

"I don't."

"Men's traditional clothes, mostly back east, Cambridge, New Haven, D.C. There's a store in Manhattan, of course."

Jake squinted a little. "You some kind of politician and I should be recognizing you and don't?"

"No," Guy said, "not at all. Why'd you say that?"

"With suits and ties like that you'd probably win if you ran, you know."

Guy laughed. "Not likely. Actually, I'm just a poor academic."

Jake's impulse was to go at him on the 'poor' part of that one, but he squelched it. Guy patted the place beside him on the little couch so Jake came and sat, feeling a little like a child doing a grown-up's bidding. He turned and looked directly into Guy's broad and now quite red face.

"What is it you want with me, man?"

Guy tentatively touched Jake's cheek, low, by the chin. "Just to kiss you."

"Well come on then and I'll kiss <u>you</u>."

He was sudden, throwing his leg across Guy's thighs, pulling his body up onto the bigger man's, cupping his face and pressing his mouth in on Guy's. His teeth made a tiny click against Guy's and then his tongue went in. In this nice soft mouth Jake tasted mint and scotch both. Guy kissed back earnestly, put his arms around Jake, hugged him close against himself.

When he'd had enough—or not quite that, more when he needed air—Jake pulled back and had another look. The man's eyes were soft, almost damp. Jake touched the soft hair, thin at the temples, brushed it back. He sighed. "You wrote you might want to undress me."

"Yes, I do want to."

"So what's stopping you?"

Jake lifted himself off Guy and stood. His sweats were tented already, cock as hard as it got. Guy reached toward it, back of his big paw grazing it lightly. Jake took Guy's hand and turned it over so he could get a decent feel, know what he was in for.

But Guy didn't get to undress him. All at once they were up off the little couch and crashed down on the bed together grappling and pulling at each other's clothes while they kissed. Frustrated, Jake stopped, sat up, kicked off his shoes and skinned down his sweats and shorts, tugged the hoody and the t-shirt off over his head together. Guy was a beat behind him, a little more fussy at first, back on his feet getting his own clothes off, aligning the seams on the legs and folding his pants over the back of a chair, unbuttoning his shirt and undoing the cuffs, then suddenly he was standing fully naked before Jake. He was lightly tanned, a low-slung bathing suit line running across under his belly. On Craigslist he presented himself as early sixties. Probably true, give or take two or three years. Jake lay back in the pillows at ease, naked, hands lightly cupping his nuts, watching. Trying not to strategize how he was going to deal with Guy—let that come as it would—just enjoying the sights, heart thumping.

"You play football?" he asked.

"In high school I did. In college I finked out."

"You've got a nice body."

"You too." Guy came around the foot of the bed, his own cock filled out now, thicker, bigger than Jake's, though maybe not so adamant.

"C'mere."

Guy seemed to hesitate.

Jake laughed. "I only want to kiss you again, man. Jees!"

Obediently then, tugging a little at his foreskin, Guy kneeled on the bed next to Jake. Impulsively Jake reached up and grabbed Guy's nipples and pulled him down to his mouth. Guy took it sighing, and Jake held him there with a firm two-finger grip on both nips.

"What'd you call these?"

"Those? Those are my tits."

Jake scrunched over and let Guy lie down beside him and run his hands all over him, down his legs, along his sides, lightly grazing his cock again, kissing into Jake's chest fur and finding his nipples and getting them wet. Jake closed his eyes and raked Guy's fine hair through his fingers. A heaving, different sigh. Fucker was looking up at him, had tears in his eyes.

"Remember what you asked on the phone?"

"What was that?"

"You said you were hairy and asked did I mind."

"Well? And?"

Pause. Then Guy said, "Well the answer is not at all." He leaned forward and tasted the head of Jake's penis, then swallowed the whole thing. Jake could feel Guy's throat muscles working at it.

"That's the way, that's the man." Thinking he might just blast off right there, right down the fucker's throat. But no, no fear, it was only the thought.

Back and forth then, back and forth. Mouth on mouth, mouths on nipples, kissing randomly on warm flesh. Equal hungers. Guy maybe a little surprised when Jake got to his knees and cupped Guy's balls, then bent and grabbed his penis and put it in his mouth.

Jake himself also a little surprised. He'd thought about whether he'd ever suck dick or not and hadn't been able to come up with a reason not to. At some point. But none of the other men he'd messed with had tempted him.

"Would you get up over me?" Guy asked. "Give it to me in the mouth?"

Jake moved promptly, straddling Guy's chest, inserting his cock. He pushed in, pulled back, felt a rush of hot feeling. "Uh oh," he whispered, "if I don't stop now, I'm gonna come, you know."

Guy, mumbling, "I want you to."

"Yeah," Jake laughed, "but I don't want to yet."

"Go on."

And almost at once Jake let go in big spurts. Guy drank it down, then licked all around Jake's cock for more of the juice.

"Can I get you off?"

"Sure," Guy said. "What did you have in mind?"

"You say and I'll do it."

"You could lay up behind me and kiss me and jack me off. It won't take much, I can tell you."

So Jake turned the bigger man on his side and nuzzled in at his neck kissing and licking and felt for Guy's penis.

*

They were lying back in the pillows, arms around each other. Guy had pulled a deep brown top sheet up, but only to their thighs.

"What is it you like most?" he asked.

"To fuck ass. Older guys only, though."

"Well that's a piece of luck, isn't it? This older guy likes to be done that way. Very much."

"And is it men around my age pretty much? Not twinks?"

"No, no twinks, thanks. Back in the day there were some somewhat younger men too, close-in graduate students I was sure of." Guy laughed. "I mean, they propositioned me."

"Oh, that's right, I forgot. You're 'just a poor academic.'" Jake cast his hand up in a sweeping motion, taking in the room, the house.

"Well, I do a little consulting too."

And clip coupons and have a stash of some considerable size too, Jake thought. "Do you manage your own portfolio?" he asked.

Guy propped himself up on his elbow, gazed down at Jake. "This isn't going to be a problem, is it?"

"What? Your having money?"

"Well, if it's any consolation to you, there's not that much really. In fact, we try to live on my income and fail so my wife works, which lets us come out about even."

"I wasn't—"

"No, let me go on a minute, since you brought it up. There is this house, it's true, and the one across the way. But I have two sisters and a brother and we own the property jointly. The big house is currently a liability. It's over a hundred and ten years old and my siblings are senti-mental about it and don't want to see it sold. They <u>say</u> it should become some kind of conference center or something, but basically they just want it restored to its original condition—which is going to cost a pret-ty penny—so it can stand as some sort of monument to our parents and grandparents and the great grandparents who built the thing."

Jake was ashamed of himself, and a bit scared. What had he been thinking, that he could prod at this guy and get him to squirm without there being consequences? Typical Jake mouths off error.

"You know what I think?" He pulled Guy back down so they were face to face on the pillow, moved his hand down and pushed into the soft flesh at the crevice where Guy's thighs came together. "My uncle had the flower business up on Green Bay—"

"Guarani's?"

"That's right. And I think we maybe delivered over there at your parents'."

"Entirely possible. Remember when that might have been?"

"In the nineties? Middle nineties? A debutante party maybe, springtime, snaps I think, in big wicker baskets—"

"Maybe my sister's coming out."

"There was a lady, I remember her for a big denim skirt nearly down to the ground."

"My mother."

Jake had a memory of a voice saying 'Put them there, and the others—let's see—over there.' A rich old bitch standing by some kind of carved pillar with a dark figure on top of it barking at him, him head down just getting through it as he always managed to. Maybe in the end she thanked him, he couldn't recall.

"No," he said, "I can't say I knew her. Maybe I <u>dealt</u> with her. Once. Twice maybe."

"The house always had flowers. So still—"

"What?"

"It's a coincidence, isn't it?"

"I guess." Jake shrugged it off.

*

They were dressed and Jake about to leave when Guy asked if he didn't want to take a look around the big house. Jake checked his watch. Shit. The gym was closing already. "Maybe just a short one," he said.

Guy put on a jacket and got a flashlight and they set out through the trees in silence. The cooler night air felt good against Jake's face, and now there was a small slice of moon half behind clouds out over the Lake.

They went around the side of the big house and Guy unlocked the kitchen door, then moved quickly across to disarm the burglar alarm. By flashlight they made their way into the main hall, where Guy flipped on a bank of electric switches. The place revealed was fucking huge, in what Jake recognized as a variation on the baronial style favored by the old Chicago millionaires. Overhead an opaque skylight with cut-glass trim, a gallery with pillars running all the way around the second floor, matching staircases to bring you halfway down to an ample landing, and then a much broader set of stairs descending to the marble inlaid ground floor. There, atop carved posts were four-foot black metal young ladies with barely-covered titties holding light globes aloft. But the clear bulbs in the circular chandelier overhead cast only a dingy light, and the place had an unkept-up look, window shades pulled to different levels, furniture stuck in the middle of the room, some pieces under cloths, others not, an oriental carpet rolled to the side and left there.

Houses in this condition were always a little sad to come across. Jake had a good deal of experience with them. If called upon and given the budget, he would know pretty precisely how to bring this one up to current code without destroying any of its original aspect or impact.

Upstairs only about half the switches Guy flipped made lights go on. Jake mentioned he could detect a faint electric burning smell. "Yes, I know," Guy said, "they think the rats have chewed some of the wiring. I probably shouldn't be turning anything on." He led Jake into what had been his own room when he was a boy, also a neglected place, two single beds with ratty, sun-bleached coverlets drooping off them, a desk and a goose-neck lamp, but also three windows which overlooked the Lake and faint in the moonlight a lawn between the house and a row of shrubs which marked the edge of the bluff.

What would it be like to wake every morning to that view? Sunlight pouring straight in, or rain or snow lashing against the glass, the wind off the water buffeting even a house as ponderous as this one. Like growing up on board a ship. But maybe more lonely than grand. The mother (if that was who the woman Jake remembered was) had shown him no sign of pleasantness, and if you can't be kind to those who wait on you then you're not likely to be any warmer to your own children.

Jake moved toward the windows and looked down, aware of Guy coming up close behind him.

"So is it ok to ask where you do this academic thing?"

"I'm at Northwestern. Actually, I'm a dean at the moment, so I'm somewhat less 'academic' than usual and more administrative than I'd like to be."

"A busy man, I guess."

"True. I also serve on too many boards of things, which eats up a lot of time."

"Like?"

"Several charities—right now I'm on the board of the Lyric as well."

"The opera?"

"Yes."

"I'm impressed."

"You needn't be. I'm not trying to impress you."

"Then what are you trying to do?"

"Let you know me. Or at least a little about me. You did ask."

"Well OK. That's fine. What I meant was I'm impressed you can stand boards, committees that kind of thing. Isn't it boring enough to turn a man into a toad?"

"I have plenty of sitzfleish."

"Which is?"

"Sitting flesh. Didn't you notice?"

Reaching around, Jake touched Guy's flank, moved over, felt his ass crack through the soft corduroy. "I noticed. The minute I saw it, I wanted some of it."

"You should have gone after it then. Want some now?"

"I do, but—" Jake sighed. "I'm afraid I got to get going here." Wondering where could he say he'd stopped for a beer, who from work say he'd run into? While Earl might pretend not to pay any attention to his comings and goings, catching Jake in an inconsistency or a lie might make his day.

"Another time then."

"OK."

So the dude imagined there might be another time. Good. Better than good.

They were halfway down the driveway from the big house, the night significantly colder than it had been going up, when Jake dug around in his pockets and found he didn't have his keys. Stupid. He knew exactly where they were. Put down on a counter in the butler's pantry when Guy had wanted a kiss there in the dark on their way out. They trudged back up the incline and Guy went back through the routine with the burglar alarm, Jake really anxious now, fidgeting.

The keys were exactly where he'd thought they were.

There in the dark, they kissed again.

"What's that smell on you?"

"Other than sex you mean?" Guy said.

"Yeah, your aftershave."

""'It's an old one. Bay Rum. I've always used it. My folks would go to Jamaica for their winter vacation and that was what my father wore. I just started dipping out of his bottle when I was home from school and first going out with girls… So he started bringing me my own bottle."

"Well, I like it. A lot. It makes me—"

"What?"

"It makes me want to jump you."

Guy laughed. And then Jake was all over him again, nearly climbing on him, pushing his dick against Guy's belly. His tongue went in Guy's mouth, his hands roamed Guy's ass, finding the crack again. Jake yanked at Guy's belt and got his pants and shorts down to his knees and turned him toward the counter.

He was about to go in when he remembered. "I got a rubber in my pocket. You want me to glove up?"

"Would you? Here, give it to me."

Guy ripped the packet open with his teeth and put the rubber in his mouth. Then, crouching, he found Jake's cock in the dark and slid it on, using his lips to extend the rubber down as he went.

He was easy to get into, soft, hot. And he knew how to stand and how to move, elbows on the counter, ass grinding back against Jake. Even in his excitement, Jake kept smelling the musty oldness of the place. He kissed Guy's neck and beat on his cock while he fucked him, and was rewarded with a handful of the man's goo the moment before he himself shot off.

On the way out again, Jake put his arm around Guy's waist and they proceeded side by side, like old, trusting friends. In a rush, Jake felt a kind of loony pride of ownership, as though Guy were some big ticket item, a Skidoo or a refrigerator he had coveted and was having wheeled out to the Home Depot lot for him.

Tripped by their approach, Guy's front entrance light came back on, delineating in a ghostly way the modern masterpiece behind. By Jake's car they kissed again, Jake conscious now of the cars out on Sheridan, the flashes of their headlights strobing in through the elms.

They agreed the best way to communicate would be email. "I'll send you my cell number too," Guy said. Then he said, "May I ask something?"

"Sure."

"It's only an idle question. What made you choose a name like 'Eugene Gorham'?"

"I don't know. It just popped into my head. I used to know some Gorhams here in Winnetka."

"Did you? I know some too. Funny we've never run into each other before, isn't it?"

"I don't know. How old are you?"

"Sixty-five next week."

"Well, there's 25 years in there, isn't there?"

Jake got in, started the Volvo, powered down the window. "Thanks. I had a really nice time."

"Me too."

"And thanks also for the tour of the big house."

"And the little trip down memory lane?"

"Yes." Although Jake wasn't as enchanted by that part—the 'coincidence' of his having been there before—as Guy seemed to be.

"Another time we wouldn't be able to meet here, of course."

Jake laughed. "And not at my house either."

"So," Guy went slowly, "a motel? Or a hotel downtown? That wouldn't be too sordid for you?"

"I like motels. They make me feel sexy."

"Is there a time you don't feel sexy?"

Jake thought about it, looked ahead. "No, I guess not."

THREE

Even when he was worn out, Jake slept fairly light. Came awake to any sound in the house or against its shell, even the most ordinary, the creak of wood, a tree branch in the wind scratching a wall. So it was unusual that Angela managed to make it in, get Lisa down for the night, herself into a nightgown and to slide up under the coverlet next to him before he stirred.

"Enjoy the show?"

"Oh yes. Magic."

She was all warm and sweet, breasts pressed against him, palm lightly on his belly, foot rubbing against his ankle.

"Too bad I'm not capable of appreciating culture."

Angela laughed. "I caught that one. Well, at least you have potential as a chauffeur."

"Yes. I wonder if she'd require me to wear a cap."

"Probably the whole uniform."

She snuggled in closer against him, began kissing against his neck. She turned her head up and he kissed her, a little surprised at how ardent she was. Despite the way he'd spent his evening—or maybe because of it—he had no problem getting hard. He pushed her nightgown up, she lifted, helped get it off over her head and he got up over her. It was a dreamy, long fuck, just the way he liked it, unthinking, no menu, his mouth everywhere, hers too, long slow thrusts, shorter ones for a while then back to long, Angie breathing hard, gasping, sucking on his mouth, biting some at his shoulder. This—he was pretty sure Angie had gotten there too—a place they'd discovered long ago where he didn't care about when he came and her cunt stayed very wet and hot and apparently she was having either one long continuous orgasm or a whole series of little ones. Sadly also a place they couldn't always get to anymore and even sadder often didn't even try for.

A little after four AM when he got up to pee, his cock stiffened up again. JE-sus! He shut the bathroom door and sat on the toilet seat and worked on it in the dim glow of a seashell nightlight. Images of Guy's super-modern place, his parents' giant house dark and cold, Guy's butt packed so nicely in his corduroys, his slightly pendulous little man's titties, the sun-browned belly, its feel in Jake's hand when he had the big man bent over before him leaning on the pantry shelf. Almost painfully hot, he shot as soon as he could, feeling force in the cum as the spurt hit his palm.

*

One of the things Jake admired most was the way Angela dealt with his family's big gatherings, Guarani eat-a-thons as he called them. From the time she first met his parents, she seemed to understand trying to please them would be like trying to shimmy up a greased pole. So she concentrated her attention on his sisters, all three of them so much older than Jake they could easily have been his aunts. Nida and Yvonne in their sixties now and even Claire, the youngest, fifteen when Jake came along. No one ever exactly said he'd been a mistake—his mother's loyalty to the Church would have ruled out any sort of family planning—although when he was a kid his sisters told him everyone was "surprised" at Mom's having a child so late.

The girls took to Angie, taught her how they cooked, which pleased Jake of course and meant her contributions to Guarani events were always lavishly praised. Big breadwinner in the family that he was, Jake was more or less expected to spring for the wine or a couple of bottles of classy booze at these gatherings.

That warm first Saturday in October the occasion was his father's 90th birthday, being held not at his parents' but a block away at Claire's. Jake parked and helped Angie carry stuff into the house, already filled with grownups variously related to him and hordes of kids out chasing each other around Claire's large shady backyard. Angela could greet even the most peripheral of them by name, in-laws and cousins and their offspring. Coming from such a tiny and blasted little family herself, she took special pride in keeping track of every minor branching in Jake's family tree.

Yvonne had married a Greek named George Panas from out in Naperville, so for years now fifteen or twenty of his gang were always invited to their functions, including an ancient aunt in black and a tiny uncle in a suit and a fedora, neither of whom spoke a word of English. On the big food tables on the back porch alongside Nida's famous meatballs and all the cold cuts George's people laid out their dolma, zucchini salad, filo spinach pies, a propped-open bakery box of baklava. When Jake greeted the white-haired old ones in Italian, they would brighten and shake his hands and answer him sweetly in what must be the appropriate Greek.

The majority of his grown male relatives congregated on the benches in the arbor out by the garage so they could drink and smoke and talk Bears, Cubs, Sox, or Bulls depending on the season. And some trash anytime, of course. Jake liked only a few of them, Nida's husband, a couple of his cousins. The rest he smiled upon and held in casual contempt. Nephews nearly as old as he was, plump, seedy guys with sideburns always nudging at him to drink along with them, as though he planned to end up as fuzzed out and useless for the rest of the day as them. They joked about his 'foreign' cars, implying he had become a yup, and then in the next breath they'd brown-nose him, imagining he might put in a good word for them with Mike Tanner or some other builder. Fat chance. When the badgering to get him to commit to deer hunting with them the weekend before Thanksgiving came along he dodged, saying maybe when he meant no way, not mentioning the Wisconsin pheasant shoot with his Skokie buddies he had already planned.

Back in the house his sisters were all worried because their parents hadn't shown up yet. They were about to call over to the folks' apartment. "Don't," Jake said. "I'll just go around and get them."

He liked walking the four or six square blocks of his childhood, even though it also always put him off some. Superficially the neighborhood had hardly changed—same comfortable but not-at-all grand old houses set back some from the sidewalk, even most of the same trees, though the trunks had thickened and they had extended their reach out over the streets. But no raggedy weed-filled yards anymore, not a single house or falling-down wood fence in need of propping up or a coat of paint, no junkers half under tarps pulled in off the alleys. At the intersection of Prairie and Park, the little corner store where his mother once sat all day in the gloom behind the counter selling candy to kids and milk about to expire to grownups was no more. Bull-dozed fifteen years ago and a house squeezed onto the odd triangular lot. Almost no working class left, all lawyers and managers and medical types these days. The Victorian with the cupola at 157 Prairie where his pal Ian had lived was gussied up and inhabited now by a lady named Fort, widow of an anthropologist and one herself, retired from Northwestern. The survival of the stack of three railroad apartments where Jake's parents still lived was like a mistake, an oversight. Like his sister Claire, who could afford to go on living around on Park only because her late husband had inherited their house from his grandfather free and clear. She said when she had the family over her new neighbors spied on her from behind their blinds. "They think we all must be Mafia," she laughed, "so I let 'em."

Out of habit, Jake went around the back. He ran up the wooden steps to the second floor and banged on their door. They were there in the kitchen, his mother hunched in a plain brown dress, his father sitting very straight in a chair with a cane resting between his legs and his big leathery hands turned palms up on his knees, so thin and bony you'd think he was starving. Jake's mom pushed her face up for him to brush his lips across it—their version of a kiss—but his father did not have anything but a grunt for him.

The place was the same as ever, worn linoleum, old laboring refrigerator, scratched sink. Jake's mother was a fanatic for soap and bleach and hard brushes so they maintained, but never sought to improve anything. The excuse was them being renters, the truth more that they feared and resented any sort of change. Pushed back into a corner of the counter still in its box was a Braun coffee maker Jake and Angela had given Mom two years ago for Christmas.

"What are you guys waiting for? Everyone's over there already."

They had no response to that. Jake offered to help Dad up, but his father shrugged him off, staked his cane and rose. He was two or three inches taller than Jake and probably forty pounds lighter, hollow-cheeked, his bald dome spotted with faint brown splotches.

Jake watched them both down the stairs and along the pavement out to the street. Once they got going neither of them really had any trouble walking, despite his mother's complaints about her rheumatism and Dad carrying the cane these days. When they got to the party, in the larger circle of family, they managed at least a semblance of sociability. His sisters' version of them was more forgiving than Jake's. Not that they tried to claim Mom and Dad were warm people, but the girls would call up what their parents must have endured just putting bread in their mouths during the War, and how alien and threatening America must have seemed when they first arrived. So was he wrong about them? Or was it him? Or him being a boy? His dad was fifty when he was born, his mother's real age unknown, her secret. Did they merely regret his showing up when they thought they were done with the bother of children?

About three-thirty the women brought out an enormous sheet cake with "90" in stand-up plastic letters and a blaze of candles so great it sent a pulse of warmth through Claire's little dining nook. Pop puffed out his cheeks until he looked like a blow fish and blew and blew while the younger grandchildren and the great-grands jumped up and down and the grownups raised their smart phones and snapped away. Angela took over cutting and distributing, though she wouldn't have any of it herself, being a snob about what she called 'Crisco icing.'

Different as they were, Jake's appreciation for each of his sisters was pretty much across the board. Though Claire was the only one still at home when he was little and Yvonne and Nida both busy starting their own families, all three of them had tried to convince the old people to lighten up some on their baby brother. More successfully, they recognized how much he needed affection from somewhere and gave it to him from their own supply. Claire joked that she had been more his mom than Mom ever was, but Jake would say, "No joke, huh?" Her being in the cafeteria at North Shore Country Day the three years he and Ian were students there together was a big help. When he was in dutch with a teacher or due in the headmaster's office for acting up in class he would sneak off to the kitchen and if he could get Claire alone, unmanly as it was he would just hide his head against the starchy front of her uniform and let her hold him for a minute.

As payback, at least partial, nowadays he tried to help the girls out whenever they asked. Not with money, they didn't beg off him, but usually with stuff like fixes around their houses. He would find a Saturday or Sunday to do the work himself rather than sending one of his men, since what they really seemed to want most was just some time with him.

As he was digging out ice cream and plopping it on paper plates, Nida ghosted up beside him. Claire, she said, her voice low, was hesitant to speak to him, but she sure could use a little assistance right now trying to figure out what to do with Stefano.

"I noticed he wasn't around. Is he home?"

"Up in his room. She says he hardly leaves it anymore. Up all night playing video games, asleep all day. Won't come down even for his meals."

"Stevie," as they generally called him, was also a late child, Claire's one and only. Fourteen when his father died, seventeen or eighteen now, Jake wasn't sure which. He had fondness for the boy, who was smart. Also sensitive. Not in any girly or sentimental way, but if there was a vibe, you could count on Stevie to absorb it. While his father was in the hospital, Jake took the boy fishing a couple of times, more than anything else to get him a few hours away from the gloomy atmosphere at home.

"What about school?" Jake asked.

Nida said, "Apparently he stopped going some time back."

"Well that's fucked. Isn't he supposed to graduate?"

"In June," Nida said. "But now they're saying there's no way." She moved in closer. "The doctor thinks he ought to go in for some days of observation."

"For mental?

"Yes."

"I'll go up."

"Would you, Jake?"

Plastered to the door to Stevie's room were various KEEP OUT signs going back as far as the boy's childhood. A warning to anyone entering without knocking that they would have their faces eaten off by insects surrounded by a decorative border of large black interlocked ants. Jake pushed and the door swung open. Dark, the window shut and the shade pulled, a rancid smell. Too much sleeping and too few showers. Computer on but inactive, under the covers on the bed a long lump. Not saying anything, Jake crossed over and pulled up the shade and cracked the window.

The lump turned, thin long hands snuck out, clutched the covers and pulled them up. The bed was high, a plywood platform on four-by-four legs with a thick slice of foam as the mattress. Jake hiked a little and perched on the edge, one foot dangling. He waited, listening to Stevie breathe. The sounds of the party down below came up, children laughing and calling, music.

The form on the bed rolled suddenly and Stevie pulled up and propped himself on his elbows. His hair was much longer and blacker than Jake remembered, almost to his shoulders, and his lips were smeared black too, as though he'd been eating licorice.

"Hey, Uncle, here's a question."

"What's that, Stevie?"

"How do you stand it?"

"Stand what?"

"It. Them. Our family."

Jake laughed. "Let me tell you one. There was some kind of event, it could even have been your <u>nonno's</u> birthday some year before you were even born, and I started noticing something peculiar so I asked your grandmother, 'Where are his friends?' And she said, 'He doesn't have friends.' So you see?"

"No, I don't. What?"

"The reason to get up, put some clothes on, comb your hair and come down is because your poor grandfather doesn't <u>have</u> anybody except you—us."

Stevie let out a big sigh and crashed back down on his saggy, over-used pillow, face turned away.

Again Jake waited, unusually patient, listening this time to his own breathing. Finally he reached over and shook the boy's shoulder. "Stefano? Did they tell you about the plan to hospitalize you?"

Stevie rolled back, but stayed flat, eyes out from under the sheet but mouth hidden. Muffled, "I heard. What about it?"

"So what do you think? You a danger to yourself?"

"Who's saying that?"

"Look, I remain in the dark here. Are they on you just because you've taken to wearing black lipstick?"

"That's part of it I'm sure." Stevie shut his eyes.

"You're not becoming a goth or anything, are you?"

"Oh please!"

"Well— I don't know these things you know," Jake said. "Tell you what I <u>do</u> know though. Psychiatric evaluation is usually 72 hours to begin with, and then if you can prove you're quite the interesting specimen you might get an additional 35 days—no sharp objects, no matches and truly lousy eats."

"Internet?"

"Doubtful. Half an hour a day maybe? Max."

"I'd rather just stay here then."

"Get your mom to bring your meals up for you? Her with her arthritis? I'm sure you would. And I'm sorry to put it this way, Stevie, but that's kind of a chicken shit solution in my humble opinion."

Silence.

Jake said, "Let me ask this. Is there a love interest in the picture here somehow?"

"There was. Maybe. I don't know."

"Serious?"

"I thought so, but—"

"But what? What happened?"

"With the love interest? I've probably blown it."

"Well I would think, huh? Frankly, Stevie, guys who can't get out of their jammies and get their three a day spoonfed from their mommies— Well, it's just not very sexy, is it?"

For that, Jake got a little smile out of his nephew.

*

What Jake wanted really was for the boy to make a clear statement about whether this 'love interest' was male or female.

Funny, of course, himself in the very moment of launching out into the world of men who do it with men not having the courage or whatever to put it to his nephew as a direct question. If that was what

Stefan's going into hibernation turned out to be about then Jake was fearful for him. And not fearful for himself? After last night? No. Yes, of course. But there was a difference. In his innocence, Stevie would probably figure he had to come out or something and Jake wasn't planning on making any such mess of his life.

On the way downstairs, he glanced at his watch. Nearly five, almost an hour he'd been up with Stevie. Still plenty of people in the house, but it was less noisy, the party beginning to wind down. Time to collect Angela and Lisa and get going. He took a brief look around, but didn't see them.

Claire was leaning against the kitchen sink rinsing plates with her free hand. Jake took the last two of them, dried them and put them in the rack, then turned off the water and asked her to come walk with him. Out back tree shadows had extended across the grass. They went as far as the gate to the alley in silence, then started slowly back.

Claire had one piece of information. The 'love interest' was some young lady who'd graduated already and gone off to college. To Dekalb actually, Jake's old school. But Stevie was finding it almost impossible to get to see her, even the weekends the girl came home. There were other suitors nosing around and the girl's parents lived out in Glenview so Stevie not having wheels of his own put him at a real disadvantage. Plus the parents had developed a low opinion of the kid.

"What am I supposed to do with him, Jake?"

"I'd say the best would be _you_ do precisely nothing, Claire. At least for the time being."

"But—"

"I laid out the possibility he might find himself locked up in the mental ward at Cook County for a while, but Stevie was not impressed. I tried shaming him—"

"Over what?"

"Worrying his mom half to death."

"Oh—"

"Doesn't matter. He's too depressed to be thinking much about other people now anyway."

"What's going to happen to him, Jake?"

"Well, I offered him to come out and work for me."

Claire stopped. With her big mouth and tight-in naturally curly reddish hair, she had never been any kind of beauty. If people were attracted to her, it was for her kindness.

Again Jake went light, avoiding anything that would seem to put blame on her for hanging on to the kid too much. At the moment, he said, trying to get Stevie to finish out school he didn't think worth the effort. Not going to happen. Best thing would be if the boy could earn a little money, maybe buy some wheels of some sort, then get out and try living on his own.

"But how'd he do that, Jake?"

"I don't know, maybe with friends somewhere?" He did not tell her Stevie had mentioned his buds had taken an apartment together closer in to Chicago where maybe he could crash for a while. "I told him to call me beginning of the week. I have a couple of guys out at the site we're on right now who live in Evanston and maybe one of them could stop by in the morning and give Stevie a lift."

"What time do you start, Jake?"

"I'm there earlier, but the men are due by seven or so."

Claire laughed. "Stevie won't even have gone to bed at that hour."

"Do this for me. Don't go up and shake him to get him going, OK? This'll only work if the kid's willing to try it on his own."

"And you can just put a man on like that on your own say-so?"

"Sure," he said. Though in fact he couldn't. Not officially. For the time being there'd be nothing on the books. Should Stevie actually show up, Jake would have to pay him out of pocket, at least for a while.

*

No one seemed to know where Lisa had gotten to. Nida thought maybe her grandfather had taken her for a walk. Angie had gone looking for them.

Jake went out and surveyed the sidewalk in both directions but saw no familiar figures either way. A toss-up how to go. He chose right, toward town and his old elementary school. The afternoon was cooling off quickly and he moved along fast, just short of breaking into a jog.

At Linden down the tunnel of the trees he spotted what he thought was all three of them turning the corner off Wilmette Avenue and starting toward him, Angela in the lead with Lisa by the hand. His father shambled along about ten feet back, head down, using his cane.

"Hey! Came looking for you."

Angela kept walking. Jake fell in beside her. "What's going on?" he said.

"We need to get going now."

"I know. We'll go. What happened? Where were you?"

But she didn't answer. Red in the face and reproachful, Lisa didn't say anything either.

In Claire's kitchen Angela scraped the remains of her white bean salad out onto a plate, rinsed the bowl, then went in and ran hurriedly through her goodbyes, brief hugs for each of his sisters, not a word to his mother, a sharp look and nothing more for the birthday boy standing there with his hands dangling.

She remained silent in the car, looking ahead, not open to questions. At home she got Lisa plunked down in front of the TV with some chips, shut the door into the den, opened the refrigerator, closed it, then turned to Jake.

"And where the hell were you?"

"Upstairs talking with Stevie, then with Claire. Why? What happened?"

Silence. Then she said, "You know, had I known what I know now about your family, I never would have married you."

"Well that's a fairly fucked thing to say, isn't it?"

"What do you mean?"

"You make it all sound so hopeless."

"What's the 'it' here?"

"Us. You know, our life together." He spread his arms.

She glared at him. "Well maybe that's the case."

"You think? No hope?"

She looked down, finally shook her head as though to cast off the thought and stalked out of the room.

It took him a while to piece together what had gone down at Claire's. His father, it turned out, had taken Lisa on a little walk on some vague promise he might get her a present. Once Angie missed the little girl, she couldn't immediately locate Jake to help find her. Somebody said they thought they'd seen Lisa leaving with the old man, so Angie got in the car and drove around the neighborhood, but didn't find them. She came back, still didn't see Jake, and took off again on foot. Eventually she spotted Dad up on Wilmette near Green Bay loitering in an alley next to the Ace Hardware and occasionally peeking out around the corner. Lisa reported that he had taken her as far as the stoplight, told her to wait for him and then just disappeared. She stood there a long while watching the cars go by before it came in on her that she'd been abandoned. She was there, leaning crying against the metal stoplight post when Angie finally got to her.

Jake's father made it all worse by his apparent failure to understand what made Angie so angry. He just stood there, eyes lowered shaking his ancient nearly bald dome, and all he would say was, "The girl will need to learn."

What in hell did that mean? Angie wanted to know.

Unfortunately, Jake knew well enough. His parents complained they were raising Lisa in a bubble. Their own view was it is a mean world we live in and even a little child needs to be on guard against what may befall her at any moment. Abandoned on a street corner by your own grandfather? To them that was a life lesson.

*

Angie fixed Lisa a little supper, but she was still all jacked up on cake and ice cream and at the same time exhausted by her scary adventure. It was only dusk when Angie took her up, got her bathed and down, surrounded in bed by all her stuffed animals and favorite dolls. Jake watched from the doorway. Angie switched on Lisa's nightlight, turned off the overhead and brushed past him. By the time he got to their bedroom door, it was shut. He heard her turn the lock.

"Angie?" Softly.

No answer.

He went down, made himself a drink, sat in front of the TV, flipping. After fifteen minutes he went back upstairs, tried their door and found she had unlocked it. Though relieved, he didn't go in. Back downstairs, more TV, but nothing caught his attention for very long. He replenished his drink, dozed in the leather chair. By ten he was crawling in beside her. Angie sighed and rolled away, but when he put his arm over her and snuggled in against her backside, pressed his legs against her soft upper legs, she didn't tell him to go away.

Jake was about through grade school before he could finally admit to himself that his mother must be nuts. She hit him sometimes for no apparent reason and with no warning, a slap to the side of his head which staggered him and made his ears ring. In exchange for his attempts to please her—or appease her—real, prolonged beatings. The notable occasion was when he was ten and saved up his money to buy an electric popcorn popper for her birthday. At first she refused to understand what the little machine with the plastic dome was for. But once the girls got it through to her, she became a fury. Why had he wasted his money on that thing she would never use? In front of everybody she yanked his pants down and started whacking away, calling him stupido, a cretino. The girls had to pull her off him while his father sat by watching, doing nothing.

One time when Jake and Angie ended up short a sitter they foolishly asked could they leave Lisa with his parents for the evening. The next week Lisa started waking up in the middle of the night crying and calling for them. Angie finally led it out of the little girl that her grandmother had told her when she was a child back in Italy the rivers overflowed and the ocean washed up through her village and for days the water stayed waist-deep in their house and she and her sisters were marooned, unable to get out of the bed they slept on. The crabs and the sharks and all the sea creatures—monsters—were circling around and around them night and day and if their hands or feet drooped out over the edge of the bed while they were sleeping, they could get bitten off.

"You know they came from up in the fucking mountains," Jake said.

Angie nodded. "But what she told Lisa was the water could come up around _her_ bed too without her noticing, so if she doesn't want her hands bitten off she should always make sure they stay under the covers. Poor little thing's so freaked out she's been trying to keep herself awake all night to protect her hands."

*

Once he had things rolling at the site Monday morning and a couple of fires damped if not entirely put out, Jake called Olivia Livieros, Cheryl's mom. Maybe from her many years with Mike Tanner, Olivia had become a fan of notable Chicago-area architecture, seldom missing a charity opportunity to traipse through some Oak Park Frank Lloyd Wrights and grab a cookie and a cup of tea in the garden of one of them. Without thinking about it, Jake had memorized Guy's address. Reciting it to her for a moment felt as though he was letting Olivia in on a wonderful secret.

"Hang on a minute, can you?" she said. "Let me get my book."

He waited, then heard rustling, Olivia efficiently paging through something.

"Oh sure, the Baer mansion. Erected 1893 as a summer residence, remodeled and enlarged and occupied as a year-round residence 1910. Pearson was the original architect, and it seems he did the expansion too. Private. Not open to the public. Why'd you want to know?"

"Oh, just interested. I had my little girl out riding around with me yesterday and going by that place I got a strong impression we must have delivered flowers for some party there when I was a kid."

"Hm," Olivia said. "Is there still a hedge? The photo I have here is tiny but the house appears pretty much hidden from Sheridan Road."

"Yeah, you don't get much more than a glimpse."

"Says here's there's also a later house on the property, a Don Erikson from 1960. That's one I'd like to see. Is it visible from the road?"

Jake said if so he hadn't noticed it. Feeling bad about wading deeper into lies with someone who cared about him, he told Olivia he had another call (one additional lie), thanked her and got off.

Several Guy Baers on Google. The one Jake was concerned about was 66 years of age, BA from Brown University 1966, USMC officer 1967-1971 (lieutenant), PhD from UC Berkeley 1974, Johns Hopkins School of International Studies Fellow, 1975-76, current position Professor of History and Dean of Intercultural Studies Northwestern University. Author of Adam Clayton Powell and the Bandung Conference and another book called The Idea of the 'Emerging' Nation, both available on Amazon, although only used. Two wives, three children, two of them girls it seemed. Union League Club and University Club of Chicago, United Way, boards of directors including the Lyric Opera, as Guy had mentioned.

Over and over then while he was opening his email in the couple of seconds while the messages loaded Jake would get all antsy. Then when the screenful of listings came up, disappointed. The fucker didn't write. And Jake had decided better not for him to initiate himself. What if there had been some misunderstanding? The professor actually turned off, uncomfortable, just hanging on by his manicured fingernails and getting through the sex with the hairy dumb cluck who had to go on the web to find out who the fuck Mary Cassatt was. (Jake didn't believe this, but had to consider the possibility.)

It rained three days in a row, heavy rain, then turned off colder than you'd expect for October. Thursday after work when Jake got home Angie and Lisa were out. He put keys, wallet, and change on the dresser and lay on the bed shoes off but still in his work clothes, hands behind his head, staring at the ceiling. What a girl you turn out to be, he thought, mooning over what is not to be. Not at all tired, he wandered the downstairs, got a glass of milk, took it in to his computer in the den.

"Would you have some time tomorrow afternoon, Friday? Around three? I can book a room. Hope Evanston is convenient. Reply here? Apologies for the late notice—Guy. And then a little farther down in the queue, "On second thought, why don't you call my cell when you have a moment?" and a phone number.

Jake had an impulse to wait, even if only for five minutes, but squelched it.

"Hello?" In the background there was white noise, rushing.

"Hi, this is Jake. OK time to talk?"

"Sure. I'm stuck on the Edens." The man's voice sounded friendly, rich.

"Tomorrow is fine. I'll have to move some things around a little, but I can make it."

"I'm very pleased. Do you know the Gavilan European Inn?"

"White building, flags out front?"

"That's right. It's not the most elegant but it should do us. In fact, it's where we sometimes put up prospective graduate students we're trying to woo."

"So they know you there."

"Oh, highly unlikely. The secretaries make the reservations— although in this case I made it myself, of course. Do you need the address?"

"No, I know where it is."

"All right. Tomorrow then."

"At three?"

"At three."

What Jake had to do then was call around and put a meeting with John Heinemann and two of the younger project managers over to Monday. He was still on the phone when he heard the kitchen door open and Lisa and her pal Trudy coming in the house.

He also had to remember to deal with Stevie. There had been a pleasant surprise Wednesday morning about eleven, a knock on the trailer door and then his nephew standing there in a light wool jacket and soaked sneakers, no socks, hair streaming. Grinning, half pleased with himself, half dubious. He had hitched, he said. Jake got him a towel and stuck him in front of a portable electric heater for twenty minutes to warm him up. When the roach wagon came he took him out and got him a burger. No use putting the kid outside without adequate clothing and some boots, so Jake had him straighten up around his work space for the rest of the day. He had thought of Friday after lunch as a time to show Stevie around the new building, but no reason not to do that while the men were eating. Opportunity to introduce him to the fellows he thought might be willing to stop by and give the boy a lift in the a.m.

Friday turned off sunny again and warm. At three on the nose Jake sauntered into the cavernous lobby of the Gavilan carrying his leather AWOL bag with nothing in it but his shaving kit. He had to take off his sunglasses to adjust to the dark. No one present but two pairs of old ladies in chairs gabbing intermittently and the clerk behind the big front counter who had a book and did not look up. Jake walked around a little, appraising. Arches and big columns, ceiling a painted garden of flowers, vines and medallions in relief, the kind of plaster work immigrant craftsmen did in the 1910s or 20s. All four old ladies following him with their eyes when he approached the desk.

"I have a reservation."

The clerk put a marker in his book, stood. Skinny, almost bald fellow in a vest spilling sandwich crumbs. "Name of?"

Caught out. "Um, the secretary made it for me."

"You Mr. Gorham by any chance?"

Jake smiled. "Yes. Eugene."

"Here," the clerk ran the mouse for an older computer screen around a bit, "I have it here. Arrival time three p.m."

Jake paid cash.

The room on the third floor he was given was large and looked out on the street side of the building. He pulled the shades down against the afternoon sun. The bathroom, also large, had older porcelain fixtures and marble-hexagon tile flooring. Not sordid certainly, or even cheesy exactly, just older, worn. Clean-looking, though. Jake paced, then with a start realized what he needed to do and called Guy.

"I'm here. It's Room 314."

"Oh, all right, fine. Sorry I'm running a little behind. But I'm on the street and I'll be up in a minute."

Then Jake couldn't figure how to occupy himself. He took off his shoes and socks, put them by the bed. Got out the shaving kit, stationed rubbers and a squeeze bottle of lubricant at bedside, felt a little embarrassed so he returned them to the kit, left the whole thing on the little table with the lamp. Should he strip down to just his shorts? That seemed too eager. So he pulled back the flimsy coverlet, propped a pillow against the headboard and lay down to wait. Heart beating, lump in his throat, lump in his pants, but the picture of casualness, or so he hoped.

A knock. He'd forgotten he'd have to answer the door. When he did, Guy came breezing in in slacks and a sports coat, already pulling at his tie. Jake stopped him. "Here, let me do that."

He had also forgotten how significantly taller Guy was. He had to reach up a little. The older man bent to him and they kissed, then hugged, hard, and Jake led Guy to the side of the bed and went on conscientiously undressing him.

Which, as Jake thought later, turned out to be exactly the right move. They talked only in brief bursts ('Sorry I was held up,' 'Doesn't matter, man,' 'How was your day?' 'Good, yours?' 'Hectic, but I soldiered through,' 'I've been looking forward to this,' 'Me too') and then Guy was standing there before him entirely naked. Good and hard himself. He got Jake to sit on the edge of the bed, shucked his pants and shorts off him, then got on his knees and sucked a long time. When he got up, he lay full out on the bed and asked would Jake screw him. Jake skinned out of his shirt, pulled on a rubber and got the grease. Guy said he'd like to try it on his back if he could manage to keep his old legs up for a while.

Jake got up on him and went to work, long slow warming strokes, feeling pretty much entirely in control, Guy below him eyes closed, smiling, drawing him closer now and then, taking long kisses when Jake came in to deliver them.

"You OK with this?"

"I'm fine."

As it got more urgent for Jake and he started going faster and harder, Guy shut his eyes and moaned, then begged, "Just fuck me now, man. OK?"

"I'm going to come then."

"Do it! Please!"

Once it was over and Jake had calmed down, Guy lifted up and gently removed the rubber, then lay back against Jake, pulling Jake's arm across his own chest. He sighed, gently ran his hand over the hair of Jake's forearm.

A long moment of quiet before Jake said, "So how're we going to get you off?"

"Oh, that'll be easy if you can stand me taking it in my mouth some more."

"Stand it?" Jake laughed.

He got up and washed his cock in the bathroom sink and patted it dry. As soon as he got back on the bed it began to stiffen again. Guy came up between his legs, licked his balls, then took Jake's penis in his mouth. Jake breathed easy, enjoying the feel of Guy's very warm chest and belly against his thigh and lower leg. As Guy got more worked up, Jake realized suddenly he was about to come again himself. He reached down and pulled out of Guy's mouth, squeezed the head.

"Umm...put it back."

"I'm going to blow again, man."

"Yes, fine, do it." Guy opened up, Jake jerked himself a couple times and shot in his mouth. A big moan and Guy shot off into his own cupped hand.

*

They were lying face to face with their arms around each other, Jake drowsing and Guy's breath heavy, the mildest snore. Jake kissed the older man's forehead and Guy started awake. "Is it time?"

Jake rolled, got his watch from the lamp table. "Four-twenty. I'm afraid I got to get going."

"Yes, me too."

"I'm going to shower off. You want to go first?"

"No," Guy said, "I can do that at home. She won't be there yet."

Guy was already dressed when Jake came out of the bathroom again. He sat on the side of the messed bed and watched while Jake toweled off and put on his clothes.

"Next weekend I have to go to Denver," Guy said. "So it may be a little while before I could see you again."

"That's OK," Jake said, though for some reason he felt dread. "Family?"

"A reunion with old pals from the Marines. We try to get together every five years."

"You were in Viet Nam, right?"

Guy raised his eyebrows. "You've been checking up on me then—"

"No." Then Jake said, "Well, only the first stuff that comes up on Google."

Guy nodded, got up smiling. "Couldn't find <u>you</u> there."

"No, I don't think you would."

Jake dropped his shaving kit in the AWOL bag and they headed together for the door. Guy started to open it, then shut it again, leaned down and gave Jake another long kiss.

"I really enjoyed myself. Thank you."

"I had fun too. Guess you could tell."

"Enough fun you'd consider making this a regular event?"

"Sure." Then Jake said, "The only thing I should tell you is I'm not looking to change anything about my family situation or anything like that."

"Well," Guy laughed a little, "as I'm sure you've already figured out that's the case for me too."

Jake nodded curtly.

Guy nodded too—was he making fun?—and said, "You ready then?"

"I'm ready."

So that was it, Jake thought later, the pact between them.

They chose to walk down. On the stairs, Guy noticed Jake's leather bag. "Were you planning on staying a while?"

"No, I brought it along so it'd look like I was actually checking into the hotel."

"More practiced at deception than I," Guy said with a little laugh. "And here I've been at it longer."

At the foot of the stairs there was a little hall and an arch leading out to the lobby. Jake said, "You want to go first?"

"Why? I don't think it matters who sees us here, do you?"

As they came toward the clerk, his head jerked up. Jake deposited the key on the counter, nodded to the man, and walked out beside Guy feeling watched.

Guy's little Beamer was half a block down, Jake's blue Mike Tanner truck parked two streets over. The sidewalk was strewn in places with still-soggy yellow leaves. At Guy's car, Jake suddenly said, "I should have served, but I didn't."

"In the army you mean?"

"Yes. But at the time I could have enlisted I had my head screwed on backward."

"Your time would have been what?"

"Iraq, or Afghanistan I guess. Fucked up as this country may be, I happen to love it and I realize now I should have gone in its defense."

"Oh—" Guy looked down, then up into Jake's face. It seemed he was going to have more to say, but he checked himself, clasped Jake's hand, winked at him, gave him a smile and said goodbye.

*

Sunday nine days later at about sun-up Jake was pacing along crunching gravel beside a single set of old railroad tracks outside Sayner, Wisconsin. He wore a heavy wool coat and a red checked cap with the fur-lined earflaps down and sticking out. The hat made him feel like Goofy, as he mentioned to Mark Sherra, an old friend from Dekalb who was tromping along beside him. Both men had their shotguns over their shoulders. Mark's trained dogs, a Labrador called Ralph and a golden called Sissy, came with and sometimes a little ahead of the two men, breathing clouds of anticipation.

Ordinarily the sun would have come up right into the men's eyes. But the day was beginning ominously clouded and the sun presented itself only as a thin smear the color of scrambled eggs wedged between the pines along the horizon and the troubled gray overhead. It had been cold in the night—it was cold now. Thin laces of ice edged the little pockets of wet alongside the roadbed. As the men trudged through the ice crackled. The brown fields on both sides of the track were dead still, the waist-high grasses and weeds sparkly with frost. If either Jake or Mark looked up and glanced over, the dogs came to full attention, noses up, ready.

"You having a good time?" Mark asked in a low voice.

"Doesn't it look like it?"

"You seem a little preoccupied."

"Well that I am."

"Job?"

"<u>And</u> family, and bills, and—"

"The usual?"

"No worse than the usual, certainly," Jake said. "No problem so big it can't be solved with a nickel, you know."

"I thought we'd agreed money doesn't buy happiness."

"Not that kind of nickel. Nickel as in the cost of a single bullet for a .22."

Mark clumped along head down. Jake could hear his breathing.

"You're not considering offing yourself, I hope—"

"I run through a lot of emotions, man, and one that comes up is suicide. I'm not perfect, you know."

"No, but—" Mark stopped.

Jake put his hand around to Mark's far shoulder, patted there a little. "Don't worry, pal. I'm not about to succumb to anything so easy. Way too much to live for. My little girl, for example. Need to see her through to flourish, don't I?"

"OK. So just don't scare me, all right?"

"I promise."

The farm where they were hunting belonged to relatives of Leonard Probst, another friend Jake had kept since college. Highly likely Leonard was still snoring away in his sleeping bag at the summer camp of some rich Texas people on the lake three miles to the north. Leonard's cousin Jack worked as the owners' guide during the season and had permission for Leonard and his friends to bunk there one weekend every fall. The pipes on the property had been drained for the winter so there was no running water, but the four of them each chipped in a little on propane so they were allowed to use the big gas stove and sit around the kitchen work table to keep warm evenings and mornings.

What Mark had mainly picked up on, Jake was pretty sure, was him not drinking along with the rest of them. But if he'd been paying attention, Mark would have noticed that fact on the trip several years ago when Jake's tapering off began. He liked all three of his companions well enough (the fourth was Fred Staten, a Cook County sheriff who lived on Jake's block), but over time the others seemed to have forgotten the purpose of the long weekend was pheasant, not Wild Turkey. Jake was patient, none of the rest of them seemed to know how so he cooked the meals, at night nursed two or three glasses of wine while they got sloppy in their talk and insistent about trying to draw him in. But these days Mark was often the only one Jake could manage to round out and get going at first light.

Not the right moment to be cooped up with other people. Even home life, which appeared on the surface to be going fine, Angie OK, LIsa OK, had him on edge. What he really wanted was time alone. To think. About? Guess! Not really having enough data on Guy yet to make up a real whole picture, Jake stuck on worrying small facts, little discoveries he'd made. That tan line slung under the man's handsome little belly. Oh right, those with the dough go on vacations in the sun any time of the year they want, don't they? And don't fret about their trunks being skimpy or even what might hang out. At $600 a night at the remote private beach on Maui no one's about to give you the fish eye.

Mainly, though, what he had in hand was questions. What does it mean that a big old former Marine wants more than anything to get bent over and take a cock up his ass? Not that Jake wasn't grateful for that, the symmetry between his desires and Guy's which made the sex so hot. To be penetrated. Does that mean somewhere deep down at least in bed the man really wants to be the woman? Concerning his own butt, Jake was sure he didn't want anything up there. The strange discomfort of the doctor's gloved and greased finger feeling around for his prostate for even a few seconds every few years was plenty enough to prove that, thanks.

More and worse. Despite how happy it made him to have found Guy, why did he feel somehow put down? Diminished? Guy had to go to Denver, he was a few minutes late, he had things to do. And Jake? The implication seemed to be Ol' Jake could just wait with his dick in his hand.

Mark stopped suddenly, head raised, something on the wind. He clucked to the dogs and Ralph and Sissy pushed in side by side close against their master's leg and sat, noses up, the look in their eyes like human pleading. Mark indicated to the right with his finger and the dogs started carefully into the weeds two or three paces apart. The men took their guns from their shoulders, cracked them, loaded shells from their pockets, closed them, put them underarm and started in after the dogs. Scratching sounds, brambles, tagalongs, Jake could feel the prickles as they raked and rasped at the canvas of his Ben Davises.

Thinking, Should have gotten in on the fucker first, told him <u>you</u> were going to be gone hunting. Let <u>him</u> wait on <u>you</u>—

*

In the night he waited in the dormitory's freezing blackness for his pals' breathing to change. They were snozzled again, so it didn't take long. One by one and then they were all out and Jake could turn on his side in his bag, reach down into his shorts and begin gently squeezing his cock. He willed up hot snapshot moments of the two sessions with Guy, but those were not enough and as he went on images of Angela joined the mix, her face hot against the back of his hand once when he touched it as she apparently was coming one more time unexpected- ly in a hotel room somewhere. And then faces and bodies from long ago, women he'd gotten to know through pushing on the sex, finding out what turned them on and then doing <u>that</u> as well and as much as he could. Jake the pleaser. The corruptor of the not-so-innocent. The pusher.

He understood how seriously his method was frowned upon. Face to face clothes on hands in your lap talk in the candle flicker of snotty restaurants—that was how civilized people got to know one another. But he alas was an animal ('Raised by wolves, didn't you listen when I told you?' he would say to Angela), so instead of drawing him closer, the recitation of the problems of the woman across the table often merely turned him off. A man's daily burdens are his own, and a woman's her own too, right? All he wanted was to break in and say, 'Why don't we go someplace? We can get naked and I will lead you and lead you further along until I make you happy. At least for a while. OK?'

Meeting up with Angie in Paris that time it came as a surprise to find himself hungry not only for her body but for whatever more he could learn about her. Any little thing. It was this wanting to know which led him to the conclusion he must be falling in love with her.

Very near coming now, breathing down into the sleeping bag' flannel lining just to be sure he didn't wake anybody, hot all over and so close to sleep he could have just let it go if he wanted. No urgency. The thing about men—no, he corrected himself, he meant only the thing about having sex with Guy Baer—was the way their body hungers seemed to mesh, their desires fit. Though Jake was considerate, asked before he did, he felt pretty much one hundred percent sure in the sack Guy wanted whatever it was he wanted. To please the pleaser. No negotiation, no holding back, no part of the body out of bounds.

*

Monday was the load-up and the drive back down, so no more opportunity to hunt. Up before the others, Jake took two buckets down and filled them with soft lake water. One he washed his face and hands from and then left out by the kitchen door, the other he took inside and put in the sink. He made coffee in a big blue enamel pot, fried all the rest of the bacon, put aside a dozen eggs, some bread and a stick of butter, then packed up the rest of the food and stowed it in Fred's truck. Still no noise from the dormitory up the way, so he took his coffee cup out on the main house porch. Yesterday's clouds had gone away and the sky was clear, empty, the sun already raking through the birches east of the camp clearing. On the lawn running down to the lake were fifteen or more deer of different sizes and ages, the two bucks hanging back more toward the trees, watchful. The does and fawns looked up, but Jake did not seem to frighten them at all and they went back to tugging up tufts of grass and chewing.

His friends came banging out of the dorm together talking loud, but as soon as they saw the deer they quieted down. Jake brought out the pot and cups and they sat on the railing and the steps warming their hands and watching the animals. They had non-resident pheasant stamps, but no one had yet renewed his out-of-state deer license. More to the point, they hadn't brought along rifles. Leonard mentioned there wouldn't be a lot of sport involved in shooting these trusting ladies from the porch anyway and the talk turned to going three days without a bath and Leonard and Fred went to sniffing at their armpits. 'Pure perfume,' they announced. Jake, who showered every day at home and sometimes twice, didn't mention he could smell cum on himself and felt grungy and itchy all over. On impulse he kicked off his boots, skinned out of shirt, pants and socks and in only his boxers made for the lake on a dead run. Startled, some of the deer jerked up and backed off, but then others seemed to think Jake was a leader of some sort and came loping down the slope after him. Jake's bare feet hit the planks of the little boat dock hard—bang, bang, bang!—and he ran down to the end and dove in.

He surfaced quickly, yelling and laughing. The water was bitterly cold, numbing, but he got to the ladder and pulled himself up and came trotting back down the dock. The deer had dispersed and the other guys were sauntering down the incline toward him, shaking their heads over him. Fred held Jake's shirt out for him to get into. As he was buttoning up, Jake glanced down. His soaked shorts were clinging to his legs, perfectly outlining his junk if anyone wanted to notice.

*

Tuesday was catch-up time at the job, which had Jake moving fast. On top of regular stuff, he had to get ready for his trailer to be lugged twenty miles over to the Miller brothers' location. Having their plans and their permits all in order, the gentlemen were antsy for him to get ahead with principal material ordering <u>and</u> with getting their foundation hole dug out or at least started before the ground froze. He told them several times how much better it would be to wait until the spring, but the brothers were not buying. Jake had a suspicion the financing for their new building was not as entirely committed as they let on it was. Both of them were increasingly concerned about the finish date he had given them, questioning him about its reality in every conversation. They'd probably already contracted rental space with an occupancy date written in. Luckily, they did seem to be taking to Kevin Tanner, which had certain advantages. Jake stepped far enough to the side to let Kev sweet talk them through some of their less critical nervous-nelly phone calls.

All week Jake hopscotched, meeting with the surveyors who were laying out the Miller site, making sure the place for the trailers was level enough and near enough to the power hookups, getting calls on his cell that forced him to run to Evanston to confer with Mike, then back to Barrington to solve problems his men should have been able to deal with on their own. But he carefully carved out an hour at the end of the day Wednesday to drive around and look for a motel that had in-room hot tubs and was close enough in so a Northwestern professor could take a little detour there coming from work and still make it home to Winnetka in time for supper. He finally located a Comfort Inn on the Lake side of the Edens in the direction of Glenview, not the world's spiffiest place, but with parking you couldn't see from the highway and one room with a Jacuzzi, their "deluxe suite" as the manager called it. Jake reserved it for Friday in his own name.

Thursday, the day he expected to hear from Guy, there was nothing. Friday at noon he had to call and cancel the Comfort Inn reservation, very angry but telling himself he had no reason to be. Nothing to be pissed off about, no one to be pissed off <u>at</u>. He wrote Guy an email which said "<u>Did you die</u>?" and then deleted it. Monday he was on the way to the Miller brothers' property with Stevie beside him in the little Toyota when his cell rang and it was Guy's deep pleasant voice asking how he had been and if by any chance he might be free for lunch and for an hour or so afterwards.

Jake said, "I'll need to get back to you. In ten minutes or so?"

"I imagine you've got somebody with you at the moment."

"My nephew," he said, giving Stevie a smile.

"OK. I'll wait to hear from you then."

At the next stoplight, Jake saved the number to the contact in his directory which he had named "Gene Gorham."

For more than two weeks now, Stevie had been showing up nearly every morning at seven, catching a ride with one or the other of the Evanston men Jake had introduced him to. The couple of times he was late it was only a matter of ten or fifteen minutes and because he had been forced to hitch out to the job. He arrived with his father's old beat-up black lunch box, the domed kind with the thermos in the lid, packed by his doting mother. (Claire called Jake at home one evening and said, "What have you done to my son?" "What'd you mean?" Jake said. "He wolfs down a huge supper and then reminds me to be sure to call him by five and goes upstairs and goes to bed.") Jake was a little surprised at the early bedtime too, since he still had Stevie in the office answering the phone, entering some stuff for him, and hadn't yet stationed him outside for any really physical work. The cash he put in a brown envelope Fridays for Stevie was coming out of his own pocket, but he thought he saw a place he could put a non-union guy on payroll in the next couple of weeks.

Leaving Stevie to receive the men hauling the bigger of the two trailers over from Barrington involved some risk, but Jake didn't think that much. He'd already paced the location with the driver, but he went through it again with Stevie, showing him the flags that had been set out to mark exactly where all four corners of the trailer should land. Stevie was plenty smart and he had his own cell so he could call Jake if the men started screwing up and wouldn't listen to him.

In profile the coffee shop where Jake told Guy to meet him looked like a big chrome check mark, enormous 1950s expanse of plate glass in front, an inclined roof down to the center beam, then a shorter uptick in the back which housed the kitchen, bathrooms, storerooms. As he pulled into the lot, Jake caught sight of Guy waiting just inside the front doors. They shook hands a little formally, like old friends or business associates. Guy had on a suede jacket and a shirt so brightly blue it was a little distracting. The place was roaring loud with the lunch crowd, but Guy said he'd been told it would only be a few minutes for a table.

As they were being led to a booth in the far front corner, Guy seemed to favor one leg. The hostess seated Jake with his back to the wall, but being by the big window made him uncomfortable. He apologized to Guy. He hadn't been thinking.

Guy half-turned to look around. "What's wrong? This seems fine to me."

He sometimes brought his daughter here for breakfast on the weekend, Jake said, when her mom wanted to sleep in. He and his little girl had several of these "secret places" as they called them, meaning his wife wasn't told where they were going or where they'd been. On Saturday and Sunday the cooks would make kids pancakes in the shape of animals more or less and his daughter got a kick out of trying to keep a straight face while telling the waitress things like, 'I'll have one raccoon and one kitty, please.'

Talking too much. Shut 'er up, he thought.

Guy had been surveying the menu, but Jake's sudden silence drew his attention. "So your home life is happy?"

"Yes, very much so."

And off Jake went again, loping all over the territory, apparently unable to keep it short and simple, glossing over some of the rougher stuff. What an unexpected pleasure having a daughter turned out to be, what a great mom his wife was. Hell, what a great <u>person</u> she was, how he admired her, <u>had</u> admired her long ago, in high school when he'd thought she was not attainable by the likes of him. A brief admission that he himself hadn't had much material stuff growing up, as maybe Guy could guess, so now how a lot of his happiness came out of being able to give his daughter a life where she had what all her little friends had.

The waitress appeared to take their order. Once she was gone, Guy said, "Mind if I ask something a little more personal?"

"You can ask me anything, man."

Guy's face brightened, as though Jake had made a pleasing little joke. "Is your sexual life at home also pretty satisfactory?"

"Yes, entirely. No complaints in that department. On either side that I know of."

"So that's not the reason you decided at your age to—what should I say?—branch out some?"

"Not at all."

"You told me right off the bat you didn't have a lot of experience."

"No. It's only in the last year—" Again that amused smile, so Jake asked, "What's funny?"

Guy shook his head, looked down. "Just thinking. You certainly must be a fast learner."

"Thanks. I'll take the compliment."

"I hope so."

"What about you, man? Is it OK to ask?"

"Of course," Guy said. "Just put the question."

"What about you? You happy?"

Guy drew breath, sighed. "You know Italian, don't you?"

"My parents spoke it at home, yes. How did you know?"

"I've been thinking some about when I used to go into Guarani's for flowers or whatever. The gentleman in charge—?"

"My uncle Gio."

"Mr. Gio, that's right. He and the gentleman in the back, the thin one, spoke Italian with each other."

"My father."

"Really? Huh!"

When the platters with Jake's sandwich and Guy's cheeseburger arrived, Guy took the catsup and pooed out a big blob down at the end of his fries, dipped one, popped it in his mouth. "Hot!" he said, "Watch out!" He drank water and then picked his over-sized burger up in both hands.

"Why'd you ask if I spoke?"

"Because with regard to happiness I wanted to say '<u>La storia mia non é breve</u>.'"

"So give the long version," Jake said.

Guy lowered his burger without biting into it, held it just above his plate. "The long version of my happiness…." He considered, sighed, looked out on the gray day, the slowed traffic along the highway.

What came out initially was Guy saying that it was certain his second marriage was happier than his first had been. He and his wife had daughters they were very proud of, one in college and the other starting the graduate program in public health at the University of Michigan. His wife was a professional fund-raiser, by chance at the moment also at Northwestern, although only to serve out a contract with the university held by the firm she was with. Unfortunately, they both worked a lot, too much for their own good probably. He traveled some on business and his wife did as well, but they still enjoyed each other's company when they found time for it. "Over the years we have become really quite tolerant and forgiving of each other's foibles, I think," Guy said.

"All of them?"

"Well not all, no. She doesn't know anything about me and men."

"Would she be forgiving if she found out?"

Guy shook his head. "Doubtful. She takes a lot of pride in being put together and successful as a professional but also as a 'real' woman, and my not being entirely monogamous I think would come as a serious blow to her." He hesitated, then said, "Although——." He began again, "Well, we _have_ talked about how things have been getting somehow dry and less what?—less _tasty_ between us in recent years. And she agrees with me on that point."

"You're talking about sex?"

Again the broad smile. "Oh, there hasn't been much of the physical between us for some time. Which doesn't have anything to do with my outside interests, by the way. _They_ began long long ago."

"During your first marriage?"

"Well before." Guy drank water. "Do you mind if I go on a little?"

"No, please—"

"To say my second marriage has been happier is too easy."

"Because—"

"Because the first time out it went very badly. My first wife and I were lovers in college, too young really to know what we were doing. We got married under the gun of me going off to southeast Asia. I was out there eleven months before I saw her again—Lois—and that was for a three-day leave in Oahu. During which, in spite of the madness— some of my brother officers were there too and there was a lot of partying—we managed to conceive a child. A boy. The sweetest thing, a poetic little kid I want to say, the way he turned out. After the Marines I felt I was behind somehow, so I devoted myself to building a career. Worked like a demon—grad school, two post-docs in D.C., first book, first job. We moved nearly every year for a while, jumping around from university to university, and I left making a home and a personal life for us almost entirely up to her. She didn't say anything and she tried, but she was miserable a lot of the time. Alone. Or alone with no one but the boy. And so in a way it's not surprising that where the unhappiness eventually manifested itself was in my son. He developed an eating disorder. He was thirteen and at first we just thought he was putting on weight because adolescence was coming on and he was having trouble fitting in at his latest new school. Then he lost weight, to please us we thought, and they caught him purposely throwing up his lunch at school. The doctors weren't much help. They were slow to say he was bulimic because at the time they still conceived of bulimia as only a malady of young ladies."

"And what happened?"

"We lost him. Whether he did something to himself or whether he just choked on bile in his sleep was never determined. But he was gone when I went in to make him get up for breakfast one morning, and had been gone for some hours they said.

"Lois blamed me, and at the time I accepted her judgment. Though I don't anymore, I think, not entirely. We both failed the boy, separately but somewhat equally."

"I'm sorry."

Guy shrugged, looked down at his food. "It's OK, thank you. That was a long time ago, you know."

Silence, both men gazing out the window. Jake wanted to look at Guy's face—he had the impression Guy was on the border of tears—but felt he shouldn't.

They turned to easier subjects, Guy's reunion in Denver with the men from his old unit, Jake's pheasant hunt and his sudden desire to take a refreshing dip in Star Lake. Guy's limp? A bit of an embarrassment, he said. Late one evening he and his Viet Nam buddies decided to play a little touch football out back of their hotel and he tripped over a lounge chair and banged his knee. Painful? Painful reminder he was no longer 24 years of age, Guy said.

When the check was presented, Guy picked up the folder, reached back for his wallet. "Let me get this. And remind me also to give you money for my half of the room at the Gavilan, would you?"

"Oh sure," Jake said, "I'm going to make you pay up on that one, Mister. Or should I just take it out in trade?"

"That would be fine."

Guy smiled, put the folder down with a credit card sticking out. "Have I talked too much, blown through the time we could have had that soak in the hottub you mentioned?"

Jake consulted his watch. Almost 1:45. The time he had freed up was ticking by, but maybe he could clear some more on his cell on the way to the motel. "No," he said, "not at all. I made a reservation on my way over here."

"Good. You didn't eat the other half of your sandwich."

Jake thought to say, 'I wasn't that hungry,' but instead he leaned forward and said, 'Couldn't manage it. I want you too bad."

In his Toyota, keeping Guy's little silver Beamer in his rearview mirror, slowing and tugging on his blinkers at each turn while calling around to locate John Heinemann, Jake was convinced he had said the wrong thing. In the old days with women he frequently got what he wanted by being direct. But you can't look a man straight in the face and admit you want to fuck him, can you? Or maybe you can. Guy had smiled, hadn't he? Maybe even reddened up, blushed a little?

*

Halloween night Lisa came down the stairs with her wide skirt swaying like a bell and her scepter in hand. Her white gold hair, usually let go long down her back, Angie had pinned up into a French roll. When Jake applauded Lisa condescended to a minimal regal bow, touching her plastic crown to keep it from tipping.

Jake waited on the sidewalk in the wavering circle of his battery lantern with the coat Lisa had refused to wear over his arm, chatting some with neighbor parents out on the same watch. As though driven by the cold persistent wind, Lisa and Trudy flew from house to house in little changing gaggles with their pals collecting chocolate bars and Cellophane cones of candy corn and the occasional do-gooder's apple or toothbrush. Overall the loot was much higher quality than what Jake remembered from Wilmette when he was a kid. And though Angela commandeered Lisa's bag as soon as they got home, she had managed to stuff in enough sugar on the run that it took Jake until after 10 to get her to lay her little head down for good.

Angie went in to go to bed, but Jake was still wide awake. He poured out a big glass of one of his reds, then sat down in the den to a two-inch stack of envelopes he had stashed in a cubbyhole behind his desk. Sorting bills into piles he thought of as PAY-NOW and PUT-OFF was one of his end-of-the-day tasks. Having it done sometimes helped him sleep.

Angie had a checking account of her own which Jake never saw, though he got the impression the balance was small, little gifts from her mother and more rarely a couple hundred from her father. Jake and Angela's savings and their family checking account were both joint. He wished he could push a thousand or even five hundred into savings every month, but as he had told Ian Stiles, they were spending every penny of his take home, and any refund coming their way April 15 either from state or federal he put to paying down credit cards.

Angie knew perfectly well how to balance a set of books, she had done it two or three years for the lawyers she worked for in Santa Barbara. Jake kept thinking if she could only see right there on the page where every cent was going, she might reconsider her own weekly yak with the therapist or Lisa's ballet class or her piano lesson or—

But Angie refused to have anything to do with the household accounts.

At least Earl had turned 21 and supposedly was now about to get entirely off the tit. The bulletin was he had a kitchen or order window job at an oven grinder place downtown. But there were still more than occasional checks for fifty or a hundred dollars noted by Angie in the stubs as "presents" or "birthday."

She thought they should have everything they wanted and live on credit like everybody else. Jake detested credit. When she said, 'But that's un-American, Jake!' he would laugh and say, 'You're right, it's unpatriotic of me. But in some part I'm still just a fucking peasant from

Calabria like my parents you know. Credit was invented to bring people like me to our knees and make us eat dirt.' He brought home stories about the shitty things that happened to men who worked for him—having to pull their kids out of out-of-town college, sell the boat, losing their homes—but Angie only shook her head back and forth with the kind of distracted irritation you see in a person when the gnats are out on a summer evening.

She was going to a new shrink. The old one, the lady with the colored Kleenex billowing from the straw box who had bestowed upon Jake the gift of anger management, had determined Angie's troubles were no longer psychological, they were spiritual. "Good!" said Jake. "So that means you're cured?" Angie said no, what it meant was that her therapist was sending her along to a woman who had been trained as a shaman.

"That's a witch doctor, right?"

"No," Angie said with strained patience, "Molly's a Native American woman with training in Chippewa ways of divination and curing. She follows the path of the Bear Spirit."

"How much?"

"What do you mean?"

"What's it going to cost me, the 'path' here?"

"A hundred and twenty-five a visit."

"Couldn't you have stayed psychological? It was only a hundred a shot to go down that road."

The shaman's first bill had arrived, brown ragged-edged paper with a black bear claw and the name "Molly Longshanks" imprinted at the top. Blue handwriting, round, school-girl letters. Four sessions, five hundred dollars. And then below

SAGE TREATMENTS (2) (LISA) $80.000

When he went upstairs finally he found the light on, his wife sleeping half sitting up, half leaned over slumped onto his pillows, her book open in her lap and her hand spread across the pages. He turned out the light and snuck in on his side and she sighed and cleared the book off and pushed down under the coverlet without really waking up. If she had been even a little awake, he would have asked her about the 'sage treatments,' but as it was he just lay over against her in the dark inhaling the faint flowery smell of her hair, his hand cupping one breast, listening to her breath rise and fall. She had on a shorty night-gown with lace on the bodice and narrow little straps like a slip. He pressed up closer, gave her shoulder a big lingering wet kiss, ran his finger under one of the straps. He hoisted his leg over hers, moved his free hand down to her crotch, let it lie there lightly. Flesh of his flesh. Her little spurts of dieting now and then seemed silliness to him. Not that he wanted her to turn into a cow or anything, but that wasn't going to happen.

He lifted the hem of the nightgown to get his hand up underneath and her breathing changed. Stillness, silence. Then she said softly, "It's all right if you want to."

"That's OK," he said, "I'm half out myself."

"Really?"

She must be able to feel his cock lying hard against her flank.

"Really."

But in the morning when he came out after his shower, in the narrow patch of bathroom light across the bed he could tell she was full awake so he dressed quickly, hoping to get away before anything bad happened. He was at the door when she said, "Honey, do you have any cash on you?"

He blew out air, came back, took two twenties from his wallet and dropped them on the bed. "That hold you?"

He turned to go.

"What's wrong?"

"Nothing." He stopped. "You know I don't like you to panhandle me. You can line up at the auto-teller just as easy as I can."

"I know. But Lisa is supposed to bring money to school this morning for their trip to the—"

"To the what?"

"Oh forget it." She picked up the bills and held them out to him. "I don't want to make you short."

He didn't move to take them. "You won't."

"What are we doing here?" Angie said. "Let's don't argue about money."

"Why not?"

"I don't know. Because there's something sordid about it. Common."

"Well I'm common. You knew that. Didn't you?

Nothing.

"I happen to have the 'common' problem that I seem to be the only one even trying to keep this goddamn family from going down the chute. And meanwhile I'm hemorrhaging money."

"What is it this time?"

He stopped, tried to control himself, make his voice reasonable. "Just tell me please what's involved in these 'sage treatments' I seem to need my little girl to have."

"Oh," she said, and then again, "Oh. Well, she was so upset after being abducted by your father, bad dreams and the whole thing, that I asked my new therapist what to do. And she said bring Lisa in and she would 'smoke' her in the traditional manner to clear away the bad experience. It seems to have worked, by the way."

"And you couldn't have mentioned it to me before you went out and spent my money on the witch doctor?"

"Your money," she said with contempt.

"My money our money—don't give me that. You know what I mean."

"But that is the issue isn't it, Jake? You get to have your toys—"

"What toys? Do I have toys? I didn't know."

"Your guns, your motorcycle, your fishing gear, that fully outfitted woodworking shop out there you never use—"

"When do I have one minute for—?"

"Look," she said, "here's the bottom line. If I can't spend a little of 'your money' the way I see fit from time to time—"

"Then <u>what</u>?"

She was silent. He waited, then said, "I have to go, I'm late now."

"I'm sorry if I made you late."

She didn't seem to mean it, her voice was mocking. Then she said, "What I really need, Jake, is—"

"You know what you need?"

"What's that?"

"You need to get off your ass and get out and get a job that makes at least a small contribution to the situation around here."

*

For three days they spoke only enough to make Lisa think everything was all right between them. Or concerning logistics, him to pick the girl up from ballet or whatever. A surprise that Angie didn't lock herself in the bedroom or ask him to sleep downstairs as she had other times. At night some sort of ceasefire went into effect. She didn't object when he moved over and their bodies touched. But if he tried to nuzzle in and kiss her when he thought she was asleep, she would turn her head away and sigh.

Thursday after work she asked would he come into the kitchen for a short conference. In a voice flat and indifferent she informed him she had a therapy appointment scheduled Friday afternoon and she'd OK'd it with "Molly" for Jake to come along if he wanted.

His first thought was what if Guy wanted to get together? But since he hadn't called or emailed yet, Jake agreed to the session.

It was a trap, obviously. While trying to convince him it would be unprofessional for her to play favorites, the Chippewa hippy mama would back Angie one hundred percent. But he felt sure he could withstand her, and a third person in the room might make it possible to get out more of what still needed to be said.

Molly Longshanks practiced in an office with a separate entrance beside her home on Edgebrook, a quiet residential street off North Hiawatha in Wildwood. (When he first read the directions Angie had written out for him, Jake said aloud, "Hiawatha? You gotta be kidding!" but no one was around to hear him.) No shingle hung out, but luckily their Volvo was already there, motor running, Angie sitting in it. He ran through the freezing rain and got in with her. She was slowly eating crackers. No conversation, but she did hold the open box out to him.

The room the little lady therapist ushered them into was pretty obviously a garage converted on the cheap. Dry wall and a ceiling let in, but no real flooring, the brown flecked wall-to-wall most likely glued directly to the original concrete. A window had been cut out in the far wall, giving a view of the house's backyard, dead tomato vines tied up with rags clinging shivering to old broomsticks, rake and hoe handles. Taking a beating.

Almost as soon as they were settled into their chairs, Angie began confessing it made her miserable to fight with him, how she couldn't eat, how impossible it became to think consecutively about anything else. She couldn't even give her daughter the attention deserved, she said.

Big admission coming from Mrs. Perfect Mom, he thought. But he said nothing. He was looking evenly at Molly Longshanks' wide face, the broad nose, the concentrating but strangely vacant or at least even and noncommital expression. Hair parted down the middle and in thick braids snaking down over her giant breasts, a squat woman in a floor-length skirt, many silver rings and bracelets. Plump but light on her feet, energetic. He'd noticed that coming in.

"And what about you, Mr. Guarani?" Molly asked. "Similar feelings?"

"Yeah, I don't sleep well at all when we're fighting. Go to work with a lump in my throat, come home and it comes right back."

Then another confession. Angie told Molly the sex she and Jake had was often still really good, but that sometimes she begged off because of some battle she was having with him and because she knew how not letting him have it hurt him.

Molly turned to him. "So Jake, if that's all right—"

"Sure," he said, "call me whatever—"

"Jake. Is this true, you're a horny toad?"

All three of them laughed, and Jake admitted that he was indeed one horny toad.

"You know that's not necessarily a bad thing," Molly said. "Good sex with someone you care for can carry with it a huge load of self-validation."

"I've heard."

The therapist was regarding him in a fixed way that made Jake uncomfortable. He turned to Angie beside him and said, "Does it make you feel better about yourself, honey?"

"Sex?" Angie shrugged, shook her head a little. "I suppose. I'd have to think—"

Pause, maybe renewed tension. Then Molly went off on a thing about how it might be more difficult for Angie because of how her first husband treated her, and given that first marriage represented a betrayal on so many levels. When Molly asked Angie what her thoughts were, Angie again clammed up, wouldn't say.

Because she felt criticized, he imagined. A turn maybe the bear-path lady might not understand. And Molly in fact dealt with Angie's head-down silence by launching into another speech, this one about how in our society the advertising and the media hammer away at a woman's sense of her body and tell her she's inadequate and not sexy unless she looks pretty much like Angelina Jolie, and as a result women often begin to seek elsewhere for their sense of their own worth, get it more from rearing their children, from the compliments they get for their casserole at the potluck, from less conflictual associations with other women instead of from men.

Time was going by too quickly and as Molly's ideas rolled on out Jake had trouble staying with her. "Seeking elsewhere,' he thought. Ah yes, that. Once or twice Angie had dangled before him the possibility that when she lived in California maybe there had been some warm moments between her and another woman. But when he said, 'You mean pussy bumping?' she shut him down, told him he had a foul mouth.

The office had a pleasant but fairly dominant sweet smell. Not pot or patchouli, and not church incense either. Sage? Briefly he wondered if the little lady across from him with her hands in her lap really could have magic. What if she saw straight through him, could tell somehow he recently had another man's balls in his mouth?

He watched Angie's face, the calm, nodding way she took in the therapist's words. Tried to imagine how she would receive the news her husband had turned to sucking cock. But that was hard, like trying to imagine the world falling apart.

Then Molly was calling on him. "So I need to know if you're in favor of that too. Jake?"

"I'm sorry? I missed that."

"I was saying, Jake, that I need to know if you are in favor of this marriage of yours, of things improving for everybody concerned, you, your wife, your little girl—"

"Me?"

"You."

"I'm very much in favor of it."

How wimpy he sounded. It was as though the words came from outside him.

"Excuse me," he said, all polite, "but we need to back up a little. Why am I being asked whether I'm 'in favor' of my marriage? Is there an issue there?"

Silence again. The women eyed one another. The collusion he had expected revealing itself at last. A pause, then Molly said, "There's nothing exactly new here, Jake. You've known for quite a while that your wife sometimes has trouble being with you."

"Right. Putting up with me she usually calls it. Angie thinks I'm a crook, you know."

Angie said, "No."

"OK, you took that one back."

"Not a crook exactly, but maybe a chiseler of some kind. How's that?" She looked down at her hands.

"Also a pretty shitty thing to say."

He glanced over at the therapist. Was there maybe some help coming from that quarter? Nope. The lady was leaned forward as intent as a spectator at the Open at Forest Hills.

"I'm sorry," Angela said. "Not a chiseler then, Jake. But for sure you are one tireless negotiator. Whatever's on offer you always want to see can you bring it down a notch, so anybody up against you is always going to wind up one less somehow. With zero, or close to it if you had your way."

"And the life we have together, our house, everything I've provided for us, is that nothing too?"

"I didn't say that. And besides, a house in itself is not a home, you know."

"Like the song says. But go on—

"Go on what?"

"Give us the next line too."

He waited while she thought, ran the first line again silently. Then she said, "'When there is no one there...'"

"'...to hold you tight,'" he finished. "Right?"

"Yes, right."

The hour or the fifty minutes or whatever was winding down. For her part in the creation of new mess Molly seemed quite satisfied with herself. But at the same time, maybe to earn her hundred and a quarter, she told them in several different ways how much she appreciated both of them being so honest in the session. 'So real' she even said.

He thought it was the end when they were all three on their feet and Molly had pulled them together in a group huddle, heads down, arms around each other's waists. But no. Molly said she wanted to extract a pledge from both of them. Could they keep 'I don't think so tonight' and all current feuds out of their bedroom for a month? Or until Christmas, maybe, or even to the end of the year? "A man and a woman's bed should be a place of refuge and comfort and pleasure," Molly said, "not a battleground. OK?"

Angie murmured, "We can try that," and Jake said, "I would like that too," and Molly Longshanks reached up and cupped the back of their heads one in each hand and held them there together forehead to forehead for a long moment before she allowed them to break out of the huddle.

*

"Funny," Guy said, "I wouldn't even have been able to tell you the name of this place."

"It's called Bigelow's."

"So I see, it is." Guy peered a little closer at the check. He had again reached for it ahead of Jake and now had his own thick black and gold ballpoint in hand and was deciding what tip to write in.

"You don't have to worry about leaving a paper trail?"

"No, she never sees the bill for this card. You?"

"My wife enjoys spending money," Jake said, "but not keeping tabs on it. Although I have been making a point of using cash."

"Because you're a careful fellow."

"Or paranoid."

Guy appraised him. "I sincerely doubt that. More likely a man who avoids letting people know his business if they don't have to."

"That's me alright."

He had thought of getting Guys' opinion about him and Angie going to the therapist. His own suspicion was that in order to get him to change his ways Angie wanted to hang the threat of divorce over his head but lacked the courage to do it herself. So she had finagled Pippi Longstocking or whatever the fuck the lady's name was into putting that question about whether <u>he</u> wanted his marriage to continue. But it was all such crap, so confusing, that he decided to keep it to himself.

Guy had only mentioned lunch, nothing about afterwards. It made Jake anxious, but he wasn't willing to push it. If it was what they call friends with benefits developing here, meaning sometimes lunch with no nookie, he was prepared to suffer that frustration.

Veterans Day, so Bigelow's was less busy, families with multiple kids around the big tables at late breakfast and bundled up old folks hunched over their soup, nibbling like mice at their half sandwiches. The waitress wanted to know where that sweet little girl of Jake's was. Didn't the kids have the day off school? Maybe time (if there was to be a next time) for him and Guy to find a new venue.

The union men got the holiday, but putting in three or four hours at the office on Monday holidays was normal with Jake. So as far as he could tell laying it on Angie he was going in to catch up on paperwork hadn't aroused any suspicions. When he asked about Guy's wife, he said she was preoccupied about a fund-raising event she had in Milwaukee in the evening and was out the door this morning well before he was even dressed.

Outside the restaurant's double glass doors, both men surveyed the clouds, considerably darker and lowered in than they had been an hour before. "Certainly <u>wants</u> to snow, doesn't it?" Guy remarked.

"I ran into some flurries, just the lightest stuff, on the way over."

"Not the weather for parades and laying wreaths and such."

"Were you ever in one?"

"A Veterans Day parade? No." Guy laughed. "I was however forced back into uniform for the dedication ceremony when they moved the Doughboy Statue to Soldier Field. Quite embarrassing, as it seems I've grown over the last thirty-some years and all in the outward direction, especially in the can. Finding a dress uniform that fit took some doing."

They strolled on out into the lot. Jake had parked Angie's Volvo halfway down the row beyond Guy's BMW.

Guy said, "I think I know the way, but maybe I'll still follow you again anyway, if it's alright."

Jake let out breath, couldn't help grinning. "That'll be fine."

At the motel he waited idling while Guy went into the office, then followed him around back to park. The room with the Jacuzzi was taken, but the one they were given was nearly its mirror, same flower-pattern upholstery and darker flowered drapes, only the bathroom smaller. Jake kicked off his shoes, skinned out of his shirt and pants and sat on the sofa in his underwear.

"Undress for me, will you? I want to look at you."

"I'm not going to dance around if you're not providing any music."

"That's OK. Just do it casual, as though I wasn't even here."

Once Guy had done as he was told, he stood close enough so Jake could stroke the backs of his thighs and up to the round of his ass. Jake caught the whiff of talcum powder or at least some kind of light scent in the older man's pubic hair. He blew on Guy's penis but didn't take it in his mouth.

"How's the knee coming?"

"Pretty good, thanks. Better."

"Can you get down on it?"

"Sure. Maybe a little cushioning would help."

Jake grabbed a square sofa pillow and thrust it at him. Guy settled himself gingerly onto it and said, "Now what?"

"You'll see."

Jake reached for his pants and whipped the belt out through the loops. Getting up, he came around, put Guy's large soft hands together behind his back and wrapped the belt around his wrists tight—or at least tight enough—and tucked in the tail. He stood in front of Guy, pushed the waistband of his shorts under his balls and tempted Guy with his cock. Guy's mouth opened and his tongue came out as though to catch it. Jake stepped back. But after a moment, he moved forward again and allowed Guy to take the thing in his mouth.

Beflre they got over to the bed he took the belt off, but remained demanding. He started with Guy up on his knees with his head down, then pulled out, turned him on his side and held the older man's leg up to get back into him. Each time he banged up against Guy's butt, Guy breathed "Oh!" Jake reached around and stuck fingers in Guy's mouth and Guy sucked hard on them. It was so hot Jake's mind went off somewhere and then he was coming in big spurts deep and under him Guy was shaking like a wet dog.

"You OK?"

"I'm fine, thanks. Better than fine."

They were still, Jake now half up over Guy's backside and kissing randomly along his neck and touching his hair until his cock softened enough to slide out. He rolled off, dropped the rubber on the floor, and Guy turned over to him and kissed him. When he reached down, Jake found Guy's cock all soft and wet.

"What happened to you?"

"I came too."

"Just from me jamming you?"

"I think so, yes. Haven't had that happen in a long time. Years."

Jake propped himself up on the pillows, the smell of his own goo and the thinner stuff Guy had produced on his hands. Guy leaned back between his legs with Jake's arm protectively across his chest. It was how they had lain before, at the Gavilan.

"This is where if we still smoked we'd now have a cigarette," Guy said.

"I could never really get into smoking," Jake said, "although God knows at one point I tried my damndest."

"You're a lucky man. I had a hell of a time kicking when I did finally." Guy sighed, his eyes up on the nubbled, off-white expanse of the ceiling. He ran his free hand lightly over Jake's hairy forearm again. "You don't have to go right away, do you?"

"I'm OK for a while."

"I'm glad." Then, "I was really pleased once I was sure I was actually going to get time with you today. This often isn't the best of holidays for me."

"Because of Viet Nam?"

"More specific than that. Because I was responsible for men who were lost. Through my own stupidity—"

"What do you mean? It was a war, right?"

"Six men from my platoon."

"I still don't see—"

"Do you mind if I tell it to you?"

"Of course not."

"We were green, hadn't been in country long, two weeks, just getting our noses bloodied as they said, and they sent us out on night patrol. What was called a 'go get'em,' based on intelligence that the enemy was definitely all around and on the move."

"This was in jungle?"

"No, savannah, open fields, waist-high grass, some little water channels and some muck and suck to get through, trees off in the distance. And black, no moon, no light of any sort anywhere. I told the men to fan out the line and I kept to the center so I could stay in close contact with my radio man. We couldn't see a thing, so I passed along an order to put up some illumination grenades, and just then the radio man got word they had been spotted in the trees off ahead of us—I could hear the voice in his headphones three feet from me—and then the sky bloomed into light and the bad guys opened up and four men on one end of my line were shot and two on the other. Dead before any of the rest of us could get our faces down in the dirt."

"I still don't see how that makes you responsible."

"I lit them up so they could get shot. In my desire to see what in hell was going on." Guy breathed and then his breath seemed to catch in his throat. "It's an ongoing surprise to me the survivors from that platoon should even want me along when they have their get-togethers."

Jake patted Guy's chest a little. "I suppose it's no use my saying you're being too hard on yourself."

"No, that is helpful and I appreciate it. Thank you."

Guy's hand closed on Jake's forearm and held there a long moment.

"I probably shouldn't have gone in the military to begin with. Not really my thing."

"Why'd you do it?"

"At the time it didn't seem I really had a whole lot of choice. My family expected it of me, they're military going back a hundred and fifty years. Navy mostly. And Marines. And the only alternatives to the draft available then were to run off to Canada or sign on for Officers Candidate School if you happened to feature yourself too good to be an ordinary grunt."

THREE

*

Jake looked ahead on the big calendar on the pegboard by his desk with some dread. The holidays. Thanksgiving he liked well enough. In the past they usually went to his family at Claire's, but now that his folks had fucked that option, his mother-in-law was condescending to come all the way out into the wilds of Skokie to eat with them. Still, at home Jake made the turkeys, so he'd be able to hide out from Alice first in the kitchen and later in the den with football and most likely Earl the Lump for companionship. Christmas he tried mainly to get through by holding on, the way you suffer with your heart beating to the finish of a bad dream. Other people's stricken faces in the stores as they handed the checker the credit card and their piled-up crap came crawling forward on the belt. He stayed away if he could. But even if he left all the buying except her own present to Angie, there was little he could do to keep out the media's noisy promises of magic time. No way to defend a vulnerable creature like Lisa against the dismay and let-down when the joy to the world didn't come rolling on in as promised.

The big unknown was when—or how often—he might get to see the professor from Northwestern. He remained convinced it was not part of the deal that he could call or email to ask for a meeting. Where had that rule come from? Despite the fact he was learning how to turn the fucker on, Jake still did not have as much sense as he wanted of what the man's life was like. Busy, yes, as Guy said, moving from meeting to meeting, luncheon in the Loop followed by board of directors of this or that. Many swishy evenings in that After Six in his closet Jake supposed, the opera or the symphony or the Art Institute or whatever. Charity balls. In the office most likely a slim young lady in slacks and scarves to keep book on him, sweetly remind him where he was supposed to be next, hold out sheaves of letters for signature on his way to the elevator.

Not to say that between work and family and brief intervals at the Comfort Inn Jake's life wasn't full up, but he was convinced there existed a critical difference between them concerning time. Guy would get in touch when he found the opportunity.

Or not. What if the heat was really only on Jake's side and Guy was already like little shrunk-down Alice in Wonderland (or was it when she was super tall?) feeling along the wall for the exit door—it was here somewhere just a minute ago, wasn't it?

For a couple of days after a session, though satisfied and calm Jake remained all turned on, having untroubled sex with Angie (sex she seemed to like too) and also taking it out and jacking off when he got twenty minutes alone in the house. But then anxiety and impatience would set in again. He cursed himself for the stupidity of tying Guy up with the belt and ordering him around the way he had. Couldn't he have guessed Veterans Day might be a hard time on the man? Jake figured himself for being tough and a realist and maybe an asshole but not an insensitive asshole or a dumb one.

But Guy could have called off that little scene and didn't, right?

It was only a week—actually eight days—before he was ready for Jake again. When Jake phoned for a reservation, the buxom day manager with the trace of a German accent asked almost at once did he want the Jacuzzi. A little creepy she'd recognize his voice, he thought, but he didn't say anything about it to Guy.

They were lying face to face on their sides, arms over each other after they had made love. Jake said, "Is it OK if I confess a little?"

"Have you sinned, my son?"

"I have, Father. Well, maybe not. Do you count being a jerk when you're eighteen as a sin?"

"That's a human condition, not a sin."

"When I told you I should have gone in the military out of high school but didn't—?"

"Yes?"

"The reason was I had a pretty clear idea who the drill sergeants would be and in those days I couldn't see myself taking orders from some black guy. Or even a latino."

Silence. Guy reached up and brushed Jake's hair off his forehead. "Is that it?"

"It's not anything I'm proud of."

"Pretty standard North Shore white-boy way of thinking it sounds like to me. Maybe you had your prejudices a little more articulated than some, but... You get to be close pals with a lot of black kids at New Trier?"

"Oh sure, lots and lots."

Guy's face was so close Jake could feel his breath soft against his own cheek.

"It's not a prejudice I have anymore. Now that it's too late."

"You don't have to apologize to me for not serving in the military, you know."

"Is that what I'm doing?"

"As far as I can tell. Isn't it?"

Jake fell silent and Guy's big hand ran up and down his backside in a friendly, soothing way, pausing to cup and hold one cheek of his ass, then fingers playing up along the bumps of his spine, moving back down again.

"You clean down here?"

"I showered this morning."

"Hop up on your knees for a minute then."

Jake did as he was told, but then sensing Guy moving over behind him, he said, "You're not going to try to fuck me, are you?"

"No, I only want to eat your ass for a while."

At first when Guy spread his cheeks and began blowing warm air, it only tickled and felt funny. But there followed wet kisses and licking and Guy's tongue pushing up inside him and Jake relaxed and gave in to it. Why such an intense pleasure? Because the ass is the sensitive part that gets so little attention? Or because we think of ass-licking as dirty? He couldn't tell. When he threw another chub, Guy put spit on his hand, reached through and gently stroked it, then pulled it back between Jake's legs and went to sucking it. It wasn't long before Jake shot off in Guy's hand.

While they were getting dressed, Guy asked, "Had that done to you before?"

"Getting the salad tossed? Let me think. In my younger years maybe. I seem to remember a couple girls who were into doing that."

"So not memorable, hm?"

"Them? Not really. You, yes."

They closed and kissed and Jake thought he tasted something on Guy's lips. Nothing ugly, just his own musk.

*

The Tuesday of Thanksgiving week the late evening news readers were full on into that dramatic alarm they project when they have drummed up a big weather story. Huge cold front coming out of Canada and bearing down on the upper Midwest. Overnight temperature drop, snow by Wednesday afternoon, holiday travelers scurrying to get out of Chicago before it hit and stranded them. Film of restless lines at O'Hare, anxious eyes turned up toward the big departure boards. The satellite pictures showed a large white mass moving stop-action jerky but rapidly across Alberta, Montana, and down through the Dakotas.

In the night Jake woke to a restless cracking sound coming every minute or so from different parts of the house. The ground freezing, the foundation locking. Once he had the source identified, he lay awake for a long time with his left hand on Angie's belly. She did not stir, so he was alone listening to the sharp reports and then the wind, a high constant whistle through the trees. Nothing he could do really. The Miller brothers' site stood at pretty much dug out, a dirt ramp in place along one side to get the heavy equipment and the trucks down in and out with the rest of the clay. The wood forms for the base concrete were due to arrive Monday. So if the hole got two feet of snow in it and then the beginning of December warmed back up, the men would have to slog around in an icy swamp until Jake could get pumps and hoses down in to suck out slush.

As he was passing O'Hare the next morning the blackness overhead was still spotted with the lights of planes going out and coming in, the ones on approach seeming to float as they came down. But snow was beginning to dance fiercely in his headlights and stick to the roads. At six forty-five there were no other vehicles at the site yet. He sat in his truck in the glow of his personal cell, motor chugging and the inadequate little heater putting out what it could. A text from Guy written only fifteen minutes before asking him to call when he could and giving his office number.

"You're up and at 'em early."

"I am."

Guy wished him a happy Thanksgiving, and then said, "I've been hoping I'd get to see you, but I didn't think there was going to be a possibility. Then just last evening I discovered I have some hours free today and I was wondering—"

"Sure," Jake said. "When?"

"It would have to be around noon and only for a couple of hours sorry to say."

"OK. Comfort Inn?"

"Well, that's the complication. I'm downtown this morning, and for us to get any decent time together we'd have to meet closer in."

"All right. Just say where."

Guy gave him the address of something called The Metropolitan, a sauna on West Montrose between Albany Park and Ravenswood. There were private rooms you could rent, he said.

Jake figured he would need 40 minutes to get there. At a quarter-to-eleven that morning the Miller brothers appeared unannounced to peer down into their excavation and put forth questions. Some of the men had already gone off to buy the family bird or (more likely) get a few stiff ones in them to brace against the storm or against the relatives coming Thursday, but enough were still there and busy to reassure the brothers. For a half hour Jake addressed their frets about whether the weather would cause delays without mentioning he had recommended they wait on construction. Luckily, Kevin Tanner's Lexus nosed up onto the gravel just about the time Jake needed to start making excuses in order to get going. Mike had fished up a big possibility at Northwestern, a whole new research laboratory he needed Jake's help to get together a bid on. He counseled against informing the Millers that Jake would be taking on another project if it came through, but Jake had already been forced to glide out from under them a couple times and leave Kevin to cover. The Millers seemed to appreciate the younger Tanner and the high-end places he chose to take them to eat.

The wind had cut out and the snow was coming down in that blinding determined way it has when it seems determined to shut down the whole world. The Metropolitan turned out to be on the end of a half-block-long row of shops. The front where the others had display windows was bricked in and there was a small parking lot off the end of the building. He found Guy inside in his overcoat leaning against a high counter, behind him a small dark woman in a sari and big gold earrings. In the wet heat Jake smelled chlorine and what must be mold. They were handed large, much-washed white towels and a key. The woman seemed to understand English but not to speak it. She did smile at Jake though, showing a mouthful of very white teeth and three or four gold caps.

Down a gloomy hall to the back of the building. Under the orchestra music piped in and a rushing sound of water, Jake could pick out no voices or movement behind the doors they passed. Were they the only customers? How did Guy happen to know about the place? What was the clientele?—mostly gays, or were there also straight couples who dropped in for afternoon delights? Anyone ever come just to soak and relax? The room Guy opened them into was tile-lined, very bright. Hot tub, glass-enclosed shower, pegs on the wall for your clothes and a raised tile platform to lie out on and cook yourself under a sunlamp on a timer.

"I know it's tacky, but is it <u>too</u> tacky?"

"I'm fine with it, man."

"How are you on time?"

Their constant question. Given the weather and the likelihood of snarled holiday traffic they agreed to be out of the Metropolitan and on the road by two at the latest. They turned off the overhead lights and made love first in the hot tub and then on their towels spread out on the platform. A row of glass bricks up on the back wall turned the room a silvery twilight blue. Hard as the tile was on his hip when Jake lay on his side or on his knees when he got up on them, he quickly came to see the advantage of the platform. There was no way for Guy's body to evade him, slip away from him a little (he was thinking back to the relatively slack bed at the Gavilan). The man under him seemed to like it this way too, chin raised, tongue reaching out, mouth begging to be kissed. So Jake obliged, deep-in kisses, Guy's hands on his butt pulling, apparently wanting as much of him as there was.

After they were done, they rearranged the towels—one under them and one for Guy to pull up over himself—and lay together, Guy behind, big arm over Jake, hand down cradling Jake's softened cock and his balls. Jake listened to Guy's gentle breathing against his neck, knew from the change into a soft wheeze when he dozed off. They had nearly an hour still, but for safety's sake he decided to stay awake.

But then he too fell asleep.

Guy was up first, across the room fishing his watch out of his pants and turning it toward the faint light when Jake came to.

"Time?"

"We have twenty minutes or so."

Guy padded back, watch now slipped onto his wrist, and climbed onto the platform again. They resumed their positions, Jake snuggling back, head pillowed on Guy's upper arm.

"Did you wonder how I happen to know such a low place?"

"I did."

Though they had intuited each other's bodily desires before, it struck Jake this was the first time Guy had read his mind.

Guy laughed a little. "An up and coming young Shakespeare scholar introduced me to the Metropolitan."

"A long time ago?"

"Five years maybe?"

He couldn't remember? Did that mean there had been an army of male lovers? A batallion? Or only a platoon or so?

"What happened to him, the Shakespeare guy?"

"He was only here for a year, a visiting professor. Back at Arizona State, poor fellow."

"What's poor about that?"

"Phoenix. A city without virtues as far as I can tell."

Jake lay still, surprised at the wave of jealousy washing around in his gut. He longed to ask a lot more questions, but all he could imagine was Guy laughing at him and stonewalling in some polite way.

"There's something that's come up I thought I better tell you about."

"What's that?"

"Mike Tanner, my company, is going to bid on those new biology labs Northwestern wants to build."

"The Belknap bequest? The complex down toward the Lake?"

"I think so, yes. And I'm supposed to be involved. If we get the work, I might well be the manager on the project, or at least one of the team."

"Well that's good for you, isn't it?"

"Sure. But I wonder if it would make you uncomfortable."

"Why would it?"

"If we ran into each other on campus—?"

"We'd say, 'Hello, nice to see you,' and maybe shake hands, right?"

"But isn't that a cause for suspicion somehow?"

"I still don't see why."

"Why would we know each other? We're from different worlds."

"Oh, not so different, do you think?"

"Yes, I do."

"But you know the Gorhams and I know the Gorhams—"

"Yes."

"Well?"

"OK, if it's not going to make you uncomfortable—"

"Not at all. Though I appreciate your concern."

On their way out, they heaped their wet towels up on the counter in front of the still-stony Indian lady. There was now almost a foot of snow on the ground and cars were pushing gingerly along the street, their lights dumb fingers poking at the constant falling white blotches. The city's roar was dampened down.

Jake and Guy shook hands and wished each other a happy Thanksgiving again. Almost to the corner in his direction, Jake heard himself called. He went back and met Guy on the pavement past the Metropolitan by its little half parking lot. The silver Beamer's door stood open, its headlights casting only the faintest circles against the brick wall.

"In my hurry I left my lights on and now it won't start."

"Let me give it a try."

The red leather seat was pushed all the way back so Jake had to scrunch down some to reach the pedals. He turned off the headlights, closed the door, checked to make sure the car was in neutral, then tried it. And got only the weakest hum and an indifferent attempt to turn over.

He climbed out shaking his head. "I'm surprised," he said.

Guy said, "I'm not. That battery's old and I was meaning to get a new one and—and I let everything get in the way of doing it."

"I don't have jumpers with me. You?"

"No."

"Towing? They'll start it, bring a new battery if you want."

Guy's face, disappointed as a child's these last minutes, suddenly brightened. He lifted his coat to get out his wallet. "Triple A."

"It may take forever in this weather with everybody—"

Guy glanced at the card, then up at Jake. "It's one my wife handles. But the address of the service doesn't appear on the bill, does it?"

"Yes, it will. Or it might. I'm not sure."

"Shit!"

Jake took out his cell phone, punched in a number. Waiting for it to ring, he said, "If the jump doesn't work or I can't get them to bring a new battery, where would you like to have it towed? Where're you supposed to be by now?"

"What are you doing?"

"I'll just put it on my card. No problem."

Then, surprisingly quickly, the operator cut in through the background music and was asking Jake for name, card number, location, what the problem was.

Guy was thinking, snow coming down on his head, his shoulders. Thirty seconds later, he whispered to Jake, "I'd be back at the university by now, I suppose."

"Campus Drive?"

Guy nodded, so Jake conveyed the information to the girl. When he asked she said she was in Oklahoma City, no snow, though they were having some awful cold wind this afternoon.

Jake sat in with Guy to wait. Cut off from the world by the whited-out windshield and the clouded-over side windows, they were warm enough in their coats. Guy occasionally tapped the steering wheel with his gloved thumb, Jake slowly turned his automobile insurance card in his hands.

"I hate making <u>you</u> late due to my stupidity."

"I'll be all right, man," Jake said. "Don't worry about me."

"Have your excuses all in order?"

"I guess." There were two messages on his cell from Angie but Jake didn't want to deal with them yet.

Guy announced that after Christmas he'd be going to Vail for a week or ten days. He asked did Jake ski, and Jake said he had, more in the past though. He really liked cross country, he said.

"You certainly have the legs for it."

Then there were long silences. Jake thought hard about what he could launch to fill in the gap, but everything he came up with—his little Lisa's triumph in her solo at parents' night, other sweet stuff—in the moment it all seemed terminally trivial, stupid, not worth even the expenditure of the words. Guy continued to drum on the steering wheel, both thumbs now in some kind of bongo-drum rhythm. Suddenly he gripped the wheel tight and clung to it and murmured, "Fuck!" His face was all puffed out, red, angry, his jaw working.

"What's wrong?"

"I just hate it when my sloppiness comes along like this to trip me up. And now you too—"

"I told you, I'll be OK. Don't worry on my account," Jake said.

He reached over and lightly touched the older man at the crook of his arm. Guy breathed, sighed, stared at the wheel, then moved enough to get Jake's hand off him. It looked as though he was going to cry.

"You know," he said, hesitating, "the trouble with me is so much of the time I'm just entirely up in my head. So the practicalities get left behind. I hate that."

"It's OK, man, it's OK." Jake spoke softly, in a calm voice that often worked when Lisa was in one of her little pets. There was some comment he might make here—about how out of his head and entirely into his body Guy got when they were balling—but Jake caught himself. Clearly not the moment.

Unsettling, watching the man go off like that on himself entirely without warning.

It was three-twenty when the tow truck finally came, raking the Beamer in its headlights as it bounced into the lot. Once Jake had given the guy his information and his card to swipe, there was no further need to hang around. Hurrying toward his truck, he pulled up Angie's messages. In the first one she said only, "Where the hell are you?" But the second was calmer, asking if he got this would he please stop at the store for her.

Nearly five o'clock by the time he got to Skokie. Trudy's mom was there and the girls were clumping happily around in new boots purchased just that afternoon. The fact that Jake came in and pulled butter, parsley, and two crinkly packages of cornbread stuffing from a grocery bag got him a sweet kiss from his wife.

*

Christmas fell on a Tuesday that year. Lisa's dance school had scheduled its dress rehearsal for the Saturday before and the recital itself for Sunday afternoon the 23rd, thus assuring maximum inconvenience for everyone concerned. Saturday Angie had lunch out with her mother and last-minute shopping, so Jake had to drive Lisa and Trudy and a third girl to the Winnetka Community House, a century-old building with fake half timbering. It was a style originally adopted to give the "Village," Winnetka's dinky downtown, a quaintsy English look. He and Ian Stiles had sometimes gone Saturday afternoons to kids' movies at the Community House. Jake sat for a while on a folding chair in the back of the hall in a glum, impatient gaggle with other parents. Continuous banging came from behind the stage curtain and in rooms nearby two pianos played different numbers over and over. Above the racket a woman whose daughter was in Lisa's group said she'd been informed it would be at least another hour, so if Jake wanted to go walk around or something, she'd be glad to watch out for his girls. He thanked her and headed for the door.

Outside it was cold and very clear. In the western sky only two long parallel contrails painted orange and gold by the sun as it set. The snow from the Thanksgiving storm hadn't held, as Jake had predicted it wouldn't, and ten warm days in the beginning of December made soup in the bottom of the Miller brothers' hole. Since then two more seasonable cold fronts had come down on them, both with significant snow. Roads were clear now, though, the pavements shoveled off and slick in places with hard ice. Unless there was something new cooking up north, they were in for a somewhat tired-looking white Christmas.

Walking the center of Winnetka brought up many of the same feelings he got from his old Wilmette neighborhood, pleasure at what remained the same and sourness over the changes. Winnetka had always been for the rich, but Jake didn't remember it stinking of money the way it did now. His uncle Gio's business on the other side of the steep declivity where the commuter trains ran was long gone, eaten up by serial additions to the luxury condo complex called the Winnetka Mews. Jake happened to know what a 'mews' was, so the name struck him as majorly fucked in its pretention.

At times (now was one of them) he got a physical pang out of the way he missed his uncle. The maestro and role model. Jake was years working in the shop before he began to understand about the plump little man's "office," a tiny slant-roof room, more of a shed really, located in the back by customer parking. When Gio went out there, you weren't allowed to knock or even call in to him, he was effectively gone. But why'd he need a separate office, given that he did all of his ordering and his books at the counter in the showroom up front?

The answer? The tiny cramped space with its sweet air-freshened smell, ratty rectangle of oriental rug and the slouchy couch was where Uncle Gio did the ladies of Winnetka and Kenilworth and a number

who came down from Glencoe or Lake Forest as well. Some had out-
standings at Guarani's they wanted knocked down a little, but from
what Jake figured out only in his junior year at New Trier, the major
draw was the quality professional experience Gio provided.

Occasionally it would be a pink-faced senior gentleman Uncle
would come back up to the showroom with, the two of them chatting
easily, innocently, Uncle's tongue darting out to sweep his lips with
wet. Although apparently Jake's stone of a father never caught on,
around the shop the cat was long out of the bag about Gio's ladies (and
the man himself dead and in the ground, mourned by his widow and
children) before Jake realized how likely it was Uncle had also been
servicing—or being serviced by—some of those old codgers in their
tennis whites. After seeing one fellow to the door and holding it for
him, he turned back to Jake, his dark eyes lit with amusement and said,
'Remember we're an entirely equal opportunity shop!'

So was it genetic, then, Jake being the way he was? Just following
in his uncle's footsteps?

For some reason a consoling thought.

Conney's, the pharmacy on Elm, was still pretty much as Jake
remembered it, the aisles busy this afternoon, the inevitable beamed in
Christmas standards filling the air. He waited for the girl in Cosmetics
to finish with another customer, suddenly uncomfortable with the fact
he had wandered into potential Guy Baer territory. Any of the willowy
ladies in the high-heeled boots outside climbing in and out of their

Audis or their Mercedes could be the wife, although he pictured her for some reason a little less manicured and lacquered and obvious than these cougars. He might brush up against her at check-out. ('Hm, that my husband I smell on you?' 'Yes, ma'am, it is. His cum.') Not that he bore her any malice. He hadn't yet thought about her much. Maybe a twinge about Vail, one moment in the stalled Beamer imagining how it would be <u>him</u> instead of the Mrs. Baer rolling over and waking Guy in an isolated sun-bright A-frame up high in the blue of the Colorado mountains, whispering, 'Mister? You got a place I can put this?' and pushing his dick hard up against Guy's thigh.

The girl was finally ready to deal with him. What he was looking for, he said, was Ma Griffe. It was a favorite perfume of Angie's. He needed to get her something bigger too, but hadn't quite decided yet what that would be. Maybe a Bose radio for her little sewing and projects room. The clerk said, "Not sure we have that one," but went about sliding doors, stooping, rooting around in the cabinets at her back anyway. A small old lady in a head scarf and big stadium coat with a fake fur collar had come tottering along. She hooked her cane onto the edge of the counter and stood staring down into the lighted case, patience itself.

The girl straightened and came back to him. "I'm afraid not, sir, no Ma Griffe."

"Oh," the old lady looked up, "try again, dear. Conney's has always carried it."

The throaty, classy voice was what Jake recognized. But as he was turning to her, Nancy Stiles asked, "Jake?"

"Hi, Nancy."

"Oh," she said again, now a little amused, "to think— Here! What a lovely surprise! Merry Christmas!" She brought both arms up in a kind of circle to hug him, but Jake got there first and enclosed her lightly in his. She turned her cheek to him and he gave it a faint kiss.

"Merry Christmas to you, Nancy."

She pulled back to regard him. Even lit up with pleasure, she looked bad, thin and worn out, darker than ever under her eyes, the skin across her forehead drawn taut, a pulse beating visibly at her temple. She turned back to the counter and grabbed it for balance and let out a sigh.

But then she recovered herself and, while the girl stood waiting, asked after Angie and remembered Jake had a daughter. Though she'd never met Lisa, Nancy asked after her too.

"And you, Jake, what's up with you?"

"I'm good, Nancy. Thanks. Everything good."

"Ian will be so pleased…oh, and Fleas too! They're coming, you know that."

"I didn't, no."

She seemed puzzled. "Not for Christmas," she said faintly, almost to herself, "couldn't get away. Families. But right after, yes. The 27th, for the eggnog party. They'll both be there, and they'll so want to see you. You remember the eggnog party, Jake—"

He did. An annual occasion where the Stiles opened their home to all their friends, a buffet, turkey and ham, fruit cake and cookies, Peter Stiles tending bar for all those who joined him in his aversion to egg-nog. For a number of years Jake himself had been the one elected to get up on top of the kitchen stool in his socks and lift down Grandmother Bowen's silver punch bowl and ladle, then hand down one by one the sixteen matching cups for Nancy and Mary the cook to polish.

"You and Angie will come, won't you? And bring your girl too, there'll be the undoctored kind for the children—" Then, trailing off, "As ever—"

On the back of her right hand lay a square tan bandage, large enough to cover most of the visible tendons and blue veins.

The clerk had taken up a little bottle and was dabbing the stopper on the inside of her wrist. "Sir, see what you think of this. It's one I like." She held her pale arm up to him.

The scent was spicy and powerful enough to make his nose twitch. Jake shook his head, was about to explain that it wasn't just some per-fume he needed, when Nancy said earnestly, "There, dear!" She point-ed. "Second shelf toward the side, white with green stripes, don't you see it? They're diagonal."

The girl bent into the cabinet again, moved things around and came up with a small, dusty cube. Placing it on the counter, she said, "This?" and brushed at the top of the box a little with her fingertips.

"That's it," Jake and Nancy both said, then laughed and glanced at each other.

There was no price on the box, so the girl went off to ask her manager, leaving the Ma Griffe on the counter. Nancy picked the box up and sniffed at it.

"Get anything?"

"I can't tell. Maybe. Angie's right to like it. Ma Griffe is a fragrance I have always admired myself."

"Then it should be for you, Nancy—"

"Oh thank you, but no—" Her hand pushed away from her body in defense or maybe rejection.

"You were the one who spotted it."

"Yes, but— No, just tell Angie to put a little on for the party, all right? I'll enjoy it all the more on her—"

Then, although there wasn't much else to say, it felt OK just to stand with Nancy waiting for the clerk, looking down on the lady's still hands, the familiar diamond and her wedding ring together on one, the distressing big Band-Aid on the back of the other. OK, although Jake kept hearing her say 'As ever—'. Christ! Refusing the offer of the perfume was her style of course, but he couldn't help thinking she also must have developed that horror of acquiring new things people get when they're on their way out.

*

"You're certainly a happy boy these days," Angie said in the car on the way home from the Tanners.

"Why not? 'Tis the season to be jolly, right?"

"You drunk? Want me to drive?"

"No. I am somewhat fucked up, but not too much to drive. You are too, you know."

Angie considered. "Not so much anymore I don't think."

"But you were putting it away there for a while."

"Yes, but then I stopped."

Another yearly event, the Tanners' cocktails and stand-up supper, usually the Saturday evening before The Big Day. When the company was smaller and Mike and Meg still had their huge spreading home in Evanston, it was an everybody affair, kids running around, all the favored subcontractors and their wives, Mike's two goldens and Meg's woolly little Bolognese in and out of the crowd on a constant lookout for dropped food. But now that the Tanners had taken the 10th-floor Gold Coast condo with the spectacular view of the Lake's curve, the party had become adults only, coat and tie (and John Heinemann in his kilt showing off his knobby knees) and for a smaller upper-echelon group from the company and the real old-timers like Olivia Livieros. Usually some serious drinking went on. Meg admitted to getting her shrimp trays, her beef, pull-apart rolls and layer cakes from Costco, but Jake saw nothing wrong with that. She always corraled him to come out to the kitchen to oversee cooking the tenderloins and then to slice them for her.

Even when Jake was keeping certain facts from her, Angie still basically read his moods right. Despite the shock Nancy Stiles gave him in Conney's in the afternoon he <u>was</u> pretty much happy boy right now. What Angie didn't quite get anymore was how his emotions rocketed around, the roller coaster effect he thought of it as. At the Tanners', for example. After he got Angie out of her coat he made her stop with him a moment so they could inspect themselves in the long gilt-framed mirror in the entry hall, both in clothes bought more or less with this occasion in mind. Jake in a deep blue silk and poly Italian suit, but cut with softer shoulders and a less severe outline than the Italians usually provided. Angie with her hair up showing off her neck and a single-strand garnet necklace Jake had given her, a velvet dress the bright green of billiard-table felt, tight to her thighs but not hobbling, up top a lot of flesh and even a hint of pushed-up breasts on display.

As they strolled into the living room, the other guests turned to look and for a moment talk went almost dead. Jake shook a few hands in passing, but his eye was on Mike Tanner boiling right across the room to enclose Angie in a big bear hug and plaster her with a kiss. Ten minutes later Jake was out with Meg, jacket off and wearing an apron, searing the long tongues of the meat, while Meg, already pleasantly whacked, repeated what she'd told him any number of times before: "Many people have thrown a lot away just for the great pleasure of telling Mike Tanner to go fuck himself, Jake. But I was smart. I married him so I can do it with no penalty!"

A flare appeared red, staked in the middle of the farthest right-hand lane. Jake checked the rearview mirror and then tentatively began touching his brake. Another flare, this one on its side and nearly burned out. In the fog ahead then red blinking lights, the shape of the back end of a police car stopped dead in a lane. Jake slowed to thirty and they swept by a two-car collision, shadows standing by the side of the road out of harm's way, no bodies or even blood. No ambulance yet.

Jake regained speed.

"Mike loves you, Jake. And Meg Tanner too. Like family."

"So it is always said."

"Oh come on, just accept it, will you?"

"I know they do. Only when push comes to shove, maybe it won't be enough."

"When will that be?"

He didn't answer. The bad luck that comes from predicting bad things. When? When Mike got stomach cancer. When his heart gave out. When Mike impulsively decided to throw it all in and move Meg to Florida to make their last stand there. Maybe even sooner. When Kevin's brat appeared. In the kitchen the minute Meg heard Kevin's voice she broke off from Jake in mid-sentence and went hustling out toward the hall. Jake followed, wiping his hands on a towel. If Meg and Mike imagined old Kev had completely given up on pills or powder or whatever, they weren't looking very hard into his eyes, tonight aglitter like little pinpricks of diamond. Kevin's skinny, dark-haired Jody, also a one-time world traveler and loafer, had Kev's same dopey tell-tale smile on, despite the fact she seemed about to tip over forward from the huge ball of future speedy little Tanner she was carting around under her dress.

For more than two hours then, all through the food and out into the cake, coffee, and the brandy, Jake's mood was so bleak he could hardly be civil to the bozo squad from the office or their wives. It didn't take a shrink to tell you that Jake Guarani had been a sucker for the generosity of Mike and Meg Tanner because in the beginning they acted like the parents he had longed for and had missed out on in life's big lottery. It was a confounded pattern in him. At an earlier date Peter and Nancy Stiles had filled the same want in him.

But once he attained a steady level of drunkenness, he cheered up. Let the worst happen, whatever form it was going to take. He didn't care. He, after all, had come with the most desirable woman in the room, the one over on the little margin of wood flooring by the front windows being earnestly fox-trotted and relentlessly squeezed by that douchebag Pat Nellums.

Well squeeze away, old Nellums, he told himself, none of that juice is for you!

Now in the car, Angie put her hand over and laid it on the inside of his thigh. "Honey?" Her voice was small.

"What?"

"I don't want you to be disappointed."

"About what?"

"I've thought and thought, but I haven't come up with much for you for Christmas yet."

"Oh," he laughed, "you don't need to worry about that. I'm the same, you know. I was going to warn you too."

She sighed and leaned over against his shoulder. He could smell booze on her, not unpleasant at all, and fainter maybe the cigarette she had snuck with Olivia out on the Tanners' freezing balcony. She clutched his leg, rubbed. "You know what I <u>could</u> give you, if you want—"

"What's that?"

"I could fuck you really good."

"Tonight?"

"If you want. Tonight, tomorrow night—"

"Take off your clothes for me all slow and sexy? Suck me off, chew on my nips?"

"All of it," she said. "Whatever you like."

*

"Ummm, you smell good, dear. Come close." Nancy Stiles put her hand up somewhat tentatively, touched Angie's shoulder and drew her nearer, took a whiff. "Is it Ma Griffe?" she said, looking over to Jake for confirmation.

Angie laughed, in as she was on the story of the chance meeting in Conney's and Nancy's request for her to wear the perfume to the party.

Nancy looked somewhat better today, hair shiny, done up, the darkness under her eyes less, the open sad droop her mouth had Saturday somehow propped up into a fairly constant smile. She was wearing her own mother's watch on its chain and had stationed herself just inside the living room to greet her friends once they had left their coats on the rented racks set out in the hall. Ian and Fleas waited nearby with Fleas' husband Leonard in his gray tailored English suit, none of them hovering exactly, but watchful. Peter Stiles was over by the huge fir that filled one corner of the far end of the room, his white shirt turned mottled rosy by the lights and reflections from the tinsel and the big silver balls. Between him and his guests stood his portable bar, a 150-year-old mahogany table on skinny long X-crossed legs. It struck Jake briefly that Ian's dad looked a bit like a street-corner three-card monte hustler.

"Oh my goodness!" Fleas exclaimed, "Angie Moore!" She descended on her old friend with big hugs and kisses, reintroduced Leonard, did a nearly as big squeeze-and-smooch number on Jake, insisted how great both of them looked. She and Angie fell to toting up how long it had been since they'd seen one another. Unless you knew about Fleas' constant urge to wring what pleasure she could out of a given moment, you would think she'd not been told what this year's eggnog party was really about.

Ian's turn then. His greetings were less theatrical, his pleasure in seeing them more believable. Angie turned one cheek up for Ian to kiss, then offered him the other one and he kissed that too and they both laughed. A joke they had from the old days about which one of them had become more frenchified. As Jake shook hands he asked, "How long you here for?"

"I'm out of here early Sunday morning."

"Any chance we can get together?"

"Sure. We'll make time."

There were new arrivals waiting behind them, so Jake and Angie moved out into the already noisy crowd. Peter Stiles' head jerked up and he looked directly at Jake, then quickly turned away.

The years had whitened the hair of many of the Stiles' friends and made their faces vague, so Jake could only bring up a few of their names. But in his own generation were school pals from Country Day and later who he recognized easily. What Jake had forgotten was how much pride old money takes in its own dowdiness. Men whose holiday finest appeared to be ancient Harris tweeds, khakis and L.L. Bean moccasins, ladies in bunchy wool suits and baggy stockings, all of them looking somehow as though they had given themselves a light dusting with the contents of the vacuum cleaner bag before setting out for the Stiles'. Angie had been right, in this crowd she in the green velvet and he in his new blue stood out.

"We're overdressed."

"I saw. Do you care?"

She laughed. "Not really."

In the dining room the table had been pushed back, leaving only a narrow space in front of the sideboard for the hired gentleman dipping the featured beverage out of Nancy's flared silver bowl. As Jake recalled, the recipe was also a treasure handed down from the Bowens, potent, the eggs and extra yolks and cream turned beige by the heavy-handed pouring of bourbon.

Ian came in from the hall bringing with him two tall men in shirtsleeves and red vests. After a moment, Jake recognized the older, white-haired one. Lewis Keyes, the Harvard guy who'd been an usher at Ezra's wedding and, when Jake came out of the shower waited, to get a gander at what was under his towel. The younger man, a skinny redhead in his 50s with a prominent bobbing adam's apple, was named Jay Carlson. He shook hands with Jake and said, "We've met," and then turned to Angie and said, "But this one, I don't think—" and gave her a big smile. So Angie was introduced to the two gentlemen.

Ian said, "Jay and Lewis drove all the way up from Hyde Park."

"Well yes," said Lewis Keyes, "for the chance to see everyone—"

"Nancy especially," Jay Carlson said in a lowered voice.

The possessiveness bugged Jake. But it wasn't the guy's fault. He seemed sincere enough. Not Jake's type certainly. He wondered what Lewis Keyes saw in him. Not enough meat there for an honest banging really, either giving or receiving.

Then all at once what he dreamed last night came back. He and Ian and Fleas were teenagers again, up in Fleas' room, her passing around a joint while the grownups partied down here. When they came down, Peter and Nancy were there, but younger. And there too in the middle of the crowd were Guy Baer and his wife, cocktails in hand, the wife scary because her face was a blank, featureless, smooth pink skin only, like a graft of some sort. Guy kept glancing at Jake and seemed to be asking 'Should we know each other or not? You figure it out.' But Jake couldn't, and the threat of exposure made his heart race relentlessly like a motor being fed too much gas.

*

Nancy, it seemed, quite reasonably wanted to occupy as much of Ian's brief time at home as she could. Finally on the phone Ian asked Jake, "How about Saturday morning early? No one gets up before ten around here anymore except Leonard to catch the business news."

They decided on a parking area at the Skokie Lagoons between Tower and Willow, a much shorter drive for Ian than for Jake, but Jake didn't mind. When he arrived just at eight with two large take-out coffee containers, there was only an older Buick Regal in the lot. Peter Stiles' car. The day had broken very cold but both men had big thick coats and scarves, so they sat out hunched on a picnic table facing the dry rushes and the iced-over expanse of water beyond, the early sun on their backs and both hands warming around their paper cups.

He had no trouble filling Ian in on his story, although as he was talking Jake became acutely aware of how lonely it had felt before with no one he could tell it to. He'd met a man, he said, older guy, also married, also kids, though his were grown. Had been seeing him regularly now for nearly three months. Sex once—first time—at the guy's house when his wife was out of town, but now usually at a motel. Sometimes lunch together before the deed. Excellent love-making, a hot and really admirable fellow. Professor type, in his middle sixties, smart, author of books, list of accomplishments twice as long as your arm.

"Actually," Jake said, "you might know him. Or your parents might. He's Winnetka too. Your set, not mine."

"In that point-five percent is he?" Ian asked.

"Right there."

"What's his name?"

Jake hesitated, then said, "I'm not going to tell you. It's not that I don't trust you—"

"No, I understand."

"—just I don't figure it's my business to bring anybody out of the closet, even to you."

"It's ok. It was a kind of <u>idle</u> curiosity on my part."

Though it was the weekend, not far beyond the Lagoons the Edens was already roaring with traffic. Nearer in to them there were clutches of shrill chattering winter birds in and out of the trees.

"Funny," Jake said, "when I was a kid and they talked about nature I always pictured the Lagoons."

"Me too. What's funny about that?"

"How artificial all this is. Reclaimed for nature you could say."

After another silence and some pulling on their coffee, Ian said, "So, is it all good with—well, what shall I call him?"

Jake laughed a little uncomfortably. "I sometimes think of him as the boyfriend—"

"All right."

"And no, not all good. It's entirely confusing. Things have fallen out in ways I had no idea they could."

"Like?"

"Like I find I have feelings for the guy."

"What do you mean? Are you saying you're in love with him?"

Jake looked away, smiled to himself, ducked his cold chin for a moment in the warmer v- at the top of his coat. "There's a part of me that resists saying it like that."

"Why?"

"The part of me that still doesn't think a man can love a man in the same way you love a woman."

"Oh Jake—"

"I know, I know, I'm a Neanderthal, right? I suck his dick, don't I? And if that ain't love—"

"I used to wonder if for some weird reason when the dentist says, 'Open, please,' he can tell if you've ever had a penis in your mouth." Ian raised his eyebrows, gave Jake a little smile. "OK, I'll be serious. Is there something wrong here I'm not getting?"

"I can't get him out of my mind. I obsess about him."

"Does Angie notice anything? Loss of interest on your part?"

"You mean sex? No, our sex life has been good—sometimes better even since the boyfriend came along. I get all charged up, if you know what I mean."

"Sure. But in your daily life with Angie, with your daughter?"

"We go along. I told you, it's sometimes pretty rocky between me and Angie, but we hang in there, do what we can, like most marriages I guess."

"And she doesn't ask why you're preoccupied?"

"She thinks I've got work worries. Which I do, of course. But I keep up a pretty good front."

"That's funny. Maybe I've just known you too long. You seem pretty unhappy to me."

"Do I?" Jake stared ahead.

"This morning at least. At the egg nog party you seemed buoyant."

"Was I? Well, I knew by then I was going to get to see him again."

"When was that?"

"Yesterday."

"And that didn't make you happy?"

"Shit, man! I can't believe what happened."

"Well OK, Jake, I don't want to be accused of trotting out my professional manner, but you need to go on now."

"It came as a big surprise. He's going to Colorado with his family to ski and I didn't think I'd get to see him until sometime into the new year. But he wrote me an email saying he saw an opening yester-day afternoon and he knew I probably wasn't available, but— And it happened Angie and Lisa were off to "The Nutcracker" down in the city with her mom, so I <u>was</u> free. We went to the motel we go to and everything started off fine. Better than fine, it was hot. Our holiday fuck. Except then I was just getting ready to put it in and I go to kiss him and he turns his head away, clearly doesn't want that. And I lose it, completely."

"You got angry you mean."

"No, man, I lost my fucking erection."

"Oh, OK. So then what happened?"

"Well he was all 'it doesn't matter, don't worry,' and all that crap, the complete gentleman. And he went to sucking me and eventually in fact we both got off."

"When you were making love other times, had he wanted to kiss?"

"Oh yes, a lot."

"So what do you think is going on?"

"I don't have a clue, my friend. Maybe he's gearing up for the big see-ya-later. Or he's figured out I'm just a dick to him, a convenience fuck, and he's stepping back."

"Do you really believe that?"

Jake thought a long time, then shook his head. He wondered if Ian could see there were about to be tears in his eyes. Would he think it was the cold that produced them? Then he felt Ian's arm come warm around his shoulder, Ian squeezing some, so he smiled a little.

"Afterwards, in the parking lot?"

"Yes?"

"We shook hands and wished each other a happy new year and then you know what he said, the boyfriend?"

"What?"

"Fucker says, 'You are the best thing that's ever happened to me you know.'"

FOUR

To get the constant buzz out of his head and the agitation out of his heart, Jake tried simplifying. He would tell himself it all came down to the fact that for him the average was about two to three days after a meeting that he got so horny for the boyfriend again, but the man in question only seemed to need a nice shagging every fourteen or fifteen days or so. A standoff kept in place partly by Jake's own rule that to avoid looking needy he himself wasn't allowed to call or write to book time together.

So. Once out of the blue in the middle of January the day after Guy got back from skiing tan and wind-burned and hungry for some loving. Hot and heavy, plenty of tongue in the kisses, dick in working order. Then a big hole in the schedule because the professor was on the road for the university, at Rockefeller in New York, at the National Science or National Endowment or something in D.C., a hiatus of almost a month during which Jake decided several times the whole thing was just too nuts-making, better to give it up than to be so frustrated, time to migrate to greener pastures, whatever. Then today, February 13th, probably in The Man's eye a special treat for the eve of the buon San

Valentino, and at Guy's house again (wifey again conveniently away, this time on business).

But not in the king-size bed upstairs. Where Guy led Jake was into one of their daughters' snug little yellow ground-floor rooms.

As soon as they walked in, Jake recognized something about the layout of the house which he could have figured before. To get those showy wide open spaces—the living room, the master bedroom—even an architect with a blank check in front of him would need to stint elsewhere. Among the new rich (and even among some of the old) it was always the kids who got shafted. Bigga vista for Mom and Dad, dank little caves for the offspring.

The low ceiling, shelves full of massed teddybears and some Barbies and the rows and rows of ruffles produced a powerful acidy, cold feeling in him. "What?" he said. "I wasn't good enough before for prime time?"

"I don't get it, Jake. What do you mean?"

"I flunked so badly in the grownups' bed I only rate this?"

Guy came to him, tolerant smile, got hold of him, kissed him, said, "Will you turn it off for just a little while? The only reason we're in here today is I imagined we might mess the sheets and I don't even know where the clean ones are kept. OK?"

"Sure," Jake shrugged. "Forget it. I'll believe you."

So then there was no question about performance. Jake stayed hard as a nail and didn't even have to think about lasting because, despite what Guy said, he remained a little put off. There was an oval mirror at a vanity against the wall which gave a perfect view of his buttocks in profile tensed then relaxing as he pumped away.

All done up, rubber wrapped in Kleenex, juice patted off his cock and back lying all tangled up legs and arms with the big warm man, he murmured, "Want some help to get you off?"

"No, I'm perfectly happy just to be here like this with you," Guy said. A few minutes passed, nothing but the sound of their breathing, and then he said, "You took your time today."

"Yeah? Was that OK?"

"Sure. Fine. It felt good. I just wondered."

Jake laughed. "I'll tell you, but you may laugh. I was getting off on the sight of my own ass in that mirror there while I fucked you."

"Funny. I was watching that too."

"You were?"

The windows were a narrow stretch of glass panels at shoulder height along the room's west side. Through them the winter sun cast a slanting blood-orange stripe down the far wall.

After a while, Jake suddenly started.

"What's wrong?"

"Maybe I better get going here."

"Really?" Guy pulled him closer, snuggled against him. "How come?"

It was of course luck that the couple hours after work and before Jake had to hit his mark at home were also within Guy's occasional window of opportunity. Otherwise, what? None of this would ever have happened. Jake took pride from the fact he had never yet had to turn Guy down. If the time suggested was completely impossible, he came up with alternatives until they got something. What a truly obedient dog you are, he sometimes told himself.

But between the Miller brothers and getting together the Belknap proposal with Mike and Angie's various legitimate calls on his time, his wiggle room seemed to be shrinking. This afternoon, for example, once out of Guy's some real boogeying lay ahead. Down and out almost all the way over to O'Hare to pick up the Guatemalan girl Angie was taking on as a maid and babysitter, in rush hour a matter of 40 minutes if he was lucky, then back to Skokie to collect Lisa from her tutoring session, get both of them home, then shower and change and him and Angie out to a long-planned dinner with the Statens.

I.e., domestic stuff, everyday problem crap not worth mentioning to Guy. Jake sat up, put his feet on the floor, looked around in the near dark for his socks. "Probably shouldn't have left my truck out there in your driveway."

"Why is that? Even this time of the year there's not much of a view you'd get from the road."

"Yeah, but I never know for sure anymore. They've taken to fucking with me about my whereabouts."

"At work?"

Jake nodded. "I'm out standing in line at the DMV and I get a call on my cell. It's Rae, the dispatcher at our yard, old bud of mine. 'Hey,' she says. 'Hey," I say, 'what's up?' 'What you doing at the DMV?' 'Who told you where I am?' 'A little bird.' 'Well what's the little bird want with me?' 'I don't know, Jake. They just called and told me to get hold of you and find out what you were up to all the way out in Niles on company time.'"

"Who is this, Jake?"

"The guys in the main office. One of them'll happen to be driving by and happen to spot my truck so they make a chicken-shit game out of it. They've done it before."

"Are they trying to put you on edge?"

Jake shrugged. "I don't know. At least they want me to know I'm under surveillance."

"And this is coming from your boss?"

"No," Jake said, "pretty clearly <u>not</u> from him. It's the others. And they should leave it, you know. I bring in too much business to be jerk-ed around like a fish on a line."

"Did you ever think of looking for something else?"

"At this stage, for a guy like me not having a college degree is really crippling."

"Hard to believe you dropped out of DeKalb."

"Why's that? Because it's such a shit school?"

"Not at all. Good place, Dekalb, in my opinion. And you have such native intelligence."

Was that a put-down? Jake had to struggle with himself to believe it wasn't.

"Problem is in any kind of academia I stand out as <u>not</u> a native. Of any sort. Always very uncomfortable for me, college. And too bad, because that piece of paper was something I really wanted."

"You left because of finances?"

"That's what I said. But I could have hacked it. I was already managing smaller jobs summers and even some while I was still technically enrolled and taking classes. I could have done it, even without any scholarship, just on my own. But I couldn't concentrate on my studies. It was awful, it made me feel awful. I didn't drop out. I fled the scene."

"And you've never thought of striking out on your own?"

"In the past I did. Not recently. I'd be at a real disadvantage, no capital, no equipment, no way to pay even myself to begin with, make the nut I need to hold my family together."

"But you do have a nice set of contacts, or so you told me. Clients who trust you—"

"It's true. But what they'd have would likely be big projects, and whether they'd feel secure in going with a stand-alone I just don't know."

"I would," Guy said. "I mean, should I happen to have a building I needed built."

A sweet thing to say, freebie though it was. Jake thought about the remark again as he was getting into his duffle coat by the front door. Will a dude say anything when he's just had your dick up his ass?

Too cynical, man. Back off a little. Here it was, what he'd wanted, a few minutes at least of easy confidence, kind of thing you'd expect there to be between friends, so why do you hurry to turn it to crap?

Guy wanted to hold him—man in shirtsleeves to smaller man bundled up in coat and scarf—wet kiss him, brush his hair up off his forehead, look at him. Jake had trouble not shying away.

Outside the sky had gone nearly dark. About a foot and a half of snow covered the ground and the crisp dry cold of the last few nights was rapidly setting in again. Guy came crunching out after Jake and stood at the driver's side window, hands in his pocket and breathing out clouds of milk-white vapor.

"You better go in."

"I know I should."

"You in for the night now?"

"No, I have to go back into town."

"What for?"

Guy laughed, looked down, scuffed the hard snow. "You've heard of the Maskers?"

"No."

"Well, that would probably please them, since it's supposed to be such a secret society. Though it isn't of course, not any more. The Maskers go way back. In the 19th century they were a kind of leading businessmen's club, very hush-hush, that put on balls and big public torch-light parades, especially at Mardi Gras, like the ones in St. Louis and New Orleans. All in masks. But by 1900 the street displays started dying out, I think because the German immigrants started celebrating their own Karneval before Lent, which made the Maskers' struts all somehow less special, so they quit. Then in the Twenties people began to complain the Union Club was no longer as restricted as it was meant to be, so they resurrected the Maskers as a kind of snootier-than-Union thing. You have to be a Union member with ancestors who were in the original Maskers."

"Which is you, of course."

"Me and my brother, yes."

"Do you wear robes?"

"On occasion we do."

"And what's tonight? Off to burn a couple crosses on the South Side?"

"No." Guy thought, smiled. "Though I suppose some of the Brothers might be of a mind to institute a ride or two now and then. Tonight in fact is the dinner dance where this year's crop of 'Virgins,' the members' debutante daughters, are put up in the block one by one to see if the Masked Sultan should want to buy any of them for his harem."

"The Masked Sultan? Is that you?"

"Well this year it happens to be, yes."

"Another world, man." Jake shook his head, laughing, and started his engine. "I guess you enjoy it though, huh?"

"It's foolishness, Jake. Clap-trap. But we do manage to raise a considerable amount of money for good causes. Upend the Brothers who have it and shake it right out of their pockets."

"You ever allowed to bring along a guest? I mean to the all-guy secret evenings?"

"There are occasions like that. Smokers we call them."

"You should take me along one time."

"I'd be honored to, Jake."

"Some night when they're having a circle jerk."

Guy cocked his head as though considering. "I'd put that up to the Activities Committee at the very next meeting except for the fact I wouldn't want to share you with any of those geezers."

"Aww—"

Guy's nose had reddened and he was shivering.

"You go in now, man," Jake said again. "Don't stand out here like a fool, OK?"

*

The exit from the Blue Line where Angie promised the girl would meet him was a brightly illuminated glass and aluminum box which appeared to hang off the edge of the Harlem Avenue bridge over the Kennedy. At this hour the freeway was running bumper-to-bumper under Jake, nothing but a sluggish river of commuters' headlights in the dark. He was more than half an hour late and had no idea what this Luz was supposed to look like. No Guatemalan girl on the pavement, no nobody. Cars having to get around him honked and he caught glimpses of some angry faces as they passed. One kid gave him the finger. Jake sat at the curb working the inside of his cheek against his teeth, gathering spit, swallowing it. Inside the station a skinny Latino guy with a green backpack at his feet kept ducking his head and glancing out at Jake's truck. Two ragamuffin boys repeatedly circled the room and then threw themselves up against the man, who paid no attention to their assaults.

Then a young woman in a black coat with long black hair came hurrying up the stairs, consulted with the man, ran to the glass door, cracked it, then called back in to him. The man corralled the children and brought them and the backpack. The woman, still half in and half out, stooped to kiss the kids and then stood as though she was going to kiss the man, but instead just took the heavy backpack from him and came out and approached Jake's truck.

"Luz?"

"Yes, I am."

Jake was out and around to help her struggle the backpack up in the well and then her into the cab and to make sure the passenger door locked right.

Angie had warned him that the girl might not speak much English. But she had also claimed Luz was single and had no children. Glancing at her at the first stoplight, he saw she was pretty, definitely very nervous and, despite the efforts of his little heater, freezing. She might be 17 and she might be closing in on 30.

"Sorry I'm late. Did you have long to wait?"

Nothing. "_Tardo_," he said. "_Io. Perdone._"

"_No, no_—" she protested. But then no more. She shrugged, shot him a look, smiled helplessly. He shrugged back. Oh well...

Being unable to talk left him free to concentrate on getting through traffic. A couple of times when he saw a break and charged around a corner Luz got thrown up against the door, so she braced herself, hung on, one hand flat against the dash, arm stiff. No matter how he drove he was going to be way late for Lisa. All he could hope was her session hadn't started on time, had run over. It was a bullshit thing anyway in his opinion to declare a second-grader a "slow reader" and send her to a commercial agency to "improve her comprehension skills." The problem was not with the girl. When she was five Lisa was already reading aloud to her mother and him. It was the books they were given at school. Lisa herself said they were dumb. She only went along with the small-group tutoring because the last couple of months she had gotten it into her head—sometimes at least—that she needed to become a model child.

The offices of <u>Excel!</u> were in an older block of stores with the parking in front. Cruising in, Jake saw only a couple of cars down by the end where the pizza place was. <u>Excel!</u> looked closed up for the night, half-strength fluorescent panels on overhead, no movement he could discern inside. What the fuck? He pulled up, ran to the door anyway, rattled it in case he could rouse someone in the back. Nothing.

He didn't have his cell, couldn't in the moment even recall where he'd left it. What had the fuckers done, just locked the doors on their little hustle and walked off leaving a seven-year-old on the pavement? He half-ran down the line in the direction of the pizzeria. Would Lisa have the sense to go and ask permission to stay warm in there? A big green Chrysler idled in front of the pizza joint emitting vapor, someone intermittently tapping the brake lights.

Inside, a teenager with iPod wires in his ears danced to his own music behind the register, but there was no Lisa and the boy claimed not to have seen her.

"Mr. Guarani?"

When Jake came out, a tall woman in glasses was unfolding herself from the driver's side of the Chrysler.

"Yes?"

"What in God's name do you mean <u>abandoning</u> this child as you have done?"

"I didn't abandon anybody. I was late, OK?"

"It comes down to the same thing, doesn't it? If I hadn't stayed—"

"And let me ask, who are you?"

"Mrs. Lyons. I'm Lisa's tutor." She began again, "And if I hadn't moved heaven and earth in <u>my</u> private life, your little girl—"

"Well, and I thank you for that."

Lisa was out of the car but not letting go of the passenger-side door, trying to get it to shut without making a noise. Jake went toward her.

"Oh, you'll pay, you know. My time is professional time, sir, and you <u>will</u> be billed—"

The big woman followed him around the hood of the Chrysler, hovering, spewing righteously. Jake scooped Lisa up, held her tight against him, her face up next to his. "Hi, baby," he whispered.

"—it <u>will</u> appear!"

"OK, good, thanks, whatever."

"Your wife is on the way down here—"

"Aw shit! Could you call her, tell her I've got the child now, she doesn't need to—"

"I will do that, yes."

"Thanks."

He carried Lisa down the walkway to his truck and put her in next to him. On the way home he tried 'Daddy's sorry' and 'I got stuck in traffic' and 'Were you waiting long?' but Lisa wouldn't come around to him at all.

Setting it up a week night out with the Statens had sounded like fun. They were good, solid neighbors, Loren Angie's pal, Fred the sheriff Jake occasionally hunted and fished with. At the restaurant without announcing it Jake led Fred along into getting toasted with him. The ladies talked on, and Jake saw nothing particularly out of the ordinary about himself, he had always made a point of holding his liquor. He did catch Angie eyeing him once or twice, however, maybe because it was unusual for him to drink during the week given the time he usually got out of the house in the a.m. Fred didn't stand up to the booze quite so well and outside afterwards there was a short set-to between husband and wife, Loren demanding the car keys and Fred swaying, head down and truculent as a steer unwilling to go in the stocks. Angie and Jake gently encouraged him until he dug in his pocket and handed over his keyring.

At home while Angie occupied the bathroom, Jake assessed himself. The alcohol left him in a gentle fog, which was what he had wanted from it, allowed him to function on automatic. He wandered down the hall to look in on Lisa, pulled up her comforter, touched her hot cheek.

So. His father thought little girls needed to learn you can't trust grownups, and now the son whose guiding principle was <u>not</u> to be like his old man in any way had forced the same bitter lesson on his own daughter. But she was a usually sunny girl, and God knows huge amounts of love had been laid on her, so maybe she wouldn't remember tonight forever. How sweet it would be to take her aside and explain how the real fuck-up was her mother hiring this nice-enough latina lady from down on the Near West Side who was so fresh off the boat she didn't yet know how to transfer to a bus, forcing <u>him</u> to drive all the way into the city of Chicago in rush hour before he could circle back for her.

But he couldn't tell Lisa that truth any more than he could tell her the other one: The fact is, honey, your old man was out pleasing himself, not just French-kissing and then boning another man but also shooting the shit with him long after the time I should have been on the road to come for you, my precious girl, because that was such a pleasure too.

Between two and three he woke up dry mouth, clammy, and in a full-on panic. What if Guy died? Since Jake didn't read the paper every day, how long would it be before he found out? No email from the man, no phone call, Jake figuring he'd been 86'd and the asshole didn't even have the courage or decency to let him know. So what if he broke his rule then? The briefest flag: *Hey, my friend, how's tricks?* And then what? A pause of several days, a week, and a terse message from the widow: *I don't recognize you among my late husband's associates. Please let me know how you knew him. What was your relationship?*

A really good question, huh?

*

Half a flight of steps down from the kitchen at ground level a previous owner had added on a small room. Whoever did the work had run an additional forced-air duct off the house's blower so the room got plenty warm. They had also plumbed out to install a half bath. When Jake and Angie were first married, they used the space as an extra bedroom when Earl's little buddies were allowed to sleep over. More recently it had become the storage place for stuff in transition from being useful to becoming junk. Since Luz was her project, with no complaint Angie took on clearing out the room and fixing it up. And though a substantial number of items ended up piled on Jake's workbench in the garage, he chose not to bitch about that. The promise was that in addition to help with Lisa and the housework, Luz's being there when Lisa's school let out would allow Angela to concentrate on getting a job.

She reported that Bear Spirit Lady or whatever the therapist's name was had determined they had entered on the "mature" period of their marriage. Jake said, "Uh-oh, does that mean no fucking?" Angie laughed him off. Their lovemaking was not a sore point between them at the moment. Like other things, steady enough, chugging along at normal, at least in Jake's opinion.

He wondered though. Earl barely out of their hair when Angie brings in someone else to live with them. Them never really by themselves anymore. In bitter moments past she would claim his anger made her afraid to be alone in the house with him. 'Oh come on,' he would say, 'I have never hit a woman in my life. You know that.'

"Yes, but your yelling sometimes is so frightening I get sick to my stomach."

If she really felt unsafe around him—ever—that was fucked.

As far off as Luz was, if she got up to use the bathroom at night Jake heard her. In the daytime she padded about in her little black slippers so quietly he kept coming on her unexpectedly, as though she were a ghost. Apparently being unobtrusive was her thing. When she was washing dishes she ran only a dribble of water, never turned it on full force.

Lisa took to her almost at once. Jake pretty much gave up on trying to talk with Luz, but she and Lisa worked out some kind of arrangement between languages and were always bent together over things, confiding in whispers.

"Well," Angie said, "I'm not being patronizing, you know, but there are ways in which Luz is still really just a little girl herself."

"With two kids of her own, and some sort of a husband or boy-friend or whatever too."

"No. What makes you say that, Jake?"

He had told her about the man and the children at the Harlem Avenue station, but Angie waved him off. Well where had Luz come from in the first place, he asked, an agency or something? No, Angie said, from her mother. The recommendation was from the Mexican guy who did Alice Moore's gardening and maintenance.

*

Nancy Stiles died the last day of March at home. Felicity had been there ten days before and arranged for Hospice to begin coming in. Thinking there was more time than there was, she then left for a planned vacation with Leonard. But she alerted Ian so he was able to get off work and be back in the States with his mother the evening she died.

Through the winter, even with Nancy in and out of the hospital, Peter Stiles continued trudging off to work every morning. But though he objected to what he called 'strangers in the goddamn house,' the arrival of the Hospice people signaled something to him. Without saying anything to anyone at his office, he stopped going downtown. One of his colleagues called and asked if he wanted to retire. It would certainly be the appropriate moment to do so, and he wouldn't even have to come in to collect his things. His friends at the bank would be glad to bring his pictures and desk stuff out to him. Peter said no, thank you, he was not quitting, he would be back—and slammed down the phone.

In the end, once the Hospice nurse adjusted her morphine drip level properly, all the agitation and trembling seemed to wash out of Nancy's exhausted body and she lay very still. Ian sat on one side of the hospital bed they had moved in for her and his father on the other, silent for a long time, each of them holding one of her hands. You might have thought they were trying to give Nancy some kind of transfusion, their life's blood to keep her going just a little while longer.

Even so very thinned out and drawn, to Ian she looked not only serene and beautiful but girlish. At one point he got up and went down the hall to Fleas' room. She had left photograph albums and manila envelopes full of family pictures spread across her old bed. Ian was able to lay his hands on what he was looking for right away, a snapshot of his mother at about fifteen or sixteen on horseback in sunlight at a summer camp. When he took it back into his parents' room to show his father the resemblance to how she looked right now Peter glanced up and said, "I think she's gone, Son."

The funeral was the afternoon of the first Friday in April, delayed slightly because Fleas and Leonard had trouble booking their way back from St. Kitts. Fleas called Thursday night from Miami to say they had missed their connection there but would arrive O'Hare in the morning.

There were no viewing hours at the funeral home and by the time

Nancy's coffin was brought into Christ Church, it was sealed. Peter wanted time with it anyway, so the family arrived a good hour before the service. In a drawer of Nancy's dresser Fleas had found a black lace mantilla she had brought her mother once from Spain. She dropped it over her head and sat with her father in the first pew before the sleek mahogany box while the old church began quietly filling up behind them. The afternoon was chilly and sunny. Rain had come and it looked as though spring was beginning, but then in late March one more storm dumped a fresh foot of wet snow on Chicago. It remained, heaped at street corners in dirty piles and in large patches under the trees on lawns that had already begun to show faint green. The roads were entirely clear, though gritty still with accumulated sand. Until the organist started playing, those in the church could hear the high sizzling singing of car tires below along Sheridan Road.

With his father and sister more or less trapped up front, out in the vestibule Ian found himself to be chief mourner, or at least greeter. His brother-in-law Leonard escorted ladies with canes or walkers to seats and gave out programs while Ian shook hands and received mumbled condolences. The big bell overhead in the tower was tolling, the boy in the white gloves had the crucifix already up directly before his face and the minister in his robes and a brilliant green stole was set to walk when Jake and Angela Guarani hurried in.

The doors into the church opened and the little procession started down the aisle, the minister intoning in a sonorous, projecting voice, "I am the resurrection and the life, saith the Lord; he that believeth in me, though he were dead, yet shall he live."

Among them, in his family, Ian thought, oddly enough it was his father who turned out to be the big believer. Even on bitter sub-zero Sundays and no matter how hung over he might be, Peter Stiles would often struggle up and risk the iced-over streets to get himself to early Communion. Nancy only liked going for weddings, baptisms, and the confirmation of friends' children, although for several years she and the women she played bridge with joined the patchwork choir that led the diminished congregation through the hymns in July and August.

"...and whosoever liveth and believeth in me shall never die."

If so, unfair. If any of them deserved life eternal, it should be his mother. The thought made Ian begin to tear up. Angie touched one of his arms and Jake the other and Jake said in a low voice, "It's OK, man, it's OK."

"I know. Thanks. I better go around and come in the side. I'm supposed to be up front there by now."

"OK. See you after then."

No limo or town car had been ordered to take family out to Memorial Park. Peter had been insistent about that. He also refused to let anyone go with him or drive him, and so led the procession following the hearse alone, hunched at the wheel of his old Buick. The car's windows were grimy and the body streaked with winter dirt. Ian had meant at least to get it to a gas-station carwash, but then had forgotten and ran out of time. Fleas and Leonard came after Dad in their rental, and Ian ended up several cars behind with Jake and Angie in Angie's car.

On the way out to Skokie Ian asked how Lisa was doing and Angie said fine, but didn't elaborate. Jake looked grim, stony, had nothing to add. Selfishly, Ian wished they would just talk, it didn't matter about what. Talk as distraction. He imagined himself reaching forward and cupping the backs of both of their heads and somehow having the power in his touch to make everything go right between them.

Back at Pine Street after the interment, he wondered how many of those who dropped by saw the gathering was a sad parody or at least a dark-glass reflection. Nancy Stiles' eggnog party without Nancy. Or the eggnog. Without the soft lights of the Christmas tree and fires in the fireplaces, the downstairs rooms took on a neglected look, worn places in the carpets spotlighted by the late afternoon sun. Dad sat wedged in the corner of a couch, trying to struggle to his feet when people came up to him, causing them to tell him not to trouble himself.

Without Fleas there, Ian and his father had done a poor job of planning on the food. On the damask-covered dining table sat a large plastic tray of shelled shrimp in concentric circles with a red dipping sauce in the middle and two trays of sandwich quarters. Guests brought Katharine Hepburn's brownies and chocolate chip cookies and someone a single glass plate of deviled eggs, which disappeared almost at once. But people seemed mostly to need a drink, so Dad's men's doubles partner from the old days was kept on the jump at the bar in the living room.

Ian had been gratified to see his mother was going to pack Christ Church, but the number of those who felt they needed to come back to the house made him recall her saying once, 'A lot of people seem to like me a lot more than I like them.'

Lewis Keyes and his partner Jay Carlson had again driven up from Hyde Park. No festive vests this time, somber suits and dark ties. Maybe merely looking for something to say, Jay asked about the three-tiered Seth Thomas on the mantel above the fireplace in the dining room. It was what was called a seven-day clock, Ian said, hearing himself repeating his mother's words, and was dated on the inside 1834. The story was it had been bought off a ship in Charleston harbor and carried up into the hills as a gift for his wife by Nancy's South Carolina great-great-grandfather, who was a Cutler.

Jake and Angie Guarani came up to them. Apologizing for interrupting, Angie pulled Ian's head down toward her a little and kissed him on both cheeks in their traditional way. He nuzzled in and brushed her mouth with a kiss.

She took hold of both his hands. "Why is it Jake always gets time with you and I never do? How long are you here for?"

"I don't know yet," he said. "Depends on what Dad decides to do, how long he needs me and Felicity."

Angie looked around. "What will he do? He can't just rattle around in this place by himself, can he?"

"Well, for the moment that _is_ what he's proposing."

"When you get the chance—or if—will you call me? I'm at home. Almost all the time."

"I will, sure."

"Promise?"

"Yes, that's a promise."

Jake could stay a while, she said, but she was sorry, she had to go.

"How'll you get home then?" Ian asked Jake.

"Oh, I'm OK. I stashed my truck around the corner here before we came to the church."

Once Angela had left them, Jay Carlson turned his attention back to the clock. "It runs, I see."

"Long as you wind it. My mother was religious about that. Every Saturday night right before she went up to bed. There're two weights inside and you wind them both."

"It strikes the hour?"

"And the quarter hours."

"I thought I heard that. Lovely little chime."

Ian laughed. "I used to hate it. Way back, kindergarten, first grade or so, when we still lived in Wilmette. I would wake up when the quarter sounded and lie staring at the ceiling just waiting for the half and then the three-quarters and then the next hour. I think now I would actually sleep some in between, but I believed I was awake all that time. Two o'clock, three o'clock, four." He laughed again. "Distressing to a child."

"Distressing to a grownup too," Jay said, "insomnia."

Lewis's eyes were on Ian, fond. "And tell the gentlemen the connection between your wakefulness and the nocturnal habits of the Stiles clan."

For a moment, Ian didn't remember. Then what he had surfaced in therapy almost twenty years before came shuffling back into view. And with it his recurrent surprise at Lewis having the memory he did.

"Turns out I wasn't the only one. For people as athletic as we were, we were also a strangely restless bunch. When my mother couldn't sleep, in order not to wake my father she would get up and go read in that little room of hers down off their bedroom. And even Dad, the heaviest droner among us, if Fleas came in from a date just an hour or so late, he'd hear her key in the front door and go clomping downstairs cinching his robe and demanding to know where in hell she'd been."

Jay Carlson's attention seemed to be lagging. He peered at his watch, his eyebrows went up in surprise, and he turned to Lewis and touched his sleeve.

But Lewis remained intent on Ian. A small steady smile. "And the reason for all that rambling?"

In the old days, Ian sometimes accused Lewis of being really more of a hypnotist than a therapist. Not so, Lewis said, he had studied hypnosis but ended up not liking it much. Too much about power, he said, control.

So now Ian shrugged and went on, "I remember thinking the restlessness was because we all had a bit more of the puritan in us than we'd admit."

"Meaning?"

"That we're a little more concerned about each other's sex lives than is wise." He turned a little. No one behind him, the four of them were well out of earshot of others. "It's the dynamic that led to me and Walter getting popped."

"Walter?" Jay Carlson said. "Who's Walter?"

"A college roommate of mine, now my brother-in-law."

"And what was 'popped'?"

Ian looked at Lewis, at Jake. Well, he thought, no cause for embarrassment here. "My dad came into my room without knocking in the middle of the night—the night before Christmas in fact—while Walter and I were making love."

"Oh!" Jay's hand went to his mouth and he started laughing, then suddenly stopped. "I'm sorry. I'm sure it must have been—what's the word? Disruptive?"

"That _is_ the word," Ian said.

"And what about you, Jake?" asked Lewis. "You spent a lot of your younger years in this house too, didn't you?"

"Yes, sir. I kind of lived here when I could get away with it."

"And would you agree the Stiles seemed a little steamed up over each other?"

"I'd guess we were all a little steamed up one way or another. One of the reasons I liked it here." Jake said to Ian, "I don't know whether you ever knew this or not—"

"What?"

"About Nancy?"

"What about her?"

Jake looked around their little circle, shook his head, "Don't mind me, I may be way out of line here."

"Oh come on, Jake. You started to say—?"

"Well your mom was the first grown woman I ever saw naked. And I always thought she kind of planned it for me to see."

A pause, then Ian laughed and they all laughed.

"Even back in the day," said Lewis, "it <u>was</u> what marked Nancy Bowen off from the general run of the Smith and Conn College girls."

Jay said, "Taking off her clothes?"

"No, of course not." Lewis looked his partner up and down. "You are an insolent fellow sometimes."

"I try," said Jay.

"Even at a young age what Nancy Bowen had was juice," Lewis said. "By which I don't mean only that she was sexy, though she was that too. Smart, and intuitive, and—"

"You knew her when?" Jake asked.

"At college. Football weekends nearly 50 years ago when she and Peter were just starting in together."

Lewis's voice had thickened and he was looking at the rug, as though trying to shield himself from something. He sucked in on his big mouth, then raised his glass and tossed off what remained in it and said, "A long, long time ago."

*

By near dark, a little over an hour later, most of the guests were gone. Out behind the house only a low trickle of the voices of those remaining reached Ian and Jake. They walked the flagstones to the end of the browned garden, looked down on the pool, empty except for some straw spread in the bottom against the winter. In the twilight the tall-grass field that stretched to Hubbard Road looked gray. It had long been an extravagance to keep, since developers and brokers regularly made offers on it, but Ian said his mother had felt strongly about holding on to it since it was part of the original Bowen property.

"Remember when we did the Western Expansion in school? The Oregon Trail and all that?"

"Barely," Jake said.

"You may have thought the Skokie Lagoons represented 'Nature,' but I always pictured this as the place where the pioneers stood and contemplated the prairie and the Great Trek and so forth."

"Hm. Funny. Westward ho! Tonight I swear we'll camp by the fires of Hoffman Estates!"

Ian laughed, then said, "So what is it, Jake? You and Angie hardly seem to be speaking."

"We are wading in shit, man. Or drowning in it, I don't know which yet."

"What happened?"

"She hired this little Guatemalan lady to live in during the week and help out—on the premise that she needed her time freed up so she could <u>finally</u> get out and get a job. Then two weeks ago I happen to come onto the fact she's managed to get herself—or 'us' I guess you have to say, since my name is on it too—a new piece of plastic with a ten thousand dollar limit out the door, based on the fact I have managed to keep our existing credit record relatively clean. And what has she done? Gone out the day she received the card and charged up seven thousand plus dollars for a Viking goddamn custom six-burner stove. With two ovens. And why have I not been notified? And where <u>is</u> this new appliance? It's at Angie's mother's house in Wilmette. And why? Because without a word to me Angie has in fact gone into business with effing Alice Moore in a fifty-fifty arrangement where her buy-in cost was the Viking for Alice's kitchen. And the Guatemalan girl and the 'real' job? A fantasy!"

"Whoosh! But what kind of business?"

"Didn't I say? Homemade fucking cookies. Not that they have a commercial license yet or anything. Still in the 'test phase' they say."

"So what did <u>you</u> say, Jake?"

"After I stopped tearing the wallpaper off the walls with my teeth? I told her, 'Fine. Do what you got to do.' And you know what she said?"

"No."

"She looked me in the eye and she said, 'You're fucking somebody else.'"

"And what did you say to that?"

. 246 .

Jake shrugged, laughed a little. "I denied it. Of course. What else could I do?"

Ian was silent a moment, then said, "And what's up with the boyfriend? Is he still in the picture?"

"Yeah. Same same. Good when we're in the same room together, otherwise not a lot of contact. I don't know how much longer I can keep it going the way things are."

"Do you think Angie has any evidence for that claim?"

"Lipstick on the collar? E-mails? No. I'm been super careful."

"So just some waning in your attention to her?"

"My attention hasn't waned," Jake said sharply. "It has never waned."

"OK. So is it just her intuition?"

Jake looked away, thought, shook his head. "Don't you see? I tell her 'do what you got to do' and she reads that as defection on my part."

"Isn't it?"

Jake paced, hands in his pockets. Three or four steps in one direction, then back. And again. "She lied to me, man. An elaborate, calculated, expensive fucking lie! Cookies! Goddamn Alice and her goddamn cookies!"

Symmetry, Ian thought. One lie for another. But he held off drawing the lesson.

Jake said, "You know what it is, don't you? There's a part of Angie that just wants to get rid of me, have it over and done with."

"Why do you think?"

"I guess she's tired of me, tired of putting up with me. I don't know—"

Jake's face in profile was stony. Then his mouth moved a little, as though he were chewing on something. "We were so close," he said, "in the beginning at least. And for a long time then. It was kind of wonderful. Sometimes we didn't even need to talk—we just knew. I didn't withhold from her. What's the use of keeping a secret when you believe the other person can read your mind?"

When Ian thought about Angie and Jake's relationship, usually what came to mind first was the little apartment he and Beatrice lived in before they were married. It was in the 11th, out beyond the Bastille on the Rue Paul Vert and on the fourth floor so five flights up, though being young neither he nor Beatrice much noticed how strenuous the climb was. Its not being on the front of the building meant that especially in the summer with windows open and despite curtains and shutters and looking away, your life became oddly mingled with the sounds and movements of your neighbors across the airshaft and on the floors above and below you. Ian and Beatrice's bedroom closed off, but not the study alcove Angie occupied when she came to visit. Jake showed up without warning very brown from three weeks in Italy visiting relatives he had never met before. He had six days for Paris and a plane ticket home, but not much cash left. Ian and Beatrice checked it with Angie and then offered Jake the badly sprung couch in their tiny living room. He never slept there, since he got himself invited to the much more comfortable air mattress in the alcove the night he arrived. Around dawn one morning when Jake and Angie grew especially boisterous, Beatrice and Ian discussed whether <u>they</u> shouldn't move over to her parents' apartment by the Luxembourg—her parents were in Antibes for the month—and give the new lovers some privacy. But they stayed, and all the little inconveniences of the marathon—the multiple showers Angie and Jake took, together and separately, the towels hung up everywhere to dry, the thumping and the murmuring and giggles and the 3 a.m. conversations, the naked or near-naked bodies ducking into or coming out of the bathroom—became a kind of open but unspoken joke among the four of them. It amused Beatrice that the other couple's noises excited her and Ian and they found themselves making love only slightly less often than their guests. Ian teased her. Didn't she feel any shame about the voyeuristic element here? She called him a silly American psychologist and said she only hoped they weren't keeping awake neighbors who had to go to work in the morning.

"If she wants a divorce," Jake said now, "I won't fight her. But I <u>will</u> be completely screwed."

"How do you mean?"

"When she <u>did</u> work, there in California, it was for a big law firm that handled a lot of divorce. She'll clean me out, she knows how. I've already begun relocating some of my things just in case."

"Which things?"

"My hunting rifles, my reels, some of the power tools. I want them off the table if we get to dividing up."

"Where are you stashing the stuff?"

"Some of it's with my sisters."

It was getting cold and time for Jake to go. In the living room only a couple of Ian's parents' oldest friends still lingered. Leonard Nelson had removed his jacket and sprawled with a drink at the other end of the couch from Dad and Fleas had taken off her shoes and put her stocking feet up on a hassock. Jake went and stood directly before Peter and began to say whatever he could muster about Nancy. Peter lumbered unsteadily to his feet and stopped him by putting his arms around Jake and hugging him.

Close on, held up against the big man, Jake said in a low voice, "I'm sorry I never came by to see about that pool pump of yours or whatever it was. It slipped my mind, sir."

"Don't worry, Jake. Sufficient unto the day. It's not as though we've been getting in a lot of swimming around here of late, you know."

"I'll put it on my list. I promise."

"Summer. When summer begins—" Peter said, somewhat vaguely, finally letting Jake go.

"Yes sir."

Ian walked Jake out to his little truck, parked around the corner under the tall dark hedge that ran down one side of the property.

"You're going to think this is weird."

"Try me."

"Did you ever contemplate confiding to Angie about your interest in men?"

Jake let out a short bark of a laugh, shook his head. "Are you kidding? No way could I ever do that. Where'd you ever get a nutso idea like that?"

"I guess it came out of the feeling I have that Angie's the person in your life who understands you best. And therefore she should have all the data—"

Jake got in, started his engine, turned on the lights. "She thinks I'm homophobic, you know."

"Does she?"

"Pretty funny, huh? After Nancy's eggnog thing she was all over me about how fidgety and uncomfortable I looked around your gay friends from down at the university. If she only knew—"

"See?" Ian laughed. "Just what I was saying."

Jake just shook his head and put the truck in gear. "Be sure to call me if you get any more bright ideas, OK?"

"I will," Ian said.

*

The plan was for Ian to meet Angie Guarani at noon at the Convito Italiano at the Plaza del Lago. The Convito was a combination market, deli and 'bistro' (as most restaurants in America now seemed to fashion themselves), the dining part bright with large windows, a terracotta floor, blond furniture, cheerful, spotlighted art along the walls. Angie appeared ten or so minutes after twelve with her long hair pulled back, wearing a soft cream-colored blouse and lapis earrings. When Ian said how nice she looked she appeared both pleased and a little dubious. "Really?" she said. "Much as I wanted to see you, two hours ago I nearly had to call and cancel."

"Why was that?"

"It's a real effort to get myself up and dressed and out of the house these days."

Ian waited, his eye on the menu before him.

"Did he tell you?"

"Who? Tell me what?"

"Jake. We've been at each other. I suppose he must have said something."

"Only that much, yes. But I noticed it too, in the car—"

"You noticed what?"

"The silences."

The waitress appeared, eager to recite the specials. Did they need a minute? No, Ian had had time before Angie arrived, and after only a glance at the big white page she seemed to know what she wanted.

Once the girl was gone, Angie said, "My mother claims if the Convito weren't three blocks from her house she might well starve."

"Eats here a lot, does she?"

"No, it's all take out. My mom lives gnoshing on things in little cartons grubbed up out of the back of her refrigerator. She may well poison herself to death one of these days."

Hardly a recommendation for the lady's sugar cookies, Ian thought.

In the version Angie gave, the trouble was big changes at Jake's job, the company moving away from him, out beyond his reach. He was working closer than ever with Mike Tanner—they were developing a huge complicated proposal on a research facility for Northwestern, no word yet whether they'd gotten it—but at the same time the old bond between Jake and his boss seemed to be fraying. At the job Jake was currently overseeing, a big office building, they were nearly through laying foundation when the engineers became alarmed about the quality of the substrata and insisted the whole thing had to be dug out deeper and re-enforced. The men whose job it was, two brothers, now seemed to have it in for Jake, as though the extra expense and the time delay were his fault.

"But they're not, are they?"

"Oh no. There's a suit already in the works against the people who did the original soil analysis. Still, he wakes up in a sweat in the middle of the night and can't go back to sleep. I do what I can, but as you know he's not very good with situations he can't one hundred percent control."

"Do you know people who are?"

Angie smiled, shook her head. "I try to get him to sort out what he can manage from what he can't. But he's going to have to learn to let go more."

Ian nodded, waited. Angie began talking about how much she herself was getting from her sessions with a woman who was both a licensed clinical psychologist and an adept in the northern plains healing tradition. About a weekend workshop retreat that confirmed her belief that now was the time for her to focus on her nurturing self. "Jake's all bent out of shape about our financial situation," she said. "He thinks what's required is for me to get out there and earn money."

"And you?"

"I think it would be a terrible waste of these years when Lisa still needs her mom and a stable home for me to be away all day just to supplement our income. Not to mention I was hoping for one more kid while I still can."

Listening to husbands and wives separately you almost inevitably found yourself waiting for certain facts to emerge, only to find them skipped over. It was as though you had briefly nodded through some minutes of a movie or one of the reels had never been put up.

What Jake lacked, Angie said, was any sort of spiritual dimension, which left him with very limited ability to change and grow. Circumstances changed around him, but he was rigid, couldn't change with them. What was his favorite 'explanation' for anything? Everything? 'It is what it is.'

"Sounds sort of deep at first," she went on, "doesn't it? But what does it mean? Nothing really. When you come right down to it, nothing."

At the end of the meal, she decided in favor of coffee and against dessert. But when Ian asked would she share the profiteroles, she agreed she could have a bite. Three little balls in a splotch of very rich warm chocolate sauce, the whole thing lonely-looking on the large white plate set down in the middle of the table.

Aware he needed to tread lightly here, Ian said, "Couldn't you say Jake <u>does</u> have a spiritual dimension, one that is all devoted to love and being a good lover?"

Angie sniffed, then smiled. "The therapist does call him a 'love bug.' Given his history, she's surprised he hasn't strayed any number of times."

"There's never been any indication of that?"

Angie's mouth opened, but then she hesitated, regrouped, and said evenly, "No, I don't think, no. He's had performance problems, as I'm sure you know. And maybe that's kept him on the straight and narrow. Fear of failure if he went elsewhere or whatever."

"I didn't know."

"I'm surprised he hasn't ever said anything to you."

"I'm not. What kind of problem?"

"Some time back he started coming way too soon. Hardly in when he'd go off." She laughed a little, looked at Ian. "I don't mean it made him unsatisfactory really. You know what a technician Jake is, the master of foreplay and a thousand ways to please. But it upset him, not being able to hold off like that and make it last."

"And that's still the situation?"

"Oh no. I thought the solution would be some kind of cream or something to slow him down, but the doctor prescribed <u>shots</u>. Hormones, I guess."

"And that worked?"

"Yes, all better now, thank you." Angie pushed half a profiterole around through the chocolate, forked it and ate it. "Though—"

"What?"

"Well, you know. You've been married longer than we have. It does come to seem a lot of the time you're just going through the motions, doesn't it? Not that I'd want to give up on sex or that I don't love Jake just as much as ever or anything, but—"

Again, Ian waited. Angie looked down, then away. For a moment, he thought she was going to cry. But then she came back into eye contact with him and there was a little smile on her lips.

"There was a woman I worked with in California. I worked <u>for</u> her, actually, as her assistant. Very smart, very chic, a very together attorney. It was the two of them—Jake and Lenore—who helped get me free finally from my entanglement with that asshole Alan Trevors. Jake on the emotional front and Lenore Jay on the legal and practical. She did the final stages of my divorce for me, and pretty much for free. Except not entirely."

"What's that mean?"

"Right at the end—Jake had come out and proposed and we were set to get married, Earl was already back here staying with my mom, and I was just waiting for the shippers to come and take my few little pieces of furniture—and Lenore shows up with two bottles of wine and we drink one and then she tells me she's in love with me and wants to kiss me."

"And what?"

"I let her. And then we drank half the other bottle and she wanted to do more stuff, so I let her. And then I did some stuff to her too—"

Angie's cheeks had reddened and she was fiddling with a fork, pressing a little series of indentations into the tablecloth with the tines, but she was smiling, bemused. "And I liked it," she said, "all of it. What does that mean, Ian?"

"That at a difficult period in your life you enjoy a little sexual attention from a woman you admire and who admires you? In itself, as an incident I wouldn't be able to make very much of it."

"Well you're no fun!" She put the fork down. "Here I am trying to make myself all exotic and unstable and corrupted and everything for your benefit and you won't even be shocked!"

"Sorry," he said. "I guess it's a professional liability. But let me ask you this. Did you ever tell Jake about the lady in California?"

She thought for a moment. "I've hinted at it, but never come out completely to him, no. Why?"

"No reason," he said.

She laughed. "You know men. They always suspect us of fooling around with other women anyway. So why not fan the fires a little, right?"

"And what does Jake say when you hint about it?"

Angie laughed. "Oh, you know him. He says it's entirely hot to think about. How he'd love to watch me make love with another lady and then how he'd hate it and couldn't stand it, being Italian and eaten up with jealousy and that whole rigamarole."

"Ah yes," Ian laughed, "our Jake."

She insisted on paying for lunch. While they were waiting for the check, Ian thought again of what he had imagined on the way to the cemetery. He had provided the place for Angie and Jake to fall in love. Why didn't he have the magic words to make them content with each other now?

Angie's head was bent, a large lock of her hair falling forward, while she figured out and wrote in the tip. "You know what?" she said, low, "I don't think he trusts me anymore, or even cares about me. About what I think."

"Oh," Ian says, "I don't think that's true at all. You're the one who matters the most to him."

"After his precious self maybe."

He didn't need to see her eyes, the anger was all in her voice.

*

Fleas had warned him: "Jake asked me what's the time difference Chicago to Paris," she said, "I guess he wants to speak with you." But when his cell phone buzzed in his pocket as Ian was hiking home through the Luxembourg late one May afternoon and he fished it out and cracked it, it was still surprising to hear Jake's voice so clear, so close.

Once through the how you doing, man? fine, you? getting along, getting along part, Jake moved directly to business. "I'm sorry to bug you, my friend, but I got something I got no one to talk to about."

"What is it, Jake?"

"I think I must be going crazy."

"Over what? Angie?"

"No, over the boyfriend. He's either got to shit or get off the pot. I can't hang in this nowhere with him much longer."

"Well what's going on?"

"Not a hell of a lot, that's the problem. It's the usual. I see him, we have lunch, we talk, we go rent the room, we have sex. Then nothing. I don't hear from him, a week, two weeks, not an email or a phone call even. Sometimes he's on the road fundraising for the university and when he gets back he calls up all hot to trot and wants to make a date pronto, get up on his knees and have me shove him something nice."

"Which isn't satisfactory to you?"

"Oh don't get me wrong. The sex is still excellent. Exciting. It's what keeps me hanging on, what keeps me going back. But—"

"I know. You want flowers, boxes of chocolates delivered to your doorstep…."

"Don't make fun, man." Jake laughed, a short brittle laugh. "Although you're not far wrong. Something like that. I wouldn't mind it at all if he were to court me some. Oh Christ! I'm such a <u>gurl</u>, you know?"

"What's that, Jake? A 'gurl'?"

"You know, like a teenage girl. All silly and emotional. Lisa and her little friends make fun by calling each other 'gurl'."

Ian had come out of the wooded area by the tennis courts and the marionette theater and crossed the big open promenade with the fountains and the view of the palace and was climbing the path that led up to the gates nearest his own building. This part of his usual walk home had once been peaceful, but now it was constantly interrupted by thumping feet or huffing breathing behind him and then young men and women in flashy shorts and t-shirts or tank tops streaming by, some of them flinging beads of sweat at you as they shouldered past. Ian stepped off to the side next to a wrought-iron bench and covered his free ear.

Jake was saying, "It's seven months now I've been seeing him and what can I say I know about him? Not a great deal."

"So there's no real conversation between you?"

"Oh yeah, no, there's talk. About our families, what we're doing, you know. For somebody as well placed as he is, he's a poor shmuck in a lot of ways. I have some sorrow for him."

"About what?"

"He had a son die and he's got guilt left over from being in Viet Nam, losing men in his command."

"So you <u>have</u> gone deeper with him some?"

"I guess. But no, not really. Very gentlemanly, that's the level we're at."

"And you want more."

"I do. You know, Ian, there's sex and then there's passion and I know the difference and I'll bet you know it too. And I'm not going to badmouth good sex, but when you settle for that and you <u>know</u> in some part of you that there was the chance of real passion…well that's fucked."

"And it seemed in the beginning you and this fellow might be on the road to 'passion'?"

"It did. To me it did."

"And he pulled back? Held back? What?"

Silence while Jake thought. Then he said, "I don't know, I just don't know. But there's something wrong here, that's for sure. You know what he makes me feel like sometimes? Like I'm nothing more than a dick. An occasional thing to satisfy a hunger of his."

The flow of runners had abated, at least for the moment, so Ian took to the path again.

Jake said, "It's totally unfair—I think about him all the time and I get no indication he does anything like that."

"Some of this has to do with the nature of the relationship, doesn't it?" Ian said. "If you and the boyfriend were free to be together all the time, you probably wouldn't obsess about him, at least not as much."

"Yeah, but—"

"Any chance you could get away with him, take a few days' vacation together, go someplace?"

Jake laughed again, quick, bitter-sounding. "Oh yeah, that's going to happen, my friend. No way. How could we swing that? 'Hey hon,

I'm off to go trout fishing with one of my buds at his cabin up on the Wisconsin River.' That was the excuse the two guys used in that movie, wasn't it? Except then they forgot to bring home any fish."

Coming out on the Boulevard San-Michel, Ian spotted his wife's head, her ginger hair bobbing among the busy walkers nearly a half a block up the street. Beatrice had seen him first and came striding toward him swinging her leather briefcase like a school girl. Reaching him, she gave his cheek a little brushing kiss and took his elbow, squeezed in against him. "Who are you talking with?" she said softly in English.

"Jake Guarani. In Chicago," Ian mouthed.

"Oh," she whispered back. "Say hello for me."

A break in the traffic came and they crossed on the run and headed down the little passageway between the street-front buildings toward their own building on the courtyard behind.

"I've written him a letter," Jake said.

"About?"

"Some of this stuff. But I'm not sure I should send it. Would you look at it for me? If it's too confrontational I want to know."

Sure, Ian said, he'd be glad to. Jake would email it, he said, he had Ian's email address right in front of him.

The trees in their courtyard were all in full leaf. Chopin issued from the open window of the professional pianist with the apartment catty-corner across from the one Beatrice's parents had so kindly turned over to them.

They were scheduled to go out with friends. For the occasion Beatrice had chosen that same rich plum fitted cocktail dress scooped in front to show off the smooth expanse of her upper chest. She was sitting at the three-fold mirror behind her dressing table raking her short hair a little with her fingertips when he came in. She stopped, put her hands in her lap, regarded herself evenly. Ian loved coming upon her in moments like this. The line between neurotic obsession with yourself and Rogers' positive self-regard might be a thin one, but in his opinion Beatrice walked the happy side of it. Since she was confident about her looks, she could meditate on her own reflection the way others might pray before a saint's image.

"What was it your friend Jake wanted?"

Ian did not mention the complication of his old pal's boyfriend. "Passion," he said. "He wants passion in his life."

Beatrice said, "But isn't Jake your age? Our age?"

"That's right. Is that what you think? Forty too old for passion?"

"Oh no, theoretically it could strike at any moment, couldn't it?"

"Like a disease?"

"But it is, isn't it? Passion? An abnormality popping up as it does to disturb the tranquility and order of everyday life?"

"More like the revolution then."

Beatrice paused, then nodded and said, "A period of conflict, destruction, and—inevitably—change and reordering, but in the individual rather than the society."

She turned back to her own face, took up an eyebrow pencil. Ian found himself smiling. He generally liked his wife's habit, instilled by French schooling, of building little boxes to put mess in. Even when there was something not very helpful about the result, this tidying up.

*

Dear Guy,

I told you from the first time I met you that I was fairly new at this kind of thing, which was true. I'm not a kid and I walked into it with eyes wide open, but the way it has turned out with you is not anything I expected and I am confused by that.

Some of the performance issues which have come up at our most recent meetings may be an indicator of my feelings.

I deeply appreciate everything we do together, and I don't want to knock the rock in any way. But what has happened, on my side at least, is that friendship and good sex have deepened into something else. I want to give you pleasure and have you give me the same mutually. But if that is all it is between us, then I am not sure how long I can continue. As just an object I am finally not very much good. I want to show sympathy and understanding for you as needed, and have you do the same with me if you are up for that at all.

FOUR

If all of this feels like a big imposition on you, then I sincerely apologize for my words and will step back. I do not want to lose you or your friendship, but in this case speaking from my heart is all I really have going for me. With my best, Jake G.

*

The first thing Ian asked when he called was what Jake meant in his letter by "performance issues." Well, Jake said, some of the trouble over his erection when they got ready for fucking had come up again. Or more to the point <u>not</u> come up. Though on both occasions he and the boyfriend got through it OK, since he had no trouble getting hard when the boyfriend sucked him, and sucking while he jacked off seemed to be the boyfriend's preferred way of getting his own nut anyway.

Ian said, "Tell me this. Given that you're making love with some regularity these days with a woman and with a man, which do you like better?"

"It's about the same." Jake considered for a moment. "No, I think at the moment making love to the boyfriend—if it's going right—that's more exciting, more satisfying. Maybe because it's still so new."

"It might come across as somewhat confrontational, your letter."

"Does it sound like I'm threatening? 'Come across with the emotions buddy pal or I'll stop seeing you?'"

"Yes. But I don't think that's a reason not to send it," said Ian.

So Jake went ahead.

And for a week now had heard nothing back.

Lucky that there was movement in other areas of life, a lot of it, so he didn't have much time to dwell on the silence on the Guy Baer front.

No contracts yet, but it looked like Northwestern was going to go with Mike Tanner for the Belknap Labs, which might end up a 38 million dollar job. Either that, or the fuckers were leading Mike and him down the garden path, getting huge amounts of time estimating and expertise out of them for what still might turn out to be free. The harsh words with the Miller brothers over their foundation (at one point he'd told them it wasn't his fault they'd chosen to build in a swamp) caused Jake to pass the day-to-day management of the job along to John Heinemann. They were well up out of the ground now, a significant skeleton against the sky, which brought the Millers some relief and cheered them up. Kevin Tanner continued to practice browning his nose with them, in Jake's opinion good use of the boy's talents.

And on the home front a cold truce had descended, based on no grievances getting aired. Since their fight over the seven thousand dollar draw on the new plastic taken out behind his back, indications were Angie had stopped going to Wilmette to experiment on different cookie doughs with her mother. No further word concerning the fate of Alice's business, and Jake didn't feel like asking. A credit for the exact amount of the Viking stove appeared on the card's next statement, leading him to believe it had been returned. But when he went one Saturday to pick Lisa up from her grandmother's, he saw it through the kitchen window still in place in all its burnished chrome glory. So the old girl must have come up with a check for the amount to repay Angie. Alice fed Lisa out the side door, no invitation to come in, all Mrs. Huffy and the big malocchios with him. It hardly mattered. If you were more or less permanently on Alice Moore's shit list, who cared what your current ladder position might be?

In the first week in June, the household in Skokie expanded. Now that Luz was speaking more English, Angie admitted Jake had been right all along. There were two boys and a husband or at least some kind of boyfriend down in the city. Not clear who actually watched out for her kids when Luz slept over at the Guaranis, possibly the boyfriend's mother. But when parochial school let out, Luz was suddenly in a bind. Angie set it up nicely, bringing Luz to Jake in the kitchen Saturday morning, making her ask if it would be all right for her sons to stay with her in her room sometimes during the summer. They were very quiet, she promised, and wouldn't get in any trouble.

His OK must have been pro forma, since Luz's boys arrived later that afternoon, driven out by the "husband" in a no-muffler junker and deposited at the curb in front of the house. Jake spoke a little with the man, who shook hands and volunteered his name was "Chember." Definitely the skinny guy Jake had noticed when he picked Luz up that first time back in February. Chember made no move to help bring the boys' stuff up to the house. You didn't need Spanish to figure out he and Luz were pissed at each other. The boys seemed to want to say goodbye to the man, but when the moment came they stayed by their mother with their heads turned into her skirts and he drove off without a word to anybody.

Jake ended up feeling quite at ease about having the second little family under his roof. The boys, Alonso and Beto, were close in age, probably five and six, a little younger than Lisa. Like their mother, they were experts at making themselves virtually invisible. They took to the deep shaded yard behind the house and the weeds and brambles by the back fence where Lisa and her friends hardly went. From his bedroom Jake would catch a glimpse of them galloping after butterflies or little white moths or sitting up rocking in the lower branches of the trees. Occasionally in the late afternoon or early evening Beto at least would play a little catch with Jake. One day when Luz had gone to the supermarket with Angie Jake pushed into the cramped little back room to check on the sleeping arrangements there. Luz had made what looked like nests with blankets on the floor on either side of the single bed. Jake found an inflatable mattress he used sometimes for camping, pumped it up and showed Luz how it could stow under the bed and be pulled out for the boys at night.

And then—surprise!—Angie got herself more or less real work. They were in bed, lights out, windows open but with a sheet and a comforter pulled up to their shoulders, touching, when she presented the fact to him, tentatively, almost as though she'd done something wrong. Receptionist and scheduler at a therapy center, recommended by her shrink. It was only 30 hours a week, so no benefits, but she'd be off by three and home probably around the time he was. Not at all up to the level of the job she'd had in California, and the pay was, well, diddle of course, but it should help out some—

"No, honey, it's great!" He kissed her and stroked her hair and then put his arms around her.

"Maybe it'll lead to something better—"

The Monday she started, coming out of the shower Jake found their bed empty and Angie downstairs in her bathrobe making coffee. He broke his routine to sit with her at the kitchen table and have a cup. Silly of her, she said, the office didn't open until nine but she kept waking up worrying about what to wear and what kind of time she would need to get ready.

She was one of those lucky people who look good from the moment they first get up. Even with her hair falling down over her face and still yawning some, she drew Jake's attention. When he got up to put his cup on the drain board, she rose too and he embraced her and nuzzled at the hollow of her neck and then kissed her, slipping his hand in at the v of her robe, cupping her breast a long moment and thumbing her nipple a bit.

*

It felt as though Guy always got in touch when Jake was least expecting him. Off the beat. In this case, in the middle of the Monday start-up hustle asking was he free for lunch. Jake couldn't go, he was booked solid through the day. So they made a plan for Tuesday. OK. Bigelow's? No, Guy would prefer something called Maitre Jacques, which Jake had passed any number of times but had never been in. Not a problem, though, since the French place was just about the same number of minutes from work for him more to the north than Bigelow's. Dumpy, comic-looking squat building marooned in the middle of its own big macadam parking lot at a busy intersection, fake shake roof, low cottage-style diamond-paned windows, window boxes stocked with weather-beaten plastic geraniums. A tunnel of striped canvas awning up to the entrance.

Guy was already seated at a table in the back, blazer and tie, nursing a drink. He asked what Jake would have and Jake went for a bourbon on the rocks.

As he slid into his seat, Jake ventured, "I'm really glad to see you."

"I'm glad to see you too," said Guy.

A different, more casual tone than Jake's. What Jake <u>meant</u> (what he wished he could spill out) was that in the second of the two weeks since emailing his little note he partly—sometimes wholly—came to believe he would never hear from Guy Baer again. And here he was, catching just the faintest whiff of bay rum coming off the big beautiful man across the table.

"I got your photographs."

"Yes?"

"Excellent. Thank you. Where were those taken? It looked like you were in a hotel corridor somewhere."

"I was."

"And who took them?"

"My wife."

Guy laughed. "You must have been having a good time."

"We were, actually. Yes."

Guy was waiting, so Jake shrugged a little and went on. "We got a little get-away dropped on us out of the blue. My mother-in-law had an early Sunday a.m. flight to New York so she booked herself into the Intercontinental out by O'Hare for the night before. But by the time she made up her mind to go another day, they wouldn't cancel the room reservation. So she called and offered it to us."

"Nice. So did you woo your wife with dinner and drinks?"

"Not really. She was up for it from the beginning. Although I did take her out and there were some cocktails involved." Jake paused, grinned. "Actually, she suggested we go to Bigelow's."

"What'd you say to that?"

"I told her no way, no atmosphere and no real wine list. Would have been just my luck to get a waitress who'd want to know where my regular buddy was tonight."

"And how did you end up in the hotel corridor in only your towel?"

What was going on here, Guy pumping him for details? Way back the man had asked did Jake have a nude photo he could take with him when he went on the road. Jake had tried to shoot some, but couldn't figure how to hold the camera far enough away or how to turn off the flash, so each time he was scowling and his chest and his crotch washed out.

So what did it matter? If you're happy to show the fucker your body, why withhold intimacies with Angie, especially if it would please Guy to hear about them, maybe give him some ideas?

"One thing about my wife is she's never been at all hoity-toity about the juices. In fact, I've probably been a little behind her on that one. But I'm learning, maybe from you—"

"How's that?"

Jake lowered his voice. "You know, sucking you off…it's made me more willing to go down on her when my own stuff's still all around. So after we'd been having intercourse I was down there doing her and all of a sudden she's up and getting her iPhone off the dresser and wants to take pictures of the whole thing."

"So one thing led to another?"

"Yeah. Not exactly new territory for us. In fact in a Marriott one time Angie was entirely nude pushing the 'UP' button at the elevator and leaning forward to show off her ass and the minute I took the picture the doors shoot open and a plump old guy with a brief case is standing there. His eyes nearly bug out of his head and he says, 'Oops, sorry, wrong floor I guess!'"

At the Intercontinental Jake used the video option for a little drama where Angie in nothing but her teddy stood knocking impatiently at their room door, sucking her fingers, locating her brown nipples under the sheer pink, not getting an answer. Slowly peeling off the teddy, knocking again, winking at the camera, briefly fingering herself, rapping more urgently. In the background suddenly the whoops and shouts of high school prom kids down below in the hotel patio.

She wanted to repeat the sequence with Jake as the cheesecake but him trying to look seriously horned up and fishing after his cock, coyly letting his towel slip and bending over to show his hairy crack—it was all too much and once they both started laughing he couldn't get back a straight face. So Angie switched the phone camera back to stills and caught him leaning against the wall next to their door naked, head half turned away, squeezing his revived dick in his fist in one, lifting and squeezing and showing off his nuts in the other.

"I nearly fucked up when I was sending you those."

"How was that?"

"After we got home, my wife was outside with our little girl and I went in her purse for her phone, but I had to put you into her contacts in order to email you the pictures. So I heard them coming in the house then and I put the phone back and then it was a couple hours before I remembered I needed to go in and take you off her list."

"Well that's good." Guy sighed. A silence fell between them, perhaps a moment of contemplation. Then Guy said, brightly, "I got your email too."

"You did? OK. And what? I offended you."

"No, on the contrary." Guy looked at him, down at his drink, back up. "About our being friends? I don't think there's any issue there, really. Perhaps against the odds we have <u>become</u> friends and there it is, right? I care about you too, Jake."

"Why 'against the odds'? Because of the great divide between our circumstances?"

"That's not what I meant at all. 'Against the odds' because we started out as no-strings fuck buddies as they so elegantly call it, and then at least on my side—and I'm presuming on yours too—it all just deepened on us."

"Yes," Jake said, "on my part for sure."

"I take great pleasure from your company, you know."

"Do you? I'm never sure."

"Even after some of the things I've said to you?"

What things? In the moment, the only one Jake could remember was 'you're the best thing that's ever happened to me.' He wished he had some kind of mind control at his beck and call to get Guy to say it again right now.

"You didn't figure a nail pounder can need as much reassuring as anybody else, did you?"

Guy said in a very low voice, "I've never thought of you as a nail pounder, Jake."

Jake shrugged, looked away. The waiter, a white-haired, wiry old fellow, was bearing down on them with a little tray. On it perched only his drink, the liquid shivering.

Guy waited until Jake had taken a big slug of bourbon, then said, "I suppose you've figured out it's one of my faults. Both my wives have complained about it."

"What is?"

"I'm just not very demonstrative. I think a lot more nice things than I can ever bring myself to say. I suppose that's my upbringing reasserting itself."

The cold lady at the foot of the grand staircase telling Jake where she wanted him to set down his flowers.

"Not a lot of pats on the back when I was growing up either," Jake said.

"Yet you're entirely able to express affection."

"To you maybe."

"When I was a boy my father was not allowed to smoke in the house. So every evening no matter what the weather he took his after-supper cigar out on the verandah. One night when I was fourteen or so he asked me to accompany him. Very unusual occurrence. We took a turn up and down and then he stopped and said Mother had informed him that I had started seeing girls. I admitted I had, a little. Another turn up and down in silence. Stop. And Dad said, 'Well, son, just don't end up with a millstone around your neck,' stumped out his cigar in the ashtray and went back in the house. His one and only contribution to my sex education."

After the waiter had taken their order, Guy said, "I don't think I told you, I've been seeing a psychiatrist again a little."

"Yeah? What for?"

"Not for the first time, of course. More of an ongoing motif in my life, therapy. In this instance, because I began wondering why the passive element is so persistent in me."

"What does that mean?"

"Don't you think there's something a little odd about a fairly effective man of the world who, when it comes to bedtime, only wants to lie down and take it up the ass?"

Jake thought, Why not play to your strengths, stay with what you do well? But after a small hesitation he said, "No, I don't see what's odd about that at all."

"Though you yourself aren't into it—"

"Getting fucked? No." Though he spoke barely above a whisper, Jake was suddenly grateful they were in a dark corner of an almost empty dining room. Up by the cash register a man in his shirtsleeves was bent to a little radio tuned to baseball. "I've thought about it, though, I mean I've begun thinking about it."

"You have?" Guy smiled broadly.

Confession time. The moment seemed right. Jake mentioned an afternoon a couple months back when they'd had their fun and were lying there, Guy behind nuzzling at his neck, licking and kissing at his shoulder. Then Jake noticed Guy had hardened some and was pressing it up against Jake's butt crack and Jake pressed back, squirmed a little.

"At the time I was thinking I wouldn't mind having you inside me at all."

Though in reality the impulse passed quickly. A little later they were just casually making out when Jake felt Guy's wet finger pushing against his hole, insistent, so he loosened himself to help let it in. But Guy was rough and jabbed at him and very soon Jake's ass began to sting, then hurt. He didn't say anything, but he was put off and rolled away, then abruptly got up off the bed.

"Do you talk to him about me?"

"Who?"

"Your shrink."

"It's a woman. Well yes, of course, you come up. As part of my life."

Part? He fixed on that, missing entirely what Guy was saying next. Hurt in the depths of himself where he wanted Guy entirely to himself. To be the one and only. It manifested as pain in his chest, constriction in his throat. Part. Partial. Incomplete. Unfulfilled... And at the same time his reasonable, stand-aside self continued saying, 'Nope. Never can be. Forget it, pal. You don't even really want that...' and on and on.

At the end of the meal, as they were getting up to leave, Jake said quietly, "I have the room booked if you want to go there."

Guy stopped, looked a little surprised, touched Jake's elbow. "Oh." They started forward again. "Actually, I was thinking maybe we should skip it for today. I should have said something earlier."

"No, no, it's OK—"

"Don't put any meaning on it, will you? It's just I have so much on my plate right now—I'm so preoccupied—I don't think it would be end up being much fun for either of us."

Jake said, "I understand."

A little too abruptly, causing Guy to sneak another glance at him.

They came out from the darkness into brilliant early afternoon sun. Even with traffic all around, what was it that smelled so sweet on the air? Way over by the fence Jake spotted a long hedge of lilacs in full-on bloom. Jake's truck and Guy's Beamer parked close by each other were almost the only cars in the lot.

"One of my current headaches—" But then Guy stopped.

"Is what?"

"But I don't need to lay all of this off on you."

"I'm fine, man. Whatever you want to tell me."

"Well it's something where maybe you could advise me. Remember I told you my sisters and my brother were enthusiastic about the renovation of my parents' place?"

"Yes."

"Well, they've decided to move ahead whether I want them to or not. And my wife, being unemployed at the moment, she's taken it on as her cause too. So I am effectively defeated on that one. It'll happen whether I drag my feet or not."

"But then what kind of advice do you need from me?"

"Mike Tanner is one of the companies they're going to get a bid from. Fellow named Pat Nellums is the contact. You know him I assume?"

Jake nodded. "Not the greatest, but it doesn't really matter. We'd do you a good job. You want me to keep an eye on it?"

"No, Jake. I want you to stay clear of it, OK? You being involved would be a little close for comfort, don't you think?"

"Oh yes, of course."

"Though it would be helpful to me if I could come to you with some questions from time to time."

"Sure. Whenever you wish."

Jake sat in the Toyota and watched Guy buzz out of the lot into the stream of cars going east. One-thirty. He had cleared his schedule until 3 PM, so he did what he knew he shouldn't do. He drove to the motel anyway, got the keys, put down cash as always.

Except for the one with the super Jacussi, the rooms were all too much alike. He couldn't tell if he and Guy had occupied this one before or not. He left the blinds shut, put a bedside lamp on low, lay on the bed. He had promised himself he would just jack off and then leave, so he lowered his pants and underpants to his knees and started playing with himself. But the feeling of defeat blanketed everything, made the fucking room seem darker and dingier than it was. His thoughts included the suspicion that despite the pledges of undying friendship Guy was in the opening stages of pulling away from him. Jake lay there staring at the ceiling and fiddling with his noodle, but nothing came of it. He wondered what would happen if he couldn't summon the nerve to get up. The maids will find you in the morning lying like this. Better at least pull your shorties up.

Then he slept. Ten minutes or so. And woke because his tears tickled as they ran down the sides of his face in the direction of his sideburns and his ears.

FIVE

Jake and Lewis Keyes were sitting in the yellow, beery gloom of a downtown Evanston tavern. Behind Jake occasionally the bar's front doors swung open and there would be a flash of the brighter, cleaner late June afternoon light. Some of the patrons seemed to shrink from it like snails with salt sprinkled on them.

He had acted impulsively, Jake said. Or was it compulsively? Whatever. Got himself drawn in on the Baers pretty much without thinking. Standing there jawing with Cheryl Oliviero in the main office reception area and watching Nellums and Tanner Junior in the conference room with three what must be new clients, two middle-aged women with severely short-cut hair and big pocketbooks and a man with a baby-sized tummy under his buttoned linen jacket and his hands in the pockets of his khakis. All standing, Nellums and Junior fawning, oiling, touching shoulders, bending to point out things on the plans unrolled on the table. Something familiar Jake couldn't place about the man and one of the women, not their looks but maybe the loose-jointed way they stood, the snatches of their voices coming through the glass. Him going in caused all five heads to bob up expectantly and Kevin and Pat at once to become annoyed. And then about the second woman, the skinny more elegant one, Jake suddenly felt dread.

"'Uh, and this is Jake Guarani, one of our project managers,' Kevin said because he had to. But he didn't seem to feel any need to introduce the new customers. Not that it mattered," Jake continued, "since all I needed by then to confirm my suspicions was one peek down at the corner of the top document, which read, 'BAER FAMILY RETREAT CENTER'."

Lewis grinned, raised his big winglike white eyebrows. "So. The wolf finally moves in among the sheep."

"Who? What do you mean?" Jake said. Then thought, laughed curtly. "Oh. I'm the wolf? I guess. You could say that. Not that I meant any harm. I wasn't in the room more than two minutes, but pretty much every five seconds I'd get another hit off the brother and the sister. Not that they look like Guy really, but their wrists, the little crinkle around their eyes, all the details are same same. They talk like him, they walk like him—shit, they smell like him. I'd swear Sis dips in the bay rum same as the boys."

"And the wife?"

"Beautiful in her way, I'd say. Or at least classy. But my guess is cold as a walk-in refrigerator. And nothing much to hold on to on a winter night." Jake ducked his head, took a sip out of his beer without lifting the glass off the table, and said, very low, "I'd for sure be the superior fuck. If I went in for that kind of thing."

Lewis said, "But you do, don't you?"

Big grin and bright eyes from Jake, meaning yes indeed. "I did get the sister's attention," he said.

"How was that?"

"There were a couple copies of old photographs of the big house lying around on the table, so I picked one up and said to her all casual, 'Pearson, right? And he designed the original enlargement too I believe.' Quite amazed and gratified her and made Nellums and Junior all twitchy. They couldn't figure what in hell I'd done to get her focused on me that way."

"Let's go back on the wife for a moment. Did she stir anything in you?"

"How do you mean?"

"Sexually."

"No, I told you. Cold. Stringy. Not my type at all. Why'd you ask that?"

"It happens," Lewis said, "doesn't it? The intense desire a person has for a partner migrates—in fantasy at least—into desire for the partner's partner?"

"Maybe in the gay world."

"Specific to us? You think?"

Jake smirked, looked down, looked past Lewis to customers at other tables. Lewis waited and after about ten seconds Jake said, "OK, so I did end up sort of thinking about her—the wife. I guess I had some dream where I was lying next to them watching Guy up on her going at it—it was the middle of the night—and then when I went into the bathroom to relieve myself the whole thing kind of 'migrated' as you said into him and me taking turns with her—"

"'Relieve' yourself. You mean to pee?"

"Come on, man! To whack off. Do I have to spell everything out for you?"

"Maybe you do. Him and you mounting her and then— What?"

"Well," Jake hesitating, "well finally I got a really big charge out of imagining I was putting it to her with her all wet with Guy's jizz. You know—"

"Yes, I do know," Lewis said, solemnly but also kindly.

Jake's eyes narrowed. "You are a fucking <u>know-it-all</u>, aren't you?" His voice was even.

Lewis laughed a little. "I suppose, yes. But what in particular brings forth that unpleasant judgment at the moment?"

"Fishing around in my head till you came up with me balling the wife. Even you knowing the fantasy was in there."

"But that's my business, Jake. Isn't it?"

"I guess." Jake shot back his sleeve, glanced at his watch. "I need to get out of here."

"OK. But if you have even a moment, I have one more thing I don't want to leave hanging."

"Go ahead."

"You know most gay men think bisexual men are really gay men who can't get off the fence because they don't want to lose their privileges as heterosexuals."

"Yeah? And what are those? Do I rate some kind of discount I haven't been putting in for?"

"You could put it that way, yes. All the advantages and prestige you get out of being a 'real man' that I for example don't get by dint of being a homo."

"I don't see any way in which you aren't a real man."

"Well thanks."

"And when it comes to 'advantages' and 'prestige' Mister Harvard professor and author—"

"Jake? What about you climbing down off the soapbox and letting me get to what I wanted to say in the first place?"

"OK. I can do that. Shoot!"

"Despite what the general run of gay men may believe, I'm of the other opinion."

"That there really are some real, dyed-in-the-wool bisexuals?"

"Yes. And I also think, in spite of what some people would imagine the advantages to be, that it's not an easy row for anyone to have to hoe."

"And you're telling me all this because—?"

"Because—"

The waitress was going by balancing a tray full of glasses and bottles. Jake touched her arm and made a scribbling motion in the air and she smiled and nodded and went on. "So?" Jake asked. "Oh. I get it. Because you think I must be one."

He leaned in across the table, head down but eyes up on Lewis. He said very softly, "Know what that tells me?"

"No, what?"

"It tells me you're coming on to me. You want me."

Lewis let a moment go by, then said, "Yes, of course. You know that. You've known that. But—"

"What?"

"You also know if it doesn't happen I won't die."

"Oh it'll happen, don't you doubt it. Just give me some time, man. I've got a lot on my plate right now. You know that. OK?"

The waitress was back, but as a torso only, her head above the cone of light the lamp cast on their table. She fished in the pocket of her little white apron, pulled out a wad of checks, thumbed through, found theirs and laid it down. Jake snatched it up, reached for his wallet.

"Personally I hate the labels," he said. "Hetero, homo, bi— I'm sexual, man. Man, woman, dog or cat, whatever appeals. Fuck, I wish—"

"What? What do you wish, Jake?"

"Sometimes I wish we lived on a planet where you could have sex and be in love with people, with a bunch of people if you wanted to be, and no one would think <u>anything</u> about it. Or about <u>you</u> for being that way."

Lewish sighed and smiled.

"What you so amused about now?"

"There are some things—this one for example—where your mind and mine run so very close together," Lewis said. "It's a pleasure."

"For me too. Tell me this. What was it Ian said about me when he called you?"

"Simply that his best pal maybe stood in need of help sorting things out, and I told him if a little talk now and then was anything that interested you, I'd be glad to."

When Lewis finally retired from Harvard and moved out to Jay Carlson's floor-through lakefront apartment in Hyde Park both Chicago and Northwestern offered him honorary appointments. Teach a graduate seminar or not or just be a 'presence' in the psych department sort of thing. Because Jay was still on the faculty at Chicago, Lewis took the Northwestern deal. It gave him an office but put him up at the Evanston campus only when he chose to go. To arrange an hour or so mid-to-late afternoon with Jake proved easy. They sat out in patios or at the little streetside tables of sandwich shops or ducked into near-empty bars and had a beer. Sometimes like aimless teenagers they looped around through the shady residential streets of north Evanston and Wilmette, Jake at the wheel occasionally pointing out the landmarks of his childhood, where his school had been, his sister's house, his parents' railroad apartment.

He had no trouble detailing for Lewis the fraught relationship with the man Jake at first called "the boyfriend." When he slipped and blurted Guy's name, he swore Lewis to secrecy and then became even more trusting. Some of Lewis's insights were really helpful, even if the man himself said they were really only old clichés of gay life.

The bottom is really always in charge.

Of course. Why hadn't he thought of that himself? Completely the case between him and Guy. The reason he felt so powerless and frustrated sometimes. The reason on occasion he fucked the man so relentlessly.

"Does he like it that way?" Lewis asked.

"Seems to."

"But not so satisfactory for you, right?"

"It's not? You could have fooled me."

"You don't sometimes want to just be gentle with him? Please him that way?"

"Well sure. Shit, man! And that happens too sometimes, you know. More often that not, really."

"I hope you're aware that you put the entire blame for the fact you can't break through to a greater intimacy with your lover on yourself."

Jake said, "Where else would it go?"

"People deal in different ways with sexual feelings they have which don't fit their image of themselves. Some men put all their same-sex stuff in a box and only allow the sex part, never the feelings. If they insist on compartmentalizing that way, they're not ever going to make great buddies and pals."

"I was good at that—compartmentalizing..." Jake said. "Once..."

He refused, however, to take to the notion that he might never get from Guy Baer the combination of camaraderie and good sex he longed for. "What I have with you," he told Lewis.

"What's that?"

"Ease. I feel I can talk about anything with you."

"Well good."

"Much better than I can talk with him, God knows."

"Well, there was some kind of charge between us from the beginning, wasn't there?"

Lewis gazed directly at him, a fond look Jake found himself returning, even though it was a little embarrassing. "I'm glad you remember that," he said.

"What in particular?"

"You standing there in the attic at Pine Street the afternoon of the wedding having Ian fix your tie while I dawdled through drying myself and then let the towel go so you could get a look at the goods."

"Is that always your mode?" Lewis asked.

"My mode of what?"

"Seduction."

"You know what they say about us Italians."

"I know some of the commonplaces. Which one were you thinking of?"

"Your Italian is always <u>on</u>."

Lewis laughed, but Jake's expression immediately turned dark. "Except the ones who're not. Italians who are always <u>off</u>. My parents for example."

*

Was Angie learning not to go behind his back? Or just becoming tired of Jake yelling and making a scene when she did? And what did it matter if the effect was the same?

She wanted Luz to have a cell phone, which seemed stupid to Jake. The girl was always around the house when they needed her, and though she shied away from answering the land line she would pick it up when she had to. When she and her boys were down in the city on her day off, there was a number where she could be reached. But Angie said sometimes if she called from her office Luz was out in the yard or down the street with Lisa, and it made her—Angie—anxious, panicky even.

It seemed to Jake a new variation on Angie's need to keep the umbilical cord to her daughter in place, but he said OK, go on and get the damned thing and put Luz on their plan. Jake was going to warn the girl about finding any calls to Guatemala on the monthly bill, but then while he was waiting for the opportunity, he began to notice how much the new cell delighted Luz and her boys. When it went off in the pocket of her apron—Alonso had found her the marimba ringtone—both kids gathered round to watch their mother answer and talk. Jake didn't want to be a spoilsport. Calls down to Chicago weren't going to break him, so he let the lecture about Guatemala go.

In mid-July Angie went up to Delavan for two and-a-half days to help old Alice straighten up her vacation place between groups of summer renters. Lisa got left behind so she could go to the birthday party of one of her little friends Saturday afternoon. Luz would be around the whole weekend and at least for the record Jake away from the house only for supper that evening with John Heinemann.

Poor John. Apparently after 30-some years of what seemed an OK marriage, his wife had decided she wanted out. The kids were grown and gone, so there was nothing John could think to do but take a furnished apartment and for the time being let his wife have the house. A kind of terrible heaviness had settled in on him. Maybe others didn't notice the change—John had always been short on chitcat—but it was a change painful to see if you knew him as well as Jake did.

The sun was just down and the long summer evening setting in when, after calling for her inside, Jake finally located Luz out back of the house. The whole time he was talking to her she nodded and smiled in her usual way, but remained with her little phone up to her ear. Not that there was a lot to tell her. Maybe time to go around to the next block and walk Lisa home…he himself might be a little late getting in…

All through pizza and beer, Jake couldn't make up his mind whether to bring John Heinemann onboard as his cover. It was so unlikely

Angie would ever check on how he occupied a Saturday night when she was away. And besides, he appreciated having John's respect. Their confidence in each other was a thing of almost twenty years. When Mike Tanner bumped Jake a step up above him, Heinemann showed no sign of being pissed, assured Jake his promotion was entirely deserved.

Jake waited, hardly able to think about anything else while their talk with all its pauses and spaces went jerking along, the usual slow freight. They were back pulled up in front of John's building, the man himself half out of the truck when Jake finally popped the question. "John, if anyone were to ask, would you mind telling them we were out together until somewhat later tonight?"

John consulted his watch. "It's quarter to nine now. How late do you want? I'm not much of a night owl anymore, you know."

"Midnight maybe?"

"I can do that." John was amused. "That's one I wouldn't even have to confess I don't think. Not anyone I know, is it?"

"No."

"Not Cheryl?"

"Office Cheryl? She's a kid, John."

"She's twenty. She makes up to you."

"Aww, come on. Really?"

"Don't say you haven't noticed."

Jake shook his head. He liked Cheryl, she seemed to like him. There had been a time, he was pretty sure, that he could have gotten it on with Olivia, Cheryl's mom.

"I had not in fact noticed, John. God's truth."

Easy as drawing Heinemann in proved, on his way to Winnetka Jake felt no particular relief. In movies and in books there were people who suddenly—bang!—gave up on a hot affair when the weight of their lies threatened to crush them. The reverend, the one he and Ian called Dimwitty when they were forced to plough through The Scarlet Letter in ninth grade, the guy with the tell-tale welt of the red "A" surfacing on his chest right over his heart. Sometimes it was the innocence of a little child—a daughter especially—that triggered recalling a man to his better self. If Jake had been screwing other women on the side maybe he'd want to renounce. But giving up the ladies had been a conscious sacrifice made in the full flush of love when he married Angie and he remained proud of the fact he'd never welshed on that promise to himself. About older men Jake did not find in himself any need to reform. He only wished in exchange for the skulking around and the little tricks to cover his tracks he was getting a bigger payoff with Professor Baer. More bang for the buck, you could call it.

Except for no fire in the fireplace on such a warm summer night, Guy had set his living room up pretty much the way it had been the first time Jake came over, shutters back to reveal the bar, full ice bucket, even the same old monks chanting away in their echo chamber on the hidden speakers. The sloppy, liguor-tasting way Guy went about the introductory kiss made Jake ask, "How long you been at it?"

"Couple hours. Suddenly it was evening and I didn't have a thing on the agenda but to wait for you."

"Sorry. I got here as quick as I could."

"It's not a problem."

Guy had learned by now that Jake preferred bourbon over scotch. While he was making drinks, Jake surveyed the big room again. The three Mary Cassatts were clearly markers of Guy. But the rest of it? Guy might be a neat person, but all the sleek polished glass and buffed wood surface, the near-emptiness, reminded Jake of nothing but the tailored no-quarter severity of the wife, her clothes.

He downed one generous bourbon on the rocks and held his glass out for Guy to refill.

"No need to try catching up to me."

"But I might want to," Jake said. "Just for the hell of it."

New drinks in hand, they wandered to the Lake side of the room and out through French doors onto a flagstone patio overlooking the water where there were two wood-framed adjustable chaise lounges with thick yellow pads. The little trilling and sucking sounds of the waves coming onshore ran up to them from below. It was not yet entirely dark.

Though warmed up some by the alcohol, Jake couldn't think of anything much to say. He stood close to Guy and put his arm around him. Guy laughed a little and Jake lowered his hand and ran it over Guy's butt, squeezing some.

"How's it going about you and your feminine impulses?"

"What? I don't quite understand."

Jake slipped his hand flat to get into Guy's pants and under the elastic of his shorts and touched warm, reassuring flesh. "You told me you and your new psychiatrist were exploring why there was a part of you that wanted to be passive and feminine."

"Oh that." Guy laughed again. "That didn't prove a very productive avenue of inquiry. She's more onto me now about whether I mightn't be happier if I were to clean up my act some."

"What would that entail? For openers, getting rid of me I suppose."

"No, Jake, no. More simply about me becoming more honest. The therapist wants me to think through what it would be like if I told my wife about the men in my life."

"Men? I didn't know I had competition."

"You don't. Don't be so prickly! I meant telling her my history."

"And exactly what good would that do? I thought you told me your wife was pretty invested in herself being a 'real' woman married to a 'real' man."

"Yes. But if I open up to her, then at least she'll know she's not the reason I've shown so little sexual interest in her for so long now."

"And that'll make her feel better?"

"It could."

"And then that's it? All she wrote? End of marriage? End of story?"

"Not necessarily. Laura and I have a lot of other things which bind us together—"

<u>Your</u> money for example, Jake thought.

But Guy had another inventory to trot out—their daughters, their various projects, the respect between them and the blah blah. Jake withdrew his hand from Guy's pants.

"Have you ever thought of it?"

"Thought of what?"

"Telling your wife?"

"About you?"

"About yourself."

"No."

"Not a possibility?"

"No way, man."

The same fool thing friend Ian had proposed.

What happens to a married professor and dean or whatever who suddenly decides to come flaming out of the closet? Jake didn't really know, but his suspicion was the answer was a big 'NOTHING.' While in his own world— He could see Nellums and the whole cadre of office fucks peering at him as though he was an escapee from the Lincoln Park Zoo. Mike! How would Mike Tanner take the news? And the guys on the job? Not even to start on trying to imagine Angie's face…although for some reason he could clearly see Alice Moore's little walnut mug scrunching up, her barking 'I knew it! I knew it!'

"Well," Guy said, "still. You might want to think about it."

"You know what I've been thinking about?"

"What?"

"How would it be if we were to make love out here? In the moon-light."

Guy looked up, looked all around. "I don't see any moon, Jake."

"Well?"

Guy put his hand out for Jake's glass. "I'll get you another and the stuff."

The CD player inside groaned and ground and changed and one of the old big bands with a girl singer came on. The tune? 'It Had to Be You.' Very unsettled, itchy-feeling by now, Jake tried to think it through, though his mind was in a kind of dreamy, detached state of its own. Guy who had seemed such a gift in the beginning. Was he more of a curse, a stone put in Jake's path by some weirdo of fate? A mountain it <u>looked</u> in the beginning as though the little guy could get to the top of, but then half way up the iciness underfoot made him realize this wasn't any decent mountain, it was a goddamn glacier, and besides, the evil tricksters hadn't given him enough oxygen to go the distance and he was going to run out.

Guy returned in a long blue-striped bathrobe bearing a wooden tray—two old fashioned glasses generously full up, the scotch slightly lighter than the bourbon, a white tube of K-Y, Kleenex, a small shiny array of condom packets. He set down his tray on a little metal table and as he was straightening Jake grabbed him and turned him and kissed him hard, pushing him back against one of the lounge chairs so its legs skittered against the flagstones emitting a high-pitch squeal.

"Why don't you just kneel here on the edge of this thing and I'll have you that way."

"You want the robe off?"

Jake considered as he undid his belt and started kicking off his shoes. "No, leave it. You're fine as you are."

Guy was right, no moon, but there was light enough to see. Jake liked the man's position, the robe bunched up at his waist the way a horny woman's dress might get. He also liked being outdoors for once and Guy wiggling his ass and grunting to show how much he liked it.

"Been a while, hasn't it?" Jake said, leaning over.

"Way too long in my opinion."

"You comfortable?" Guy's knees and elbows were on the yellow cushion.

"Very."

"Let's try this then—"

He unplugged, holding the condom securely to the base of his cock, and said, "Roll over, man, and put your legs up and I think I'll be able to make it, OK?"

"Yes, sure."

Guy moved to flip quicker than Jake expected and his elbow struck across Guy's face as he came up. The blow made a little crack-ing sound. Guy first winced, very startled, then moaned. Blood flowed from his nose and he cried, "Jesus!"

"Oh man!" Jake reached for whatever was handy—the snake of Guy's robe belt lying across the yellow—but the man himself already had his sleeve up to his nose. A dark patch bloomed and widened across the cloth.

"You OK?"

"No. It feels like I've broken something," Guy said in a voice that sounded funny, blocked off. He started to try to get up.

"You stay. I'll get you ice."

Jake hurried in, got the ice bucket, ducked into the kitchen and grabbed a striped dish towel, ran back out to the patio. Guy was leaning forward, which he shouldn't be doing, one hand cradling the other and the robe sleeve up to his face.

"Put your head back. Look up at me here."

He scooped ice into the towel, folded it and gave it to Guy to hold up against his nostrils. The nose did in fact look out of alignment and already there was blue in by the bridge toward the man's eyes.

While he was finding Guy's clothes and getting him into them Jake mentioned Evanston Hospital, but Guy for some reason didn't want to go there. The next place Jake could think of was a doc-in-the-box out in Morton Grove, twenty minutes away. On the road, Guy sitting with his head back and pressing the ice towel to his face, Jake tried to apologize for his clumsiness. But Guy was having none of it. He blamed himself. They got at least a small laugh over what to tell the doctor if he should ask how all this had come about.

From the moment they walked in, everything about the clinic infuriated Jake. The name "Immediate Care" was the first and obvious lie. Every seat in the waiting area was taken. Banged-up suburb kids and their parents and old folks clutching at themselves. Though Guy was allowed to register and the girl at the desk efficiently took a swipe of his credit card, it was 40 minutes before they were shunted into a closet-sized examining room and Guy was allowed to lie down. Why all the suspicion about the idea of Jake being the patient's "friend?" Was he the first "friend" who had ever brought anyone in to this particular joint? The harried physician who came in finally was bald and bearded but otherwise had the undeveloped face of a 12-year-old. His voice even piped and scratched like a kid's.

He managed to get Guy's ice pack away from him and to ascertain there was no further blood to come, at least at the moment. The pronounced crook in the nose and the blue darkness which had now spread out and rimmed all under both of Guy's eyes made Jake let go a short inadvertent laugh.

"What's so funny?"

Jake shook his head and touched Guy's hand. "You look awful, man. Like someone slugged you."

The child posing as a medic said the nose would have to be X-rayed and would probably need to be set as well, things he didn't have the facility to do here and which could wait until after the weekend anyway. He cleaned off dry blood, laid gauze and tape, making a fairly large white mask across the Guy's face, and then shaped it with smaller lengths of tape so it came in under his nostrils. Baby doc promised the bandage should hold everything in place as long as Guy didn't bang anything a second time. He wrote out a prescription for some pain pills.

Guy needed the men's room and then had the bill to sign. The waiting room was just as crowded and noisy as before, though with an almost completely new set of sufferers, now more babbling teenagers on bad trips than old folks with their tickers and the kids with their cuts and scrapes. Jake stepped outside into the night air to wait, almost without thought reaching in his pocket for his phone to check messages.

Four from Angie. Shit. The first two just missed calls 20 minutes apart while he was at Guy's, the third a half hour later with a recording: "Jake? Jake? Where are you? Call me please! There's something wrong at the house. I'm on the road down there now," and the last an hour later, "Where the fuck are you? The police are just pulling up now. I need you, Jake, I really do," her voice small.

He tried the house but the phone there just rang and rang. He called Angie on her cell, but she wasn't picking up. In the Toyota going back, Guy was at first silent, then complained about Jake driving so fast. Jake apologized, slowed for a mile, then noticed himself speeding up again. Then, as they got into Winnetka, Guy began to natter. The condoms and the grease left out on the patio…had Jake cleared any of that stuff before they left for the emergency room? No? Well thank God then they hadn't wanted to keep him overnight. What if his wife had beat him home? Hm? At the house, Guy was slow, a little unsteady getting out of the truck, fumble-bunny about finding his key. Jake walked him to the front door holding him by the arm.

"I'd come in but—"

"No, no, you've done plenty enough."

Was that supposed to be a joke? Above the bandage Guy's eyes only looked hurt, yet also strangely fierce, wounded. But then he recovered himself and said quickly, "I'll be fine now. Thanks for all your help."

"I'm really sorry—"

Guy stabbed at the keyhole a little, found it. Hearing the tumblers, Jake was ready to roll.

"Don't worry, I'll be fine," Guy repeated.

*

He tore home, not even bothering to phone there again. And though he tried to imagine what he would find, once he turned onto his own block the scene he came on still clutched him. An all-black Skokie police car was bumped up into the middle of his lawn, headlights flatly illuminating the whole front of the house, red and blue flashers still turning round and round. His front door was standing open. An ambulance waited half into his driveway, a kid in white in the driver's seat smoking. Clusters of neighbors stood back toward the trees, some of the ladies' nightgowns drooping below the raincoats or big sweaters they'd thrown on.

Jake was crossing the lawn when Lisa wandered out the front door in her pajamas, hair all mussed, face streaked red. She saw him but didn't seem to recognize him and so turned and wandered back into the house. By the time he got inside, she had disappeared. He heard Angie calling for her from the kitchen. In there two big Village officers in their deep blue at the counter, one with a notepad out, Angie sitting hunched on a stool with a glass of water in front of her. When Jake came in, both cops turned and the younger one stepped back and laid his hand on the pistol at his hip.

"Who're you?"

"I live here."

Angie looked up, blank. "He's my husband."

"Where's Luz?" Jake asked.

Angie just looked at him.

It turned out what must have been keeping Luz occupied while Jake was talking to her earlier was a breakup with Chember, the boyfriend or husband or whatever he was. According to what they could get out of the children—Lisa and Luz's boys, all three of them still freaked and teary—around suppertime Chember showed up and there was yelling and shouting in Luz's room and then Chember ran out and slammed the door and took off and Luz fell apart. The kids were playing and then as it got dark they were in watching TV and waiting for their dinner so they didn't see her, but it seemed she got into Jake's liquor cabinet and managed to consume about a half bottle of rum. She came out of the den crying and tearing at her hair and then she was tripping and falling down and "just acting scary" as Lisa said. Lisa took some cookies up to her room and got into bed and tried to put herself to sleep—not easy, since Luz was prowling up and down the upstairs hall moaning and talking to herself. Then Lisa smelled smoke and came back downstairs. Luz must have started to cook something and then forgot about it. A frying pan full of oil on the stove got so hot it caught fire. Lisa had the presence of mind to turn off the gas. The little boys were there crying and Luz was stumbling around the downstairs yelling in Spanish. She grabbed her boys and was trying to drag them with her down to her room. She had taken a big kitchen knife out of the drawer and the boys reported she kept telling them she just wanted to die. At that point Lisa ran in and tried to call Angie's cell but couldn't get her. (Angie, it seemed, had had enough of her own mom—why was never made especially clear to Jake—and was already on the way down from Wisconsin and temporarily out of cell signal range.) So Lisa called over to the Statens. Fred happened not to be working that evening so he jumped in his car and radioed his buds at the Skokie police on the way over and was first on the scene. When the Village cops showed up they helped him get the little boys out of Luz's clutches. Apparently she was so fucked up she started screaming again when they came into her room and struck at one of the officers with the knife. "Kinda frightening for a moment there, actually," Fred said, "hysterical woman coming at you that way." He and the police grabbed one of the blankets off her bed and threw it over her head and got some plastic cuffs on her and brought her out to the squad car.

Angie arrived about then. Loren Staten was already there and had Lisa and the little boys with her in the kitchen, trying to calm all three of them down with glasses of milk. The question then became what to do with Luz. Angie went out to see if she could talk with her, but Luz was all curled up on her side under the blanket in the back of the police car, hands tied in front of her. The police were willing to take her into custody, but preferred not to put her in the Skokie jail. A much better idea, they thought, if they could get her in the ambulance and take her to Cook County and see if those people could help her be more reasonable once she sobered up.

The paramedic with the ambulance said he lacked the authority to sedate the lady, so one of the officers agreed to ride along in back with Luz to the hospital. Jake walked with her as they led her out to the vehicle, trying to tell her everything was going to be all right, but she was still trembling and fearful and drunk and he doubted he was much help. When they started trying to push her down onto the gurney and get the straps over her, she struggled wildly, flailing her arms.

Once the ambulance was gone and the cops' headlights were off the front of the house, the Statens went out to encourage the other neighbors to leave. Jake could hear Fred repeating, 'OK folks, show's over, all over for this evening, thanks.' Angie disappeared upstairs with Lisa and Loren got out a broom and started sweeping up broken glass from the hall floor. Jake made a quick tour through the downstairs rooms. There was mess, chairs tipped over and end tables and one lamp broken and magazines strewn around, but otherwise not much real damage he could see. He thanked Loren and Fred and said he'd call and report in to them in the morning.

Nearly 2:30 a.m. when he finally got them on their way. The dead silence of the house suddenly seemed strange, suspicious. Jake was going through turning out lights and about to go up when he remembered Luz's boys. He went down and found the door into their room slightly ajar, a faint light inside. Alonso and Beto were half-sitting up on their mother's bed in their clothes holding each other. Both wide awake. They understood more English than their mother did, so Jake was able to tell them they should get undressed and under the covers and that their mother was going to be fine, in fact everything was going to be fine.

Neither of them moved.

They were right, of course. Nothing at all was going to be fine. Jake helped them get their shoes off and spread a blanket half over them. Then in a kind of sickening dread, he went back up into the house and tried Lisa's door. Locked. He went into his and Angie's room, shed his clothes in the dark and spread out on the bed. He didn't expect he would be able to drop off, and until first light in fact he didn't. When he started awake at seven, he was surprised he had slept at all.

He made coffee and waited, but by nine no one else had stirred. The door to Lisa's room stood open now, and she and her mother were gone. The only time they could have snuck off was in the dawn, during that hour-and-a-half Jake was passed out.

Not hard to figure out where they'd gone. Angie had women friends enough, but as far as Jake could tell not any she would ever want to bare her soul or share her troubles with. When she would threaten, "I'm going to——" and then pause, he would say, "What? Go on. You're going home to the old bag again, right?" A bitter sort of joke they had.

Her Volvo stood in the driveway at Alice's, partly obscured by the pickup truck pulled in behind it, which belonged to Manuel the gardener. Not wanting to go up and knock on either the front or the kitchen door quite yet, Jake took a little walk around the premises. On the far side of the house he came upon Manuel up on a short stepladder lolly-popping a bush and whistling softly, contentedly to himself. When Jake asked, Manny said he'd been here about an hour. Anyone up inside yet? No, or at least Manny hadn't heard anything.

Jake went back around and tried the back door, which turned out not to be locked. His wife and daughter were camped out on the two big puffy facing couches in Alice's overdone living room, Lisa's face almost entirely hidden under a pulled-up comforter, Angie's a little fun-ny-looking, vulnerable. Her mouth was half open and she was very gently snoring.

*

"So bottom line where exactly was it I screwed up?"

"Bottom line?" Angie repeated. "You weren't there."

"'I wasn't there.'" She mimicked him so Jake mimicked her, higher up and whiney. "You're the one who put your trust in Luz. With no idea where she came from except the valuable reference of our friend Manny the yardman. Don't try and lay that one off on me."

"So how was I to know the girl would go to pieces on me like that? Jake?"

She was seated on a small stone bench and he was standing close. She'd brought a cigarette from the box on Alice's coffee table out into the yard. The long filter trembled in her mouth and her hands trembled as she tried over and over to light a match.

It would be an easy thing to have some pity on her at this juncture. Try to calm her down and then patch up whatever could be patched between them, a temporary fix at least. But he wasn't exactly hitting on all eight himself right now.

He took the matches from her, pulled one, struck it, held it up to the cigarette for her. When it lit, she nodded, brushed the first smoke away from her face with a little wave of her hand.

"I don't know why you want to smoke one of those. They're always stale."

Angie just shrugged, then settled a little and stared fixedly off at the rose bushes stationed along the gravel path like spindly big-headed green soldiers.

The beating of the midday sun on top of the lack of sleep provided Jake with a monster headache.

"How was John Heinemann?"

"Oh I don't know. Fairly destroyed it seemed to me."

"Where'd you go?"

"To pizza, then to a bar near his apartment. I guess it's become his regular place."

"And why were you so late?"

"John wanted to talk."

She laughed curtly, shook her head. "That's a first."

He let it ride. There were decisions to make. He kept thinking of the two little boys alone in the house, scared, hungry probably. Maybe they'd be able to make themselves peanut butter and jelly, he'd seen them do it once. He suggested a deal. He would see if Manuel knew where the boyfriend's mother lived and whether he'd go along to take Alonso and Beto down there. For her part, Angie would go to Cook County and see if Luz was ready to be sprung and, if not, what she needed.

Jake getting Beto and Alonso and Luz's stuff gone from their house was fine by Angie, but she herself wasn't about to get involved. No hospital visit, no taking the girl one of her nighties, not even a toothbrush. To her way of thinking Luz had broken whatever bond there had been between them.

"Other people have to behave responsibly, but Angie Moore is above all that, hm?"

"Oh go, Jake, just leave me alone!"

He went out to Skokie, fed the boys some Spaghetti-Os and helped them put their things and their mother's stuff into the packs they'd come with. He got a black trash bag for the overflow. In his Toyota Alonso and Beto were silent, didn't even ask where they were being taken. It was as though they thought they somehow were the guilty parties. From Alice's house Manuel led the way down to the city in his pickup. When they reached the place, a four-story brick apartment building, he went in alone. While they were waiting, Alonso finally managed to ask Jake what had happened to their mother. She had gone to a hospital to get over what drinking all that rum had done to her, he said, but she should be coming home soon. After about 15 minutes, Manuel came back out followed by a squat latin woman with her hair parted in the middle and pulled back tight. She veered along with a pronounced limp. Jake and Manuel took the boys' possessions and the trash bag up onto the stoop and were going to carry them inside, but the woman stepped in and barred their way. Loud music issued from several open windows above them. The woman and Manuel conferred in Spanish, and Manuel turned to Jake. "She says the boys can take it from here."

"OK."

"And she says they're not hers, not really her responsibility, so she'll need money, at least to feed them on."

Jake got his wallet from his back pocket. He had only seventy bucks on him, a fifty and two tens. The woman watched as he took out the fifty and handed it over. She sniffed, waited. So he gave her the one of the tens too and she folded the bills together and tucked them away in her bosom. Jake squatted and put his arms around both boys and told them, very quietly, to be good. They said OK, then shrugged away from him and followed the woman into the hall.

He called Angie from the road. "You guys home yet?"

"No. My mother came in, and we're going to stay over with her."

"OK," he said, slowly. "And how long is this going last? Can you tell me?"

"I don't know yet, Jake. But I'll be sure to tell you when I know."

"OK."

Their house was dark and quiet. Worn out as he was, it seemed a kind of blessing to have the place to himself. He poured a glass of wine, carried it in the den and plunked down in front of the TV. He turned it on, but even as it was warming up, he decided no, and punched it off.

Monday afternoon when he got home from work, there were two messages from Angie's job, the first wondering whether she was coming in today or not, the second asking her to call her supervisor at her convenience.

So that, he figured, was the end of that.

*

Once some months back, Guy had said if Jake ever really needed to get hold of him it would be OK to leave a message with his office. That Wednesday afternoon when there was still no sign of his wife and daughter at home, Jake broke his own rule and called. Guy's secretary had the kind of pert, attentive chirp he had more or less expected. Dean Baer was not in at the moment, she said, could she take a message?

"Tell him Jake Guarani called. I'm with Mike Tanner Builder."

"Oh yes, Mr. Guarani." She asked him to spell it please.

Fifteen minutes later he had just finished washing up and changing into a pair of loose running shorts and a t-shirt when his cell rang. "Mr. Guarani?" A slightly stopped-up male voice.

"Yes?"

"Are you responsible for this welter of Mike Tanner trucks and equipment which is currently digging up my property?"

"No sir, I'm not." Then he understood. "Guy?"

"Yes."

He said he was doing OK. Sunday and Monday his face was all swollen and it looked like he had two black eyes, so he was working from home, at least for the time being. Pain? There was some. He hadn't needed to go out and fill the doc-in-the-box prescription because he happened to have Vicodin left over from some dental work and he was able to sleep a lot. As long as he stayed head straight up. Even a soft pillow against the side of his face hurt.

And what had his story for his wife been and how'd it gone down? Luckily, Guy said, he got an appointment Tuesday and managed to drive himself to the doctor's office. His own doctor's opinion, contrary to the boy physician's, was that Guy hadn't really broken his nose. There wasn't even any cartilage loose, so no reason to have to reset it. Guy's man removed the first bandage to see what was going on and redressed the area with a smaller, less alarming covering. When Laura got home that evening, Guy told her he'd had a couple of nice stiff drinks Saturday evening and dozed off out on the little deck, then rolled in his sleep and fell off and hit his nose on the edge of the chaise on his way down.

"I'm really sorry, man."

"For what, Jake? Your enthusiasm? Besides, it was my own damn fault anyway. I'm the clumsy one here."

"OK. So what's this complaint about Tanner?"

Guy's laugh came through muffled. "I was actually just kidding. They started Monday on the renovation over at my parents' and there just seem to be an inordinate number of vehicles out there and a lot of whanging and banging we're not accustomed to. Nothing you can do about that, and certainly nothing you need worry yourself over."

"Did you talk to whoever ended up in charge? Know who it is?"

"My wife did. I haven't been over there yet. I think we drew the owner's son."

"Kevin?"

"I suppose. Yes, that sounds right. Why? Not good?"

It would be entirely easy to badmouth the kid, but Jake hesitated. The job would probably turn out fine. They'd employed an architect with a good reputation so no reason to warn the client, even if he was your sometimes lover.

"You should be fine," he said.

"And you?" Guy asked. "Saturday night? What time did you finally make it home?"

"About one-thirty or two, I think."

He was going to launch into the whole Luz story, but then something stopped him. Instead he said, "I'd like to see you when you think that's possible—"

Silence. Then, "Well, it may be a while before—"

"I don't mean for sex necessarily. I'd just like to see you."

"Oh, OK, fine. Let me get my ducks lined up again and then I'll give you a call, OK?"

"Sure. That sounds good," he said, although it didn't. To Jake it sounded like maybe the brush-off.

*

"It could be for our anniversary," Jake said. "That's right, isn't it, Lewis? A year ago just now we first met?"

The early September evening was setting in, the neighbors across the way already had lights on, though kids were still wheeling and circling on bikes and skateboards in the street.

"So what exactly is it you're proposing, Jake?"

"I don't care. Two guys, both abandoned by their folks, left to their own devices. I could take a drive down there, or you could come out to my house, spend the night if you want."

"Bring my jammies along?"

"If you like. I don't wear 'em myself but I wouldn't mind seeing you in yours."

Lewis let out a laugh.

"What's so funny, man?"

"The way you hustle."

"What do you mean?"

"So relentless."

"Yeah, but so far not very <u>successful</u>. With you at least."

"Oh I don't know."

"What does that mean? That you'll do it?"

"Sure. I'd rather you came here, though, if you don't mind. My night vision isn't what it once was."

"And your partner? Where is it he's gone?"

"He's safely back in Vermont dealing with his ancient and imperious mom."

Jake said he could be in Hyde Park within the hour.

But then twenty minutes later he had to call back. "Really sorry to do this, man, but my stepson just showed up unexpectedly and it looks like he's planning on spending the night."

"So you're not coming?"

A pause, Jake thinking. "I don't have any really decent excuse for getting out of the house."

"And you couldn't just make something up?"

Jake's voice was lower. "I have an idea his mom might have asked him to come by to check on me."

Lewis sighed. "Well then, maybe tomorrow night, hm?"

"Tomorrow night I leave on vacation. But maybe in the afternoon. How would that be?"

"That's possible."

"What if we met at your office at the campus?"

"All right."

"You're not going to back out now, are you?"

"No. I was just thinking. Last month there was considerable amusement around the department because according to the scuttlebutt a female grad student and her boyfriend were having sex on the floor in one of the offices after hours when suddenly the door flew open and there were two fireman who'd come to check on the sprinklers gazing down at them."

"But this is the weekend, and a holiday to boot."

"You're right. You know where Swift Hall is?"

"Off Campus Drive there by the water?"

"That's right. You'll have to meet me out front of the building."

"You have keys, right?"

Lewis sighed. "I do have keys."

*

In shorts and a t-shirt and sneakers, all clean and smiling, Jake half sat and half leaned against Lewis's office desk and eyed the long leather couch under the bookcases.

"So?"

"So? Are we going to be shy with each other now?"

"I don't see any reason we should be," Lewis said.

"Good. Me neither."

Jake closed on him, reached up and kissed him, cupping Lewis's face between his hands. Once he had Jake undressed, Lewis stood back and said, "Let me just take you in some, all right?"

"Why?" Jake said. "You've seen me naked."

"At young Ezra's wedding I caught a glimpse of you. But now I have the opportunity to actually look at you."

"Well go quick, you're going to embarrass me, you know."

"No, Jake, don't say that. Let the old man look, all right?"

Jake shrugged, put his hands frankly on his hips. "OK?" He reached down and pulled on his already hard cock.

*

"Are you always so adamant?"

Jake said, "Adamant?"

"You know, hungry."

"I know what it means, thanks." Jake thought, then said, "Yes, pretty much. Which is not to say that you aren't special to me, 'cause you are."

"Oh Jake."

"What?"

Lewis fumbled, finally said, "I do hope you mean that."

Half an hour later as they were about to leave the office, Lewis pulled a book off the shelf and handed it over. "Here," he said. "Maybe that'll amuse you on your flight to Hawaii."

Jake read from the cover, "<u>Days at Sea, a memoir</u>. What is it? Hot sailor booty stories or something?" He turned the book over, raised his eyebrows at the photo of Lewis large on the back jacket.

"In a way, yes. Sailors and others. I hope it amuses you. Or at least lets you know me a little better."

"I look forward to it," Jake said.

After the gloom of the Swift hallways, the green of the lawns outside whited out in the sun. The Northwestern campus had a ghostly, deserted feeling.

As they were getting ready to go their separate ways, Lewis said, "I have to thank you."

"What for?"

"That was very hot."

"Was it? I could have done better, you know."

"I don't see how."

"I was holding back some."

"Really? How come?"

"Don't know really. Loyalty to the boyfriend? Something."

"So are you making a promise of some sort?"

"A promise? What of?"

"To make it even hotter next time?"

Jake laughed, looked down, shook his head. Gave Lewis a bemused 'what am I going to do with you?' look.

*

About eight that evening, Jake called from O'Hare on his cell.

"Hm," Lewis said. "I thought you'd be gone by now."

"They're about to start boarding."

"So what's up?"

"I've been thinking. I probably shouldn't have done that."

"Done what?"

"You and me this afternoon."

"Why? Did you not have a good time?"

"Oh don't get me wrong. The sex was great. Thank you."

"Then why shouldn't you have done it? Because you're a married man?"

"Don't act that way. Please. The reason I shouldn't have is because I have a lover already."

Lewis laughed. "Well, then, I shouldn't have either, should I?"

"I guess. You're right. I got to go, they're calling my section now."

"Well then, aloha!"

"Yeah, aloha!"

*

Alice's plan to take them all to Hawaii had been in the works for almost six months, so the actual trip coming up at a time Angie and Jake were on the outs failed to register with the old girl. In the beginning, Jake said he wasn't sure he could get off, they should go without him (thinking but not saying an entire week cooped up with his mother-in-law might lead to mayhem). Then he began to look forward to the time away. Alice was not much bought into the whole hiding your light under a bushel thing, so when she'd start into 'You know, this vacation is costing me a mint...' Jake would think, Good! Let's spend it up some.

Hard to dope out exactly what Alice was striving after. Long term obviously she meant to destroy any remaining faith Angie had in Jake. But she hadn't enjoyed four days of daughter and granddaughter camped out on her, so she stood opposed to the come-home-to-mama option.

About Hawaii, Jake thought he knew the drill. Tropical paradise with mai-tais, hula girls, leis, coconut palms, the sparkling blue water.

The swarms of other tourists he would have predicted, at the Marriot where they stayed on Kauai a lot of them waspy fatcats trailing packs of clueless, whiny offspring. But the constant enveloping warmth did impress him, the breezes, the jagged moony silhouettes of mountains all around, the smell of the strange flowers whacking you in the nose when you came around a corner, the instant rainbows. He got a kick out of the outdoor border plantations made up of the same indoor plants they used to carry at the nursery ('bathroom plants' Uncle Gio called them), here apparently effortlessly grown out to Martian monster size.

The suite Alice booked was a living room with kitchenette and two bedrooms, each with its own bath and little balcony with a view of the pool to one side and the harbor to the other. She took Lisa with her in the room with the double beds and ceded Angie and Jake the king-size. It was the first time they had slept together in three weeks, and Angie made it clear right away that they would be occupying the bed for resting purposes only. But even the first night in sleep she flung an arm out, touching him and waking him, and he rolled on his side and kissed the palm of her hand. Then from the change in her breathing he could tell she was awake too, at least briefly, and she did not withdraw from him. After that, although they didn't have sex, she no longer hid her body from him when she was changing clothes and Jake became hopeful Hawaii might bring an end to the freeze-out.

Daytime, the ladies were content to spend hour upon hour by the enormous pool working on their tans, gabbing with each other, gabbing with the mainland on their phones. At first Jake stayed close, taking Lisa to horse around in the waist-deep pool with him, ride his back, then crossing the path and getting her to come out and try the ocean for the first time. In the harbor the waves broke small. By day two Alice was encouraging him to go put some of what she called 'boy stuff' on her tab. He could count that as his Christmas present, she said. Through the concierge in the lobby he booked a morning of him and Lisa kayaking on the Wailua River and then for the next day a full afternoon of lessons in power hang-gliding for himself. A guy he talked with in the ABC store told him there were wild boar trophy hunts available on private land or over on some island called Ni'ihau. A thousand bucks, plus a hundred for the rifle rental. He wasn't going to stick Alice with a bill that size, but if he could arrange it for toward the end of the week he was tempted to spring for it himself.

The rest of them seemed to adjust to the time difference, but he was coming fully awake each morning at four or a little after. So he forced himself to lie there, listen to the waves hit the beach, watch the sheer curtains at the slider waft back and forth in the vague moonlight. The general run of guests rose late, but coffee urns were pulled out almost precisely at six down on a semi-circular promenade overlooking the pool and Jake and a small assortment of guys his age would be there waiting in their shorts and flipflops, mugs in hand. The others had their Bluetooths already hooked on, calls to make to their brokers or to their home offices. (Well, and also if he wasn't mistaken some extracurricular girlfriend calls, including one sour-looking guy who managed to play a little pocket pool under the table while yakking with his secretary.)

Jake had the book Lewis had lent him, <u>Days at Sea</u>. Some fairly steamy stuff about anonymous sex between men, but the story itself was pretty sad. It seemed long before Jay Carlson, starting in graduate school Lewis had a partner named Brian. They lived together 20-some years, happily, unhappily, treated in liberal Boston as a married couple, as time went by even as a stodgy old married couple. Brian taught French at Tufts while Lewis built his brilliant career at Harvard. Only a few of their gay friends knew that while Lewis worked away, Brian amused himself drinking in bars and picking up guys. He didn't bring them home, and the sex he found usually had an element of danger—public bathrooms, parks, straight working-class men out on a toot. So of course Brian more than once got himself beaten up, twice ended up in the clink. He fed Lewis's worry by insisting on telling him the details of his adventures. When Brian died suddenly at the age of 50, on top of his sorrow Lewis recognized in himself an element of relief. For the next three or four years he had the recurrent feeling that his life was also over. He started frequenting the same bars Brian had gone to and having the same kind of encounters. This double life, spotlight academic by day, prowler of dark corridors by night, was the book's big revelation.

As the dawn rose, an enormous cruise liner came into view across the narrow mouth of the harbor, all lit up and pulled along noiselessly by a tugboat. The effect was unreal, the liner so huge and near, rows and rows of lashed down lifeboats, yellow deck lights, the whole thing sliding in two dimensional like a piece of stage scenery. Whoever the pilot was, Jake admired his ability to fit that great mother into the space available.

Once the ship had passed out of view, Jake called Hyde Park. "Hi. What you up to?"

"Sitting here at the breakfast table with Jay reading the paper and having coffee," Lewis said.

"What did you eat?"

"Oatmeal. With a banana and some pecans and raisins."

Jake lowered his voice. "Bad time? You could act as though I was just calling to schedule a session with you and get off, you know."

"No, Jake, it's fine. Jay just went in to shower. What's up?"

"I'm about halfway through your book and I'm really enjoying myself."

"You are? What in particular?"

"Well mainly finding out what a whore you were. At least back then."

"I probably never should have published that book."

"How come?"

"At the time I thought of it as some sort of useful contribution to our understanding of the life of older gay men in couples and when they have to go on on their own and so forth. But the reaction, especially among my colleagues, was pretty much like yours, though in somewhat more genteel terms. And only then did I realize it wasn't only the sexual behavior that was my way of mourning Brian, but writing the book and subjecting myself to the exposure too."

Long silence. Jake waited, then said, "Hello? You there?"

"Yes, I'm here."

"So what's up?"

"Frankly, Jake, I'm having trouble going on with this conversation right now. If you want, I could just agree with you—yes, I did have a lot of sex there for a while—but the other part of me would really rather know what exactly it gets you to call me a whore."

"Oh man, I didn't mean <u>anything</u>. I apologize. It was a joke. I don't think you're any more of a whore than I am, you know that."

From Hyde Park, silence.

"I'm the biggest fucking-ass whore of them all. That's me. No question."

Another silence. This one Jake broke into sooner. "Say what's going on, will you? You can't talk?"

"No, I can."

"I've offended you."

"No, not so much. You do, however, make me think I need to be a little more wary of you. More than I would like to be."

"Join the crowd."

"What do you mean?"

"Pretty much everybody I care about comes to the conclusion they need to take a step or two back on me."

A long pause and then Lewis said, "Well, when you get on the horn to call someone four thousand miles away to tell them they're a 'whore'…"

"Wow. You really are angry, aren't you?"

"I guess I am, yes."

"Well that's entirely fucked then."

"It is, isn't it? But go on, tell me what you mean."

"Just that I'm—I don't know—but I'm really dependent on your friendship right now. You're pretty much what I've got, you know—"

Lewis didn't say anything.

"Lewis?"

"Yes?"

"Still there?"

"Yes."

"Are we going to be able to get past this?"

"Of course. Why shouldn't we?"

*

Twenty-four hours later, Jake was sitting at the same table in the same wicker chair looking out through the palms toward the harbor—briefly shining in the morning light like a silver plate—when his cell began to buzz and dance a little across the glass tabletop. It was Cheryl from the office, wanting to know first if she was waking him. No, he said, it was seven a.m. in Hawaii and he was dressed and out.

"So what's up back there, honey?"

"Lunch time," Cheryl said in a low voice. "Jake? My mom said you should give her a call. Have you got her number?"

"I do, and I will. But give me a heads up. What's going on?"

"I really shouldn't get caught talking, Jake."

"OK, I'll call your mom then."

Olivia picked up on what sounded like the first ring. She must have been waiting for him. "Jake, I thought you should know this. Mike's wife had what they think was a stroke."

"Meg? When?"

"Couple of days ago. I went to see her yesterday and I'm no doctor but I'd say she's not doing at all well."

"Jesus! Is she going to die?"

"I have no idea. Maybe not. They say they've got her stabilized. There's a lot of tubes and things in her."

"And Mike? How's Mike doing?"

"I've never seen a man so distraught in my entire life, Jake. I don't know, this may well do him in too. Or him and not her."

"And what in hell would happen then?"

"I have no idea. No idea."

Jake was on his feet now, pacing the long curved corridor. He had not liked having to listen to the other early guys with their business twaddle and now a couple of them were giving <u>him</u> the fish eye.

"Should I come? I could probably get a flight out of here this afternoon or tonight."

"I don't know, Jake. I'm so out of touch. I don't even know who's holding the fort at the office other than my poor Cheryl."

After Olivia, Jake tried Mike, but his cell phone just rang. The land line at Meg and Mike's apartment in town got Meg's cheerful answering machine singsong. Her voice made Jake want to cry. He left a brief message asking Mike to call him.

From a stand that sold breakfast stuff—hard-boiled egg at three bucks—he got coffees for the ladies and a hot chocolate and a cinnamon roll for Lisa and went up to the suite. None of them awake yet, so he sat out on one of the little balconies and let the first sunlight coming over the far wing of the hotel warm his arms and legs. Though it was short of eight o'clock, lady guests were down at the pool staking out huge family territories by draping yellow-striped towels over the deck furniture. The apartness or unreality of Hawaii, which he had been trying to overlook, came over Jake now in a rush. His feelings about Mike Tanner were complicated, but Meg he just cared about in a plain, whole-hearted way. When he closed his eyes against the harsh oncoming light, he couldn't help thinking of her lying there somewhere with the machines keeping her alive mildly beeping and chugging away all around her and again he wanted to cry.

Or to get off this fucking island as quick as humanly possible.

He heard them beginning to stir inside, Alice calling something out to him when his phone rang. He expected Mike, but it was Kevin giving him a perfunctory briefing.

As soon as the boy paused, Jake said, "Why in hell didn't you call me before this, Kev?"

"Well, we thought of this more as a family matter, Jake. And besides, you're in Hawaii, right?"

"I'm coming back."

"Oh I don't see any reason for that. Mom's in good hands and there's nothing especially you could do here."

"And your dad?"

"Dad? Oh, you know him. He's holding it together. Keep to your plans, Jake. I'll call you again should anything change one way or another."

*

Fed up with waiting for Jake to decide, Alice had gotten Hawaii tickets for herself, Angie, and Lisa and then had to purchase Jake's separately—at considerable extra expense and bother, as she did not fail to point out. Back in Chicago alone Sunday afternoon, Jake went directly to the hospital, where he had trouble finding Meg. They remembered her in the stroke unit, 'Oh yes,' they said, 'Mrs. Tanner,' but they weren't sure whether she'd been taken to their own rehab or had gone to another facility.

Wandering a little, unsure of how to get to Restorative Care, far down a fluorescent hallway Jake recognized a round figure busily chugging away from him, then turning a corner. He had to run to catch up with Mike. They embraced quickly, then walked on together, Jake all huffy in his chest as though any moment he might break up. At the moment not so much about Meg as about the consolation of Mike rapid-fire filling him in as they went. The sure thing about Mike, the great thing at least with Jake, was that he never withheld information. He wanted you on the same page with him.

They were still in the critical window, he said. If things Meg had lost didn't come back soon now, they might never come back. Along something called the decelerating curve to recovery she was doing only so-so.

They had passed out of the shiny spacious new part of the hospital into an older wing with lower ceilings, narrower corridors, less light. Worn linoleum and gurneys left in the hall and the smells of medicine and disinfectant and just plain sickness. At the door into Meg's room, Mike said, "Don't expect too much, OK? She's aphasic. You know what that means, right?"

"No."

"She'll try to talk, poor thing, but what comes out is mostly garbage."

Meg lay propped up dozing in a quilted bed jacket and surrounded by a lot of flowers. Several half-depleted hydrogen balloons floated and swayed up a foot or so below the ceiling. Someone probably meaning well had gathered her hair and tied it sticking up with a piece of thick orange yarn, which made Meg look like a clown or a rag doll. The men coming in woke her. She recognized Jake immediately and reached toward him, her good right arm coming up, the left one stirring a bit and then dropping back. Jake took her hand and leaned in close, kissed her cheek and told her how glad he was to see her.

Meg made sounds, slippery ones, the kind you'd make if you'd forgotten to put in your dentures. Almost at once she became aware of the fact that she wasn't making sense and she closed her mouth and set it and began to weep. So Jake sat by the bed with her and patted her hand and nodded at her for several minutes until she sighed and turned her head and seemed ready to drop back off to sleep.

Mike went into the hall with Jake, lugging his iPad with him. "Here," he said, "have a look at this."

On the screen a photograph of brilliant blue water, lighter blue sky, a canal or some sort of waterway, a beach and several blocks of gleaming high rises.

"Where's that?"

"Boca Raton. Condos. I bought into one. If Meg recovers, even partially, I'm going to move her there. She loves it down there."

"And what'll you do?"

"Live. Smell the ocean, for as long as we last, as long as Meg—"

"Retire, you mean."

"That's right."

They'd been vacationing down south more and more, Mike and Meg, but the place in Boca was news to Jake. When he got home he checked out comparables on the net. A one-bedroom ocean view would go for well over a million. Mike hadn't mentioned how many bedrooms they had. Two? Three? Disappointment over not having been told gave way to hurt—the very fact the Tanners had the money to throw around so they could live out their days up there in the clouds overlooking the water, or scuttle back and forth between their place on Lake Shore Drive and the air-conditioned one down there in steamy effing Florida.

Monday Jake got to work on a mountain of questions and details concerning the Belknap proposal Mike had left him and forgot to consider when he could get over to see Meg again. Angie and Lisa were home and there was flurry to get the little girl ready for school. She had already missed almost a week, but at least on the way to the Lihue airport the ladies had stopped to buy a smelly Walmart lei Lisa could take for Show and Tell her first day back.

All the specs on the lab proposal were in the main office, so it made sense for Jake to go in to Evanston every day. But the place felt a little spooky—under-populated—without the boss there steaming around shouting after Cheryl or one of the goonies for this or that. And almost immediately a difficulty arose because Jake didn't have any fixed place to spread out his materials. He used the conference room until one of the sales guys claimed it for a meeting, then he'd take his stuff into Mike's office where he had cleared himself a table in the far corner. There was a major powwow scheduled over at the university for Thursday, but Wednesday a.m. Mike called to say Jake would have to represent them by himself, since Thursday they were moving Meg to a private facility.

Under pressure then to cram his head with the figure sets Mike usually represented, Jake went trundling down the hall with his armfuls of binders and file folders and found Junior in his father's chair at his father's desk hunched over talking on the phone. Earnestly doing the school-boy 'yes ma'am, no ma'am' thing. Whoever he was in dutch with must matter some because Kevin was red in the cheeks and laying on the sincerity. Almost a minute passed before he noticed Jake in the doorway. Embarrassed, he waved Jake off. When the other man didn't go immediately, Kevin cupped his hand up by the receiver and pumped, the jack-off gesture so Jake would understand the humble pie thing was all an act.

Cheryl found a place to stash Jake's stuff and he took a walk around the block. Back at the building doors not yet through the turmoil caused by Kevin so casually dismissing him, Jake decided to hike some more. Five blocks down he stopped in and had a long coffee in a shop new to him. It was an hour and a half before he could make himself go back up to the office.

Friday when he came in at 7:30, Mike was present. Jake reported that he was very satisfied with the meeting at Northwestern. Their planning director and the guy who oversaw their electricity both had heard about Meg and sent their good wishes. Mike just grunted.

"I think they're within an inch of closing with us."

Mike bent, pulled out a drawer in his desk, peered in, shut it, sat up. "You know they're still talking with those suckasses at McClosky too."

"No, I didn't know that."

They sat in silence just looking at one another. The heavy emotions Jake had been having about Mike and Meg had somehow sorted themselves out. If Mike had been siphoning off huge amounts of money to purchase himself castles in the air, so be it. Mike Tanner Builder was not, after all, a profit-sharing outfit. Mike owned it lock, stock, and barrel and Jake was an employee. Proud of his loyalty, but an employee still. At the end of the day, what he needed to concentrate on was his personal sorrow for Meg, knocked out of the line-up like a bowling pin taking just the right hit.

"Jake, I need a favor from you."

"Sure. What?"

"Kevin has been in charge of this Baer family home job, and apparently he may have screwed it up to some extent. Or at least so the clients maintain. They're in a monumental tizzy, calling me day and night. They've already had their lawyers out snooping about the place—"

"What can I do about that?"

"Would you go out and have a look around? Swanson was the redo architect, maybe you should call and get him to go with you. The property's on the water side of Sheridan Road up toward Tower."

"I know where the Baer estate is." Even admitting that much gave him a lump in his throat.

"Will you get on it then?"

"Sure. I'll see what I can see. After the weekend."

*

Jake had a couple of little email exchanges with Guy while he was in Kauai. How ya doing? Good. Bandages off, face as good as new. Nose still not exactly as elegant as John Barrymore's, however. How's Hawaii? Kauai's my favorite island. Hope to get together soon. Me too. Hungry for you. Back on the road for the university for a couple of weeks—

But just to make sure, Jake called Guy's office. The sweet-voiced young thing apologized, yes, Dean Baer was still out of town, could she take a message for him? Jake left his name, spelled 'Guarani' for her as he'd done once before.

Leigh Swanson was perfectly willing to meet as soon as possible, which confirmed Jake's suspicion the troubles whatever they might be were for real. Swanson was a couple of years younger than Jake. On the phone he mentioned that though the Baer place was not that big a job in dollar terms, it <u>was</u> of importance to him and his practice.

They set to meet at 8:30 a.m. Monday, but Jake was in Winnetka forty-five minutes early. He parked on Humboldt across from Christ Church, jumped across the road in a brief break in traffic and hiked the block-and-a-half down to the property entrance. Amused with himself for taking the same kind of precaution with the Toyota he might take if he were coming for some hot loving. Even where the gravel road in forked, the heavy foliage hid Guy's place almost completely. Just the barest indication of that big dark expanse of down-sloping roof.

The job was supposed to be near completion. Out front the boys had made an unholy mess, truck tire ruts gouged into the oval of lawn in the middle of the turnaround, piles of crap pulled out of the building junked together with packaging for new stuff being installed. Wire, casings. Had the crews been Jake's all of this would be cleared regularly as they went along, but there was nothing irreparable about the trash and the damage to the greenery. Landscape restoration was in the budget.

The real problem was what they had done to the building itself, and if you cared about such things it was a heartbreaker. Even from the exterior Jake got a sense of what had happened, and when he found a side door unlocked and let himself in, the story only got worse. Though he had only been in the house once, and then in dim light and with other things on his mind, he remembered details, especially meticulous skill work, not only in wood, but in the laying of the marble flooring and in such things as the molded plaster ceilings in the halls and upstairs. A lot of it now wiped out, gone for good.

True that to become of use again the house needed updating, especially in its mechanical and its electrical. Certain soffits for wiring and heating ducts or recessed lighting Jake understood the reason for. In some places they broke original lines of the house or made a room look a little smaller, but Swanson had been clever in his planning and had kept these to a minimum. The trashing was not in the re-design but in the materials. Stupid stuff. Metal-rimmed production window replacements on one side of a room with no match to the handsome wooden originals left on the other.

What kind of lazyass excuse could Kevin mount? That they hadn't given him the money or the time to do the work properly? It might be hard for the boy to admit the truth, which was that when it came to craft he didn't know crap from Cremora.

Jake was up on the second floor moving from room to room with his clipboard out making note of the most obvious or possible fixes they might be able to come up with—if the Baers were willing to give them the chance to try to save the job—when he heard the workmen clunking in down below. Then he heard Leigh Swanson's voice, high, agitated, running off to somebody. Jake went out onto the gallery and to the head of the grand staircase but Leigh and whoever he was talking to had moved out of the central area below. Two workers were bringing a standard sheet of wallboard up the stairs. When they reached the top, the man on the back end popped his head around and said, "Hey, Uncle!"

Stefan in dirty white carpenter overalls and a t-shirt, hair in a ponytail, big sappy grin. He'd bulked up some over the last months. Jake was only a little surprised to see him. Once he managed to get the kid on as a regular, Stefan had moved ahead on his own. The men approved of him because he didn't shirk humping it the way some of the other younger ones did, and he appreciated being shown how to do things. "What you doing here?"

"Oh, just came by to see how things are going," Jake said.

Stefan nodded and smiled. Did he understand? The guy on the front end of the board stamped and moved and Stefan had to go with him.

Downstairs, Jake followed the trace of the architect's voice through the formal dining room with the shoulder-high wainscoting and into the butler's pantry, where he stopped, hand on the edge of the counter Guy had leaned his elbows on the first time Jake fucked him.

"Jake?" Little Leigh Swanson came through from the kitchen in a crisp check shirt, touched Jake's sleeve and led him along back into the big kitchen. Standing there were Guy's brother and sister and his wife.

"This is Jake Guarani, Mike Tanner's senior project manager, who's come over today to—"

All three of them looked sourly at Jake. "We've met Mr. Guarani," the sister said, her voice tired, flat. The wife had her cell phone to her ear.

Leigh tried again, still cheerful, "Jake is going to take a look through with us today."

The wife snapped her phone shut, put it in her jacket pocket, patted it, and said to no one in particular, "Guy'll be up in a minute."

"I'm here, honey." Guy in the dark pantry, already breezing in.

Jake watched the man's face, the separate smiles for his brother and his sister, nothing much for the wife, the slight questioning look about Jake—not asking 'What are you doing here?' but rather 'And who would you be?'

Leigh introduced them. Guy said, "Nice to meet you," but kept his hands to himself.

The tour began, Jake following along behind the others, listening, nodding if they spoke to him, writing down things they mentioned. The time he met the clients at the office, Jake thought he liked the sister best. But now she had turned into one long whine. 'This was never like this I can promise you.' 'I can't believe what they've done to this room.' 'Ruined! Ruined! I hate to think what my poor mother would say were she still with us...'

Not that any of her complaints were off target, but Jake began to wish she'd adopt the icy, silent fixed-mouth approach the wife and the brother were going for. Guy was keeping his head down, avoiding making any direct eye contact with Jake.

Upstairs finally, as they were leaving what had once been Guy's bedroom, he himself dropped behind the others for a moment. Turning to Jake, he said in a low voice, "What the hell are you doing here?"

"I was sent over. Mike Tanner personally sent me to see what we can do about correcting the problems. I'm kind of the expert on something like this."

"You are? Hm. Well tell me this then: Didn't I ask you just one favor, which was <u>not</u> to get yourself involved in this particular piece of business?"

"Yes."

"And yet here you are."

"I had the impression you were out of town."

"But I'm back, aren't I? And what? You thought in my absence you could just sneak in on my real life for a bit?"

"There was no 'sneaking' involved."

"No?"

How even and controlled he remained on the surface. Would you have to be his lover to tell how panicked the man was?

There was a connecting door half open into the next room, movement in there, work going on. And down the hall a woman's voice—or were there two of them?—calling for Guy. "Honey? Are you coming?" "Hm?" Otherwise, Jake might have waded in, tried to explain the circumstances, his boss's wife at stroke rehab, everything—

"You know what?" Guy said. "You have turned out to be everything I was afraid you might be."

"And what does that mean?"

"Uncle?" Stefan standing in the doorway, apologetic, confused. "Can I just come in and get my bucket and some nails?"

"Sure, come ahead."

"Guy? Dear?" The ladies' voices hollow from the hallway.

Guy's eye was fixed on Jake. "If you don't know what I mean, so much the worse for you."

He turned abruptly and as he scuttled out Stefan tiptoed in through the connecting door. The boy picked up his stuff, then stood in the middle of the room, goofy, waiting, as though Jake might illuminate him about the little scene he had just witnessed.

SIX

Lewis held Jake on top of him with one hand on Jake's ass, the other running lightly along the man's extraordinarily thick-muscled side. When Jake moved in even closer, Lewis felt into the hairy crack, found Jake's butthole and rested his finger at the gentle pulse there.

Jake squirmed a little and sighed. "What'd you think you're doing?"

"Do you mind?"

"Am I objecting?"

"I guess not. I just remember your saying when your boyfriend did this you didn't like it."

"No, well, but what you're doing is different." Another sigh. Jake stretching. "I wonder sometimes what it'd feel like to have eight inches up there."

"Not that it would be any eight inches, but if you'd like to experiment—"

"No. No thanks."

"You know the standard gay male wisdom about anal intercourse, don't you?"

"How would I know that?"

"Well, some of it's actually also more general straight folk wisdom."

"Like what?"

"Basically that once you break the taboo and give your ass up there's no going back, the desire to have it plugged again will take over, dominate. In psychoanalytic terms, this fear (or is it a promise?) makes complete sense. The anus is the pleasure source which is the most negatively sanctioned, so the idea is that once the taboo is breached a person will want to do it again and again, make it into an obsession."

Jake said, "I don't think with me that's going to happen."

"No, I suppose not."

When Jake got off him and Lewis started to get up, there was a sucking sound. The leather of his big office couch had stuck to his sweaty back.

Though it was the Saturday of the Wildcats' first home game over at Ryan, campus was still busy, undergrads on the paths, two separate tours for prospective students inching along, parents following the spiels more attentively than their little lambs. On the steps, Jake sniffed at Lewis. "You smell, you know."

"What of?"

"Cum. Sweat. K-Y."

"K-Y doesn't have an odor, does it? What about you? You must smell too."

Jake took a whiff at himself. "True," he said.

They stood another moment. Lewis said, "And you don't mind coming here these days?"

"Why would I?"

"Chance of meeting up with the boyfriend?"

Jake glanced down, then back up with a smile. "Fact is, I'd appreciate running into him right now. I have something for him." He fished in his back pocket and handed Lewis a folded sheet of paper. "Tell me whether I should send that or not."

It was a printout of a draft email: "*Guy: Apologies all around. Did not mean to horn in on your territory. My company's falling apart like pretty much everything else and I was sent to see what could be rectified in the botch made of your folks' house. It's you I want, not to move in on your life or wreck anything you have going. None of the rest of it matters at all. Call when you can? Jake*"

"So what do you think?"

Lewis was still making up his mind when Jake took the sheet back, wadded it and stuck it in his pants pocket. "Actually, I guess my mind's already made up. No reason to go crawling after him."

"Not if it's just for a piece of ass, even a superior one. Right?"

"I guess."

They walked to the corner. Jake's truck was in one lot, Lewis's car in another.

"Thanks for a <u>highly</u> superior time," Lewis said.

"You thought?" Jake laughed a little. "Actually, I've been thinking it's probably a good moment for us to stop meeting."

"For sex."

"No, the whole thing. Boyfriend's gone and he was the—what do you guys call it?"

"The 'presenting problem?'"

"Yeah, that. So with him out of my life I'm cured, right?"

"All right, if you say so. We could however still get together just to make love."

"Now who's crawling?"

Lewis said nothing.

"Look," Jake said again, "I'd appreciate having you for a sex partner, but I don't think in the long run it's going to be good for you. You need to get back down to Hyde Park and pay some good attention to things between you and that fellow there."

"And you? What about you knuckling down the same way out there in Skokie?"

"You know what she says?"

"Who?"

"Angie. My wife. She says by now too much has gone wrong ever to make it right again. Between her and me."

"You're very experienced at this, aren't you? You'd have to be."

"Experienced at what?"

"Making out it's for their own good when you give people the old heave-ho."

Jake looked Lewis in the eye, a glinting, appraising look, very still. Then he shook his head. "I'm not doing this, man."

"Not doing what?"

"I know I disappoint you, but I'm not going to fight with you, OK? I respect you and I admire you too much. You've been very good to me, you know, and I'm grateful."

And with that, Jake turned and walked away quickly.

*

The afternoon had turned out more summery than what you'd expect for the beginning of October, and when he let himself in at Claire's Jake decided the house needed a little airing out. So he left the front door ajar before going down the basement. And so when Stefan came home he got as far as the kitchen before Jake heard him.

"Uncle?"

"Down here!"

"Uncle? You got the power off?"

"Yes!"

"Where are you?"

"Up toward the front here."

Early for the boy to be off, especially for a Thursday. Jake could hear him clunking down the steps, crossing the floored section of the basement, softer padding when he hit the packed dirt part. The ceiling was so low even Jake had to crouch a little to clear, so Stefan must have needed to bend nearly double. It seemed Claire and them hardly came down here, thick dust all over and cobwebs on the cobwebs. Ash and clinkers spilled out the open bottom door of the old coal furnace, apparently just left like that by Walter, Stefan's dad, when they moved to an oil heater.

Jake was up squatting on a packing case so he could get at the box where the electrical came in and the fuse box next to it. He was working by the light of a battery lantern he had hung overhead. Stefan moved in to have a look. "Can I help?"

"Sure. Maybe you should change, though. It's dirty up here."

"I'm alright."

What Claire had called about was her lights flickering sometimes when either her washing machine or her dryer was starting up, the TV winking off and then coming back on for no apparent reason. When Jake showed him the boxes, Stefan saw at once the dubious patch-overs someone had made, probably as more electrical appliances came into the house. "Looks like my dad's handiwork," Stefan said, laughing.

"Is it?"

"Yep. His motto was never do anything tight if you can get away with doing it half-ass."

Well, Jake said, himself he wasn't about to risk his sister being burned out of house and home. So he'd get better wire and a bigger fuse box and be back to install it on the weekend. He put away his pliers and his screwdriver, took the electric lantern down, and they went upstairs.

Would Jake like a beer? Sure, why not? Stefan brought two bottles from the refrigerator and they settled in at the kitchen table.

"Where's your mom?"

"Oh. Thursday she helps serve the free lunch down at the Ebenezer Church."

Jake laughed. "Really? The place on Emerson?"

"Yes."

"That's a black church."

"Yeah. So? Mom's pretty cool in her way, you know. Says working a food line must be her karma. And that the majority of homeless folks are better behaved than the kids at North Shore Country Day ever were."

"That's not saying much. And you, Stefan, since when are you allowed to drink beer in your mother's house?"

"Since I turned 18 and began kicking in toward the rent. And the beer."

"Did you not work this afternoon?"

"We were at the Miller brothers' for a while, but there wasn't a helluva lot to do so they let us knock off."

"Right." Jake had been at Millers' in the morning himself. He'd already forgotten it was he and the floor manager who'd agreed to give some of the men a few hours free.

Practiced at picking up clues and piecing them together, the men often understood a lot more about what was going on upstairs than management gave them credit for. From being taken off the job, Stefan and his buddies knew the Baer mansion had been put on hold. They might well have figured out the company could end up taking it in the shorts to pull out and replace the windows, woodwork and flooring Kevin had installed. Stefan had heard about the big boss having gone to Florida, though he didn't know it was so Mike could get Meg set up and comfortable there, daycare brought in for her. And the boy also wouldn't know that at the last minute fucking Northwestern gave the fucking Belknap Labs to McClosky. Nor understand how far out to sea that left his uncle Giacomo's personal little rowboat.

Jake knew he should be on his own case every day right now, not pounding the pavement exactly, but massaging his range of contacts, hot as a hunting dog with a scent to go on after new work he could bring in. But he was balked, unable, the image of Kevin at Mike's desk shooing him off with the back of his hand recurrently in his head, the idea of having to prove his own worth yet again a burn in his chest. Sometimes the pain migrated to his stomach and a couple of times he wondered was he getting an ulcer.

At the Miller brothers' they were down to paint and light fixtures and carpeting, so there was really nothing left for Jake to do. He went for a couple of hours every day mostly out of a kind of dreamy hope that among his messages there might be one from somebody he knew over at McClosky. It would make sense for them to hustle him now, given his level of understanding of what the Belknap job was all about. And there would be nothing illegal about him making the jump, in 20 years he never signed even a single piece of paper to bind him to Mike Tanner Builder. As the days went by with no call from anybody, the desire to up and quit just grew stronger and stronger. But to get unemployment he would need to be let go.

And even then— The monthly unemployment check wouldn't even cover the Skokie house mortgage payment. Sometimes now he woke up in the middle of the night panicky. Not that it amounted to that much, but defaulting would be ten years' equity down the drain. And what would Angie do? Take Lisa, move in to Alice's. To Alice's displeasure. He fretted about Lisa forced to change to a different school, make a whole new set of friends. But why did he also worry about Angie? It seemed built in, part and parcel of who he was, what he had become.

Tentative tapping at the front-door screen followed by a moment's silence and then a small voice asking "Jake?"

Stefan got up, beer in hand, and went down the hall. Jake followed. Dapper little Charlie Villon, a long-time neighbor, stood peering in at the front door screen.

"Jake? Is that you? I saw your truck and I was just wondering if you were— Oh!" Mr. Villon put his hand up to shade his eyes. "Is that you too, Stephen?"

"Hi, Charlie."

They unlatched the screen and brought him into the hallway where he shook hands with both of them. Villon must be 80 by now. He wore short-sleeve solid-color shirts and jeans and with his sideburns and a full head of carefully-combed white hair looked like some TV singer from the era of Glen Campbell.

"I'm so sorry to bother you," the little man rattled out, "but I <u>was</u> going to go out after some groceries, unless you were planning on coming by, of course."

"I am coming, Charlie," Jake said. "Got your sticks in the truck and everything. I'll finish up here and I should be right over."

"Oh! All right. Good. I'll just wait for you at home then."

The gentleman turned to go, then turned back and for some reason shook hands with Jake and Stefan a second time. He pushed open the screen and let himself carefully down the four steps to the pavement. Stefan waited and watched while Charlie marched out to the sidewalk and made a smart little military turn in the direction of his own house.

"He caught me the other day when I was here to see your mom," Jake said. "Seems he stepped through some rotted-out wood on his back porch, so I offered to come over and fix it up for him."

"That's pretty nice of you, Uncle."

"Yeah, well— The Villons were always good to us when I was a kid, when Dara was alive. You wouldn't remember her."

"She was the wife?"

"Yes. Out back they had pear trees. Really good pears. Trees are still there. They were always generous about letting us come in and pick a bunch."

"In my time you weren't supposed to go in if Mr. Villon invited you into the house," said Stefan.

"Why was that?"

"Well it got around the old guy was offering to blow some of the older boys."

Jake feigned surprise. "Charlie?" He laughed. "And was anyone taking him up on it?"

"A lot of 'em did I think. Not me, I never partook—" Stefan laughed, "—but then Mr. Villon never asked me into the house either."

Jake took a swig of his beer, drained the bottle.

"Maybe you'll get paid for your work, Uncle."

"May be," Jake said slowly.

And what if now, this moment, together in the dark hall with the honey-warm afternoon air flowing in on them he were to tell Stefan he was already receiving old Charlie's sweet, denture-free benefits?

"Uncle? Can I ask you something?"

"Sure. Ask away."

"I don't mean anything by this, and I don't want you to take offense, but I've been kind of wondering if you think you might be turning gay or something."

"Is that something you've heard the men wondering about too?"

"Not at all. Really it just kind of came into my head that day you were talking with that guy upstairs at the Baer place. He's the owner, right?"

"One of them, yes. And what you heard was what, Stefan?

"Not so much what I heard, not the words, but the <u>tone</u> of it. Between you two. It was like lovers breaking up."

A long pause. Today, from the moment he woke up in Earl's room and stumbled forth to throw water in his face still nearly asleep and confused about why he had to go into the hall to get to a bathroom when the bathroom was supposed to be off his and Angie's room, Jake had been aware of the fact it was the one-year anniversary of the night he first went on the Baer property.

"'Lovers?'" He hastened to correct. "We were fuck buddies for a while. Quite a while. In fact, you're right. What you heard was the end of that."

"Oh. I'm really sorry, Uncle." Stefan's big handsome mouth stretched down into an exaggerated, boyish look of concern.

Jake shrugged. "No biggy. The guy was more trouble than he was worth." Then he said, "Still, I'd prefer for you to keep this knowledge to yourself if you would, my friend."

"Of course, Uncle. You know I'm in favor of all that—men showing their feelings for each other any way they'd like."

"But you haven't 'partaken,' as you would say, right?"

"No. But I would, I mean I <u>will</u> at some point, I'm sure. If and when there's a guy I care about in that way."

As he walked along toward Charlie's, Stefan's unclouded expectations for his own future good times, purely imaginary and without complication, cheered Jake up. Sex as an expression of friendship, of affection, of love—now there was a concept!

*

Fleas had arrived at Pine Street six days ahead of Ian and without Leonard along to require tending she had managed to arrange Dad's move to the new condo down to nearly the last detail. To keep her father from trailing after her or objecting, she had him confined to three areas, his bed and bathroom upstairs, the table in the corner by the kitchen windows where they ate, mostly take-out, and the chairs, couches and the better little tables she had chosen to go along with him to the Mews. Standing in the middle of the otherwise bare living room, the little furniture grouping looked like an outcast's island. Dad's drinks table was there, of course, folded up and leaning against his armchair, his bottles, glasses, and silver shaker boxed beside it. Apparently the old fellow was so flummoxed by all the motion around him that he had nearly forgotten about the solace of drink.

From the whirlwind of her own throwing-out Fleas occasionally rescued small caches or single items for others. Friends of her mother's (people who thought they had been Nancy's friends) rang the front doorbell at odd hours and came in a little shyly to be presented with the mottled antique hall mirror or the silver and crystal ink well Fleas assured them her mother had wanted them to have. Handed the fox stole with the three glass-eyed little foxes biting each other's tails, Nancy's longtime ladies' singles rival had to catch her breath before she could manage a faint 'Oh thanks.'

"Was there a list or something Mom left?" Ian asked.

"Yes!" Fleas snapped. "Did you think I was pulling these bequests out of my ass?"

Irritated as he was with her, Fleas made him laugh. "Not exactly," he said.

"What is wrong then? Did you want the Seth Thomas?"

"No. All that damned clock ever did for me was keep me awake."

She had apportioned the three-level mantel clock to herself for the library at Mayfields. It leaned against the dining-room wall with a padded cloth over it, waiting for some expert packer who was to come in Monday morning, build it a box and take it to FedEx.

"What is it then, Ian?"

"I don't know. I guess I wish we could somehow just move along a little slower here for a while."

"The movers come tomorrow, we take Dad to the new place, make up the beds and sleep there, I have cleaners contracted for Monday and the new owners are expecting us to turn over the keys Tuesday morning. Slow down here now? How?"

She was right of course. The end _was_ near, he himself booked for the Monday night O'Hare/Charles de Gaulle flight. And if Fleas was frantic, it was fairly obviously because she was now mourning not only her mother but the loss of the house and the whole way they had once lived, been. Ian's own sadness was taking a form more like his father's, low function, numbness.

An hour later he was upstairs when there was a knock at the front door, then another knock and someone calling and no one responding, so Ian went down himself.

Lewis Keyes and Jay Carlson under a single black umbrella, huddled together a bit against the day's bluster and off-and-on spitting cold rain. They had come, they said, because Fleas had phoned that she had something for Jay. Ian offered to take their raincoats, but they said they weren't staying. Ian went off through the downstairs calling for his sister and Lewis and Jay, both Peering about a little gingerly, went in to say hello to Peter.

She had been in the attic. She strode into the living room pulling off the cloth she'd bound her long hair up in and warning Jay and Lewis she was covered in dust. The things for Jay she thought she'd left up above the fireplace weren't there. Where else might she have put them? Jay, Lewis, and Ian trailed after her into the hall where Fleas said, "Oh—! In back!" and led Jay off through into the pantry and toward the rear of the house, leaving Ian with Lewis.

"Had you come by tomorrow instead, you might have run into Jake," Ian said.

"Oh yes?"

"He said he'd drop in to see whether he could help with moving my father."

"Hm. Well, probably better this way anyway."

Ian knew Jake had stopped meeting with Lewis, but was unsure what the reason was. "What happened there?" he asked. "Are you free to say?"

Lewis moved so he could keep an eye on the swinging door into the back. "You remember Jake's problem with 'the boyfriend' as he called him?"

"He thought he cared considerably more about the other fellow than the fellow cared about him."

"Right. Well, in this case a certain odd symmetry developed between the patient's real-world conundrum and his pseudo-therapist's main difficulty concerning the patient."

"Which was?"

"I was more attracted to Jake than he was to me."

"Oh. I'm sorry."

"No need. Merely another case of what the poet calls life's other sorrow."

"Which would be what?"

"'…that our hearts are drawn to stars which want us not." Lewis laughed.

"Nice. Who is it?"

"Insufficiently studied these days, the wisdom of Edgar Lee Masters."

"When I said I was sorry, in part I meant for having put you in that proximity to Jake."

"Don't be. I'm a little old to be hurt much by unreturned love. Besides, Jake and I had a good time. He <u>is</u> a star, after all, in his way. In fact, I came to think Guy Baer must be a bit of a dope not to take more advantage of what Jake had on offer."

Ian was stopped for a moment. "Is that who the mysterious boyfriend was?"

"You know him?"

"Oh sure. The Baers were friends of my parents. Guy? I think my mother dated him back in the day."

"Mother did what?" Fleas and Jay were coming through from the kitchen, Jay carrying a small cardboard carton.

"Did Mom and Guy Baer go out before she met Dad?"

"It was either him or that brother of his," Fleas said. "What about them?" She laughed. "The Baers! Proof if any was ever needed that money by itself does not alleviate dullness."

Jay's prizes were two matching cloisonné vases a little under a foot in height, flared at the top like trumpet bells. The design was chrysanthemums in dark blue and green, the metalwork and the rim glowing silver. They had stood always at opposite ends of the living-room mantel, spring to fall filled with flowers his mother picked specially for them.

Maybe Jay caught Ian's look, because he suddenly thrust the box toward him. "They're way too valuable for me, you know. You should have them."

"No, I—"

Fleas took control, pushing the box back on Jay and saying, "No, no—"

"But these are priceless pieces!"

"No, not priceless. They appraised at a thousand dollars each if you must know," Fleas said. "Mom knew you collect Meiji cloisonné and she knew you coveted—"

"Coveted? Me?" Jay glanced from one to another of the others. "But isn't coveting a deadly sin?"

"Venial maybe," Lewis said, "but not deadly. And now that you've got them, you can just <u>cherish</u> them, which is no sin at all but a kind of virtue."

"A virtue? Wow!" Jay turned up toward the brass light fixture overhead. "Nancy?" he said, as though calling on Heaven, "Look! Cherishing going on down here!"

*

Dad's movers were two burly boys barely in their twenties from down in the city who turned out to be expert psychologists. Ducking Fleas' attempts to manage them, they focused right in on Peter Stiles, made him tell them which was his favorite place to sit, installed him there, and then went through the house removing things to their van, checking in with him now and then to see how he was doing. By the time they got to his little island in the living room, they had him halfway jollied back into his old hail-fellow self. About noon the boys handed him over to Ian to take to the Village for a hamburger and whisked the gentleman's favorite chair away to their van. When Peter and Ian got to the new condo an hour and a half later, the chair was standing alone in the freshly-painted living room waiting for Dad to sit in it and watch his new life come together.

By three the movers were done, tipped, and on their way. When Ian went back for Fleas' suitcase and his own and to lock up, he found Jake Guarani out front of the house in a worn leather baseball jacket. The weather had changed again and the day had turned sunny, warm for the beginning of November.

"Sorry I'm so late. Guess there's nothing much more to do."

"No matter," Ian said. "Why don't you come by the new place and say hello? Fleas will want to see you."

So Jake followed Ian up Pine Street in his truck and came in. Dad had turned the now-designated favorite chair away from the other furniture and was sitting looking down on the late-afternoon traffic along Green Bay three floors below. He braced himself on the chair arms to get up but Jake stuck out his hand and Peter sank back before he shook it.

"I was thinking about you just now, young man."

"You were?"

"Well, about your uncle and your dad, and now me here right up from where they had their shop for what? How many years?"

"For some while for sure."

"Indeed. And wasn't there always a big manure pile out back? I figure directly below where I am now in this damn fogey corral."

"I've heard the Mews is a fairly swinging place, Mr. Stiles. Fogeys need not apply. The lonely ladies with their casseroles and their pitchers of margaritas will be beating down your door within days."

"Will I have to hire protection then?"

Fleas filled his ice bucket for him and brought it out and Peter offered drinks. The four of them toasted new beginnings, then sat together. But instead of settling in, Fleas suddenly jumped up again and said, "I entirely forgot I've got beds to make."

There was an uncomfortably long moment of silence. Though the square footage of Dad's unit was generous, every sound Fleas made bustling about the hall and the master bedroom reached them. Then Peter got up and wandered toward the big rectangle of window, gone blue now, and plunked down again in his chair. Jake called in to Fleas, "Can we do anything?"

"Actually, I could use some help here, thanks."

A new mattress and spring set stood upright beside her parents' bedstead, reassembled and placed by the moving men. Jake and Ian got the plastic wrap off and hoisted up the new springs, then the new Sealy. Jake and Fleas fitted the new mattress cover on and spread new olive green sheets and pushed new pillows into the matching cases and plumped them.

Ian went in the bathroom, and when he came back Fleas was saying, "What do you think, Jake?"

"'Can this marriage be saved?' Me, I've got my doubts. But you talked to her. What does <u>she</u> think?"

"Angie's pretty obdurate about it right now."

"You're telling me?"

"But really, Jake. Is it too late for counseling? Too late for—"

"<u>She</u> has never been willing to go, you know, unless the deck is pre-stacked entirely in her favor. <u>Her</u> therapist, <u>her</u> turf. Plus—"

"What?"

"Plus I'm not in a position to get on my knees and beg right now."

"Out of pride?"

"The hell with pride. Because I don't have the resources. Or rather I won't have probably, soon enough, once Mike gets back and screws up the courage to walk me. Or if Kevin Tanner turns out to have the balls to do it himself. Angie's got no clue, you know. She imagines herself and Lisa continuing to live the life alone in the house off my same paycheck. And her mom of course encourages her in that thinking. But the fact is there ain't going to be money for the ballet lessons and the orthodontist and the house will go back and become the property of the bank soon enough."

Fleas spread a comforter over the bed and the three of them moved out into the hall. Not saying anything, Fleas jerked her head toward the second bedroom and Jake and Ian followed her in. She switched on the overhead light and she and Jake began tearing open packets of single-bed mattress covers.

"The only one I really feel for is Lisa," Jake said. "Do you think the court would give me an injunction against old Alice? Grandma forbidden to badmouth Dad to his little girl morning, noon and night? Doubtful, hm?" Jake shook his head. "I think I could lose big in that area."

The man's awful fatalism. Ian had forgotten. Even with the upbringing he had not entirely explicable, the great contradiction in a person of Jake's will and drive.

Once they were through with the beds, Fleas determined it was time to order the pizza. Jake begged off, said he was due for supper at his sister's down in Wilmette. He did allow Ian to fill up his drink, however, and sat with them until the merry chime flourish on Fleas' iPhone sounded and it was time for Ian to go down to pick up the order.

On the stairs, Ian asked, "Have you proceeded as far as lawyers?"

"Her mom has one all lined up for her, I think. I've got a name from my friend John Heinemann and I need to call for an appointment."

"And what'll you do? Have you thought about where you'll live?"

"Think maybe I should bunk in with your old man, look after him, protect him from the hungry widow ladies of the Mews?"

Ian laughed. "You are not going to bird dog my father, not at this point. Or are you?"

Jake laughed too. "Don't worry. Joke, OK? Not to say that he's not still good-looking, but I have something pretty nice going in that line already."

"Not anyone I happen to know."

"Not this time. Although he <u>is</u> from the old neighborhood. In his eighties by now—"

"You dropping in on him tonight?"

"That was the plan, yes."

Ian laughed again, shook his head. "And the famous boyfriend? Any word from him?"

"I saw him. The ex-."

"You did? Where?"

"I had to go to campus to pick up the last of the materials we'd prepared for those ass wipes and I ran across him on the path."

"And?"

"And nothing. It was polite. He said hello, I said hello. We went our separate ways."

"So that fire has gone out?"

"Some residual pain, but otherwise I can't say seeing him again I felt a lot one way or another."

*

In 35 years of being friends, Jake couldn't remember another time he had lied to Ian Stiles. So why now? Just because when push came to shove his actual confrontation with Guy had turned out so badly?

Though Jake and Angie and Lisa were all still occupying the Skokie house, he saw very little of Lisa these days. He figured Angie had it all arranged to deny him what he cared about most. Sometimes when they were gone he would sneak into the little girl's room (<u>sneaking</u> in his own g.d. house, he thought) and set some of her stuffed animals up straight. Leaned over against one another they looked too sad. But then he'd be reminded of Guy's daughter's room the day before Valentine's, the slant of heavy orange light across the wall, their conversation all about the Maskers, him asking if Guy couldn't bring him along as a guest to one of their circle jerks. How far off the mark he'd been! Turned out Guy Baer was so ashamed of Jake Guarani he would bar the door to the Maskers' sacred precincts and set a flaming sword against him. Adam and Eve had to move east from Eden. To dreary Gary maybe. And St. Valentine too, who now they said had never existed or wasn't a saint. Decanonized, unseated, sent down. Maybe he'll be at the bar too, Jake thought, me and John Heinemann and the holy man of love all in a row staring at our own reflections and wondering what in hell happened.

Early Sunday morning, Angie still asleep, he corralled Lisa and asked did she want to go for pancakes. She seemed to hesitate, her question was this allowed? But then she ran to get ready and reappeared a couple minutes later in one of her long princess skirts. Bigelow's, their old secret place, hadn't filled up yet and they got a waitress who knew the routine, kept a straight face when Lisa asked could they make her a bear and a possum. Of course they could, no problem, the lady said.

Then, while they were waiting, as casually as he could he asked whether she knew what was going to happen to them.

Lisa stopped pressing the tines of her fork into her paper napkin and looked directly at him. "You and Mom are going to not live together anymore and you'll go someplace else. At least for a while."

"Do you know when that's to be?"

"No, do you?"

"No," he said. "But honey, I hope you're also aware whatever goes down there'll still be a lot of time for just you and me together."

"A lot? How much is that?"

"I don't know the terms yet exactly, but probably some whole weekends and vacations and some time on the holidays too."

"And you'll still be my dad, right?"

"That I will be."

"OK."

At that moment the waitress appeared with their platters and Lisa was distracted by the buttering of the plump brown figures before her and then by drawing looping designs of syrup over them. But beyond that, it seemed that she was also now heart at rest in a larger way. She wasn't going to lose him. They weren't going to lose one another.

Reassuring to have at least one person in your life who feels that way about you.

After they'd eaten, as usual he gave Lisa his change to go play the little plastic-bubble trinket machine by the cash register. Figuring out the tip, he looked up and coming toward him in the next aisle was one of the ones who <u>didn't</u> care whether he lived or died, accompanied by a blond young lady. The gentleman, natty in a car coat with a sheered sheepskin collar, slid into a booth and the girl said something and headed off toward the restrooms.

Jake came up on Guy from behind, tapped his shoulder. "Hey pal, <u>my</u> territory, right? Didn't I ask you to stay clear?"

Guy seemed mystified. Didn't he get it?

"Tit for tat, man. Right?"

"I—um—I just got my daughter from the airport and she hadn't eaten and I remembered this place. I'm sorry."

Nice, very nice, <u>super</u> in fact for once to put Mr. Cool on the defensive. But the sensation passed, and suddenly, giving away like an embankment.

"Jake, you know it wasn't really about you coming on that job, being in my parents' house."

"It wasn't? Could have fooled me."

"In the moment I didn't explain myself very well. I'm getting along, you know, and I want to see can I make my marriage work better. Try to be more of a father too if I can be."

When Jake was silent, Guy said, "What do you think?"

Jake thought, Maybe you're not only a cold fish, maybe you're a coward too. But he said, "Well good luck. With me there were so many places you wouldn't go."

Guy brightened. "What do you mean? Zihuatanejo?"

"I don't know what that is. Mexico, right?"

"Yes."

The girl was wending her way back, eyebrows up and giving Jake the half-smile you give someone you're about to be introduced to. He was remembering Ian Stiles' question: Wasn't there some way he and the boyfriend could get away together, if only for a few days? Had he fucked up there too? Would sun and sand and some cold Coronas have done the trick?

Guy was the sort of gentleman who slides out of a booth and stands to welcome his own daughter back from the ladies' room. Strangely enough, Jake he presented as the man from Mike Tanner who was going to rectify the mistakes made in renovating Grandma Baer's house. Jake saw no reason to tell him and his daughter different.

*

"So. Did you know about Jake all along?"

Ian continued looking at Felicity, but said nothing. Behind him, distantly, the soft shushing of his father snoring. Peter had eaten only a small slice of pizza, then had some ice cream and by eight-thirty announced it had been a long day and went in, leaving the door to his room open.

"Oh come on, Ian, tell!"

"All right, not all along, no."

"When then? It's OK to tell me, you know. It's not like he's ever been your patient or anything."

"How long have I known Jake Guarini might be interested in other men? A year, a little more. Actually from the evening after Ez's wedding."

"And is it one guy, or men in general?"

"That I don't really know," Ian said. "Did Angie say how she happened to figure all this out?"

"No." Fleas thought. "Oh, yes. It was Jake's <u>sister</u>—Claire, right?—who mentioned it as a possibility. Not in any mean way though."

"Recently?"

"Apparently. Angie says it came as no big surprise to her, doesn't upset her, isn't any part of the reason she wants out of the marriage."

"That's a sentiment that could change."

"Why would it do that?"

"If they get into it in the divorce? Custody battles? Visitation rights? Money?"

"Oh. Right."

"Think I should let Jake know? So he can be more careful, cover his tracks?"

"No," Fleas said. Then she said, "Don't you think it's high time we leave Jake to his own devices, at least for a while?"

"I suppose," he said. But actually, Ian remained unsure about what Fleas meant. Did she believe that they, the Stiles family, were in some large sense responsible for Jake's confusion and his troubles?

Ian himself was not at all convinced that Jake was an unhappy man.

For a time then after his return to Europe, he didn't hear from his friend or receive any news of him. Let be. Almost a year later, back in Winnetka to check in on his father, he found out Jake and Angie's divorce had gone through. Jake was living alone, Lisa staying over at his apartment with him two weekends a month. When Ian asked was he seeing anyone, Jake smiled and winked and said, "Several people."

Made in the USA
Monee, IL
19 May 2025

17763984R00225